A Midsummer's Delight

Alicia Rasley

**ZEBRA BOOKS
KENSINGTON PUBLISHING CORP.**

ZEBRA BOOKS are published by

Kensington Publishing Corp.
475 Park Avenue South
New York, NY 10016

Copyright © 1993 by Alicia Rasley

All rights reserved. No part of this book may be reproduced in any form or by any means without the prior written consent of the Publisher, excepting brief quotes used in reviews. If you purchased this book without a cover you should be aware that this book is stolen property. It was reported as "unsold and destroyed" to the Publisher and neither the Author nor the Publisher has received any payment for this "stripped book."

Zebra and the Z logo are trademarks of Kensington Publishing Corp.

First Printing: July, 1993
Printed in the United States of America

To my parents, who gave me even more brothers than poor Charity has.

And to those brothers: Mark, Greg, Dan, Rob, Chris, and Rick. Most is forgiven.

And to Deb, whose help and support while I wrote this book can't be measured.

Chapter One

May 1819

"Charity, you didn't tell me this was an exhibition of—of pornography!"

Charity Calder turned guiltily from her admiration of a sinewy thigh emerging from a gold-braided tunic. Fortunately her aunt was too shocked by the painting to wonder at the true cause of Charity's flushed cheeks.

"Well you should blush, my dear. In the Royal Academy such doings! Don't they realize maidens will see?" Mrs. Garland tried to back away from the small study of a god and goddess on a sunswept beach, but the press of the crowd kept her almost nose to knee with Adonis.

"Oh, Aunt Grace, I have—had—five brothers." Charity hurried on past her mistake. "And none of them took the least notice of my maidenly sensibilities. I've seen more than this, I promise you." And less, she added silently, for her brothers all tended toward compactness and the Adonis standing ankle-deep in the Aegean was lean but well-built, if only, alas, of oil and canvas.

"And I expect you will tell me your brothers have seen more than that?" Mrs. Garland's arm swept accusingly past Adonis's bronzed body to indict his companion, whose charms were unconcealed even by a tunic.

"Not of me, I trust. Not that there's that much of me to

see—generously endowed, isn't she?" Laughing, Charity gestured from Aphrodite's bared bosom to her own less majestic version, primly covered in rose and blue sprig muslin. "But Aunt Grace, Francis and Barry are both grown. It's not inconceivable that they've seen some other—never mind, never mind. Don't you admire the golden beach? And the sea is so clear, why, you can even see her dainty toes! And do you not think the arrow Adonis is handing her most—oh, evocative?"

"Provocative, you mean! Charity, come away from there!"

"Oh, Aunt Grace." Charity was a lover of art and, she had recently decided, of the male form, though art was the only experience she had had of it apart from a few stolen embraces with neighborhood boys. And none of those embraces, she realized now, included a male form like Adonis's here. "That is Adonis with Aphrodite, who is playing the huntress for him. She has captured him, I think. Only he thinks he has captured her." Indeed, Adonis's dark eyes were blazing triumphantly at his captor and prey. "Do you see how they are both gripping the arrow?"

"I see nothing." Mrs. Garland was speaking only the truth, for she had pressed her palms to her eyes. "And you should see nothing either."

Bidding Adonis and his arrow a silent farewell, Charity took her aunt's arm and guided her to the next overheated gallery. This was Charity's third visit to Somerset House in a week, and the first time she'd managed to squeeze past the ground-floor galleries.

The Royal Academy of Art's annual exhibition was, as usual, a royal crush. This season the dandies and dragons were using its gilded chambers as a sophisticated Almack's Assembly Rooms for gossip and glamour and quizzing. But Charity couldn't complain, for the Academy's new wealth brought in a wealth of the art she, at least, really studied.

In this gallery every inch of wall, floor to ceiling, was covered by canvases in elaborate frames. One wall was devoted to landscapes, but as far as Charity could tell, that was the

THE CHALLENGE

Charity had never in her life been able to run down a challenge, even one she knew was unintended. "Too old? You are mistaken, Lord Braden. I climbed a tree only last week to rescue a kitten. It's all a matter of skill—and privacy."

"Privacy?"

"Surely you know the rules—boys up first, girls down first."

Lord Braden considered this somberly, his brows drawn together in a frown. "When I used to climb trees, propriety wasn't really a consideration. But if you insist—"

She had never really supposed he would do it—he was lithe enough, of course, but it was rather at odds with a man's dignity, to climb a tree. He didn't even take the easy route, up the rungs, but caught the first branches and swung himself up.

She strained to look up through the concealing leaves but did not see him again until he dropped onto the balcony and leaned over the wall. He was laughing at her, holding his hand out as if she might jump up and grasp it. "Are you coming? Or have you decided to take the long way through the house?"

Charity sensed the Italian warmth now in his cool voice, and laughing down at her from above, he looked like one of his own paintings of young gods, slim and golden in the noon sun.

His recklessness was contagious. She set aside any notions of modesty and decorum and glanced around to make sure the boxwoods encircling the garden concealed her misdemeanor. She lost her sunbonnet before she reached the balcony. But her light sandals didn't slip off, and her feet stayed secure on the thick branch until, taking the hand Lord Braden held out to her, she dropped lightly over the wall . . .

ELEGANT LOVE STILL FLOURISHES—
Wrap yourself in a Zebra Regency Romance.

A MATCHMAKER'S MATCH (3783, $3.50/$4.50)
by Nina Porter
To save herself from a loveless marriage, Lady Psyche Veringham pretends to be a bluestocking. Resigned to spinsterhood at twenty-three, Psyche sets her keen mind to snaring a husband for her young charge, Amanda. She sets her cap for long-time bachelor, Justin St. James. This man of the world has had his fill of frothy-headed debutantes and turns the tables on Psyche. Can a bluestocking and a man about town find true love?

FIRES IN THE SNOW (3809, $3.99/$4.99)
by Janis Laden
Because of an unhappy occurrence, Diana Ruskin knew that a secure marriage was not in her future. She was content to assist her physician father and follow in his footsteps . . . until now. After meeting Adam, Duke of Marchmaine, Diana's precise world is shattered. She would simply have to avoid the temptation of his gentle touch and stunning physique—and by doing so break her own heart!

FIRST SEASON (3810, $3.50/$4.50)
by Anne Baldwin
When country heiress Laetitia Biddle arrives in London for the Season, she harbors dreams of triumph and applause. Instead, she becomes the laughingstock of drawing rooms and ballrooms, alike. This headstrong miss blames the rakish Lord Wakeford for her miserable debut, and she vows to rise above her many faux pas. Vowing to become an Original, Letty proves that she's more than a match for this eligible, seasoned Lord.

AN UNCOMMON INTRIGUE (3701, $3.99/$4.99)
by Georgina Devon
Miss Mary Elizabeth Sinclair was rather startled when the British Home Office employed her as a spy. Posing as "Tasha," an exotic fortune-teller, she expected to encounter unforeseen dangers. However, nothing could have prepared her for Lord Eric Stewart, her dashing and infuriating partner. Giving her heart to this haughty rogue would be the most reckless hazard of all.

A MADDENING MINX (3702, $3.50/$4.50)
by Mary Kingsley
After a curricle accident, Miss Sarah Chadwick is literally thrust into the arms of Philip Thornton. While other women shy away from Thornton's eyepatch and aloof exterior, Sarah finds herself drawn to discover why this man is physically and emotionally scarred.

Available wherever paperbacks are sold, or order direct from the Publisher. Send cover price plus 50¢ per copy for mailing and handling to Zebra Books, Dept. 4230, 475 Park Avenue South, New York, N.Y. 10016. Residents of New York and Tennessee must include sales tax. DO NOT SEND CASH. For a free Zebra/Pinnacle catalog please write to the above address.

only method in the madness of the arrangement. Ward's ominous view of a derelict castle jostled a pretty scene by Crome of boys swimming in a country pond.

"You can open your eyes now, Aunt." Through judicious use of her cherry-handled parasol, Charity made room in front of a gentle portrayal of English farmlife. "Just a Constable. And a lovely one at that."

She left her aunt gazing determinedly at the cow lounging on a dewy hillside. Charity, a Kent girl, had seen enough cows to last a lifetime and preferred more exotic vistas. So she slipped between a dandy and his acolyte and found herself mere inches from another landscape, this one vivid with the yellows and blues and reds of Italy. A village of whitewashed cottages rambled down a hillside to the sea. The terra cotta roofs were exuberant against the blue sky, and the sun spilled like melted butter on a turquoise sea. How shocking were the colors, and how right, and how very un-English.

The noisy crowd receded from her awareness. Charity laid her fingers lightly on the canvas, almost expecting to find it warm from the Italian sun. But it was cool and rough under her touch.

Then, at her shoulder, a gallery attendant appeared. "Please don't touch the paintings, miss."

The young man looked as if he expected her to pull out a knife, cut the canvas from its frame, and roll it into a tube to stuff in Aunt Grace's capacious handbag. She chuckled at the thought, and the attendant's scowl vanished to leave him looking young and confused.

"I am sorry." Charity hid the guilty hand behind her back. "Tell me, will you, what is the name of this painting? And the artist? I can't read the signature—isn't it odd that he paints the little whitecapped waves so precisely then scrawls his name incomprehensibly?"

The attendant nodded, then shook his head, then nodded again. Finally he ducked his head to study a catalog with handwritten notes in the margin. "It's *Ferendisi,* miss. That's an island village in the Adriatic. And the artist is the new Lord Braden."

The artist's title meant nothing to her, except as a village in Sussex, not far from her own Kent home. "He must be very accomplished to have been ennobled for his work," she murmured, gripping her parasol to keep her fingers from tracing the jagged line of the hillside.

"Oh, no, miss, I think he inherited the title. He's far too young to have earned such honors, though he's talented, they say. I prefer the Constables; this is too—too vibrant. Vibrating, almost." The attendant waited somberly for Charity's smiling response to his wordplay, then glanced down at his catalog. "He always paints the sea, I understand, even in the classical figures. The *Aegean Aphrodite and Adonis* in the antechamber is his also."

His gesture back toward the doorway collided with a dowager's turban and knocked it askew. As the lady sputtered and the attendant drew back in fear for his job and life, Charity stole a longing glance at the Italian village and then applied herself to setting things right. She murmured soothingly as she straightened the purple satin headdress, "No, no, the plume isn't broken at all; why, it looks quite jaunty, I'd say! Such a lovely color, almost like the heather in that Crome landscape over there. Have you seen it yet? Oh, you must, for I know you'll want to have a turban made of the exact shade of the sky." And she pointed the now-agreeable lady in the opposite direction and gave her a gentle shove.

Horrified by the use of the sainted Crome as a fashion device, the attendant started away. But Charity stopped him with an inquiring smile and a grip on his sleeve. He gazed down at her small, capable hand with its short nails and simple ruby ring, and cleared his throat. "Was there something else you wanted, miss?"

"Only a bit more information on this artist. Such dramatic use of color. Vibrant, as you said. I almost feel I am there in

Italy. It's not often, is it, that a young artist gets two paintings in the Royal Academy exhibition?"

His lips twisted, and Charity suspected him to be a bit envious. She had heard about the favoritism of Academy members and wondered if their employee here would suggest the titled painter was a beneficiary.

But he only observed, "Thomas Lawrence had two paintings exhibited when he was but eighteen. Turner was made an associate at two-and-twenty." As he consulted his annotated catalog again, Charity wished she could steal this source of all artistic knowledge. "Braden was once a student here at the Academy school—as am I!—so the Academicians would be acquainted with his work."

"Do you paint yourself?" she inquired, turning back to that Italian summer day.

"I sculpt." His tone suggested that sculpting was by far the superior art.

All Charity knew of sculpture she learned while watching the butler carve the Christmas goose, but she asked brightly, "In what medium?" Surely this question must be as important to sculptors as to painters, for whom one's morals were somehow tied to one's medium.

"Clay, mostly. I want to try marble, but it's prohibitively expensive."

Struck by inspiration, Charity said, "You should come to Kent. We have miles and miles of chalk cliffs. I wonder what an accomplished sculptor could do with them. During the war I thought a massive sculpture of Admiral Nelson gazing over the Dover Harbor would discourage French invaders. Now where did you say this Ferendisi is?"

"On the Adriatic. Chalk? Is it very malleable? Would I use a chisel, or could I mold it by hand?"

Charity murmured suggestions then took herself back to Italy.

The attendant had long since moved away, still clutching

the coveted catalog, when Charity felt an imperious grip on her elbow.

"Miss Calder! Your aunt said you were imprisoned here. She entrusted me with the message that she will await you in the lobby. And to judge by her expression, she prefers not to wait long!"

The beatific smile sat uncomfortably on Sir Ralph Bessemer's wolfish features. He was a rake of the first order, not the sort of man Aunt Grace would ordinarily entrust with a message or a maiden niece. But his father had recently died and left him in charge of ten thousand acres and three schoolgirl sisters. Ralph the Rakehell was in need of a wife, and Aunt Grace was happy to help out.

Reluctantly Charity took his arm, wishing she could be thrilled by the deliciously dissipated Sir Ralph. Not that he would ever be dissipated with Charity. She was, as he had told her approvingly at Almack's last week (word was he had to blackmail Sally Jersey to get a voucher to the hallowed hall), the best of good girls. And rakehells, unfortunately, wanted only one thing from good girls.

Mischief seized Charity as they passed the other contribution by Lord Braden. She smiled merrily at her escort. "Do you like that painting of Adonis and Aphrodite?"

"Certainly not." Sir Ralph quickened his pace, tugging her away from the immoral immortals. "Shocking the sort of things they put on public display. Why, the thought of an innocent girl like you exposed to such a sight!"

"But it's Adonis and Aphrodite who are exposed, not I." Charity knew her slightly risqué wit was lost on Sir Ralph. He gave no sign of even hearing her little jest. For weeks he had simply ignored all evidence that Charity Calder was anything but a well-bred country miss, the perfect prospective wife. He had also ignored all evidence that Charity Calder had no desire to be his perfect prospective wife.

Sir Ralph's hand tightened on her elbow as they descended the opulent but steeply curved staircase. But he was only seeking to protect her from the sort of embarrassing tumble two ladies had already taken today. He released her with an abashed smile as soon as the danger was past. At the bottom Aunt Grace beamed up at them, no doubt imagining a more ceremonial descent down the steps of St. George's, Hanover Square.

Sir Ralph must also have envisioned such a scene. After he conveyed them across the Strand to their carriage, he pressed a chaste kiss on Charity's hand and gazed significantly into her eyes. "I should like to call on you this afternoon. Sir Francis has given me permission."

Traitor, Charity thought, for her elder brother had explicit instructions otherwise.

"Come for tea," Aunt Grace, another Judas, called back cheerily as she climbed into her seat.

"Ten thousand acres in Shropshire," Aunt Grace reminded Charity as the coach lurched down the busy Strand. "Four hundred acres of park—Capability Brown designed the grounds, my dear!—and a Jacobian manor. Why, it's in all the guidebooks!"

"I won't marry a house, Aunt. Or a park, Capability Brown or no. I don't love their owner. And he doesn't love me."

"He adores you! He gazes at you as if—"

"As if I were a prize broodmare. Or a particularly comfortable armchair." From her reticule, Charity withdrew her little everyday book and a lead pencil sheathed in leather. Dismissing Sir Ralph from her thoughts, she noted down, as neatly as the jolting of the carriage allowed, Lord Braden's name and a description of his paintings. She nibbled at the end of her pencil and then added a few other artists and paintings to the list. Later she would transfer this information to her journal, where she kept close track of her aesthetic education, haphazard and unsupervised as it had to be.

"But you've already turned down five offers! Five fine offers! A marquess! That nabob just back from Bengal!" Aunt Grace's lament was accompanied by such agonized headshaking that her gray fringecurls undid themselves in the humid May air. "And Charity, by rights you shouldn't have received more than one or two! You've no fortune to speak of, and the family is well-bred but nothing special, and—"

"And my looks are nothing special either!" Charity looked up from her book with a laugh. Early in the season she had encountered a girl who looked startlingly familiar, and she had wondered for a moment if they had been to school together. Then Charity counted up the nut brown curls, the spray of freckles across the snub nose, the frank brown eyes and realized, she looks just like me! She and Priscilla had shared a chuckle at the number of healthy English dairymaid sorts just like them in London this spring.

"Oh, you're fetching enough," Aunt Grace admitted, "but no Incomparable. I must say I never expected you to be so popular with the young men, for you're hardly in the first bloom of youth!" She reached across the divide and patted Charity's hand. "I know it wasn't your fault that your season was postponed so often, of course; one can't arrange for familial deaths at convenient times. But you are rather old to be a deb, dear."

Actually Charity, who had nearly reached the age of one-and-twenty, had never felt younger. She had considered her youth ended years ago, when her mother died and left Charity the running of the household. Here in London, her responsibilities were so few she felt herself back in some lost and carefree stage of childhood. She had only to attend entertainments and remember names and receive morning callers—and afternoon proposals.

Perhaps she could find a way to beg off from tea. Aunt Grace's household accounts were in a tangle, after all. The butcher was demanding payment on three months of bills, while the housekeeper swore she'd paid him, so Charity could claim imminent litigation precluded her presence this afternoon.

Aunt Grace, reading her mind, moaned, "Charity, Charity,

why don't you accept one of these nice young men? They all like you so well!"

"They don't like me. They don't even know me. They don't even know they don't know me." Sir Ralph's offhanded "an innocent girl like you" still rankled.

"Why, of course they know you, dear. Before Chilworth offered, he wrote a letter to your vicar inquiring about your character."

"He did? He did?" Charity suddenly wished she'd been less kind when she refused the arrogant marquess.

"He was only being prudent, my dear. His title, after all, is six centuries old, and he can surely be forgiven if he takes step to ensure that the mother of the next marquess is above reproach. As you are, of course. Chilworth's mama told me the Rev. Mr. Langworth was most laudatory and regretted only that marriage would take you away from the parish you have served so well." Mrs. Garland sighed in a most mournful way. "You are so very helpful, my dear. Everyone knows that, especially these men who are so enamoured of you."

Not of me, Charity countered silently. But it was no use to elaborate, for Mrs. Garland also thought she knew her niece through and through. Charity Calder, the cheerful, capable country girl, with the rosy cheeks and useful skills, was all too easy to know.

Not for the first time, Charity contemplated accepting an offer of marriage. Sir Ralph was rich and well-born, and his wife would certainly not lack for either material things or social status. He needed her, too, or someone just like her, to take charge of his sisters and servants and eventually his children. He perhaps even needed her to check that self-destructiveness that lurked on the dark side of every rakehell.

And to judge by his reputation, Bessemer was adept enough at the arts of love. Of course, that reputation was all Charity had to judge by. Last week at the Cranmere ball, she had been intrigued when the kingdom's premier rogue suggested a garden walk. She thought perhaps this man with the seductive silver eyes might be the suitor who would sweep away all her hesitation with his passion. But when she experimentally entwined her arms around his neck, he had responded with the merest peck on the cheek, the sort she might receive from the most respectable of suitors. Then, hastily, he suggested they return to the ballroom, for he didn't wish anyone to comment on their absence. Sir Ralph had been a great disappointment all in all.

But all in all, Sir Ralph was a gentleman, despite his thrilling reputation. So that afternoon, he did not argue with her rejection beyond a quarter-hour. Finally, in utter despair, he cried, "Then what am I to do with my sisters?"

This, at least, was a situation in which Charity could help. Eliciting the information that his obstreperous sisters were ten, eleven, and thirteen, she went to the cherrywood desk and neatly wrote out a few lines on her aunt's best notepaper. "They are just the right age for going away to school. I attended Miss Falesham's Academy in Maidenhead for two years and liked it very well. My mother became ill then, and I had to come home to take care of the household. But I've always looked back fondly on my schooldays. Miss Falesham is kind but very firm and adept at turning young girls into young ladies, even without their knowledge or consent!"

Grudgingly Sir Ralph accepted the name and address of this paragon, and even more grudgingly Charity's insistence that, no, she hadn't changed her mind in the last ten minutes. Only after he took his leave did Charity realize she should also have given him the name and direction of Priscilla Barrett, her lookalike from Lancashire. Charity just knew Priscilla, in the great tradition of understudies, could step right into the role of perfect wife. Sir Ralph would probably never notice the substitution.

Breakfast the next morning was a chilled meal, though the dining room was filled with May sunlight. Aunt Grace had donned a crepe dress of lavender, declaring herself in half-mourning. She was taking the refusal of Sir Ralph with rather less grace than Sir Ralph himself. Sniffling into a gray-edged handkerchief, she announced to the footman to bring only kippers, eggs, scones, and melon, as she had no appetite.

So Charity blew on her steaming coffee and opened her mail without venturing a word to her aunt beyond necessary requests. With none of her aunt's delicacy, she was wearing a cheery yellow cambric morning dress with matching ribbons holding back her thick curls. Ordinarily a loquacious girl, she was proud to make it through letters from one cousin and two brothers without regaling her aunt with tidbits. But that final letter did her in, making her groan and sigh and then shake her head with rue.

Finally Aunt Grace surrendered. "Whatever are you reading, Charity?"

"A letter from Francis. I'm afraid it means I must return home by the week's end at the latest."

Grace put aside her pique and took the news with real regret. "You're needed at home? Your brothers aren't ill, are they?"

"Oh, no, though he says Charlie has not been attending to his lessons. And he won't be admitted to Eton if he doesn't improve his Latin. To judge by his letter, his English needs work, too." Charity picked up Charlie's ill-spelled missive and frowned at it, then hid it under the others. "No, the vicar means to cancel the Midsummer fair!"

"Is that all?" Aunt Grace shrugged and returned to her kippers. "That needn't cut your season short. You must stay until the King's birthday, at least."

Charity shook her head. The King's birthday, the traditional end to the London Season, was a bare two weeks before the fair would be held. "No, you don't understand. The vicar—well, I think he has intended this all along. When I told him I wouldn't be able to organize the festivities this year, as I would be here in London, he suggested to Mrs. Hering that she plan the fair." Charity pushed away her breakfast plate, too annoyed now to eat. "He knows how tetchy she is, and I wager he deliberately argued with her to force her to quit, and now she has!"

"But Charity, why would the vicar do that? Not just to force you home surely! After your dazzling success? The villain! He wants to keep you in that benighted backwater, ministering to *his* flock, instead of taking up your rightful place next to—oh, someone like Sir Ralph!"

Aunt Grace had worked herself up into such a pet imagining a villainous vicar that Charity hated to spoil the vision. But she was an honest young lady, and the vicar, however obdurate, was no villain.

"No, Aunt, he wouldn't dream of spoiling my chances. Indeed, I'm sure he hoped I would stay in London through most of June and arrive home too late to contrive a celebration of any sort at all!" In baleful tones, she concluded, "Mr. Langworth, you see, doesn't approve of Midsummer."

"No, I don't see. How can anyone disapprove of a holiday?"

"Oh, he claims it is a pagan fertility festival." Charity added grudgingly, "And it is, I suppose, or was. But—well, it has become quite Christianized these last thousand years! It isn't even held at Midsummer any longer, but on St. John's Day, at the very beginning of summer! But Mr. Langworth doesn't like even the tiniest suggestion of the holiday's early traditions."

"You mean the parade? And the fortunetelling? Why, that's harmless stuff, surely. Just funning!"

"Exactly. The country people love it, especially the children." Charity had a flash of memory, a taste of gingerbread, and she remembered sharing her Midsummer cake with her twin Ned, so that he would have two chances to get his wish. Then she shook her head briskly and returned to the subject at hand. "The proceeds were to go to restoring the church tower. It's in lamentable state after six centuries. Chunks of flint keep falling off, and one day a piece will strike a churchgoer on the head and kill him quite dead."

Aunt Grace considered this, then speared a piece of toast and spread marmalade across it. "Well, then I should think the vicar should want to earn every groat he can from the festival, even if it means bringing on dancing girls and dancing bears!"

"Oh, but he knows he needn't do any such thing, you may be sure!" Charity picked up her elder brother's letter and scanned it again, reading between the closely written lines. "Mr. Langworth knows that if there is no other option, Francis will, as he always does, come forth with a contribution. Two hundred pounds, that's what the work will cost. And Francis can't afford that, not this year, what with the spring floods, and my season—" She broke off, troubled to think that her frivolity here in Town might have depleted the family coffers. Francis, a conscientious steward, had assured her that they could stand several seasons, if need be, but she was too frugal to ask for another.

Carefully casual, Aunt Grace remarked, "Sir Ralph, I'm sure, would be quite generous with the marriage settlements."

Charity's head snapped up, and she fixed her aunt with a minatory look. "I am not going to marry just to get the church tower fixed. All that's needed is the Midsummer Fair, for the receipts last year, when I was organizer, were nearly one hundred and fifty pounds, and Francis can stand the rest without pain."

Aunt Grace subsided, sullenly stirring her chocolate until the steam rose in a gentle curve. "There are other options, surely, than you going home so soon! Francis isn't the only nobleman in the parish, is he?"

"Well, no. But it all falls to him, to maintain the vicarage and the church. Because he *will*, you know. Haverne—the local lord—never would. And now he can't. Though," Charity added thoughtfully, "it might help his heavenly case if he did."

"Do stop being cryptic, dear. It gives me the headache. This Haverne—" Aunt Grace frowned. "Wasn't there some scandal attached to that name?"

"Scandal. Well, yes, it was a bit of a scandal." Charity thought of Kenny Haverton, Lord Haverne, Kent's wickedest boy, wicked and boyish to the last. "He was killed in a duel in March."

Grace wasn't one to take pleasure in the tragedies of others, but her plump face brightened as she connected her niece's acquaintance with one of the prize scandals of the season. "Ah, yes, I remember now. He was fighting over a lady—or perhaps not a lady—certainly not his lady wife."

"That's the one." Charity felt a momentary pang, for it was sad, Kenny dead so young. But there was no other plausible destiny for him, she saw that now. "He was the earl and made most of his income off the land, so one might expect him to do his duty to the area. But he never cared a jot for the parish or the village. He didn't even maintain the vicar's living, as he was obliged to do. Francis, of course, has taken care of that. Kenny was a handsome rascal, though."

"Handsome is as handsome does," Aunt Grace interposed with comfortable piety. "It is a shame for poor Lady Haverne though. I don't think I've seen her about at all this season, but that's only to be expected."

Charity consulted her letter again. "Francis says she retreated back to Kent after the duel. I gather she isn't taking this well. She loved him madly, poor thing." For just a moment, Charity wondered if the rational contract her suitors offered weren't preferable to that madness. Then she shook her head decisively; one needn't, after all, fall in love with the likes of Kenny Haverton. "She was one of those wives who could never see ill in her husband. And there was so *much* ill to see in Kenny, once you got past that face of his."

"Well, the wife is always the last to know," Aunt Grace said inarguably. "What a dreadful way to find out, however."

Charity would have liked to suggest that the wife of

Grace's favorite, Sir Ralph, would doubtlessly face a similar fate, but instead returned to her brother's letter. "Dreadful is right. Listen to what Francis says: 'It's coming on three months now since his death, however, and she's never gotten out of bed.' "

"Oh, that must be an exaggeration," said the practical Aunt Grace. "She must have had to visit the conveniences at least once in three months. Now don't you start thinking that she is one more reason to go home!" she added over Charity's laughter. "I'm sure she has a family doting on her and allaying her grief, and needs you not at all."

"Anna does have a brother, at least, but it occurs to me he lives abroad." Charity frowned, for she'd never really considered that Lady Haverne's trouble might not be her affair. "We have been friendly, you know, though never really friends. She's older, close to thirty, I think. She used to have me to tea when she was playing the grand lady of the manor. Taking pity on the country mouse, you know." She soon repented such a catty comment, however apt, and rushed on. "I've known Haverne forever, of course. He wasn't a very good earl, having inherited so young—my word, little Lawrence must hold the title now, and he's but seven. They seldom set foot in the country, you know, although I gather Anna's now finding it more hospitable than London what with all the gossips." She folded the letter neatly and tucked it into her lace sleeve. "And I would go home, even were Lady Haverne the merriest of widows. The fairs have been my responsibility for years now. I shouldn't have thought to shirk it, just for a London season."

"But we've had such fun," Aunt Grace said with a drooping look. "I was so hoping you could be spared another fortnight or more, for there are dozens of dances and picnics. And you said you would see to the leasing of the Chelsea house, for my man of business has no judgment about tenants. His last choice, I am persuaded, was an opium smoker, for he left burn marks all along the parlor wall."

Charity promised to engage a tenant before she left town and to attend every last picnic and ball offered in the next couple of days. Aunt Grace helped herself to the last scone and said hopefully, "You don't suppose you could also accept an offer while you are being so conciliating? For the thought of sending you home unmarried—why, I feel as if I have failed."

Charity checked the watch pinned to her rose-embroidered bodice. "Oh, I am sorry, Aunt, but if I'm to engage tenants and attend picnics, I shan't have any time to entertain offers."

Back in her room, Charity kicked off her slippers and began to pack up her winter clothes to be sent home ahead of her. But she paused in her neat folding, her thoughts wandering. She packed the shawl carefully into the open trunk at the foot of her bed, then, from under the mattress, brought out her journal.

This journal was not the sort needing to be hidden. There were no speculations about an unknown man's intense gaze or breathless reports of stolen kisses. Would that there were! No, this journal only recorded the sights she had seen, the people she had met, to be read months from now when her memories of the season had faded, perhaps as a respite from organizing the Christmas carol service. And perhaps someday she might turn these into a little memoir, a girl's guide to the London Season.

It was a silly ambition, for who would read such a book? But Charity liked to have distant goals as well as reachable ones. So, innocent as her jottings were, she kept her journal hidden away. Life with a clutch of brothers had taught her that the most innocuous private thoughts could be turned into sport at the dinner table, and even now, sixty miles from home, instinct kept her secretive.

She smoothed the blue counterpane and sat down on the bed, tucking her feet up under her skirt. Editing pencil in hand, she read over yesterday's entry. She had, perhaps, made rather too much of that classical painting, lingering overlong on Adonis's burning gaze and well-defined musculature. A pretense at sophistication, she realized now, and perhaps an overheated and best-undefined longing. Enough, she told herself, and began an introduction to Braden's other painting, the Italian landscape she admired even more. "Lord Braden is known for—" and she immediately broke off her formal description to add a parenthetical note to herself. "(How old? Attendant said he was too young for ennobling, recently at the RA school—young enough, anyway, to inspire his envy, for a man of twenty does not envy a man of forty) his dramatic use of vivid colors and his interest, even obsession, with the sea. The sea reportedly figures in his every painting, even the classical studies. Both these qualities are in evidence in *Ferendisi*, his landscape of an island village on the Italian coast of the Adriatic. Braden is meticulous with detail. The rocky cliff, the trees bent from the sea breeze, the curling waves are precisely drawn, and the colors are almost shockingly real."

She frowned at her entry, wishing she could explain the real appeal of that landscape, that the mix of canvas and oil contained Italy in all its operatic drama. She could not, however, express in such careful words what the artist did so well in image. So she added, all in a rush, her precise lettering becoming scattered, "I would love to see a village so different from my own. To touch the Adriatic, so blue, so warm, so different from my cold gray Channel. To hear the music and laughter of a people so unlike myself."

And then she stopped, for it seemed unpatriotic somehow, as if she didn't love England, didn't love Kent and its down-to-earth residents. She did, of course, with all her heart. It was only that she had known nothing else all her life.

She put away her pencils and slipped the journal into her trunk. Already her thoughts were turning to Calder, the pretty Tudor village near the coast that had borne her family's name for three centuries. She wondered if Lady Haverne suffered more from humiliation than grief, if more flint had chipped off the church tower, if a month was long enough to organize the Midsummer fair. And with a little relief she realized that her holiday was over; it was time to go home.

Chapter Two

After two days in his sister's house, Tristan Hale concluded that very probably he would never paint again.

His Muse had ever been an exacting mistress, refusing to bewitch except under perfect conditions. He'd never been able to paint well in England, for his Muse loved best the brilliant Italian sun. And she was apparently a rather declassé sort for a divinity, preferring to tryst in bare garret studios, not opulent surroundings like Haverne House. Most important, she liked her acolyte's attention focused entirely on herself, his mind empty of all but a desire to serve her.

But a focused attention was impossible in his sister's house. He couldn't concentrate even for the hour a day he set aside for painting. His hands felt wooden, his brushes unfamiliar and heavy. His thoughts were not of art but of guilt and melancholy. He couldn't relax into mindless sensual enjoyment, for at any moment he expected to be interrupted by two screaming demons.

So now, when he needed her most, his creative Muse denied him, and he was left with only the destructive chaos around him.

Tristan had done his best, setting up a makeshift studio in the sunroom, where the morning light played so evocatively. It had taken only an hour to achieve the careful disorder he needed, his brushes scattered just so, his painting shirts hung on pegs, his easels stuck up in a semicircle near the window wall. He'd even rigged a lock on the door to keep his nephews out. But staring now at the half-finished painting of a ship afire, he could dredge up not the least inspiration. He could not even mix his paints right; the ocher he needed for the depths of the fire was a mud brown, the midnight blue of the night sky remained stubbornly black.

And whenever he raised his eyes from the canvas, he saw the fallow fields of Haverne through the windows and was reminded of his sister's far greater sorrow.

He had arrived here determined to set his elder sister's life aright, to assuage her grief and manage her household. But he hadn't counted on things being in such a state—Anna a near-invalid, her sons running wild, the house slovenly, and the grounds unkempt. No one had gotten round to the spring planting, on which most of the estate's income depended.

Tristan had grown up in London and Florence, among artists and intellectuals, and didn't know wheat from barley. But the fields visible through the great wall of windows looked melancholy, their fruitlessness only highlighted by the wildflowers that sprang up between the empty rows. So much neglect—and he was as guilty as anyone. He'd been so glad to be released from family obligations when his sister married that he'd never given more than cursory attention to her happiness.

He went to the basin and washed the paint from his hands, wishing he could as easily deal with his guilt. Then he stripped off his old paint-spotted shirt and put on a pristine one and his coat over it. He gave a last regretful look to his great effort, destined now to remain unfinished, and headed out the door.

"Uncle Tris! Uncle Tris!"

Swiftly he pulled the door shut behind him and turned the key. Then he caught, one in each arm, the nephews who catapulted at him. Lawrence, the elder, tried to squirm past to the sunroom door, but Tristan held him fast. "Now, boys," he said with a steely sort of pleasantness, "you remember I told you that my studio is off-limits. Out of bounds. Prohibited territory. *Terra vetata.*"

Jeremy was impressed with this litany, but Lawrence, as usual, objected. Flinging himself back into the hallway, he stood, arms crossed, like the arrogant little lord he was. "It's not a studio. It's only a sunroom. And Papa always let us play there. Now he's dead and you've come and you won't let us play in our own home!"

Tristan almost retorted that Lawrence's papa seldom noticed he had sons, much less a sunroom. But Lawrence was such a skinny little boy, more like an urchin than an aristocrat, his untidy fair hair reaching to his frayed collars, his thin face defiant, that Tristan bit back his sharp words. "I hereby designate the other forty-seven rooms yours, Lawrence. Jeremy can have the garden and the stables,"

"And Mother can have her sickroom. It's all she wants anyway."

Lawrence's words were so bitter they must have hurt his throat, for he swallowed hard several times and turned away. Ashamed of his anger at these near-orphans, Tristan grabbed Jeremy up in one arm and extended the other hand to Lawrence. "Let's go down to the kitchen. There's sure to be some bread and jam left from breakfast."

But a maid stopped them halfway down the backstairs. She was a bashful girl, a true orphan, the only maid left, for she had nowhere else to go. She was worn to a shade from trying to do the work of six. "Begging your pardon, my lord, but Mr. Langworth, the vicar, is here. He asked for her ladyship again, and I told him she wasn't receiving."

That understatement struck even six-year-old Jeremy as ludicrous. "Mama never receives. She doesn't even get out of bed."

"I'll see him." Tristan set Jeremy gently on his feet. "Go on down to the kitchen and get us some bread and jam. Then go on out to the stables and check on my horse, will you? See how he's settled in."

"The vicar probably wants to know why we don't go to church on Sunday." Lawrence sat down on the step, looking defiantly up at his uncle. "And I wager you won't know what to tell him."

"I'll tell him I'm your guardian and I've decided to raise you as pagans. You've got such a good start already."

Lawrence was so delighted by the prospect that he took off running after his brother. "Pagans! We get to be pagans, Jerry!"

The Reverend Mr. Langworth, waiting in the dusty small salon, was a prosperous-looking man, for a vicar. Tristan would have preferred him cadaverous, so that the contrast between pallid skin and black garb would be more pronounced. But Mr. Langworth was all pink cheeks, cornflower blue eyes, pearly teeth, silver hair, and rosy nose. His black robe hadn't the slightest impact in the midst of all the pastels.

"I am so glad you have arrived," Mr. Langworth said after they had settled themselves into armchairs and the maid had gone to procure refreshments. His sincerity was almost palpable. "Things have not been happy here at Haverne."

"So I've noticed." Tristan kicked at the couch; a cloud of dust arose, eliciting a sneeze from the vicar. "I would have been here sooner, but I was traveling in Italy and my sister's summons reached me very late." He felt a sudden need to confess his guilt; vicars cultivated that effect, he supposed. "Since the war ended, I've primarily lived abroad. I haven't kept up with my sister as I ought. But I never thought Haverne would let things get in such a state. This looks like more than three months' neglect."

"Just so. He seldom came down from London." The vicar twisted uncomfortably in his chair. But his voice was harsh, and Tristan thought, Aha, he has some Old Testament black-and-white under the pastels after all. "Like so many landowners, he turned his family heritage over to hired hands."

Tristan hadn't visited his own estate since last year, when he'd inherited it and the title from a cousin. He'd never felt any real connection to the Sussex farm, but now he wondered if his seemingly trustworthy bailiff was taking good care of the place. Uncomfortably aware that he was probably as negligent as Kenny, he told himself that he would make the twenty-mile trip to Braden as soon as he got his sister's problems under control. "I don't know how much I can do here. I've never lived out in the country, except in Italy. But I'll do what I can."

Reverting now to his customary gentleness, Mr. Langworth asked, "How is Lady Haverne?"

"Not well." Now he was the one making understatements. "I didn't realize how hard she had taken this. Oh, I don't make light of her being widowed and in such a way, but she's always gone to extremes. She used to swear she couldn't live without Haverne. Now she's doing her best to keep that vow."

A decade ago, in fact, Anna had threatened to kill herself if she weren't allowed to marry Kenny. Tristan, then a cynical boy of sixteen, thought her threat mere dramatics. But their father had surrendered immediately, for their mother had been just as histrionic, and when her bluff was called, she had very deliberately faded away. Tristan's youthful assessment was to be proven wrong again, he supposed. Anna was set on the same decline their mother had taken.

"Well, I'm not one to speak ill of the dead, but that was one man who was not worth such grief."

Tristan had to revise his earlier estimation of the vicar's character. It was an artist's failing to judge too much on appearances, to assume that vision could reveal all. But the vicar was by no means merely a study in pastels; there was some righteous darkness in there somewhere.

As his own harsh words echoed, the vicar glanced guiltily around, then hastened on, "Be that as it may, I have been quite concerned about Lady Haverne. We are not well-acquainted, for she and her sons weren't here very often. But she has always been quite kind. She is so young to sequester herself this way. And I can't think it's healthy for the little lads."

The drawing room smelled as if it hadn't been aired for weeks. Tristan crossed to the window and opened the casement, letting in the fragrant May air. It was a lovely morning. The sky was a gentle blue, the elm trees lining the avenue were decked in a pale green, pastel wildflowers sprang up around the darker hedges that crisscrossed the hills. The vista was subdued compared to what he was used to in Italy, but it had its own quiet beauty.

Then contemplation of the landscape gave way to another assessment of decrepitude: the long avenue was rutted and muddy, with weeds growing up around the unpruned elms. The hedges were unkempt, here overgrown and there sparse. The hills were covered with ragged growth instead of careful rows of wheat.

The vicar added anxiously behind him, "I don't mean to be so blunt, my lord. But your arrival is a blessing. This is the first time I have been admitted since the funeral. I would have been more insistent, perhaps, had I known what a state things were in."

"Well, I've already surveyed the damage, and I'm ready to get to work. I just don't know precisely where to begin. There's seed in the barn that must be sown, though who's to do it I haven't an idea. The hands all left months ago. And I mean to hire a nurse for the boys and get some girls in here to clean."

"I'll send Miss Calder over," the vicar said with an air of settling matters entirely. "Oh, yes, the village is named for her family. They've been the gentry here for centuries, far pre-dating the Havernes. Sir Francis is her brother. I'll drop a word in his ear, too. He's been busy with his own lands, but I'm sure he can spare you a bit of advice. And Charity can take the boys in hand for you. She and Lady Haverne were always cordial. I'm sure she'd have been here months ago, but she was in London for the social season." He brightened as if she were his own daughter. "She was a great success, our Charity. All the young beaus were taken by her—and who could blame them? A better example of Kentish womanhood can't be found. Very capable, you'll find her to be. I'm certain she can coax Lady Haverne back into good spirits."

"A miracle worker, is she?"

"No," the vicar said slowly, turning this over in his mind. "Just a good-hearted girl. And she knows how to deal with people. Never takes a step wrong." As if that settled that, the vicar picked up his hat and moved to the door. "Yes, I'll ask her to stop by soon."

That this charitable Miss Charity was a capable girl, Tristan had no doubt. But a great success in London? The vicar's fondness and provincialism must have hid the truth from him. London liked simpering, selfish little beauties, not good-hearted girls. And if Miss Charity had been a great success, she would never still be a "miss."

The vicar hesitated in the doorway, his hat gripped in one hand. "As I said, Miss Calder would be quite a help to you here. But perhaps she won't be able to spare the time, after all. She's gotten herself tied up with preparations for some absurd village festival. Midsummer Eve, you know."

Tristan found himself annoyed that the vicar had dangled this offer of aid then snatched it back. Anna might indeed do better with another woman to confide in; she hadn't been able to do more than weep on her brother's shoulder. "It's so important, this festival?"

"Not as far as I am concerned." The vicar cleared his throat, and his expression took on an unvicarly cunning that diverted Tristan. "But Miss Calder insists on earning funds to restore the church tower. I would rather save her the bother of the festival by holding a special collection of the landowners in the area. Two hundred pounds, that's what's needed." He added significantly, "Then we can cancel this Midsummer nonsense, and Miss Calder would have plenty of time to support your poor sister."

With a start, Tristan realized he was being touched for a contribution. He'd never before had the wherewithal to be a likely target for this, and he still wasn't at all sure he or Haverne could afford it, just to procure the services of some girl he'd never met. "The affairs here are in such a state I can't tell when we could make a contribution. Next fall, perhaps." That would take them safely past Midsummer, he thought. And if Miss Calder was as capable as the vicar said, the church tower should be restored to its previous glory by then.

The vicar seemed inclined to stand there and argue the point. But then the front door slammed, the boys' voices echoed shrill in the great hall, and their footsteps came stamping up the stairs. The vicar bowed and took his exit with unseemly alacrity.

Only an hour later Tristan heard of the miraculous Miss Calder again, this time from her brother. Sir Francis Calder tracked Tristan down in the plow yard, where he was staring at a plow and wondering how to hook a horse to it. Calder was a compact young man with a shock of dark hair, friendly hazel eyes, and an outstretched hand. "We live down the lane at the Grange. Thought I'd come and offer my aid, belated as it is. I came earlier, but the countess wasn't receiving. And, well, we had some flooding damage, you see, or I'd've been more helpful."

Tristan rose from beside the plow and shook the proffered hand. "No one would have known what to do with you, as I understand it. The foreman and hands quit, and the tenants weren't interested in paying for Haverne's seed, so they just planted their own acreage. Not that there are many tenants. My brother-in-law—"

"Let the place rot. Yes, we've noticed. My father was much the same, only he had me to keep the land fertile and the shot for the brandy paid. Kenny couldn't even keep a bailiff, for he never got around to paying them."

Such candor was oddly refreshing, and Tristan relaxed a bit. No need to keep up a loyal front with this one, who apparently knew Kenny all too well. "It's good land, though, do you think?"

Calder's harsh expression faded as he gazed lovingly out at the rolling hills, etched with hedgerows, washed in golden light. "Best damn farmland in the kingdom. It only needs good stewardship, you know, to offer up all the bounty God intended."

Tristan politely inclined his head at this piety. Then gesturing out at the barren fields, he asked, "Do you think it's too late to plant?"

Calder shrugged. "We were all late getting the seed into the ground this spring, for the lower fields near the rivers were inaccessible. Usually the summer lasts long after such a spring—just have to hope. You've got a fortnight before sun gets too hot for germination."

Once again, Tristan decided confession was the best policy. "I'm no wheat farmer. I haven't the slightest idea what to do. If you could steer me to a good foreman, I'd be grateful."

"You won't find a good foreman quick enough, for you'd probably have to go out of the county. Tell you what." Calder clapped him on the shoulder. "I'll send over a few of my hands to help you. They've been idle a day now anyway. A dozen or so men should do the trick." He cast an expert eye on the plow, then hefted it up with calloused hands and let it drop. "I'd best send over some plows and horses, too. Hell, I'll come myself and supervise it all, if you don't mind."

"If I don't mind?" Tristan stared at the other man, suspecting he was being touched for another contribution of some kind. But there was no vicarlike cunning in those frank eyes, and Tristan relaxed his guard. "No, I don't mind. In fact, I don't know how to thank you."

"No reason to stretch, old man." Calder kicked at the plow,

apparently uncomfortable with gratitude. "Nothing I like better than spring planting—or summer planting, as the case may be."

As they started back to the house, Calder asked diffidently, "How's Lady Haverne? I stopped by to pay my respects after the—the accident, but she wasn't receiving."

"She's still not receiving. The grief—and the scandal—have got her prostrate."

"No need for that," Calder said gruffly. "This ain't London. We don't care a fig for scandal. And besides, Kenny was ours, you know. We all knew what he was and weren't the least surprised at his end. Never expected anything else of him."

"Well, Anna did." He suspected, in fact, that self-disgust was as much a factor in her decline as grief over the husband she had so overesteemed.

"I'll send my sister over this afternoon," Calder said helpfully. "She can visit with your sister and start getting the household in order. I hear you've lost some staff."

"No more than the cook, the housekeeper, the butler, and all but one maid. Not to mention the boys' nurse. They drift away when they don't get paid."

"Well, Charity'll have things in hand in a day or so."

As they walked back to the front of the house, Tristan caught sight of Lawrence on the portico, all defiance now gone, leaning against a pillar with his head bowed. He must have said something unforgiveable to Jeremy, and now repented it. But when he saw his uncle, he scowled and ran back into the house.

Tristan felt the despair threaten again. He didn't think he could raise these boys, at least not Lawrence, who was so headstrong and angry and determined to push love to the breaking point. "The vicar did mention your sister, but he said she'd be too busy with Midsummer preparations to come."

"Too busy? Not Charity. She's got the energy of ten. She'll

find the time if you need her. And—" Calder grinned, "it looks like you need her." Calder's confidence in his sister was all the more striking for being so offhand. "She'd've been here earlier on but she was—"

"In London. Yes, the vicar told me she was a great success."

"Success?" Calder echoed with a brother's irreverence. "Charity? Oh, I suppose she did well enough. She received an offer or two. Fawcett—is that his name?"

"The nabob?" Even in Italy Tristan had heard about Fawcett, who liked to spend his Indian gold on very large paintings of very naked nymphs.

"That's the one. Such a settlement he offered! Not that I'd take anything, you know; I don't hold with auctioning off my sister like that. These nabobs come back from India where they all have slaves and think they can do the same with good English girls. And Chilworth, of course. Now him I was glad she sent packing. He sent a Bow Street Runner to find out if we were the right sort to ally with his exalted family."

"Chilworth. The marquess."

"Too high in the instep for my tastes. Though I was ready for her to accept the devil himself after she turned down Charlie Cantrell, and Ralph Bessemer, too. And some other fellow I can't remember. These hopeful suitors all tend to blend together after a time, you know."

Tristan stopped there in the middle of the overgrown path. "So many offers?" He didn't know much about English maidens, having in the main avoided the sort of girls who required chaperons. But he knew enough to know that this was inconceivable. "And she didn't accept any?"

"Well, I had high hopes for Bessemer, for he's just the sort of loose screw the girls seem to appreciate. Do you know him?"

A decade ago Tristan's father, a don at Oxford, was wont to use Ralph Bessemer as his prime illustration of the worthlessness of modern undergraduates. "I know of him."

"Always reminded me of Kenny, only Kenny hadn't any brains to speak of. So I guess it's best she saw through him, or I'd be in your shoes in a decade or so. The others, though, were right enough. Poor fools. They all trooped down here to apply to me. I felt like a physician telling 'em their days were numbered. And they were all so blasted disappointed." He shook his head ruefully. "I reckon, having decided to step right into the shackles, they expected she'd want to step in there with 'em. But she'd send me frantic notes: 'Forget Chilworth and his six hundred-year-old name!' 'Don't accept Bessemer and his ten thousand acres!' Now that one I disregarded, for I thought he was a dab hand with the ladies and could persuade her."

"An inflated reputation, I take it," Tristan said dryly, intrigued in spite of himself.

"Well, that's what she told me. Said he treated her only with the utmost respect." Calder's open face looked honestly confused. "It just goes to show. Don't the ladies always say they want to be treated like ladies? And then when we comply, they complain. It's a damned shame, for she'd be a fine wife. She's been too long raising my parent's children—we'd three younger brothers, you know. One's just twelve now, and he's been all Charity's doing."

Calder's sturdy bay was tied to a post near the portico, and they began walking that way. Calder cast him a speculative glance. "You're an artist, I hear. She likes art. She's got a stack of art books. My aunt said Charity would miss a picnic to spend an afternoon in the Royal Academy and look at the paintings."

Tristan couldn't help but wonder if she'd seen his own pictures, if she liked them. Then he realized he was being approached for another contribution, one considerably greater than the vicar's two hundred pounds. As politely as he could, Tristan said, "I'm not in the market for a wife."

"Wait till you meet our Charity. She's got a way of changing a fellow's mind. You know how you see some women and want to bed them?"

Tristan thought it prudent not to answer and was glad he hadn't when Calder continued, "Not my sister. You see her and want to wed her. You start thinking how well she'd entertain your guests and consult with your chef and raise your children. You think she'd keep your household in order and make your life peaceful—and she would. She's had a decade's worth of experience at it. I almost hate to lose her, for I can't imagine how my brothers and I'll do without her. But she deserves a home of her own, don't you think?"

Again Tristan thought it politic not to answer, and Calder nodded as he mounted his horse. "Just as well. I'd as soon not have her refuse another neighbor. She's turned down the squire's sons and his nephew, too. So the squire's beginning to think we're too haughty a family—the Calders! Haughty!" He urged his horse down the avenue, calling over his shoulder, "I'll be back later with the crew."

Chapter Three

The brisk Calder soon had five plows working the nearby fields and four men preparing the seed for sowing. Tristan found himself very much in the way and took up Calder's polite suggestion to assemble the records of the last three seasons to determine if more seed had to be ordered. He disliked feeling so useless, but he had never turned over a spade in his life and wouldn't be much help now. He resolved to find some way to repay Sir Francis. Calder would be offended by a direct offer of cash, but perhaps a fine hunter wouldn't be taken amiss. Kenny had probably left a stableful at his lodge in Leicestershire.

Closeted in the balcony-level study with three volumes of agricultural notations, Tristan was almost relieved to hear childish screeches in the great hall below. He had left the boys in care of the sole surviving groom, but they had apparently escaped again. He emerged from the study to the sounds of running feet. Then he heard a crash and knew, somehow, that it was the Sèvres vase he had given his sister on her twenty-fifth birthday. He strode to the railing, about to remonstrate with his nephews, when someone beat him to it.

"Lawrence, Jeremy! Did I break that when I opened the door?" The cheerful voice carried clearly on the lofty foyer. "No one answered my knock so I just walked in. But I never thought—well, I don't know my own strength, I vow! I mean to say, I didn't fling the door or crash it against the wall. But look on it—shards all over the floor! What an Amazon I must be!"

"What's an Amazon?" Jeremy asked.

"A very strong woman. Stronger'n any man." Tristan could hear her voice lilting with pride. But unless he hung over the railing, which he wasn't about to do, he would catch no glimpse of the unknown Amazon below him, under the balcony.

Lawrence's scornful tones, however, were all too familiar. "You're not an Amazon, Charity. You didn't break the vase. I did."

So this was the estimable Miss Calder, taking a break from her festival planning. Braden wandered farther along the railing, hoping for an unobstructed view. But he could only see fragments of porcelain scattered on the muddy parquet floor around a discarded bouquet of flowers.

"Oh, Lawrence, are you the strong one then? Did you just open the door and see the vase crash to the floor from your enormous strength?"

"No, he pushed it," said Jeremy, a boy without the guile of his brother—or Miss Charity. "He was in a taking something terrible."

Braden expected the girl to respond with the awful voice of authority, as he himself was about to do. But instead he heard only amusement. "Well, I should hope it was a terrible taking! I hope just a minor pique wouldn't inspire this sort of destruction, or we're none of us safe from Lawrence the Terrible!"

Jeremy's giggle encouraged her. "What a shame! Your mother told me once that your uncle gave her that." Her sigh was a masterpiece of longing and regret. "I was always so thrilled to see the vase and know it was most probably criminally obtained. All my relatives are so tediously honest, you know, and you get to have a smuggler uncle."

Tristan had never precisely considered his act of packing the vase carefully in his luggage and walking off a ship a crime, but he supposed it was, at all that. And his credit with Lawrence immediately went up a notch or two. "Uncle Tristan smuggled that?"

"Well, it's of no account. The excise agents would have no use for the vase now. Look at it, all smashed to bits. Lawrence, you wild man, what were you thinking, smashing your mother's vase?" There was the slightest pause, then the gentle suggestion, "Were you angry at your mother, perhaps?"

Tristan, curiously moved by the girl's unconventional tactics, waited for the boy's answer. Finally Lawrence cried, "She wouldn't see me! She sent me away! She said she couldn't bear to see me today!" In an instant his sobs were muted, presumably by a feminine shoulder.

"Oh, you poor darlings. It's been awful for you, hasn't it? I just don't blame you a bit, Lawrence, in fact I can't, for I've been just as bad myself."

"You? Bad?" Lawrence's voice was raw but retained its scoffing note.

"You would never believe it to look at me, would you? But I was so wicked—just once. No, I can't tell you! It's too bad!"

Of course, the boys were begging at this point, and Tristen himself was in some suspense. Reluctantly Miss Calder said, "You must promise to tell no one. And promise you won't think too badly of me. You see—come here, Jeremy, sit with us—"

Braden heard the swish of skirts on wood and imagined her sitting down on the floor and gathering the boys into her lap if she were telling them a bedtime story. "It was all because of preserves."

"Preserves?" Jeremy echoed.

"Yes, preserves. Strawberry, cherry, peach—my mother loved to put up preserves. It always embarrassed me to see her working like a scullery maid, and of course she made me help, too. Oh, she'd have the whole house steaming with the heat of a dozen kettles, and all the maids would be peeling grapes and plums. And I, naturally, had to stir the muck. You can imagine what that did to my elaborate coiffure."

"What's a coiffure?" Jeremy whispered.

"A hair arrangement. And I didn't have one, once preserving day was done. I never could understand why we had to put up so many pots every year, for we had shelves and shelves of them. Five brothers, I had, and we never made a dent in the supply. But still Mother had to put up more. Then she died."

"You poisoned one of the pots?" Lawrence breathed.

"I poisoned—Lawrence, where do you get these notions? Has someone been reading you gruesome German tales? No, I didn't poison anything. I wouldn't poison my mother, even if she made me put up preserves every day of the year."

"I didn't really think so," Lawrence's shame was mitigated only by his disappointment. "So what did you do that was so wicked?"

Miss Calder signed gustily. "I was so angry when she died—oh, don't look so shocked at me! You promised you wouldn't think badly of me! I know it's shameful, but I really was angry that she died. I was sad, too, but first of all I was angry." There was a combative spark in her words now—what a voice she had, Tristan marveled, wishing he could see her expression. She could go on Drury Lane tomorrow. "And I don't think either of you can tell me I shouldn't have been."

Jeremy squeaked his demurral, and, in a bit of a huff, she went on. "So the day after the funeral, I went into the stillroom—" her voice lowered shamefully, or perhaps only conspiratorially—"and I took one of the jampots and—and I took it out to the pond and I heaved it. As far as I could. Apricot preserves. My favorite."

There was a moment of silence. "That's not very wicked."

"Well, Larry," she mimicked his scornful tone, "it's not a

Sèvres vase, to be sure. But then I'm not titled. I can't afford to go about destroying my valuable possessions. But valuable or no, it made me feel much better. I even went back into the stillroom and got another pot."

"Did you heave that one, too?" Jeremy, at least, was still innocent enough to be impressed.

"I was going to. But then I saw the label. It had an etching of the Grange on it, with the big oak tree in the front, and underneath it said 'From the kitchens of Calder Grange'—we have only one kitchen, actually, but Mother thought it more impressive in the plural. She used to give the jam to all our guests. She sometimes had to press it on them, for I imagine they had stillrooms full of preserves, too. You know, I'll wager we could end starvation entirely if we just gave away the contents of our stillrooms! But perhaps," her voice grew meditative, "perhaps even starving people would get weary of forever eating grape jam."

Tristan leaned back against the paneled wall, suppressing a laugh. Lawrence was not so amused at the digression. "You didn't heave it, did you?"

"No, I didn't. I meant to, but then I thought of how much my mother loved to make the preserves and how she always told me that good jam was just like love, sweet and nourishing—that isn't very appealing, is it? Jam is so sticky! So I put the pot down and sat there in the stillroom and just cried and cried there among the jampots Mother loved so."

"Mother loved her vase!" Lawrence suddenly wailed. "That's why I broke it! She was so cruel!"

"Oh, darling, I know! Even if she didn't mean to be, I know how hurt you must have been! And you couldn't tell her so, when she isn't well, could you? So you had to break the vase instead." The slightly ragged edge to her sigh touched Tristan as much as Lawrence's sobs, and he no longer cared very much about the vase. "But I haven't the slightest idea what to do now. Can we mend it?"

"Not likely," Jeremy replied with mournful pride. "It's in a thousand bits."

"And someone's sure to notice it's gone. That's why I chose a jampot. No one would notice it was gone, for there were a hundred others. But what are we to do?"

Lawrence said, "I suppose I must confess to Mama that I did it."

"Are you sure you can? I never confessed about the jampot, except to you, of course, for I knew you wouldn't spill the soup. I wasn't brave enough. Perhaps you aren't either."

His manhood questioned, Lawrence could only aver, "I am so brave enough. I'll even confess to Uncle Tristan."

"My word, Larry, you must be careful. After all, we know your uncle is—well, criminally inclined."

I? Tristan wanted to protest but held his tongue, for Lawrence, of all people, was defending him. "He's not so horrid as you might think, Charity. He said Jerry and I could be pagans if we liked."

"Pagans?" Miss Calder echoed faintly. "Aren't you afraid he's a pagan, too? Don't they boil people in oil?" Tristan didn't know whether to be amused or outraged that she was putting such thoughts in his nephews' heads. But Larry's reply reassured him; she knew what she was about, however labyrinthine her methods.

"That's cannibals. And I don't think he's a cannibal. I don't think he'd even beat me, as long as I apologized."

"Still, to be safe, I think you might offer to pay him back. That might pacify him. Do you get an allowance?"

"Not till I go away to school. And I wouldn't want to have to give it up. I could tell him I'll pay him when I come into my inheritance when I'm twenty-one. I'm seven now, so it's only—" He halted, such higher mathematics beyond his ken.

"A very long time. Well, you can put it to him. But I imagine an apology graciously extended will be graciously accepted, and you can let your solicitors haggle over the price."

"What's a solicitor?" said Jeremy, but Lawrence shushed him.

"I can make another vase. Not a—a whatever you said, but I have some modeling clay."

"That's a good idea. But isn't there something else you should do first?" The boys remained in a baffled silence until she prompted, "The mess here. I wager your downstairs maid has enough to do without this."

"She's the upstairs maid, too, and the cook." Lawrence gave a put-upon sigh, then said with an oddly adult resignation, "I'll clean it up."

"I'll help," Jeremy piped up, for he hated to be left out.

"Do ask the maid to watch you though, so you don't get cut. I wager she'll love sitting back and watching someone else work for a change! And I'll tell you what." The boys' silence was obviously expectant, and she did not disappoint. "If you do a good job sweeping up here, I'll see if you can help me with my Midsummer work! I must build, oh, booths and tables, and I will need some able confederates. I *think* you are old enough, but—well, we shall see. Now I'll go on up and see your mother. I've picked her some wildflowers from the copse, and they can't fail to perk her up."

"She won't see you," Lawrence said with a return to his gloomy disdain.

"Oh, I shan't give her the chance to tell me! I'll just burst in like the big bad wolf and blow all her protests out the window. Now go on, you find the broom, and I'll go huff and puff and blow down your mama's door."

Braden heard the boys pelter off, then the girl's heels clicking on the oak parquet. "Ick. Little boy hands are always so sticky. Jam, jam, all over my dress." At first he thought she was addressing the maid or had perhaps discovered the listener above her. But then he saw her emerge from under the balcony and cross to the brass mirror on the opposite wall, and he realized she was talking to herself. He wondered if

44

that was a habit of hers, if she was so used to cajoling and coaxing others she addressed herself with the same cheerful purpose.

Now he recognized her as exactly the Charity he had unconsciously envisioned—a small girl with a neat figure, in a chocolate riding habit of fashionably military cut. The short jacket just skimmed her trim waist; the hem of her skirt was a little dusty from the floor. Her thick curls were of a matching brown, tumbled from their pins by little-boy hugs. What he could observe of her face was pretty, triangular, wide at the brow and pointed at the chin, with a certain liveliness around the dark eyes that accorded with her lively voice.

Her features arranged so easily into a merry smile that he thought it must be customary, along with the wrinkled-nose face she made in the mirror. She rubbed at a smudge on her cheek, murmuring, "Minx! The elegant Anna will never believe you took in London." She laughed at her reflection's reaction to this and suddenly leaned over the rosewood table and kissed herself in the streaked mirror. Then she made another silly face and vanished—or so it seemed, but Braden realized she had only run up the steps. He melted back into the shadows, for spies best remain hidden, and watched her emerge at the top of the stairs and head to his sister's room, the motley assortment of blossoms back in her hand.

Once she had knocked and entered without waiting for a response, Tristan moved closer to his sister's open door. He was not, in the general way, an eavesdropper. But this chit had marched into the house and immediately set about disciplining his nephews—very capably, he had to admit. Then she started talking to herself and kissing herself in the mirror. Of course, she thought herself unobserved, but her unconventional actions, coupled with that reference to the boys' criminal pagan of an uncle, made him wary. Now she meant to assault his sister with her unique brand of impertinent cheer.

He could forgive himself a certain unease about Anna's fate at the hands of this very managing Miss Calder.

But fascination with her methods kept him out of the room and out of sight, though still within earshot. He leaned against the wall, waiting to hear Anna's faint voice of protest. But she never got the chance. Miss Calder began chattering as soon as she cleared the threshold. "Anna, dear, how lovely to see you. But how sad, too! What a sorrowful time you've had of it. Kenny was so young. Such sad news, and the vicar told me you had to manage it all quite alone until your brother arrived. I'm so glad he's here, for I can't bear to think of you by yourself in this big house. Of course, you have the children, but they really cannot help as a brother can. You have been so brave—oh, my dear, go ahead and cry, only you'll probably make me cry, too, and I don't look quite so adorable in tears. Just look at you—it's entirely unfair how glorious you look with your eyes glistening so. Your nose doesn't redden in the slightest—however do you manage it?"

Before Anna could answer this unanswerable question, Miss Calder sped on. "I brought you some flowers. Just wildflowers. I gathered them from the copse, but they are pretty, aren't they? Have you been out to see the meadows? Full of daisies! Oh, you must see them! Kent is its loveliest in spring, you know, and that's very lovely! I'm so glad to be home when the flowers are blooming, aren't you? You really must come out to the garden, at least. Tomorrow."

Good luck with that, Tristan thought, pressing his head wearily against the wall. But at least Anna wasn't sobbing, not that she'd had time to get a whimper in edgewise.

"I'll pack a picnic lunch then. Alfresco meals were all the crack in London this season, so I've the most luscious menus. I'll tell you all about the Clayborne Mayday picnic at Ranelagh when all the London swells fell at my feet—I'd grabbed the last bottle of champagne, you understand!"

As he expected, Anna made a demurring noise. But then

the resourceful Charity changed tactics again. No longer the social director, she was regretful and a bit insulted. "Oh, I knew you wouldn't believe me. I told myself, Lady Haverne is a true cosmopolitan. She'll never believe an ordinary girl had her day in the London sun. So I shan't even tell you." This haughtiness lasted exactly a second. "Although I was hoping you'd be the slightest bit intrigued. Even proud. For you were my model. Oh, not in appearance, of course; I hadn't a prayer of suddenly acquiring inky black waves and those flashing eyes of yours. But I'd truly applied myself these last years, ever since I first met you, to determine how you'd behave always so exquisitely. I was ever such a hoyden, but I was fortunate to have a pattern of a true lady to follow. So whenever I found myself in a precarious situation, I would ask, How would Lady Haverne handle this? And I would do it just that way, and I fancy I always acted with a bit of your grace."

To his surprise, Anna finally spoke. It was a little more than a squeak, and quickly faded, but her voice showed more animation than he had heard since he arrived. "Did you really think of me?"

"Yes, I did. I never told any of the multitude who complimented me on my pretty behavior that it was all copied. I preferred they thought it was entirely natural, that I had grown up in some royal court and not a rough-and-tumble manor house. But I knew the flattery was really due you, even if the flatterers didn't."

Painfully Anna asked, "Were they all talking about—about me in London?"

"Well, I hope not!" came the gay reply. "They were all talking about me! Who is that mysterious Miss Calder? Oh, perhaps she looks as if she's just up from the country, but see how she pours tea. Exquisite, don't you think?" Her imitation of a London fop was note-perfect, and Tristan was hard-put not to announce his presence by laughing aloud.

"I mean, were they all talking about the—the duel?"

"Oh, the duel. Well, there was some talk in March, but the season was just beginning and the next thing we knew that German princess had eloped with her physician and everyone suspected he had been drugging her. So no one gave poor Kenny another thought." Ruefully she added, "Fame is ever fleeting in London, you know."

"But here, here in Calder. Everyone's gossiping, I'm sure."

"Gossiping? Come, dearest, this isn't London. People have better things to do than endlessly work over the latest scandal. Especially after the flood in April. And the Midsummer fair is coming up, and there's ever so much work to do—you know, I think your boys might like to help me with the preparations. Lawrence is quite the little Hercules. And they can go through their toys to donate a few to the jumble booth. You'll remember to ask them, won't you? They will love the fortune-teller, I know. Everyone will, except the vicar. He thinks it's paganism."

She broke off her cheery monologue, and Tristan could hear his sister's now-familiar sobs. He almost went in, but then the heartbreaking sounds quieted, and he imagined Miss Calder's shoulder was getting soaked again.

"There, there, darling. You know, this is all sad enough without you thinking yourself the center of gossip. For Kenny was ours before he was yours. We all loved him despite his faults, so we can hardly think the worse of his wife for feeling the same way."

"But I didn't even know that he had—had faults like that."

"You are in good company! Why, only this morning Mrs. Jenkinson—she buys our excess milk from us—told me that Kenny Haverton was the sweetest boy in Kent and no one would ever convince her otherwise. Of course," she continued thoughtfully, "he'd never put a snake in her picnic basket, so she could still cherish an illusion or two."

A watery giggle was her answer. "Did he really do that?"

"Yes. And much, much more. I was only eight, so—Lord, he must have been eighteen then! And still playing such pranks. At any rate, he was very sweet when he wasn't wicked, and no one blames you for loving him. You deserved better, of course, but surely you've noticed most women deserve better than the husbands they end up with."

There was a sardonic note in her lilting voice that saved it from girlishness, and Tristan recalled her rejected swains. Not particularly respectful of the opposite sex, Miss Calder. But then her tone briskened. "Now then, what's this about you not receiving callers? Not everyone is as rude as I, you know; if you tell them to go away, they will usually go away. And then you're left all alone with your sad thoughts. No, Anna, no more hiding away in your lonely tower. Your brother is here and I am here, and you shan't be alone, prefer it or no!"

Anna made some inarticulate protest, and Miss Calder laughed, an impish sound, light and teasing. "You haven't any choice, my dear, so you must get used to it. Come, give me your arm, and I'll show you. Just lean on me; of course you're feeling weak, you've been lying down forever." Her voice, when it resumed, came from farther away. "Now do you see my brother and his crew there? You have been taken over by Calders. Francis has been trying to buy that south field from Kenny for years. Now he'll get his chance to farm it, after all. He is such an enthusiastic farmer, you know."

"I'm so glad," Anna replied. "Please, take me back to bed now." There was a shifting of the mattress, and Anna's sigh. "I am glad, for I hadn't given a thought to the planting, and I doubt poor Tristan knows a hoe from a serving fork. He's not a farmer, you see."

"But an artist! Much more exciting, I think. You never told me your brother was the famous Lord Braden. I must tell you what my aunt said when she saw his—"

Tristan thought it best to cut short this artistic discussion before he heard something he preferred not to—the fate of all eavesdroppers, he understood. He knocked on the open door and entered to see his sister pale and lovely, traces of tears silver on her cheeks, her blue-black hair arranged against the white pillow. "Oh, Anna, I see you have a visitor." He was rather proud of his nonchalance; Miss Calder wasn't the only one worthy of Drury Lane.

As his sister performed the introductions, even smiling a bit, Braden got his first close look at Miss Calder. She rose from her perch on the bed, her fair cheeks flushed, but she quickly regained her composure. Her hand was small and warm in his, her smile merry, revealing a couple of dimples. Her eyes, a clear hazel, were nicely fringed with dark lashes; her gaze was direct and unafraid. She had discarded the light jacket of her riding habit, and a white chemisette hinted pleasantly at the curve of her breasts. She had no claim to beauty—there was no mystery in that gaze—but this was an appealing face, fresh and piquant and intelligent.

And the contrast between the energetic Charity and his beautiful, broken sister was almost too painful to bear.

As if she understood, Miss Calder moved away from Anna's bed and began to arrange the neglected wildflowers in the pitcher on the mantel. Tristan's sharp eye noted her felicity with the simple art; the daisies were surrounded by the deep pink hedgeroses, and a single green fern, asymmetrically placed, balanced the pitcher's spout. "Lady Haverne has agreed to come out to the garden with me in the morning. I told her she would like the flowers, but actually I'm planning to bore her with tales of my life in London."

"London suited you then?"

She looked back from her flowers, perhaps sensing some challenge, though he had meant none. The she chuckled, a pretty sound, like gold coins in a pocket. "But of course. And I suited London! I was named the Incomparable! Actually," she told Anna in a stage whisper, "I was called the Comparable, but here in the country they don't understand such distinctions and think it a fine title indeed."

Anna, he was glad to notice, made a brave show of feminine curiosity. "Did you fix the attention of any special gentlemen?"

Miss Calder set the pitcher of flowers on the night table and wrinkled her nose in dismay. "Oh, tomorrow when we are in the garden, I shall confess all. Now I must take my leave and go back to the church. Oh, Anna, Lawrence has a matter to take up with you. Please don't be too angry with him, for he's a boy, and boys are inclined to be troublesome." She cast a mischievous glance at Tristan. "Of course, you only had the one brother, and I've no doubt he was a paragon. But mine weren't so good, and Lawrence is no worse than the best of them—or no better than the worst, is that what I mean?" She picked up her jacket and gloves and bent to touch Anna's cheek. "Till tomorrow, dearest."

"I'll see you out," Braden said in response to the speaking glance the girl gave him.

As he had expected, the silent invitation was extended for purposes less lascivious than instructive. While they walked down the staircase, Miss Calder quickly outlined Lawrence's crime and punishment. She gestured to the dingy parquet floor of the foyer. "You see, he's swept every bit. So if you could just—oh, forgive me. I shouldn't tell you how to handle your own nephew. I've so many brothers, you see, that I tend to play big sister to any little boy. But he really was very sorry."

Tristan promised not to give Lawrence the thrashing he no doubt deserved. "They have no nurse, you see, and have been let to run wild."

"I'll send over my old governess Cammie. She's been sadly underworked since Joey—since we grew out of the schoolroom. But of course, she reared us, so we've never been able to let her go. She'll enjoy staying with the boys till you find a permanent nurse."

"I would be in your debt," he replied, with a humility that

was entirely new to him. He was unaccustomed to such open generosity as these Calders had shown. "My sister is already a world improved."

She tugged on her riding gloves as they reached the front door. "I'll arrange some visits from the ladies of the church. Does she sew at all? She can make rag dolls to give away to the poor children at the Midsummer fair. Busy hands mend a troubled heart, you know. Well, of course, you know that, you're an artist. Do try to admire her, won't you? She's probably missing all the compliments she usually garners—some women waste away for lack of flattery, I think. And Kenny darling—what a snake he was—Kenny's end must have been a great blow to her pride. If you tell her she's still lovely, perhaps she'll think she's still lovable." She wrinkled her nose again—a childish trait, and rather endearing. "Of course, she'll be mighty suspicious, hearing such twaddle from her brother, but the ladies do appreciate flattery, no matter what the source!"

Awkwardly he said, "I don't know how to thank you."

"Then don't." She walked briskly through the door he held open. "You'll no doubt be wanting to curse me in a day or two, calling me an interfering baggage. Will you remind her I'll be by at eleven? I'll bring lunch. Join us if you like."

This invitation was delivered with candid amiability that was hard to suspect. But in his experience, unmarried girls didn't invite men to lunch so casually, and he recalled her brother's speculative comment, "You're an artist—she likes art."

But before he could ready a polite refusal, she was running down the stone steps, her light farewell floating back to him. Not waiting for his help, she used a rail of the fence for a mounting block, and in a moment, never looking back, she was cantering down the avenue. She rode well, her back straight, her hands light. Yet another accomplishment of this most accomplished miss.

Anna had sagged back on her pillows but raised her head when he returned. "Isn't Charity a very good sort of girl?" Her eyes misted as she touched a daisy chain Charity had left on the counterpane. "And she hasn't any reason to be. I never paid her the slightest mind. Oh, I invited her and the other gentlewomen to tea, of course, whenever we were here, but we were never here. But she and her brother—they're just being kind, aren't they? I'd forgotten that sometimes people are just kind."

He took her hand, hurt by the transparency of the skin over her fragile bones. "It's the country way, I suppose. A little village like this must weave a web of kindness if it is to thrive."

"Oh, but I haven't ever been part of it. I've never cared at all for the place, so slow and dull compared to London. And yet, my friends in town—"

Tears clouded up her voice and she broke off. But he could finish her thought: her London friends had sent her pro forma letters of condolence and forgotten her. He'd never had the slightest illusion about the nature of such relationships, but Anna was honestly hurt by their defection. He forestalled her returning melancholy. "Miss Calder certainly is a helpful young lady."

For some reason, Anna took this as an insult. "Oh, I know you think she is too managing. I saw that critical look of yours—you always used to look just so when Father put on his tyrannical performance. You narrow your eyes and raise that eyebrow even while you remain perfectly polite. I am your elder sister, don't you forget, and I know all your ways."

As she asserted her seniority over him, she pulled herself up straight against the headboard and tugged her hand out of his. Pleased to have elicited such a spirited response, however unintentionally, he amended, "Not managing, precisely. Competent."

"Competent. Well, that sounds very dull, and she isn't in the least dull. And I don't remember her getting the least bit forward before this. I guess I brought out the nurse in her. I seem to recall that she does sick calls for the parish. And, of course, her mother died young, and her father suffered a lingering death a few years ago, so she's plenty of experience. I think their deaths postponed her come-out for years. She must be nearly of age and only just had her season!"

For a moment, her voice faded; she was doubtlessly remembering her own glorious season a decade earlier. Then she roused, pouting a little as her thoughts returned to Miss Calder. "And she came home unmarried. How sad! I just don't understand it. You would think one man in London at least would have noticed what a fine wife she would make. It's not as if she is an antidote, after all. She has a lovely smile and a fine little figure," Anna observed with the objectivity of a woman of fabled beauty. "I suppose there wasn't much of a dowry, but surely not every man this season was a fortune hunter. And yet she received no offers!"

"Why do you assume that?"

Anna regarded him with sisterly disdain. "Tristan dear, girls without fortune or beauty can't pick and choose. If she had received an eligible offer, the banns would have been posted before the suitor left the house."

With great restraint, he forbore to correct her, knowing Miss Calder's revelation of her conquests would enliven the picnic. He only commented, "She doesn't seem to be shrinking away in response to rejection. In fact, she appeared to be entirely self-assured."

"I knew you would say something of the sort, and in such a tone!"

Tristan thought his tone had been impersonally admiring, but he didn't object, for Anna's eyes, so recently lackluster, were flashing in response to his perceived offense.

"Of course, you're judging her bold because she speaks up clearly and looks you directly in the eye and doesn't practice those mysterious die-away airs all your flirts cultivate. Men!"

Her spirited charge had quite dried the tears in her eyes,

and Tristan laughingly held up his hands in protest. "I am not judging her at all. I concede that she's a fine girl. She's cheered you and that's enough to earn her my regard. But you must admit, Anna, that she is a bit—"

He let his voice trail off, and Anna obligingly filled in the blank. "Talkative? Oh, I imagine she is, but she is most amusing, isn't she? I know you don't like that sort of girl. You'd prefer her to communicate entirely in significant looks and wistful sighs."

"How do you know what I'd like?" he demanded.

"Because you are my baby brother, and your tastes haven't changed since you were thirteen and fell in love with that mysterious French emigré who turned out to be a jewel thief—"

Tristan hadn't thought of Madam Daumier in a decade, but for his sister's sake he reminisced, "The perfect woman. She opened her mouth only for kissing."

Instead of shock, Anna responded with a big sister's skepticism. "How would you know? And I heard she also opened her mouth to smoke opium."

"No wonder I worship her still. An opium-smoking jewel thief—the stuff of dreams."

Anna's laughter dissolved into tears, and he held her against him as sobs racked her fragile body. She was still so beautiful, even after three months shut away in grief. Their mother had been just the same, heartbreakingly lovely even as she died of sorrow. But Anna wouldn't, not if he could help it. He waited for her tears to abate, then gently urged her back on the pillows.

"You must rest now. You have a picnic tomorrow, do you remember?"

"Oh, Tristan," she whispered, "I can't."

"You must." He rose abruptly and went to the door, then forced himself to turn back with a smile. "If you aren't ready to celebrate at eleven, your Miss Calder will have my head.

And I know you'd never consign your baby brother to such a fate."

"She's really very nice, Tristan, she is!" Her faint protests followed him out the door. He heard his nephews thundering up the stairs and thought Miss Calder's old governess couldn't arrive too soon to suit him.

Chapter Four

"I worry about you, Charity," the Reverend Mr. Langworth said in his avuncular way as they walked through the nave of the old church. The morning sunlight streamed in through the stained-glass windows, outlining every mote of dust their entrance had stirred up. "Taking on so much, with your usual household duties, and the poor work—just preparing your brother for Eton will take all summer! I wish you would not have cut your time in London short, for I'm persuaded you need a holiday far more than we need this rubbish about Midsummer."

"Oh, a season in London is hardly a holiday." Charity stopped by a battered pew and with her handkerchief rubbed off a bit of gumdrop from the seat back. After Midsummer, she thought, I must get all the ladies to come in and scrub down every pew and beat out the kneelers, too. "I have gotten much better rest since I've been home away from all the traffic noise. And you needn't worry about me! You've always said I have too much energy. Why, if I hadn't the outlet of the church work and the Midsummer fair, I don't doubt I would have to take up smuggling just for diversion!"

"But to come home early from your grand season for such a trivial purpose! Why, I heard Mrs. Williams just yesterday lamenting that with another week you might have made the acquaintance of some respectable man that you could have joined in life."

The vicar's sigh was quite well done as he continued down the aisle, his hands clasped behind his back, his head bent so that Charity couldn't see his expression. But she could imagine it: wily, cunning, a bit shamed.

Unfair, she thought, and almost said it aloud. Instead she followed him past the altar toward the sacristy. Her boot heels set up an angry clatter on the worn granite; deliberately she slowed, smoothed her steps, just as deliberately softened her tone as she spoke. "Mrs. Williams said that? I'll have to thank her for taking such an interest in my life. But I think I met every respectable man in London, and a few less respectable ones, so I missed little by coming home. And Midsummer isn't trivial. Why, it's the most important festival of the summer, and the whole parish looks forward to it! Especially after the terrible spring floods, I think we need something to cheer the village folk, don't you?"

They went on fencing like this in the church parlor, Charity and the vicar. She kept her voice light and her manner cheery; Mr. Langworth maintained a gloomy mien throughout. It must have been better than a play for the housekeeper, Mrs. Ferris, who brought in lemonade and biscuits and stayed to polish the gleaming sideboard, her ear bent in the direction of the tea table.

Now that Charity had volunteered her services as organizer, Mr. Langworth could not credibly insist on cancelling Midsummer. But he could and did object to every proposal she made for entertainment.

An orchestra for the Midsummer Eve banquet would be too expensive; Charity smiled and agreed, knowing that Mr. Perry, the mason, would donate his fiddle playing in return for getting the contract to fix the tower.

The St. George and the Dragon mumming play planned for after the banquet offered a violent example to the village children; Charity pointed out that St. George was Britain's patron saint, thus the tradition had patriotic as well as religious significance.

"What if," she said, as if struck by inspiration, "we follow it with a more devotional sort of play, one the children perform themselves? If they are desperately trying to remember their lines for, oh, say, Jonah and the Whale, they will pay no attention to the St. George story."

The vicar could hardly accuse her of lying about the devotion of the church's children, and he could hardly cancel Britain's patron saint. So in bad grace he said, "I shan't hear of any fortune-telling. That's paganism, and worse, it will remind people of painful conflicts of the past. It wasn't so long ago that witches were burned, you know."

That ominous warning wouldn't deter Margo Ashton, Charity knew, for the baker's wife loved to dress up in her gypsy costume and frown at her cards, intoning bad tidings in an eerie voice. But Charity would find some place for her, if not along the green where the concession booths would be located.

"No fortune-telling booths then." Charity sighed, as if making a great concession. "But I do worry what Mr. Ashton will say if we not only deprive Margo of her fortune-telling but we also don't put in our customary order for destiny cakes from his bakery. There's no witchcraft in destiny cakes, surely, only a bit of amusement."

And so it went as they nibbled their biscuits, Charity conceding a little bit and keeping a great deal, the vicar glowering, knowing he was being cheated but too fond of her to point it out. But on one point he stood firm.

"No kissing booth. Absolutely none."

Mrs. Ferris, whose daughters wanted to staff this booth, stopped polishing long enough to hurrumph her agreement, but the vicar was caught up in his righteous wrath and didn't notice.

"I would be the scandal of the diocese if I sanctioned such depravity as the girls of the parish kissing the boys of the parish!"

"But, Mr. Langworth, they are doing it anyway." Charity's thoughts went inevitably to Lord Braden, wondering if he would purchase a kiss at a kissing booth if she were the kisser. With a wrench she forced the picture out of her mind and brought her attention back to the vicar. He was already pink with outrage, but practicality required one last effort. "At least with a kissing booth, the Tower Restoration Fund could benefit from the depravity."

"Not another word, Charity Calder!" The vicar, who was given to theatricality, raised his hand as if warding off temptation. "You'll not persuade me that the tower's foundation is so paltry it needs to be propped up with kisses!"

"Well, kisses will hardly bring it down, either!" Charity had never hoped to win the kissing booth, lucrative as it might have been. Still she sought a concession in return for dropping this demand. "We will need something to keep the young men occupied and peaceable. Sporting endeavors surely during the afternoon. An ale booth also—"

"You think ale will keep them peaceable?" The vicar, of course, had been known to heft a mug of ale on a hot summer afternoon, but in his Old Testament wrathful role, he disregarded this. "More likely it will lead to brawling and tendentiousness!"

"With Mrs. Hering regulating the supply?" Triumphantly she produced this trump card. "You know her own sons and nephews are the likeliest brawlers—" That was true; the Hering boys were known for their pugilistic predilections but were all cowed by the family matriarch. "And, Mr. Langworth, you know it might be a conciliatory gesture to ask her to take charge of such an important concession, after your little disagreement with her."

The vicar muttered some annoyance to himself but said

nothing more, and Charity knew she'd scored another point. Squire Hering was an important man in their little parish, and Mrs. Hering nearly as integrated into the church benevolence as Charity herself. The vicar could not long be on the outs with them. As Charity knew he would, he nodded grudgingly. But he made one last attempt to divert her.

"You did go out to Haverne, didn't you, to help the countess? She is in a sad way, isn't she?"

Charity nodded, wary of his direction.

"Fortunate that her brother has arrived, of course. But I don't know that a man can be a great help in this sort of situation. Another woman, one as gifted in sympathy as you, however, can work miracles." The vicar smiled in what he must have thought was a conspiratorial way. "That is, at least, what I promised Lord Braden!" Somber again, he finally got to his point. "You must not lose sight of what is truly important, Charity. Organizing this Midsummer festival in meaningless compared to perhaps saving Lady Haverne from—from the ultimate despair."

Long adept at controlling her temper, Charity did not object to this cynical use of Lady Haverne's grief. She only smiled sweetly. "You need not worry, sir. I shall have no trouble coordinating the two duties you have assigned me. Indeed, by the Midsummer fair, I promise you, she will be well on the way to health again."

With that bold prediction, she left the vicar to write his Sunday sermon, which would no doubt condemn Midsummer, paganism, revelry, and ale, and include a few barbs about kissing, too.

In the old church hall, Charity found the blond Ferris girls, daughters of the rectory housekeeper, engaged in their monthly task of washing down the whitewashed walls and plank floor. The floor was still slick from its washing, and Charity picked a careful way to the center of the hall. She turned around, imagining how many banquet tables it might hold. It was every bit as large as the church sanctuary but barren of pews.

If Midsummer arrives wetly, Charity thought, we can hold the entire festival in here. But then the dance circle of twenty-four candles might burn the place down around their heads. She would just have to pray for sunshine, she decided, and hope that the Lord would dismiss the vicar's prayers for a hurricane.

In the meantime, the stage under the rose window, where the choir practiced, would make a good rehearsal place for the children's play. Over by the entry there was room to store the lumber for the booths; she would have to order the wood from Mr. Milton's yard after lunch. Perhaps he would see fit to donate the nails and lend the tools and even help out with the building, if she promised him one of their new retriever pups.

The Ferris girls were still scrubbing the west wall, one kneeling, one standing, one on tiptoe, all glancing over their shoulders at her. When she finally said, "Hullo, Polly. Molly, Dolly," they halted in their labors and turned eagerly to her.

"So," the eldest and boldest inquired with bright interest, propping her mop against the door, "do we get to do our kissing or no?"

"Polly, do you think me a miracle worker? I couldn't even get the words out before he thundered that he would never allow it. Your mother was quite in agreement, to judge by her expression."

Dolly, the youngest girl, giggled, but then, when Polly shot her a stern glance, she hushed and backed away into a pail of soapy water. Her apologetic murmur was barely audible in the clanging echoes the collision set up.

"Dolly, you are such a gawk." Polly dismissed her sister with a wave of her hand and turned back to Charity. "St.

Ann's Parish, I hear, earned forty pounds from its kissing booth. Did you tell the vicar that?"

"No," Charity replied dryly. She picked up the discarded mop and used it to sop up the spill of soapy water before it stained the oak. "I thought he might come back with the amount the resulting parish bastards cost St. Ann's. It was never more than a gamble, Polly, you knew that. And—" She cast a knowing look at the other girl. "I shouldn't think any girl needs to shill for the Tower Restoration Fund to get a man to kiss her at Midsummer."

"But it's more fun in a booth with everyone looking!" Molly, the middle girl, had dreams of a stage career, and Charity, fresh from her aunt's box at Drury Lane, had to agree that kissing practice would probably further that ambition.

"Molly, you will just have to audition for the role of the princess in St. George and the Dragon! In the end, when you are saved by the brave St. George, you can throw your arms around him in a demonstration of gratitude."

Molly was pleased enough with the picture, but Polly, more discriminating, broke in. "Who's to be St. George then? If it's Malachi Morgan, Molly may have him. But I might give her a bit of a contest, if St. George is.... mmmm—" She glanced mischievously at Charity. "Crispin Hering, perhaps."

"I'm sure he'd love to be fought over." Charity kept her tone neutral; Crispin had always been one of her best friends, even after she rejected his marriage proposal.

"Or that new lord in the neighborhood. Him I'd kiss for free! Lady Haverne's brother, what's his name?"

"Lord Braden," Molly supplied. "I hear he's ever so handsome. Could he be St. George?"

"I don't know." A vision of Lord Braden in armor flashed in Charity's mind, bringing with it the glimmer of an idea— two ideas, really. "What would you think, girls, of a St. George competition? Among the young men?"

All three of her advisors looked blankly back at her, and Charity sighed inwardly, wishing her tongue could keep up with her mind. "I mean, of course, what would you think of a contest, let me see, of swordplay and dragon-killing? A St. George sort of endeavor. The young men of the parish could demonstrate their skill, and the most proficient would be chosen St. George in the mummery play. No, Polly," she added, guessing the question hovering on the girl's full lips, "kissing will not be the skill tested."

Polly shrugged her disappointment, then brightened. "It's a thought, Miss Charity. All them young men gathered, stripped to the waist for the boxing—"

"No boxing," Charity said faintly, imagining the vicar's reaction. "Just—just fencing. St. George kills the dragon with his sword, after all. What do you think?"

"When will it be held?"

"Say a fortnight. That would give us time to get the word round. We could do it in an evening, and all the men—bachelors, only, of course—would be invited to compete."

"It's a lovely idea, it is." Dolly spoke up for the first time. "Men like to compete, they do, and if you charge an entry fee—"

"Dolly, you are a genius." Charity smiled warmly on the abashed girl. "An entry fee. Just a few shillings, but that will pay for supplies to build the dragon. Now who do you think will want to compete?" She considered her brothers: Francis would never risk winning and then having to dress up in costume—he was so very stuffy. Barry, if he could get down from Oxford, would think it a great lark, but he was too gangly to be much of a swordsman. Ned, now Ned would have loved it, competing with his friends, garnering the congratulatory kisses of the ladies afterwards—

"Crispin Hering would never turn down a dare," Polly remarked. She smiled in such a way to suggest that she had dared him once and he hadn't failed her, and Charity wondered just what form that challenge had taken.

"His cousins, too," Molly put in. "All the Herings love to fight. Who else?"

"Malachi." Dolly's voice dropped into gloom at that last syllable; the innkeeper's son was obnoxiously competitive.

"What about Lord Braden? Is he adept at—at swordplay?"

Polly looked archly over, and Charity realized that she had been designated expert on the elusive artist, having met the man once already. "I don't know," she snapped, turning to leave and colliding with Dolly's bucket. Then she recalled her second brilliant idea. She turned slowly back to the girls. "Why don't you ask him yourself? You can, if you go up to Haverne Hall and help me put it to rights. It needs—oh, just a bit of cleaning."

"Just a bit?" Polly picked up her mop and turned back to stretch for the cobweb in the corner above the doorframe. "How long's it been since the housekeeper left? Two months?"

"Perhaps more than a bit," Charity admitted. "But if they haven't paid a housekeeper in two months, the pay is likely to be more than a bit. In fact—" She clapped her hands as if she had just been struck with a joyous thought. "Lady Haverne's going to be in mourning dress forever. I wonder ... she has no lady's maid to be given her old gowns. I might persuade her to give you a few silk dresses in time for the Midsummer Banquet."

This last incentive swept away all of Polly's unspoken objections, and she tossed her mop to Molly, who caught it and gazed at her with scant comprehension. "You finish the floor. I'll get the wall done, and then we'll go earn our silks."

"I never had nothing silk," Molly said, wistfully ducking her mop into the bucket of water. "Does it feel lovely?"

Charity moved back into the doorway before Polly's energetic swiping splashed dirty water on her new dress. "Silk feels exquisite. Especially to men. They just love to let silk run through their hands."

"And they call me wicked." Polly looked back, laughing. "Is that silk you're wearing now? Is some man going to run his hands through it? Her ladyship's brother maybe?"

"It's only muslin, worse luck." Charity glanced deprecatingly down at her peach gown strewn with violet knots, refusing to let Polly discompose her anymore. After all, they had known each other all their lives and compared notes about the kisses of every one of the squire's boys. So she answered back in the same teasing way. "I couldn't justify silk for a picnic. Not in Kent. In London, of course, a picnic calls for a satin court gown, near enough!"

She made a last surveyal of the hall, then went out the door, calling back over her shoulder, "You'll be up this afternoon, then? I'll tell them to expect you. Silk, remember. You must do an impeccable job to deserve it!"

Cammie, the Calder governess, was waiting as arranged by the front gate of the churchyard, sitting on the wall, her round face raised to the sun, a carpetbag at her feet. Charity felt a moment's unease, seeing that carpetbag. It seemed so permanent, as if Cammie were leaving them forever. And perhaps she would leave, for once Charlie went off to school there would be little for her to do. If Joey were still at home, of course, she'd have stayed for him.

But Haverne needed her more now, Charity told herself firmly. "Cammie, let's go!" she cried, and the old governess rose and gathered up her bag.

"Yes, we'd best get on."

And so they set off at a goodly pace down High Road. At the west end of it, a quarter-mile away, Haverne Hall rose in a great block like a sphinx crouched over the village. But Cammie wasn't cowed, not by the hall or its inhabitants. Indeed, when Charity paused to tug up a clump of weeds from around the signpost that announced "Entering Village of Calder," Cammie snorted with some impatience.

"Come, girl, if we linger much longer, we might not be in time to save the ancestral legacies from the new earl's mischief!"

Chapter Five

In fact, they arrived just in time to preserve the suit of armor in the munitions gallery. Mrs. Cameron took one look at Lawrence hanging on the handle of the mace and said, "Off. This instant."

The voice that had cowed six lion-hearted Calder children had a predictable effect on young Lawrence. His hands opened slightly and he dropped to his feet, his shoulders hunching around his dirty face. Jeremy sidled toward the door, where Charity stood laughing silently. "Who's that?" Jeremy asked, in what he supposed was a confidential whisper.

"That is my governess, Mrs. Cameron. Mrs. Cameron, Cammie, we always called her, this is Jeremy, and that miscreant is Lawrence."

"What's a miscreant?" Jeremy asked.

"Something we'll have no more of." Cammie was a round, comfortable woman with plump arms and a welcoming bosom under her crisp white apron. But her face was as austere as a nun's now, the full mouth pursed as she stared down at Lawrence. "I don't believe in bad boys."

"You don't believe in them?" Jeremy repeated, for Lawrence seemed to have been struck dumb by this new acquaintance.

"No, I don't. I only believe in boys who need healthy outlets for their energy. Like schoolwork."

Lawrence's mouth opened and closed in wordless protest. But Cammie continued inexorably, "And chores. And—" she added when Lawrence started to speak, "dogs. Puppies, to be precise. I do value precision, don't you, Lawrence?"

"Puppies?" Lawrence looked wary, for he'd spent most of his life in London, where puppies did not thrive.

"Yes, puppies. Sir Francis's retriever had eight. He's sent two over for your birthday."

"My birthday was last month." Lawrence's eyes filled with tears, and Charity knew that he was the only one who had remembered.

But Cammie only shrugged. "Lawrence, they weren't three weeks old then! We could hardly give them to you before they were weaned!"

"No, I suppose not." Lawrence rubbed away his tears with the heel of his hand, leaving dirty stripes behind. "What about Jeremy? His birthday's in August."

"He has to get his present early, for his new pets must meet their new master before they become too enamored of Calder Grange. Puppies form attachments very early, you know. You don't mind, do you, Jeremy, getting your gifts early?"

"No, ma'am. What about the others?"

"Oh, two are for sale, I think, and two are staying with our young Charlie. He's right fond of them already. And he's already fulfilled the first duty of ownership for them, which you'll have to do straightaway. You must give your pets names."

"Now, Cammie," Charity interposed. After a decade together, she and her governess worked in perfect tandem. "Lawrence's and Jeremy's puppies already have very fine names. The boys needn't go to the trouble of coming up with new ones."

Jeremy nodded, for he was a deliberate boy, and coming up with two puppy names might take him all day. But Lawrence was more adventuresome. "What are they named now?"

"The first is named A, and the second B, and the third C, and the fourth—"

"D!" Jeremy shouted triumphantly. "And then there's E and F!"

He might have gone through the whole alphabet if Lawrence hadn't broken in. "Those are stupid names! I won't call my puppies A and B!"

Charity looked doubtful. "Well, they sounded fine to me. Here, A! Sit, B! Don't you think that sounds fine?"

Cammie ignored her former charge and turned to the young earl. "I am in entire agreement with you, Lawrence. A and B are perfectly good letters but lamentable names. We shall get out an atlas, and a dictionary, and a book of constellations, and find some proper names for your puppies. Let's go meet them and see if inspiration strikes or whether we shall have to make a search for just the right appellation."

The boys trooped off obediently after Cammie, Jeremy asking, "What's an appellation?"

Charity went back out to the carriage yard, wondering if Jeremy would grow up to be a lexicographer or merely obnoxious. Having loosed the puppies in the empty stable yard, Jem, the Calder coachman, was waiting near the gig with the rest of Cammie's luggage and Charity's luncheon things. She asked him to take the luggage up to the schoolroom. "Do be careful on the staircase," she added. "Those boys have probably greased the treads."

Alone again, she hauled the picnic basket out of the gig and carried it around the east wing of the hall to the weed-choked gardens. She skirted the stagnant lily pond, enjoying the flutter of her heart as she thought of Lord Braden somewhere in the house. It was altogether too wonderful that the artist of the paintings she so admired would become a neighbor and that he would turn out to be so very attractive. Perhaps—

But she cut that wish short. Charity was too sensible to hold to superstitions, but there was no use tempting fate by imagining the most glorious outcome of this nascent acquaintance. She decided to be happy if she only got to ask him about his painting and to watch the play of mood across his sun-gilded face.

The terrace flagstones were muddy from the recent rains, and the wrought-iron table and chairs were speckled with dirt and dead leaves. Charity wrinkled her nose and surrendered to necessity. She was soon equipped with an apron, a mop, a pail, and lots of soapy water. She set her sandals on the wall overlooking the garden, hitched up her skirt under the enveloping apron, and tied back her hair. If her gown and her coiffure survived this work, she deserved to win the heart of Lord Braden, she told herself. "Too soon," she scolded aloud, swishing the mop around the flagstones. "You'll hex your chances for certain."

It was a perfect day for cleaning a terrace, sunny with a hint of a breeze and the scent of jasmine teasing the piney fragrance of the soap. She made short work of the mud, and with a few minutes still lacking to eleven, she returned the apron and mop to the maid's closet. In the necessary room of the vacant housekeeper's office, she paused to straighten her dress and wash her hands. As she scrubbed the dirt off her nose, she made a face in the mirror and wasted a moment longing for hair as pale as a sunbeam and eyes blue like a peacock's feathers. She had the dreams of a girl like that, but the appearance and character of someone far more prosaic. Lacking a comb, she ran her fingers through her hair and tied the violet ribbon in a dashing bow just north of her ear. She hid the locket she always wore under her bodice, so that only the gold chain showed. Then, giving the prosaic girl in the mirror a forgiving smile, she ran off to set the picnic table.

The sun was warm on her bare arms as she smoothed down the white linen tablecloth. She removed the china plates—three, just in case—and the silverware, just the everyday tableware for an everyday sort of picnic. A handful of daisies in a tumbler served as an everyday sort of centerpiece. And if the slivered ham and melon were a bit elaborate for everyday, it was only because the usual picnic fare of cold chicken and corn pudding did not leave a lady at her best advantage.

"Oh, Charlie is my darling, my darling, my darling," she sang softly as she made last-minute adjustments to the pretty display. "Oh, Charlie is my darling, the young chevalier."

"I knew you were too good to be true. Your secret vice is Jacobitism."

That deep voice she had been listening for came from the open French doors. From the sunlit terrace, she could not discern more than a dark form there in the gloomy library. But she could call his image up so clearly, even after only one encounter: his lean figure; his austere face, all angles, with its paradoxically tender mouth; the burning dark eyes—Adonis's eyes, she realized now.

Then his reality emerged to join his image in her vision, only the reality was so much more intense. There was something indefinably exotic about his slender, graceful form, even in a casual gray riding coat and supplely fitted buckskins. And there was something foreign in his slanted brows and narrow straight nose, in the contrast between his blue-black hair and fair skin—for he tanned golden, not dark. He and Anna had an Italian mother, Charity recalled suddenly.

She heard Italy in his voice, too, now that she listened for it. Having studied Italian in school, Charity recognized that the usually crisp English consonants were a little blurred, the vowels more musical. She could almost hear him whispering silken endearments—*mia cara, mi' amore* . . .

She dropped her head to hide her blush and returned to her innocent table setting. The spoons were not precisely parallel to the knives; she rectified this as she puzzled over his greeting.

"Oh, you heard my song!" There was no reason now to blush, for she had always been told she had a pretty voice and had been lead contralto in the children's choir for six years. But she felt her cheeks burn anyway and hastened to explain. "The Bonnie Prince isn't the Charlie I meant. My younger brother is named Charlie, and I was singing it this morning to tease him. It drives him mad, as you might imagine. And Francis, too, for he's the very opposite of a Jacobite. He can't abide the Stuarts, says they were a cursed family that visited a curse on Britain."

"Infuriating two brothers with the same tune—quite an accomplishment, I'd say. Sir Francis has opinions about such subjects, does he? And I thought only agriculture kept his attention."

Charity looked up to his sardonic gaze and returned in sharp defense, "You are wrong. He may look like a mere farmer, but Francis took a First in history at Oxford." She was about to add that Lord Braden would do well to try to rely less on first impressions where people were concerned, but the hesitance in his dark eyes made her pause.

He was unsure of himself here in the country, that was all, unused to helpful and interfering neighbors, uncertain how much gratitude or irritation to feel. So he had retreated into that arrogant observer role so common to city folk, and to artists too, she supposed. If she didn't understand his reasons, and if his black hair didn't curl so wantonly over his forehead, she might take offense. As it was, she immediately went to work soothing over the discord.

"Though, of course, farming is his first love. He was up at the crack of dawn, plotting out his campaign to save Haverne's harvest. He has always believed he could do better with the land than the Havertons have done. It's so seldom that one gets the opportunity to make good on such boasts."

Her warmer tone worked, for Lord Braden smiled, genuinely this time. "It's kind of you to pretend we are doing you a favor letting you work so hard. What a pretty table you have set."

"Careful. The flagstones aren't quite dry yet." Then Charity felt those flagstones wet under her own feet and drew in her breath. Her sandals were there on the wall, just beyond

Lord Braden. At least she had put the mop and pail away before her host had arrived.

But he had caught her quick glance at the wall and followed it. When he saw the sandals he considered them thoughtfully, and even in her embarrassment Charity was fascinated. He had a wary face, his dark eyes shadowed by long lashes, his expression ever watchful. She supposed it was the artist in him that made him pause to study things so.

But his study now brought him right to the conclusion she had hoped would escape him. He transferred his gaze to her bare feet, just visible under the ruffled hem of her gown. "You washed the flagstones yourself, didn't you?"

Charity only shrugged and, slipping past him, retrieved her sandals. She sat on the wall and put them back on, taking great diligence to fasten the buckles so that she wouldn't have to face that delicious scowl.

"You shouldn't be doing such work yourself, Miss Calder. We don't use our guests as scullery maids." He was angry now, his dark eyes flashing, and Charity suppressed a sigh of pure delight. The Italian was there, surely, in his sudden passion, the fire burning in his eyes like the Mediterranean sun.

She rose, shuffling a little to adjust her sandals, joy blossoming in her heart. Oh, perhaps he was the one. She answered distractedly, "I don't mind in the least pitching in. There's nothing shameful in housework, after all—oh, I wish my mother could have heard me say that! I doubt she ever imagined all her lectures on the subject would ever take root!"

Lord Braden's anger had dissolved into consternation—almost as enjoyable, as it introduced the dearest frown between his dark brows. "You are surely not accustomed to doing your own housework there at the Grange?"

"We have a staff, of course, but I supervise them. I can hardly assign duties to a maid without knowing what it is she must do. Else how will I know what standard I can expect her to attain?"

Charity shrugged and began dusting the chairs off with her handkerchief. "At least if my fortunes turn sour, I shall be able to hire myself out as a scullery maid! Or as a cook!" Her laugh faded as she saw the puzzlement in his eyes. She shook out her handkerchief, observing, "I wouldn't feel right watching others work while I was idle."

He would consider her a drudge, the sort who liked working better than waltzing. And she wasn't really that way at all. But she had never been good at self-defense. "I'll go entice Anna out of bed. Do you think she will be able to walk down the stairs?"

In the end, Anna had to be coaxed out of her room and Lord Braden had to carry her to the terrace. Though she was a tall woman, Anna had always been willowy, and she was lighter than ever now. Charity kept up a steady stream of chatter as they walked, but faltered when he carefully set his sister in a chair. In the black wrapper she insisted on wearing, Anna looked as pale and lovely as Ophelia, and just as distraught. She shrank back against her brother, whispering, "The sun is so bright—"

From the picnic basket, Charity produced a dashing black bonnet with a high brim and dangling black ribbons. "I'm just out of blacks myself—my father died only Christmas last—so this is the latest crack in mourning fashion."

Lord Braden courteously stepped out of the way so she could kneel and place the bonnet on Anna's dark hair. She tied a big bow under Anna's chin then sat back on her heels to survey her work. "Oh, you look lovely. Your skin looks just like pearls, so deep and glowing. Now, would you like some lemonade? Some ham? Try the melon—I found it in Folkestone yesterday, shipped all the way from Morocco. Fit for a princess!"

Apparently Anna never suspected the motives of flatterers; those pearly cheeks were pinking now under the dramatic black bonnet. Thus did Kenny keep her in thrall, Charity thought cynically, taking the adjacent seat. She hoped she would be more skeptical, did anyone ever compare her skin to pearls. She looked up to meet the enigmatic gaze of Lord Braden and flushed. He was not so easily gulled as his sister. He knew that Charity's compliments were mere manipulation, if of the kindest sort.

Embarrassed as she was to be caught in such a trick, Charity was nonetheless excited. So few people saw below the surface of human converse to recognize underlying motives and methods. But Lord Braden's slight smile told her that he understood her cozening ways rather too well for comfort. No doubt an artist learned to read people in order to capture their essence with paint and canvas.

Charity felt a warm rush of gratification. So handsome, so talented, so observant—so intense. This was a man she could admire, a man she could respect. And, she thought as she gazed into his stormy dark eyes—Adonis's eyes—he was a man she could desire.

"Please join us." She gestured at the extra place. "I brought enough for all three of us."

That moment of communion vanished. He moved back a step, wariness replacing the amusement in his eyes. "I meant to get started on sorting out Haverne's books this morning."

He thinks I've set my cap for him, Charity realized. For all that she had just decided to fall in love with him, Charity was insulted. She tilted up her chin and gave him a look utterly devoid of regret. "Just as well. I've so much gossip I can't imagine relating in mixed company."

Now amusement flickered in those speaking eyes of his. She was diverted for a moment, for she was learning to watch his eyes for the emotion that he masked with those chiseled features. But she regained her hauteur as he took a seat beside her and held out his plate. "Say on, then. Please pay me no mind, except to spear me a bit of that Moroccan melon of yours."

"As you wish." Charity forked a slice of melon and dropped it carelessly on his plate. Then, taking him entirely at his word, she turned to Anna. "Have you heard about the Abshire twins?" She did not even glance at Braden, although she was burningly aware of him. "Twenty-four-year-old identical twins. By identical, I mean identically tall, blond, handsome, and wealthy. They arrived in town in search of brides. Then they announced they would only accept a pair of twin sisters! Such despair you would not countenance. Priscilla Barrett and I thought we might pass ourselves off as twins—"

"Who is Priscilla Barrett?" Braden broke in.

As if Anna had asked this, Charity favored her with a smile. "Oh, Priscilla looks nearly as much like me as Abshire One looks like Abshire Two. But she and I couldn't decide how we would divvy them up, or how we would keep them divvied after that. For they are very mischievous, and it would be just like them to switch off occasionally, just for variety!"

"Charity! What a thing to say!" Anna inclined her head in her brother's direction, but Charity ostentatiously paid this no mind. Even when Braden refilled her glass from the jar of lemonade, Charity kept her smile focused on her hostess and her gossip as scandalous as possible.

She ran through all the stories she could remember which had naught to do with straying husbands and fatal duels, and succeeded in diverting the countess. Lord Braden made no further attempt to intervene in the conversation. But she knew he was listening, for she heard his quiet chuckle whenever she said something particularly outrageous. She still hadn't forgiven him, but she was conscious of his gaze on her face, could feel its heat right there above her cheekbone. Sometimes, out of the corner of her eye, she could see his hands. Slim and graceful as they toyed with utensils, here and there stained with paint, his hands fascinated her. They created the art she admired so much. She longed to see them at work, longed to touch them—

Anna spoke little, but finally she managed an inquiring

smile. "But Charity dear, you haven't told me the least bit of gossip that included you!"

Charity gave into the spirit of mischief yet again, bringing her hand to her cheek in mock chagrin. "You've heard then? Oh, that's the last time I trust a tsar who promises not to kiss and tell!"

Anna gasped, then blushed and slapped Charity's hand lightly. "The tsar? Oh, Charity, you are horrid! And I recall you as ever the prettiest-behaved girl!"

"Blame it on Alexander then. I never said such things before I experienced his royal Russian charm."

Anna gave way finally to laughter, a weak series of chuckles that barely shook her frail shoulders. But Charity knew from the rusty sound that the countess had not used this reflex for months now. And so she redoubled her attempts to amuse, making risqué plays on the word *Russian* that had Anna helpless with giggles.

She had almost forgotten Lord Braden, as much as she could forget a man whose image had haunted her dreams all night long. But as she leaned over to pour a glass of lemonade to soothe Anna's laugh-roughened throat, Charity saw his face, so vivid, so austere under the dark curls. As he witnessed his sister's amusement, his eyes were stormy now with some anger Charity couldn't comprehend.

But she felt rebuked again. Perhaps she had gone too far beyond the acceptable with her last sallies, however successful they were with Anna. So she only handed the countess her lemonade and bade her drink, then concentrated on buttering her a slice of rye bread. But her silence reminded Anna of her original inquiry. "Come, Charity, tell me," she said, her breath coming in little gasps of laughter, "wasn't there any man short of royalty who paid you special attention?"

Charity felt Braden's gaze on her again and murmured something negative. Anna, not entirely lost to nuance, did not press the issue, doubtlessly believing Charity to have been an utter failure in London.

But to her surprise, Braden took up the question even more bluntly. "No suitor then? Not even one?"

This stung like a slap; for the first time in a half-hour, she faced that dark gaze levelly. "None I care to name. I am not like the tsar, you see. I see no sense in boasting of my conquests."

"Oh, I knew you had conquests! And you did promise yesterday to tell me of them!" Anna cried. Then she dismissed her brother with an imperious gesture. "Tristan, dear, you must leave. She won't say a word when you're about."

"I beg leave to doubt that," Braden observed coolly, "as she's favored me with three months' worth of scandal in thirty minutes. Miss Calder, do not shy off now. Or do you gossip only about other people?"

Hurt, trapped, Charity could only bite her lower lip and then, addressing Anna, said quietly, "No one I thought to marry, obviously. Terence Wetherby. His father the general liked me, and Terence, I think, wanted to incur his approval. Which he's never had, poor boy. And Bessemer," she concluded in a rush.

"Bessemer?" Anna's echo plainly expressed her incredulity. "Surely you don't mean Sir Ralph—"

"He has three little sisters, you see." Charity tilted her head wryly, more in control now. "I gather he's fond of them in his way but has no idea how to go about rearing them. Why he thought I would, I can't imagine. Now if he had three little brothers, I might be tempted, for that is my field of expertise."

Anna shook her head in wonder. She might have married for love (however foolish that seemed now), but her subtle disapproval indicated that a girl like Charity should not be so choosy. Braden, however, would not let the matter rest. "Only the two?"

Charity refused to dignify his taunting with the truth. She had no need to boast, after all, for there was nothing very much to boast about. "I am so sorry to disappoint you, Lord

Braden. Anna, dear, thank you for your company and your garden." She scraped their bread remains into a bowl then carried it to the wall and tossed the crusts into the weedy tulip bed for the birds. Returning to the table, she briskly stacked plates into her basket.

After a stunned moment, Braden must have realized that he had no maid to call to clear away, and rose to help. He gathered the silverware into a linen napkin and wrapped it up safely. Anna only sat there musing over Charity's foolishness. Finally she looked up. "Oh, dear, you aren't leaving, are you? I would so love to hear if Sir Ralph went down on one knee and vowed to slay dragons for you."

"Of course not! He saves such dramatics for more intriguing propositions! And I must go; I've lumber to order, and then I'm to start planning the children's play. We're doing Jonah and the Whale—do say Lawrence and Jeremy can help with the rehearsals. They might even get parts as Jonah's disloyal shipmates. And, Anna, you must help also; Mrs. Hering expects sixty rag dolls for booth prizes, and I shall never have time!" Before Anna could protest that she couldn't, she just couldn't, Charity turned to Lord Braden, letting the slightest hint of malice enter her merry voice. "And your brother can paint the set for my play! A backdrop of the sea, with a great whale rampant!"

She smiled sweetly at the horror that dawned on his face and hardly heard Anna's hasty agreement to the rag doll proposal. Then she turned briskly back to her packing, wrapping the lemonade jar carefully in the tablecloth, covering the plates with a napkin. "The Ferris girls are coming up to clean. I hope you don't mind that I promised them a silk gown apiece. They wouldn't take on this task for mere money!" She closed the picnic basket with a definitive snap. "I'll come round tomorrow to see how Cammie has fared against the boys. I'm taking wagers on her knockout in round three. I shall make my fortune, I think for the boys have some fervent advocates in the stables who are ready to give me odds."

So, leaving Anna smiling tremulously but truly, Charity hefted the laden basket and crossed to the French doors. As she fumbled with the latch, Braden came up behind her and took the basket's handle. "Let me carry this to your gig."

Charity was entirely capable of carrying the basket all the way back to the Grange, but she had no desire to brangle further with him. Instead, she stayed silent, nursing the hurt in her heart, as they walked through the house to the front door. Her heart actually ached, she thought with a mingling of alarm and excitement. And all because he had spoken to her in that slighting way.

Finally, as they emerged into the sunlight, he broke the silence, not to apologize, but only to thank her again. "I thought I'd never hear Anna laugh again. But you had her giggling like a girl. I don't understand," he continued, raising his hand to signal the elderly coachman. "I am her brother, and yet I can do nothing to ease her pain. And you come in like—like a sunbeam, and she brightens again."

She realized now that his disconcerting anger had been self-directed. He wasn't incomprehensible after all; his thoughts only took some interpreting. With a secret thrill, she attributed that to his Italian side. "Oh, it's not so hard to understand. I'm not associated with any happy or sad times in her life. She risks nothing by letting me close."

Jem, yawning from his afternoon nap, had brought the gig around, and Braden handed him the basket. Still frowning, he said, almost to himself, "Yes, I suppose that makes sense. She expected nothing of you, so your kindness is a gift. But from me, she had a right to expect more than—than a letter every three months and an annual visit in London when the Academy had its exhibition."

Charity paused with one foot on the gig's first rung. She felt every sympathy for widows, but she saw no sense in Braden's getting caught up in the snare of Anna's helplessness. "But you have your own life. And your own work. You will do her no favor, you know, by making her dependent on you."

"I didn't mean to do that."

"Oh, but if you sacrifice for her, she will become dependent. For if she doesn't need you, your sacrifice will seem meaningless—"

She broke off, disoriented by her own insight. Braden was about to speak, but she forestalled him. "I saw your paintings at the exhibition in London. I was intrigued—and that was before I knew you were almost a neighbor! You must not let your sister's troubles upset you too greatly. She would hate to think she had interfered with your success, for I'm certain she takes great pride in it."

This long speech had the effect of diverting him from whatever assessing comment he meant to make. Instead, Braden smiled ruefully and shook his head. "Very nice, Miss Calder. I suppose you think susceptibility to flattery is a family trait? But having observed your technique with my sister, I am wise to your ways. You will not persuade me that my sister's well-being depends more on my finishing a painting than straightening out her finances. No, no!" He raised his hand, laughing. "Don't volunteer to do it for me. We have presumed on you enough already."

Was he implying that she took too much on herself, pushed to help where she wasn't needed? Her aid had never been turned down before; most recipients were, in fact, all to happy to take advantage of her talents. But Lord Braden was probably used to minding his own affairs and expected others to mind theirs. His reluctance to join her little lunch, his challenging comment about her number of suitors—perhaps he felt pursued and was warning her off.

In the moment or two it took to reach this supposition, Charity had climbed nimbly in beside Jem. She just wanted to be gone from this difficult man who regarded her so coolly out of those burning eyes, who suspected motives she didn't quite have, who let her have only tantalizing glimpses of his thoughts. Even as she welcomed her own painful disorientation—surely it indicated intense emotion!—she felt cheated. She had always known that falling in love would hurt. But she had not reckoned that it would be humiliating, too.

Rejection was new to her. So she retreated into a familiar role, holding her hand out to him with a smile. "It was a lovely lunch. Thank you. Tell Anna I hope she will let me return her hospitality very soon."

"But you provided the lunch—"

She withdrew her hand from his and nodded to Jem, who urged the horse on before Lord Braden could complete his objection.

Chapter Six

Steadying his hand with a long-held breath, Tristan etched a fine black line along the charred mainmast. Then quickly, before he ruined it, he stepped back from the ship. Tomorrow he would begin filling in the background that he had so far neglected.

He emerged from his creative trance to the sounds of a household in operation. His studio, opening onto the long south balcony, was entirely too noisy on such a warm day, when every window in the house was open to the light breeze. But for a change the noise was pleasant. The new gardener below whistled a popular tune in counterpoint to the birdsongs; the foreman borrowed from Calder shouted instructions to his workers in a nearby field. A maid sang to herself in the hallway. The boys, taking their lessons on the terrace below, chanted their spelling words vigorously, Mrs. Cameron murmuring praise occasionally, corrections more frequently.

And Tristan thought if he listened hard enough he could hear his sister in the nearby drawing room, chatting with a few church ladies as they sewed rag dolls for the Midsummer prize booth. The great day was less than three weeks away, and Anna was sewing rag dolls as if her life depended on it.

But one voice he didn't hear—the cheerful one belonging to the girl who had organized all this humming activity. Today Charity's voice was silent. In the past week, Tristan had heard her brisk instructions to a new downstairs maid, her confidential whisper to the gossip-hungry Anna, even a trace of her laughter amidst the boys' gleeful shouts.

Never, however, did he hear a friendly greeting directed his way or a sudden observation that made him suspect she had read his mind. He never got close enough to her for that. Her visits always coincided with the early afternoon hours, when the light was so white and gold it seemed almost Italian, when Tristan surrendered himself to painting.

In fact, her visits were so perfectly timed that Tristan suspected she was avoiding him. And now, as he soaked his brushes and scrubbed his hands, he thought he knew why.

He had offended her during that picnic lunch. She had read his hesitance to join her and his quizzing about her proposals as warnings to steer clear. And so she had, all through the picnic, all through the week. Now he was weary of the game, weary of feeling like a villain, of sensing her presence and finding her gone, of hearing her voice and having to imagine her face.

He went out on the balcony to clear the paint fumes from his mind. As he gazed south, straining for a glimpse of the sea between the hills, he saw instead a small feminine figure cutting across the corner of the Haverne Park. She squeezed through a gap in the unkempt hedge and emerged into the avenue that wound down to the village.

From her quick light steps as much as her direction, Tristan knew this was Miss Calder. He narrowed his eyes, shading them against the sunlight, and saw that she must be returning from some homely parish duty, for a goodwill basket was hung from her arm. From this distance, he could distinguish only the faded blue of her gown and sunbonnet, a pastel as subtle as today's sun-blanched sky.

She had appeared as if prompted by his conscience. So he answered his own cue expeditiously. He changed into a pristine shirt, yanked on a coat, and bent to chip a paint spot off his Hessians. Then, mindful that the boys would soon be released from their lessons and beg to go along, he took the secret route, out the balcony. Without giving himself time to think, he swung his leg over the wall and slid down. Then he hung there for a moment, looking down at the ground a dozen feet away, contemplating the likelihood of breaking his ankle. He felt the rough stone scraping at his hands and decided better a broken ankle than a scabbed brush-hand, and let go. He landed safely on the soft, overgrown grass, dusted his tingling hands, and crossed the lawn to the elm-lined avenue.

Miss Calder was walking briskly down the slope toward the village. With its crooked streets, white and black houses, red and yellow and green square gardens, spread out like a display in a toyshop window, it was as neat and pretty and unique as the girl who served as its mainstay and source of energy.

He was just in time to see her quick figure vanish, as if the village's needs and demands had swallowed her up whole, like the whale with Jonah. But he knew where she must have gone, to that cross-shaped church with the deteriorating square tower, that tower whose expensive restoration so occupied Miss Calder's time.

She was not in the hushed, dusty church, so he walked across the yard under the ancient oaks to the hall where she had said some of the Midsummer preparations would take place.

The hall was Tudor, like the rest of the village, far newer than the Norman-era church. As he came alongside it, he heard Miss Calder's laughter through the open casement window and knew he had come the right way. He glanced in through the rippled glass then hesitated there on the side of the hall, reluctant to call out. For on a raised platform that resembled a stage, beyond three stacks of pine boards, she was kneeling as if in prayer, her back to the room, her head bent.

But then he heard another voice, raised in laughing protest.

She wasn't praying; she was hard at work, and not alone. She raised a hammer aloft in what in a less-amiable woman might have seemed a threatening manner, and indeed, the boy in front of her, holding the corner of a wooden frame with exaggerated gingerness, was giving a good imitation of fear.

"Crispin, you're such a coward! I promise you I won't hit you, no matter how much you deserve it!"

Her brother, Tristan thought, recognizing that form of abuse. They were building a huge canvas, the backdrop for *Jonah and the Whale*, perhaps, the one she wanted him to paint. They'd do better to construct a triptych, he thought with professional interest, then the canvas wouldn't sag in the middle and the effect would be more macabre. As Miss Calder's hammering echoed in the hall and escaped through his window, he envisioned a Hieronymous-Bosch-like scene: a distorted seascape, a monstrous whale with seamen dangling from its teeth, feet kicking, arms flailing. Not his sort of painting, but it would be effective with the provincials.

The blond boy gave an exaggerated sigh of relief as the last tack secured the canvas to the wood. Then Miss Calder propped the frame, as tall as she and at least eight feet wide, against the back wall and surveyed it critically. The boy, however, was watching her. Not her brother after all, Tristan decided, annoyed. A brother wouldn't stand quite so close or watch her so intently or reach out and brush the stray curl back from her cheek like that.

Miss Calder only pushed another tack into the canvas frame and raised her hammer. "Cris, don't crowd me, or I shall have to hit you after all." Sullenly he drew away, and with a few swift blows she dealt with the last tack.

With this delicate operation concluded, Tristan went through the great rustic plank doors and, ignoring the boy entirely, said, "Miss Calder, I thought I would find you here."

She turned, startled. Her expression, before she assembled it into the familiar cheerful lines, was one of dismay, and he determined then and there that he couldn't abide that, couldn't let her respond so to his presence. If the words twisted his throat, he would apologize for his inadvertent offense; he would say what he must to make her regard him as she had when first they met, with that open willingness to be pleased.

The boy made no such attempt to hide his emotions; he took the hammer from Miss Calder and hefted it, more boyish than ever as he favored Tristan with a hard look, as if he meant to challenge him to a duel with building tools. No, he was most definitely not her brother.

"Yes, the lumber was delivered today, and I put Crispin right to work." So saying, Miss Calder put the paper twist of tacks into Crispin's free hand, abjuring him, "You be careful with those now. I don't want the children stepping on them."

The boy flushed dark, and Tristan knew an unwilling sympathy for him, treated so casually, as if they were brother and sister after all. But that was better, Tristan thought as she made swift introductions, never really looking at him, than to be treated as a stranger by a girl who had never known a stranger.

Crispin acknowledged him with a barely civil nod, then crossed to a stack of lumber and pulled a six-foot board off the top. "Come on, Charity. You said we had to make something to look like Jonah's boat or the children will never agree to rehearse."

Miss Calder gave Tristan a swift, unreadable glance from under her lashes before she replied. "Don't bother, Cris. I decided just to borrow a rowboat. But you can start building booths. We'll need a dozen at least for all the concessions." She untied the scarf from her hair, shook free the tangle of curls, then rolled down her sleeves. "I think I've mangled enough of my fingers for the day, but I'll go home and wake Barry and send him over to help you!"

Tristan noted that she did not bother to ask for his help, and, provoked, he broke in. "Perhaps I can walk with you then." She opened her mouth, and he said what he knew would forestall her demurral. "You mentioned that you needed someone to paint the backdrop of the whale. I thought of a rather dramatic scene, but I don't know whether it would be appropriate for Midsummer."

His volunteering came as a surprise to them all, an unwelcome one to Crispin, who immediately said with some belligerence, "Charity, I told you I could paint a whale. *Anyone* can paint a whale. You don't need," his youthful voice dripped with sarcasm, "the Royal Academy to paint a whale."

Tristan ignored him, for the impulsive offer had done its job. Miss Calder was regarding him more charitably now; in fact, she even smiled at him as she gathered up her basket and donned her bonnet, leaving the ribbons undone to tangle with her dark curls. "Thank you, Cris, for the offer. But you've already volunteered to do so much. Just the booths will take a fortnight or so of evenings, for you know your papa will not be happy if I take you away from your duties every day like this."

Crispin's muttered protests grew louder as Tristan held open the door for her. Fortunately, relief arrived in the form of a familiar formidable matron in a prowlike bonnet just ascending the steps: Mrs. Hering, the lady who was keeping Anna supplied in rag doll material.

Miss Calder called back over her shoulder, "Oh, Cris, here is your mother!" They stood in the doorway then, exchanging greetings, while Crispin banged petulantly inside. "Mrs. Hering, Cris is going to build the booths, and I think he should start with the ale booth, don't you? Perhaps you can tell him what dimensions you want."

Ignoring her son's dismay, Mrs. Hering agreed and sailed past them, stopping to inspect the nearest pile of lumber then beckoning the boy to her. "Come, dear, have you got your tape measure? And where are your spectacles? You know you can't judge distances well! What are you thinking, leaving your specs at home? You'll probably pound your hand instead of the nail!"

Mrs. Hering's adjurations trailed Tristan into the soft afternoon, and he hid a smile as he followed Charity across the green to the street. There were some benefits to being orphaned, after all.

Villagers stopped them every few steps to say good afternoon, so Tristan wasn't immediately called upon to explain his offer of painting services, and even had a few moments to consider how to rescind it. As they crossed the main road in front of the half-timbered inn, the village school was just letting out. The stream of a dozen or so children past the black-garbed schoolmaster was diverted their way as soon as one sighted Miss Calder and cried, "There's Charity!"

They ignored Tristan altogether, pushing past him to gather round her on the village common, tugging at her skirt and calling her name. One little boy boastfully recited his alphabet and demanded her approval; a little girl held up a dirty bandaged finger, which Charity gravely examined. Finally, laughing, she dipped her hand into her basket and came up with a handful of paper-wrapped peppermints. With remarkable efficiency, she distributed them with a quick personal word to speed each child on the way.

As the children scattered, the schoolmaster Mr. Greenaway came forward to be introduced. They exchanged meaningless pleasantries, Tristan thinking that he had met more people in the ten minutes he had walked with Charity Calder than the ten days he had been in this village. *She is so popular*, he thought with an odd pang, watching her toss the last peppermint to the biggest boy and display her empty basket to the schoolmaster. *I shall never have her to myself.*

It was an aberrant thought, but one he had no chance to chase. Mr. Greenaway was holding out a sheaf of papers. Something about his low, urgent tone and the careful way Miss Calder took the pages made Tristan study the schoolmaster's sharp face. He saw jealousy there—but not jealousy *for* Miss Calder, as the luckless Crispin had shown: jealousy *of* her. But why? Because his pupils preferred her?

Instinctively Tristan moved a step closer to her on the path, interposing his shoulder and arm between her and the schoolmaster.

It was a needless gallantry, certainly. Mr. Greenaway was a weedy young man with anxious hands that flexed and fluttered as Miss Calder skimmed his Jonah and the Whale play. He was harmless, no doubt; Tristan had met many like him in Italy, those nervous literary types hired to shepherd the sons of earls through the Grand Tour. The little lords usually thought the tour pretty grand, for the tutors were wont to drape themselves on various Roman ruins and write sonnets, leaving their charges to catch dread diseases from black-eyed pleasure girls. Lord Byron, Tristan always thought, had done Italy a great disservice, inviting in every pale English versifier who had ever read *Childe Harold's Pilgrimage* and aspired to similar heights.

This versifier must have been particularly unlucky to end up at a village reciting Milton to cobblers' sons. At least Greenaway took some pride in it, it seemed. He still wore the short black academic robe that proclaimed him a university man, though with his short thin legs in black pantaloons it made him look rather like a sparrow. His sharp, twitching eyes, now focused on Miss Calder, completed the birdlike image.

"Do you think it will do for Midsummer?" The tension had not left his voice; the young Miss Calder might have been Leigh Hunt or some other important London publisher assessing this for publication.

"How considerate of you to do this!" Charity looked up from her reading and favored the schoolmaster with a bright smile. Then she packed the play away in her basket. "If I had known you were of such a mind, I would have asked you from the start and consulted with you as you planned the play! It's fascinating, I'm sure. Of course, it will have to be modified somewhat, as it will be children performing it, and such verse as this might be too elegant for their little mouths.

Perhaps some tightening would be in order, too. But what a kind thing for you to do!"

Perhaps Tristan was more sensitive to Miss Calder than another would be, having observed her closely during their few encounters. But he sensed a reserve under the warmth of her response. Mr. Greenaway did not; his anxious hands clasped together, finally still, and he beamed as if she had promised a performance at Drury Lane. "Of course, make whatever changes you deem necessary. Perhaps the Greek epigram in line 67 ought to be translated."

He was still calling out instructions as they walked up the lane towards the Grange, and Miss Calder, in a low voice, said, "Iambic pentameter, would you believe, and heroic couplets.... But—" She started briskly toward her home, pushing the basket with the offending manuscript up to the crook of her elbow. "I will contrive something out of it that the children can get their mouths around, even if I must burn the midnight oil over this epic."

That did it. If the schoolmaster was going to write the play and young Hering to build the set, Tristan would have to paint the blasted backdrop after all. Otherwise he would never get Miss Calder to concentrate on him long enough to set things right between them.

Why that was so imperative he didn't care to pursue. It was enough that she had been welcoming to him, and more than kind to his sister, and had put the household straight enough that he could paint again in good conscience; he didn't want this angel of mercy to think him a devil.

"This backdrop you wanted has been occupying my thoughts lately. But the scene that keeps appearing—well, it would require another two canvases, as I envision a triptych. And I fear it may be as unsuitable as Mr. Greenaway's epic meter. Only much more gruesome."

This gambit worked. Her steps slowed on the lane, and she looked full at him for the first time. "Gruesome?"

As he describe his triptych, he watched her expressive

eyes. They widened when he mentioned the monstrous whale, sparkled when he described the seaman's legs twitching between its jaws. She was laughing when he finished.

"Oh, the children would love that! They are so gruesome themselves, you know. I just heard Daisy Sillitoe tell Mary Adams that St. George's dragon could burn the flesh right off her bones and that her blood would rise in red steam. They have not been happy about having to do Jonah instead of the dragon, and seeing Mr. Greenaway's script, I can hardly blame them."

Then she gave him the smile he had been aiming for, that open, generous smile that set the dimples dancing at the corners of her mouth. "But when they see this picture, they might even wonder if perhaps the Bible isn't more entertaining than they had thought!"

As they passed through the iron gate to the Grange and she waited to make sure Tristan latched it back securely, her smile faded. "The vicar now—vicars don't often think the Bible is meant to entertain, you know."

Tristan didn't know, having had little contact with vicars, but he could have guessed from the tasteful churches that dotted this pretty countryside. "Yes, I can tell Mr. Langworth lacks the appreciation for the macabre that Italian priests cultivate. If you think my whale is gruesome, you should see some of the crucifixes in Tuscany churches, dripping red blood and black sweat."

"Oh, I would love to! And the statues, too—all the gilt and glory—" She broke off, glancing up at him and away, as if she were confessing some guilty secret. "I have read about Italian religious art and seen some engravings, but I know the effect is diminished in reproductions. It's such a very different view of religion, so unrestrained, so—so intense."

"It is that," he agreed. "But Italy itself is different from England, so its religion must needs be a thing apart. Like wine and milk."

"You mean," she asked, her eyes thoughtful, "one is intoxicating and the other is—is nourishing?"

It was as succinct a summary as he had heard of the distinctions between his two worlds, between his mother's land and his father's. We realized that together, he thought suddenly, the two of us talking like this.

He wanted to pursue this, but they were already at the circular drive in front of the whitewashed Tudor house, and she had returned to Jonah's accursed whale, making her decision in preparation for bidding him farewell. "Perhaps you could tone down the gory aspect just a bit and keep it covered when you are not working on it? Or would you like to take the canvases home with you to paint?"

That would defeat his whole purpose. "No, no, it's too unwieldy to move about. I'll paint it at the church hall. I'll need your help, of course," he added as if in afterthought. She likes art, he recalled Sir Francis saying. "I can't spare more than a few hours a week, and I'll never get the background painted in time, so if you don't mind picking up a brush yourself . . ."

He had thought her smile open before, but this one was better. It had the radiance of the sun bursting to life over a sullen sea.

"If I don't mind? Oh, no, I don't mind. I would love to help you paint—I can't imagine anything more—" She broke off this unprecedentedly inarticulate assent as they came to the granite steps. "Thank you. Will tomorrow be too soon to start?"

"Tomorrow is Sunday," he had to point out, knowing that Charity Calder would obey the commandment and avoid work on the Sabbath, at least what work could be postponed.

"Oh, yes." The golden light dimmed in her eyes, and the hazel became merely brown again as she seemed to take out some mental appointment book and scan her coming week. "And Monday I've the household linens and the church linens to see to, and Tuesday I will be starting work on the play and determining the booth arrangements. . . . Another day perhaps. Send me a note when you will be ready for my help, and I shall set aside some time."

It was too equivocal a note to let her go on, but there she was, her hand on the brass knob. She was poised to escape, already wrenching open the heavy door, when he touched her upper arm. It was slim and firm from hefting goodwill baskets, and he had an instant to decide that all this walking would have worked the same magic on her legs, before he realized from her startled expression that he had crossed some unseen border.

Having already broken the rules, he tested them further, sliding his fingers down her slender arm before he dropped his hand. "Stay a minute. I want to apologize."

She didn't let go of the door, but she hesitated there on the threshold. Tristan filed that away for future reference—apparently no woman could leave a man on the brink of apology. "For what?" she asked warily.

He had to think how to couch the apology without giving greater offense. "For—for teasing you so at lunch last week. Your brother had boasted of your success in London, you see, and I knew Anna would enjoy hearing of it. But it seemed you didn't mean to tell her, so I fear I gave into impulse and teased you into addressing a subject you didn't want to address."

She relaxed then, her hand sliding up and down the door as if checking the consistency of the varnish. "I grew up with a household of brothers, Lord Braden. I hope you don't think I am so poor-spirited I take offense at a bit of teasing."

If it wasn't that, then, he wanted to ask, why have you stayed away all week? But she had forgiven whatever it was, and it made no sense to go on apologizing.

That proved to be the best course, because after a moment she must have found his silence unnerving and broke it with a quick invitation. "Do come in and have tea, won't you? Francis will be in soon, and I know you must have things to talk to him about."

He couldn't think of any, but he liked the thought of tea with Charity. So he followed her into the big central hall. Flashing him a bright glance, she left him at the arched entry to the drawing room. "I'll send for Francis. He'll be with his bailiff."

He smiled as she stopped beyond the staircase and, thinking herself unobserved, kicked off her boots, tossing them into a wooden box beside the door to the kitchen. Then she ran off lightly in her stockinged feet, her skirt swirling to reveal slim ankles.

But then, this was the sort of house one might go barefoot in. There was no pretension here, no Adam staircase or elaborate Belgian wainscoting; it was only a comfortable old place of walnut half-timbers, oak floors, and low, long mullioned windows.

Even the formal drawing room looked like it was meant to be lived in and not just visited. He ducked his head instinctively as he entered, for the ceiling was a bit low in the style of the Elizabethan architects, crossed with rough hammerbeams that echoed the half-timbered exterior.

He was drawn to an elaborate medieval tapestry of a king's hunt hanging between the mullioned windows. It was so ancient that the purples and roses and blues had become muted, subtle, like a J.M.W. Turner watercolor. That part of his mind that dealt with art collectors wondered if the Calders knew how valuable their family heirloom was. But he knew them well enough to know they wouldn't sell it, no matter what the price. The drawing room just wouldn't look right without the tapestry that must have hung there since before the Queen Anne chairs were new.

This was nobility without ostentation, and he would have recognized it immediately as the home where Charity Calder had grown up.

The wall across from the windows was lined with bookcases, and he remembered that Sir Francis was, against all expectation, an erudite man. He wandered past the shelves, running his finger across the gilt-titled volumes, noting with distant appreciation the absence of dust. His father was wont to claim that a bookcase's contents reflected the owner's character. Erudite and tidy, then, that was the Calders. There were history books aplenty, Sir Francis's, of course, but also volumes of natural philosophy, too, with an emphasis on geology, and well-thumbed editions of Shakespeare and Milton.

One shelf was filled with a surprisingly extensive collection of travelogues, arranged meticulously in alphabetical order. He was not surprised to open a recent guidebook of Italy and note the penciled notes in the margin. He recognized Charity's neat hand, though he had never seen it before. "Dante's tomb" appeared next to the description of Ravenna. "Not worth the visit," he wanted to write underneath, having made the pilgrimage himself as a child in his mother's wake.

But the door opened then, and he turned. Charity was no longer barefoot, he noted with some regret, but he could not find fault with her. She couldn't have been gone ten minutes, and yet here she was, her hair neatly combed, her old dress exchanged for a pretty frock of lilac dashed with white flowers, two new brothers in tow. He was too used to women who took two hours to emerge from the boudoir not to be impressed.

"Francis will be in soon. These are my younger brothers, Charlie and Barry." Charlie, the one she liked to tease, was twelve or so, but seemed young for his age, with the slim sturdy proportions of late childhood and a boy's careless dress. He glanced shyly up at Tristan, then at Charity, who smiled encouragingly back. "This is Lord Braden."

"Tristan Hale," he corrected automatically. He wasn't yet used to his title and out of some confused democratic tendency reserved it mostly for getting better service in inns.

The older boy, compactly built like Francis but with Charity's smile, took his lead, grinning and holding out his hand. "Good to meet you, Tristan. I'd've been over earlier, but I just came down from Oxford last night. You an Oxford man yourself?"

Tristan had lived long enough in Oxford to recognize school-fever, and this undergraduate looked to have an especially bad case. A Trinity College scarf was knotted casually about his neck, and the pocket of his riding coat gleamed with his club pin. No doubt he really believed that one could tell the cut of a man by the colors of his college scarf. "I am not a university man."

"Lord Braden studied at the Royal Academy of Art." Miss Calder's expression suggested that he might do a better job of establishing his consequence with her brother.

But the candid Barry only shrugged. "Could be worse. Could be Cambridge. Might as well be, if it's not Oxford."

Tristan smiled at Charity's exasperated sigh. "Actually I know the place well. My father was a maths don at Merton College, so I spent half my life in Oxford. Naturally I would have hanged rather than matriculate there."

"What a sorry shame! You could hardly cut up a lark with your old man right there every minute."

"Barry hopes to take his degree in cutting up larks," Charity observed ironically. "I hope he can, for he hasn't time to study anything else, between rowing practice and applying for exeats to come home at the week's end, who knows why."

Barry flushed dark, and Tristan wondered which of the fabled Ferris girls he was home to visit. He took pity on him and changed the subject. He remembered the guidebook in his hand and held it up. "I gather someone means to visit Italy."

Charity made an instinctive, immediately checked reach for the book, and Tristan worried he'd offended her again. If not, Barry was quick to provide reinforcement. "Oh, that's Charity's," he said with a smirk, sprawling on the couch, leaving just enough room for Charlie to squeeze in. "She reads all those travel books, though she's never going to go anywhere."

"I might go to Italy this winter, in fact. With Cammie." The door opened, and Charity flushed as she turned to take the tea tray from the maid. She set it on the teak table and began to pour tea into sturdy china cups. Tristan took the opposite chair and set the troublesome travel book on the table. Miss Calder kept her eyes on her hands as she gave him a cup, as if this routine transfer were fraught with peril. Look up at me, he commanded silently, but she didn't obey.

"With Cammie? That's rich." Barry helped himself to a half-dozen thumbprint biscuits, and started licking the apricot preserves out of the depressions. Between licks, he tormented his sister, as if the sight of his tongue wasn't torment enough. "Cammie can't look at the Channel without turning green. You'll never get her on a ferry. Besides, you'd have to wait till after Christmas, so you could get all the poor baskets put together and the carol service prepared, and then you'd have to cross the Alps in the blizzard season. I don't think so, Sis."

"You could sail and see the Rock of Gibraltar." Charlie, having broken his silence, immediately resumed it by cramming a biscuit into his mouth.

"You and your rocks. Say, Tristan, do you like fishing? Charlie and I can show you our favorite spot. Sunrise is the best time."

Tristan was glad Barry had dropped the subject, for he didn't like to see Charity embarrassed like that. But the prospect of spending dawn with a talkative undergraduate and a silent schoolboy did not appeal. It would be just his luck that they'd bring along the other two brothers Tristan hadn't met yet. "Fishing isn't one of my sports. Are you leaving?" he added in some dismay as Charity rose and began tidying up.

She picked up the guidebook along with a linen napkin, dusting the volume off and crossing to the bookcase to reshelve it. "I hear Francis coming in. Barry, do leave some of the sweets for Lord Braden and your brother, won't you? They've business to discuss and will need sustenance." She waited for her brothers to take the hint and join her at the door. "Thank you for bringing me home, Lord Braden. Please give Anna and the boys my best, and tell them I hope to see them at church tomorrow."

So he was left there, trying to formulate a few intelligent questions for Francis, wondering why she had colored up so when Barry teased her about Italy. Perhaps she thought his point that the village couldn't spare her made her seem conceited. But Tristan could not accuse her of that; he had been in Calder long enough to know how essential she really was, and to admire her for it.

Chapter Seven

"I can't, Tristan." Anna halted just outside the church door. Lawrence and Jeremy didn't notice; well-scrubbed and wet-combed, they were following Mrs. Cameron down the central aisle to the oak-and-velvet pew reserved for the earl.

Tristan could not see beneath the black veil his sister insisted on wearing, but he could just imagine the tears trailing down her pale cheeks. "Of course you can," he replied through gritted teeth. "It's just a church service. God knows we suffered through enough of them when Mother went through her Blessed Virgin devotion years." Of course, that was Roman masses they had endured; their mother returned to her mystical papist practices whenever they were in Italy. Even now he could not breathe in the heavy sweet scent of incense without seeing his mother's perfect Madonna face raised up with a martyr's joy. Three years, that passion had lasted. This service, God willing, would only take an hour, if he could get Anna to cross the threshold.

Anna took a sobbing breath but didn't protest as he took her arm and drew her to the Haverton pew. She gathered her skirts and sat down, staring straight ahead, unable yet to acknowledge the respectful nods of the other parishioners. Lawrence and Jeremy, Tristan was pleased to note, were quiet and well-behaved. But then he suspected Mrs. Cameron could have quelled even Bonaparte's mischief with one reproving glance.

"Look." Jeremy's loud whisper to his brother brought one of those glances from Mrs. Cameron, so he resorted to mouthing, "Charity," and pointing at the organ to the right of the altar, not a half-dozen steps from their pew.

Tristan was unsurprised to see Charity as the church organist. He wouldn't be surprised, in fact, if she stood up and gave the sermon. She looked small at the keyboard, though it was a tiny organ, too small to hide the figure of the boy pumping the bellows. Charity was frowning with concentration as she approached the end of one of the simpler Bach fugues. As she pressed the last key, her shoulders lifted in a silent sigh of relief and the vicar entered the reverberating sanctuary.

Tristan was lulled by the familiar cadence of the mass, though he was used to hearing the words intoned in Latin. He and Anna had been baptized Anglican, of course, but their father had been a free-thinker who thought their religious education should best end there. Their mother always threatened to have them baptized again by their cousin the archbishop in Naples, but she never carried through. Such an absurdity, all this anguish about the true church. His mother loved her statues of tormented martyrs; Mrs. Cameron would think them vulgar, preferring Anglican saints too sensible for martyrdom. Why should either have to give way?

The vicar wouldn't hold with such tolerance, Tristan thought, as Mr. Langworth stood at the pulpit, frowning at his sermon notes. Apparently he found something amiss, for with a righteous snort, he balled up one page and flung it away into the recesses of the pulpit. Then his pink face turned red as he pierced the congregation with a glare and reminded them not to flirt with the devil. How inscrutable people were, after all. When they first met, Tristan had thought the vicar the most amiable of men, a pastel study of gentleness and mercy. And here he was, thundering like Jeremiah about paganism—as though paganism could stand a chance in cautious Christian Kent.

Mr. Langworth's gaze seemed to fix on Tristan for a moment before passing onto another churchgoer. Could the vicar have heard of Tristan's classical paintings? But surely even the vicar would understand that the classics weren't pagans, precisely; of course, the gods weren't Christian, but—It didn't matter, Tristan told himself firmly, but he had to smile, imagining the vicar's certain response to the Aphodite painting. Pagan and nude, besides. He would probably collapse in apoplexy.

Tristan rubbed his forehead to hide his grin, then noticed Lawrence's less successful attempts to contain his mirth. When Tristan nudged him, the boy could only nod in the direction of the organ. Charity was sitting up straight, innocently attending to the vicar's sermon. But then she darted a glance at Lawrence and made a face. He dissolved again into silent laughter, earning a sharp glance from Mrs. Cameron. Charity, her eyes bright at her own escape from reproof, turned back toward the pulpit. But for an instant her eyes met Tristan's and her expression faltered. Then she raised up that stubborn chin and focused every ounce of attention on the vicar.

The service was concluded, the recessional hymn only an echo, before she looked back at their pew. She ran lightly down the altar steps, taking Anna's hand, drawing her out into the sunlight to greet the vicar, keeping up a soothing stream of chatter, even convincing Anna to push back her veil. A few other ladies came to say hello, but most kept their distance, only nodding respectfully at the new widow.

Francis Calder stood, hat in hand, at the edge of the church steps, staring wistfully at the pale vision in black. When Tristan took pity on him and presented him to Anna, the normally hearty Calder could only stammer his way through a few pleasantries. But Anna responded to this flattering awkwardness, lowering her eyes and holding out a fragile hand.

Immune to his sister's attractions, Tristan for the first time observed how stupidly men responded to beauty. Even the vicar, pagan denunciation forgotten, hovered about her like a great black moth, inquiring solicitously of her health, bending close to hear her faint answer.

Tristan liked to think that as an artist, he took a more objective attitude toward feminine beauty. But then he recalled a contessa who had kept him cooling his heels one sweltering summer in Rome. He glanced around, wondering if Charity would be able to read his thoughts if she saw his face. But she was gone from the little circle around Anna.

He heard her light voice mixed with childish shouts, and located her off to the side of the church lawn within a wedge of wisteria bushes. She stood in the center of a circle of children, extending her hands in front of her then out as if she were swimming. "Swim, swim, Jonah! Swim away from the whale!"

When the children took up her cry, she changed from coach to whale, swimming purposefully across the grass as the children scattered, shouting with glee. Her fashionable blue bonnet was hanging down her back; sunlight glinted off her hair. Her cheeks were flushed, her eyes abrim with laughter, as she pretended to grab Jeremy out of the swirl of children around her.

She belongs so well, Tristan thought. Wherever she is, she makes her home. Whomever she's with, she makes her own.

Near him two stately matrons stood, commenting on the service and the weather, watching the children play. "That Charity Calder," one remarked significantly—Mrs. Dalton.

Tristan pretended to be absorbed in watching his nephews gambol with the village children. But really he was waiting, daring her to call Charity a hoyden, to disapprove of her high spirits and unladylike display, so that he could rise to her defense.

"That Charity," Mrs. Hering agreed, shaking her head, and then proceeded to demolish his assumptions about the narrow-mindedness of country folk. "Such a very good sort of girl. Look at how well the children mind her. Little Lawrence—why, he's an earl, and she has him apologizing for knocking down the blacksmith's boy."

"Well, the Calders have never held themselves too high. I'll wager it's a relief for you, isn't it, Agatha, that she's come back as organizer of the Midsummer fair?"

Mrs. Hering glanced around for the vicar and, finding him gone, snorted. "Well, I got no joy in the position! She's the only one, it's true, who can get round the vicar when he's put his back up. And he's got his back up with this festival, right enough." Lowering her voice, so that Tristan could barely hear her, she added, "My Crispin, you know, is set to offer for her again. She refused him once, but he was out in his timing, for her father had just died. She's out of mourning now, and she's had her season, and I imagine she must have decided Kentish men are just as good or better as any she saw in London."

"Well, I wish him the best, I do. If she married your boy, she would be able to stay here in the village where she belongs."

Tristan knew a pierce of resentment as these women assigned themselves ownership rights to Charity, as if her birth in this village gave them first claim on her. But he was surprised at his own proprietary sense—as if somehow he should have that first claim, if he chose to exercise it.

Just then Charity detached herself from the children and ran up the stairs. "No, no, Mrs. Hering," she cried breathlessly, waving the ladies away. "I'll take care of the altar. You go on home to your dinner. I have to talk to the children's parents about the play anyway."

Tristan wanted to reach out and stop her, to hold her back, to force her to stop working just for a moment and give her attention to him. But she only tilted her head to the side and smiled as she went past him into the church. He refused to chase her into the sanctuary, determined to wait until she came out.

After their long afternoon together, he had expected more communication with her than a greeting and that quick smile. But she'd paid more mind to the blacksmith's boy, behaved more flirtatiously with Lawrence, smiled more warmly at Mrs. Hering. But then, none of their encounters—had they really met only four times?—had followed any pattern he recognized. When they did connect, he felt comfortable yet always intrigued, on edge—not a combination he expected with women.

Young Charlie Calder, who had been one of the altar boys, came out of the church then and, casting a quick glance at Tristan, leaned on the iron railing beside the steps. As the younger children scampered over the lawn, calling out challenges to each other, Charlie's thin face grew still. Tristan knew an unwilling sympathy for the boy. He was so wiry, as thin as a reed, his thick dark hair the most substantial part of him. How unlike his siblings Charlie was. They were all so gregarious and confident, and Charlie's shyness was that much sharper in contrast.

Tristan didn't want to reach out to this boy; his own nephews were expensive enough for a man who couldn't afford much emotional expense. But Charlie looked so lonely there, waiting for his sister, watching the children but unable to join them.

"What do you plan for your holiday, Charlie?"

At least the lad could respond to a direct question. His voice was low and quiet as if each word came considered. "I'm supposed to study Latin. That's in the morning. I have chores, too, of course. And rock hunting. I collect rocks and fossils, and the like."

"And you fish, your brother said." Tristan felt a bit of triumph that they were having a real conversation. Charlie even looked up at him.

"Well, Barry fishes. Mostly I tramp around in the water,

looking for interesting pebbles. Barry doesn't like it. He says I scare the fish." The boy's rare smile flashed; for a moment he resembled his sister, all bright irony. "But he'd rather not get any bites at all, than to spend the time alone. Barry hates being alone. He doesn't care if I don't say a word or if I fall asleep, as long as he can chatter away."

"Where are your brothers?"

"Francis is right there." Charlie gestured toward the knot of people still around Anna. The eldest Calder was standing protectively near. Tristan supposed he ought to feel guilty, to let another man keep guard over Anna, but he felt only relief.

"And Barry stayed in bed." Charlie ducked his head and smiled to himself. "He went to the Rose and Crown—that's the public house—with the squire's boys last night. He said he couldn't face the day. He turned green when I yanked open his drapes and let all the sun in!"

"But aren't there five of you? And Charity? Where are the other two?"

The laughter left Charlie's eyes and his face grew still again. "They're—they're out there. Out back. Charity's there." Then, with an apologetic bob of his head, Charlie slid down the iron rail and ran off down the lane.

Tristan meant to propose a meeting with Charity to start the Jonah painting, and besides, he was curious to discover the reason for the boy's odd manner. So he walked through the empty church, his footsteps echoing in the quiet. Light streamed through the prismatic stained-glass windows, painting the gray stone floor with color. The altar cloths had already been put away; Charity was nowhere to be seen. He stood indecisive in a pool of rosy light, then walked on, automatically genuflecting in the papist way as he passed the altar.

At the end of the altar rail, beyond the statue of St. Christopher holding a lamb, was an arched door. This led through a small passageway to an exit out the back of the church, away from the village.

The steps led down to an old brick walk through the old graveyard. On either side of the path leaned headstones, most worn smooth with age. Charity stood before a group of newer ones, a bouquet of the altar lilies in her hand. She bent to place a bloom before each of three stones. One was a doubled arch, like Moses's tablets—for her parents, no doubt. The other two were smaller. She put a hand on the smallest and patted it, as she might pat the head of a child, then repeated the action with the other simple stone. Then she stood there silently, head bowed, the remaining blooms dropping unnoticed from her hand, her pale blue skirt rustling in the light breeze. The only other sound was the distant cries of children.

Abandoning his original intent, Tristan turned and pushed back through the door before she could see him. But he found no answer in the empty sanctuary. All the prisms disoriented him, all that dancing color in the gray stillness. The place seemed to echo with color, with the last solemn note of the Bach fugue she had played, with the secret sadness of a cheerful girl.

Chapter Eight

Monday the two eldest Calders shared a working lunch at the white iron table in the courtyard. Behind them the Grange spread out, comfortable as a dowager, its two wings edged with centuries-old gardens. If they looked up from their papers, they might see a sunlit meadow complete with grazing cows and a brook reflecting the angelic blue sky. But they seldom looked up; it might be a landscape worthy of Constable, but it was home, and not worthy of note.

Francis and Charity often met for lunch in the brick courtyard to exchange village news and make plans for the household. This camaraderie was relatively new; they had never been close as children. Four years separated Francis from the twins Charity and Ned—an unbridgeable gap in childhood. And Charity had always been fonder of her high-spirited twin than of sensible Francis.

But she was ever old for her age, and those four years shrank as her responsibilities grew. Francis had been helpful when Ned died, when they had to unite to keep their father from drinking away the estate in remorse. A year or so ago Charity realized she actually liked Francis. She didn't want to, for he possessed too many of her boring virtues—steadiness and diligence and thrift—and none of her cherished flaws—cynicism and guile and secret romanticism. And Francis was stuffy, no doubt about it, in a way she had never been. Even this morning, when he expected to spend the day in the fields, he wore a starched neckcloth under his riding coat.

But Francis had a fine intellect, even if he used it primarily to make agricultural progress, and a dry sense of humor that occasionally, on certain sorts of days, struck his sister as hilarious. And when she was being very honest, Charity admitted that it was good to know someone as reliable as she was herself. She never worried that Francis would bankrupt them with some crazy investment or that he would miss dinner without sending word or that he would plunge into melancholy just when planting started, requiring her to set her own shoulder to the plow.

They dealt together so amicably that she seldom remembered that when Francis finally decided to make someone a wonderful husband, Charity would have to surrender her home to another woman.

But today her worry about the future extended only as far as the next three weeks, culminating in the Midsummer fair. Actually, the festivities would all take place on Midsummer Eve, June 18, starting in the afternoon with athletic events and an open market. The great evening banquet would cap the day's revelry, culminating in the plays and the parade and a great bonfire after darkness finally fell.

Pencil in hand, Charity was deep into revisions of one of the plays, the one that was to keep the children out of mischief. She had set aside the lists of duties yet to be delegated and booths yet to be assigned, and now stopped editing only long enough to sip her lemonade, which was growing warm in the noon sun.

Mr. Greenaway's *Jonah and the Whale* was just as fearsome as she had dreaded, full of intricate metrical patterns, labored classical imagery, and odd but ingenious rhymes. She wondered how a schoolteacher could expect children to rattle off the likes of "Forcible bears the great Leviathan/to yon trim brig we few rely upon." She changed to "The whale is ramming the boat! The whale is ramming the boat!" and hoped Mr. Greenaway wouldn't notice the substitution.

Weary of the whale and his chronicler's heavy hand, Charity sighed and with a sense of relief took up the booth assignment sheet. This was a more delicate task than might be expected, with the need to accommodate longstanding village rivalries. Neither Mrs. Hering nor Mrs. Dalton could be trusted with the pie booth, for example, for each would be sure to give her own pies the most advantageous placement and sales pitch, while making vaguely foreboding observations about the cleanliness of the other's oven. Mr. Petrick, the local magistrate, had asked to run the children's bean-toss game again, but Charity thought him too rulebound. He never countenanced "helping" a beanbag into the bushel basket, so last year only three children won prizes.

Charity nibbled on her pencil, then inscribed the magistrate's name on the line for the bottle-smash game, which attracted a raffish set of older boys. The kindly Mrs. Petrick could take on the bean-toss booth, and Mrs. Hering could have the ale concession. Charity smiled, remembering the fiasco one year when her own father had been put in charge of that booth. At least Mrs. Hering could be trusted not to drink up most of the supply, give free samples to all her friends, or end up standing on the barrel declaiming bawdy poetry.

"What do you say to a family excursion Wednesday?" Francis asked, looking up from his perusal of the day's post.

Charity knew better than to commit herself; she had accompanied her brother on excursions before. "I say no, if it means standing in a barley field while you discuss some farmer's new way of processing manure."

"It's not my idea. Comes from your artist."

"Lord Braden?" With elaborate unconcern, she raised her pencil and returned to her booth diagrams.

"You have other artists? Yes, Braden. And don't pretend you aren't curious. I see your little ears prick up." Only after she put down her pencil with an exasperated sigh did he explain. "Braden writes very kindly to ask if we—I expect he means the lot of us, but Barry's gone back to Oxford, he'll be glad to hear—will join the lot of them—I expect that means the little demons, too, worse luck—on a picnic luncheon in their Greek folly on Paige Hill." He tossed down the paper in disgust. "Blast, they've remembered that execrable folly after all. I was hoping they'd forget it was ever built and one night I could send Barry and the squire's boys to tear it down. You would think, wouldn't you, that an artist like Braden would see what a travesty that temple is and rid Kent of it once and for all."

Charity let him run through all his oft-stated objections to good English landowners who defaced the good English landscape with bad copies of foreign buildings. She was too busy contemplating what this invitation might mean to take much note of his dissertation: "A druid structure like Stonehenge, well, I could abide that, and anything Celtic, for the Celts were the earliest British race, and, I suppose, even a Roman ruin, especially here in Kent where they ruled, but Greek? Greek?" She looked up only when he spoke that infuriating word—"A *pagan* temple, only a stone's throw from our fine Norman church."

"You're as bad as the vicar!" she commented acidly. "Always worrying about the pagans. Well, what is so dreadful about the pagans, I ask you? They didn't recognize our Savior, but then, that hadn't occurred yet. And it seemed to me they had a deal more excitement in those temples than we do at St. Catherine's of a Sunday!"

Francis opened his mouth to object, then closed it again. Finally, laughing, he said, "Charity, you heretic. Mind your tongue or the vicar will cut it out and have you burned at the stake. He's had enough difficulty swallowing all the Dionysian revelry you've got planned for the Midsummer fair."

She went back to her work, leaving him to chuckle over the vision of his sister, the church organist, roasting on the heretic's spit. But finally he rattled the letter to remind her of the question at hand. "So what about this pagan picnic? Would you like to go?"

Charity bent her head to hide her expression as she contemplated what sorts of things might transpire on a pagan picnic. Not much, she concluded, with the families present. Even pagans had some limits. And duty, as usual, reared its dissenting head. "I don't know as I can spare the time. The fair is only two weeks from Friday."

"You told the vicar yesterday you had it all under control. Of course, you've doubtlessly got the Christmas carol service under control, seeing as it's only six months away."

"Yes, well, I didn't want Mr. Langworth to bring up cancelling again. If I should venture to complain that Mr. Greenaway's version of the Jonah story is a bit—complicated or that the nails for the booths are too short, he will brighten up and say not to worry, he will just make an announcement next week before the sermon, and all my problems, and the Midsummer fair, will be gone."

Francis gave her a sharp, assessing look. "You aren't having any trouble, are you? If it's too much work, you need only ask for a bit of help. Mrs. Hering—"

"Is helping a great deal, for she's taking care of making all the prizes, and Mrs. Dalton is organizing the marketplace, and Crispin promised to build the booths—I've little to do, actually," she said more cheerfully. "Just the games and the banquet and the plays. I do wish I hadn't suggested that we have a preliminary go-round this Saturday. It will earn a bit of money, and the children will enjoy rehearsing the sporting events. And we will come out of it with someone to play St. George. But it's one more thing to plan this week, and I'd best get that done before I contemplate any picnics."

Francis put his hand out. "Give me a sheet of that paper. I'll make up a list of the games for Saturday and put an adult's name next to each to give lessons, and that will be that. The ladies will all bring pies and lemonade of their own accord, and the prospective St. Georges will bring their swords, and everyone will contrive to have fine time. There." He wrote one last name with a flourish and tossed the pencil down. "Now you have no excuse not to go to the picnic."

Charity took back his scrawled list and frowned thoughtfully at it. "Well, I've been over to Haverne near every day to help Cammie, so this won't be very different, will it? And it is our duty to help poor Anna get out more into the fresh air."

"Our duty. To Lady Haverne. Nothing to do with her brother."

Charity mistrusted her brother's grin, which, lacking only a trail of cream, resembled a cat's. "Anna is at last emerging from her cocoon. I was so pleased to see her at church yesterday. You were too, I noticed."

There, that got him back. Francis flushed and dropped his gaze back to the note. "Half after eleven, Braden says. You will get plenty of time with him," he added with his version of a wicked leer. "Says he will be back from an overnight visit to his estate today—significant, don't you think?"

"No," Charity answered crossly.

"He's probably walking through the place right now, noting all the dust and decay, imagining how comfortable and homey it could be if only you were there to supervise its operation. Crack the whip over the maids, refurnish the drawing room, match the linens."

For an instant Charity wondered if it were true. I should never have let him see me mopping that terrace, she thought bleakly; he must think me some sort of *haut ton* housekeeper. To her brother, however, she aimed a scornful look. "You're being absurd, Francis. We haven't met above four times, and he's never shown me any sort of particular attentions."

"Seeing you in that bedraggled sunbonnet and walking you home anyway isn't particular? And staying for tea even after he met Barry? I'd call that pretty particular. I'd call it downright gallant."

By particular, Charity had meant passionate stolen embraces under a moonlit sky, but she could hardly tell her brother that. There was no need, anyway, because Francis had his own ideas about courtship procedures. "Anyway, near as I can tell, a bachelor needs only two encounters with you to decide you are destined to serve tea in his drawing room for the rest of his life. Any day now, Braden's going to throw caution to the wind and beg for your hand. And I hope you accept this one, because for all he doesn't know a plow from a platypus, he'd make me a good brother-in-law."

Charity took a restorative drink of lemonade, obscurely depressed by this prediction. She didn't want Braden to behave like the rest of her suitors. For he was different, and he made her feel different, too. He was fascinating to look at and to listen to, with those hot Italian eyes and ever-so-slight Italian accent.

He was intrigued by her, too, she had reason to hope—but surely not just for her domestic skills! He found her amusing, challenging. The ironical remarks that passed over most of her suitors made him laugh, and he wasn't a man free with his laughter. Besides, if she hadn't yet experienced his "particular attentions," she felt thrilled enough at his smile to imagine the excitement his kiss would arouse.

So when Francis suggested it was all of a piece with the other courtships, instinctively she rebelled. No, it was different. Braden was different. He was artistic, romantic, Mediterranean. He was extraordinary, and he could take her away from the ordinary.

"I expect we should accept the invitation, Francis." Charity piled her utensils neatly on her plate and rose, shaking the crumbs off her napkin. "A picnic expedition would be good for Anna. And it will do Charlie some good, too, to be out with other boys. At least Lawrence and Jeremy can help him scout for rocks on the hillside."

"No benefit to you, of course, in this picnic, is there?" As she walked back to the house, Francis's brotherly taunt followed. "That's our Charity, never thinks of herself—or never admits to it, anyway."

The Calder laundress had hung the altar linens up to dry earlier, and Charity folded them, still warm from the sun, away into a basket. Along the short walk to the church, she let questions play through her mind: was Lord Braden's house in Sussex indeed in decrepit shape, and what did he plan to do about it, and would he request her help, and what form would that request take?

She hadn't enough information to answer any of those questions. So it was something of a relief to find a diversion ready for her as she approached the church, in the form of the vicar, pacing back and forth, his cassock sweeping the flower petals from the path.

Before she could climb the steps to the church hall, he pounced on her. He held up one of the notices the Ferris girls had distributed over the week's end, announcing the audition and games rehearsals to be held Saturday in front of the church. "What's this, Charity? More revelry? Isn't Midsummer enough for you?"

His cassocked form blocked the way; Charity couldn't dodge around him. So she just smiled and shook her head in a deprecating way. "Oh, sir, it is nothing. Just a chance for the younger children to learn the games. You know, carrying an egg on a spoon across the green does not come easy to a six-year-old, and I thought they might do better with a bit of practice."

The vicar's usually benevolent expression was a glower now. "I saw the announcement you inserted in my notes at Matins yesterday. You thought I would read it out unawares during the sermon, didn't you? This—this audition. What is that? Are Drury Lane theater directors coming to make Hamlets and Portias of our parishioners?"

Charity hid a smile at his heavy attempt at sarcasm. "No, sir. It's for the mummer plays. You remember, *Jonah and the Whale?*" She meant to start rehearsing the children's play immediately, before the week's end, but she thought it best not to tell him that.

But Mr. Langworth was too sharp for her. Peering at the notice again, he observed with that labored irony, "What an unusual Jonah play you must be planning. For you are announcing a fencing contest. Why, I must read my Bible again, for I remember no swordplay by Jonah."

Charity feinted to the left, but the vicar saw and moved a bit to counteract her. She sighed and resigned herself to standing in the sun until he had had his say. Shifting the linen blanket to the other arm, she said, "Yes, sir, that too. We'll need a St. George, you recall, to slay the dragon. I thought that at the least we could use an earlier competition to earn a bit of funds to defray the cost of putting on the fair."

The vicar snorted. "That's all well and good, but encouraging swordplay among our young men is not a duty of the church!"

"The foils will have buttons on them, of course, so no one will be hurt." Charity added innocently, "If you would prefer a pugilistic contest, I will devise a boxing ring—"

"Pugilism? Certainly not! I vow—"

Fortunately, before the vicar could make his vow, he was interrupted. He looked over Charity's shoulder and called, "Why, Lord Braden, what brings you here?"

"I am here to start the Jonah painting."

Trying to appear nonchalant, Charity turned slowly. Lord Braden was striding up the walk, the afternoon sun outlining his slim form and blazing a halo around his black hair. A satchel was slung over his shoulder, a length of canvas rolled up under his arm. He must have returned from Sussex and decided to use the afternoon light on her project rather than his own.

From a dedicated artist, this was a gesture so generous she knew it to have some higher significance, and Charity felt a swelling in her chest that almost cut off her breath. What was this emotion that seized her whenever she saw him? It was thrilling, this feeling: airy, fluttery, but somehow disorienting. She was not used to this; usually she could marshal her emotions like little soldiers to do her bidding. Now she could hardly control her own breathing.

But that part of herself that was always observing noted that the vicar was struck silent by Lord Braden's announced intention. Aha, Charity thought, Mr. Langworth faces a collision of principle and interest! He would like to proclaim against paganism but does not want to offend the parish's richest family.

She knew principle had lost out when the vicar stepped to the side, letting both Charity and Lord Braden enter the church hall. He trailed in behind them, watching suspiciously as the artist unloaded his supplies onto a makeshift table contrived from a board set across two sawhorses. "You are to paint something for this play?"

"The backdrop." Lord Braden cast a swift glance at Charity, and as if that was enough to realize her need for support, he added casually, "The work for this Midsummer fair has been good for my sister. You would be amazed at how very hard she is working on those rag dolls. I was hoping that if the entire family became involved, she would find even more to occupy her during these difficult days."

"Well, if Lady Haverne is comforted by her church work— well, God loves to keep us busy, he does. Painting the backdrop, are you?" The vicar couldn't entirely give up his sternness, even for a lord. "I hope you mean this backdrop to be appropriate for a Christian occasion."

Charity could hear the undertone of laughter in Lord Braden's voice as he answered, "Yes, yes, my art is always appropriate."

The vicar apparently decided to disregard the ambiguity of that answer and turned to Charity. "I am glad to hear you enlisted Mr. Greenaway also. He told me that his script is true to its Biblical origins. He made several copies and means to let me have one."

Charity swallowed back a sigh. How like the schoolmaster to make copies of his magnum opus. Now she would never be able to burn the original and claim her own version was a faithful replication. But at least the vicar was accepting the fair and the plays as inevitable. With restored good humor, she smiled at Lord Braden, her savior, hoping he might soften the vicar to the activity at week end's, too. To give him an opening, she asked, "Do you think your nephews would like to learn how to play the Midsummer games? We are having instruction from veteran sportsmen on Saturday. The entire village will turn out, I think!"

"They saw the notice this morning, and bedeviled Mrs. Cameron until she agreed to bring them. I think if you add your invitation, Anna might come, too." He glanced at the vicar, his voice entirely serious now. "Coming to Matins yesterday was a great step for her. I think Saturday, if she has motivation enough, she will come and even enjoy herself, and then perhaps she will realize that she has friends here." Awkwardly he added, "I know the Havernes have never taken much part in the parish, and I am grateful that the parishoners nonetheless have been so welcoming."

The vicar couldn't be blamed for beaming at this, and Charity, too, was warmed by the thought of lost lambs gathered back into the parish flock. You see, she wanted to tell the vicar, this is why we have fairs and festivals; this keeps the church in the center of our village and makes faith a joyful thing. But she knew better than to hammer home the point; she held her tongue and let Mr. Langworth declare that he would call upon the countess in the morning.

Arranging his brushes on the board, Lord Braden murmured that she would like that. "On Saturday, I might even be drawn into the games. That fencing exhibition—might a visitor join in?"

"Oh, my lord, you are not a visitor," Mr. Langworth said. "You are one of us, surely, no matter where your home might be."

Charity sensed Lord Braden's slight withdrawal as he held up a brush to study it and then tugged a few stray beaver hairs from the tuft. He's not sure he wants to be one of us, she realized. He is too used to being alone. To cover the awkward silence, she asked, "Do you fence, then, Lord Braden?"

He glanced up with a grin. "A bit. I would be better for some practice, I think. But I hope to get that Saturday."

The vicar, recognizing his defeat, folded up the notice of Saturday's revelry and stuck it in his cassock pocket. "Doubtlessly I will see you then, for I—" he shot a warning glance at Charity, "I will be overseeing the activities. We wouldn't want them to get out of bounds."

He departed to prepare for evensong, and Charity found herself alone with Lord Braden. Even as she told him of her family's acceptance of his kind invitation to luncheon on the morrow, she realized how free social relations were in the village. In London, she would never have been left indoors, unchaperoned, with a bachelor. But the vicar was hardly one to neglect the proprieties. He knew Lord Braden was unlikely to try to ruin her right here in the church hall, with the graves of her ancestors visible through the windows and church ladies wandering in and out at will. Still, as she busied herself putting away the linens in the cupboard, she glanced back over her shoulder at him, waiting for him to approach her with lascivious intent.

But he was kneeling down, rolling out the canvas in the middle of the floor. "This will be the center panel. Can you help me?"

Less relieved than she ought to be by his restraint, Charity joined him, tugging her skirt up and kneeling across from him to tug the huge canvas straight. He had already begun work, she saw with appreciation. With quick flowing lines he had sketched the outlines of the whale, a formidable bulk almost five feet across, its great mouth open in a fierce grin. "Where will the boat go?"

"Half here." He was stripping off his blue coat and yanked

one arm out of the sleeve then pointed to the corner of the canvas. "And half on the right panel. The whale's tail will take up most of the left panel. That way the image will flow from one panel to the other, you see. Continuity is essential for a successful triptych. So are frames," he added. "We'll have to build two more."

"Oh, I'll get Crispin to do it when he comes by this evening."

She was surprised when he frowned at her careless words. "I can't wait for this evening," he said, a hint of hauteur entering his voice. The temperamental artist, she thought. "I cannot begin painting until the canvas is stretched on the frame. And I mean to begin painting this afternoon."

So it was that Charity found herself once more pounding nails as a young man held the frame in place. She was no stranger to carpentry, having built treehouses with Ned and display boxes for Charlie's rocks. And with Crispin she had worried not at all about smashing him with her hammer, no matter how he cringed and complained.

But she felt more dangerous this time. When Lord Braden held the frame, his long slender fingers only inches from her hammer, she had to bite her lip to keep the tremble from her hands and the hammer aimed true.

If Lord Braden worried that his talented hands were destined for destruction, he gave no sign of it. But she relaxed only when she could set down her hammer, tilt the two new frames next to the one she and Crispin built, and survey the start of the triptych. "It will be very large, won't it?"

"All the children should be able to fit in front of it. That way it will frame the action, in the Renaissance fashion."

"The Renaissance fashion?"

It took a bit of coaxing, but Lord Braden explained the term as he went to his makeshift table and began mixing the gray paint for the whale. With the same slight diffidence he answered her other questions: what special qualities triptychs had, and whether Hieronymous Bosch was as mad as his great triptych made him seem, and a half-dozen more, until she felt as if she had been privileged to attend the Royal Academy School herself.

She halted her inquiries when he took his palette and brushes to the triptych. "Here," he said, holding out a wide brush dowsed in gray-blue, "just swab that on that first canvas. Just the top half." When she hesitated, holding the brush up to keep the paint from dripping on the dropcloths, he added, "Go on, Miss Calder. You won't hurt it. That's the first thing I learned at art school: how to paint over mistakes."

At first tentatively, and then with gathering confidence, she daubed away at the great expanse of white. It was rather like painting a wall, she thought, then stole a look at Lord Braden. He was not painting a wall, she realized, as she saw the whale take shape under his deft hands.

When she had covered the top half of the canvas with paint, he stopped his own work to study hers. After a moment of intense concentration, he nodded. "We'll let it dry until I paint the boat underneath. Then we'll have to add some shadow and contrast. You did well for now. Don't forget to rinse your brush in the bucket there, and then in the oil."

She was too pleased with his laconic praise to retort that she, of all people, would never forget to rinse out her brush. But that done, she had nothing to do, and couldn't bring herself to leave.

Lord Braden gave no sign that he wasn't content to let her watch him paint. Occasionally, as if he were tutoring a student, he pointed with his brush at some point on the canvas, explained why he chose this shade of black for the shadowy wrinkles above the eyes, or how he meant the open mouth to look like a tunnel into hell. It was all fascinating to her, listening, watching, as he worked.

So though she had a dozen tasks to complete, Charity gave into temptation. She sat quietly on a pile of lumber in front of the window, her hands for once still in her lap. Even when he fell silent, she didn't let her mind dart about in its usual fashion, checking its list of unfinished duties, planning the rest of the week, crafting letters to her correspondents. No, there in a pool of sunlight she felt as warm and content as a cat. But like a cat, she was intent under her deceptive laziness, intent upon the artist making art before her.

She liked to watch his slim hands, one balancing the gray-smeared palette, the other with an easy grip on a thick brush. His brush hand moved in small precise arcs along the outline of the whale, sometimes halting, then backing up to correct some infinitesimal mistake in an earlier arc. These were not the knobby splayed hands of a Kent farmer, neither the white exquisite hands of a London nobleman, used mostly for taking snuff and pulling on gloves. They were a working artist's hands, strong, hard, but elegant nonetheless in their grace and power.

Finally she let her gaze drift to his face. He was so serious now; as he studied his work, his dark eyes narrowed and his straight brows drew together, but not in a forbidding way. Rather he seemed to confine his focus entirely to that square of canvas and paint, making minute unfathomable calculations and decisions, then acting to put them to effect. He no longer seemed to know that she was there; he might have been all alone, as intent as if this children's triptych were a fresco in the Sistine Chapel.

Watching the play of light and shadow across his face, she wondered if such a concentration was uniquely masculine or uniquely artistic. She certainly could never shut out the world as he did or lose herself so completely in one activity. It was seductive, that solitude, that concentration, and sitting here, silent as he worked, she could almost imagine what it would be like to be so very alone and yet so content.

But the world was too much with her. When the sonorous church bells ran the call to evensong, she sprang to her feet. Half after five o'clock! She had been sitting here two hours, doing nothing! Her mind filled with the duties she had been neglecting: Mr. Greenaway's manuscript, the jumble booth collections, Charlie's lessons.

But then she saw Lord Braden, standing slim and straight at the canvas, still frowning thoughtfully at his work. The great bells which called men in from distant fields were tolling only a hundred feet away. But he didn't hear them. And so she knew he wouldn't hear her slip out of the hall, to return to the world from which he had spirited her.

Chapter Nine

Francis's many virtues had never included subtlety. They had hardly finished lunch in the striped tent (the Greek folly had been deemed too spider-ridden for entry) before he began culling out the crowd that separated Charity from what he called her "prey." Cammie and the three boys were the first victims, ruthlessly sent on a nature walk in the adjacent woods. Anna was invited to climb up into the church tower, Francis declaring that once she saw the Greek monstrosity from above she would surely order it demolished before some neighborhood ruffians did it for her.

Though she looked wary at the mention of the church tower, Anna joined into the conspiracy. With elaborate unconcern, she told her brother, "Show Charity your studio. She will enjoy that."

So Charity and the amused Braden went off obediently toward Haverne Hall. As they crossed the sun-filled meadow, she silently cursed her interfering brother. I would like to choose my own suitors, thank you, she thought righteously, kicking aside a pebble that lay in her path. But since very likely she would have made the same choice, and she did want to see Tristan's paintings, she thought it best not to make an issue of her brother's machinations.

Lord Braden looked back at his sister, picking her way down the path to the church, her arm held securely by

Francis. "I thought you said the whole point of this Midsummer fair was to fix the church tower. Are you sure it's safe for them to go climbing in it?"

"As long as they climb inside, they'll be safe enough!" She stopped to point out the distant tower, a gray block in the sunlight, looming primitive and ominous over the pretty village. "It's only the masonry around the outside of the windows that needs repair. It keeps chipping off and falling. You must know cautious Francis would never put Anna in any danger! Except—" she glanced sidelong at him, "how does Anna feel about spiders?"

"Hates 'em."

They exchanged laughing glances, and Charity said with some satisfaction, "It will serve Francis right if she shrieks and faints and must be carried all the way down the stairs!"

From the hill in the distance came childish shouts. The boys were embarking on their nature walk. With a shock Charity recognized the merry one as Charlie, laughing at one of the Haverton boys' interminable bickers. She had almost forgotten what Charlie's laugh sounded like—startled and boyish above Lawrence's shout.

Lord Braden laughed, too, hearing the children. "It was kind of you, by the way, to give my nephews parts in your great production. I understand you have tapped their greatest talent."

"What do you mean?"

"I asked if they had any lines to speak, and they said no, they are only to wield an oar on the boat. And to bellow with fear. They do," he added ruefully, "bellow very well."

"Well, they were agog to see your painting. All the children were. But I thought it better to keep it covered. I've promised to reveal it when they've all learned their parts."

"I'm to be an incentive, am I? I had best redouble my efforts, then, so as to be worthy of the wait." As he held open the hedgegate for her, he said suddenly, "Your brother and my sister think they are being very clever, arranging so deftly to send us off alone together."

Charity took advantage of the moment he spent latching the gate to gather her thoughts. She recalled his instinctive withdrawal at the last luncheon they had shared, when he thought she was setting her cap for him. Had he decided he liked the idea after all?

She was used to reading people instinctively, but she could not quite translate Lord Braden's signals, even as they applied to her. He was so much more enigmatic than most of the men she knew. She still didn't quite know why he had sought her out recently, whether it was merely out of gratitude or some other, more interesting emotion—and whether he resented or appreciated such transparent attempts at matchmaking.

But his smile was rueful as he rejoined her on the walk. "I have lived abroad for so long, I am no longer accustomed to being ordered about by my big sister."

That was safe enough, talking about Anna, who was so much easier to interpret than her brother. "Doubtless it makes her feel stronger to dictate to you. It is kind of you to submit so."

"And are you just being kind, to submit also?"

Confused, she dropped her gaze to the path they were taking across the rolling lawn. The groundskeeper she had recommended had cropped the grass, she noted with absent approval, but he hadn't gotten round to the finishing work yet. Bending down to pluck a handful of weed, she used the moment to gather her composure. "Kind? Not at all," she answered calmly, flinging the weeds away. "I just couldn't turn down a chance to see your work. Do you work on more than one painting at a time?"

This response seemed to disappoint him. It was a moment before he said, "Yes, I like to have several canvases started. But my dealer in London is demanding one to show a special client." He cast her a speculative glance. "I'm certain the conspirators mean for us to stay away a good long time.

Would you like to help me choose which painting to finish first?"

Charity's mood suddenly brightened. Something told her that this special client might be very special indeed. A *royal* client, perhaps? "There's nothing I'd like better! If—if you don't mind, of course."

"Why should I mind?"

"Oh, because if I must *choose,* I must then tell you which painting I like best and which I don't like quite so well. Though I'm sure," she added hurriedly, "that I will like them all very well."

Lord Braden shook his head. "If you like them all, then you will be of little help to me. Come, you must promise to be honest! You could never be as brutal as my teachers have been. I had one who used to rap me on the head with a palette because I used more red paint than any other student." He rubbed the back of his head, as if even the memory hurt. "After that, any critic who didn't hit me won my appreciation. Artists can't get through their training, you see, without developing a thick skin. A thick skull, also."

"Well, you won't need either one, if I am to be the critic. I will like all your paintings."

This promise made him pause on the path, reaching his hand out and taking her arm to stop her also. "How do you know that you will like them? How do you know I am not some hack-handed novice? Oh, I know you have seen my masterpiece, 'Jonah's Whale'—"

She was about to demur, but with a laugh he forestalled her. "Yes, I know you have been checking on my progress with the whale. I saw this morning how perfectly squared the cover was over the painting. I would never be so neat."

There was no profit in denying her guilt, so she only observed, "The whale is nearly done, and it is done very well."

"Ah, but perhaps that is the limit of my abilities. Perhaps I can draw nothing but whales."

There was a teasing light in his eyes that entranced her,

and even as they resume their walk she kept her gaze on his face. How easily he laughed with her now. His smile was almost carefree, easing the austere lines of his face. He could even make jokes about his own art, which Charity knew to be the most important thing in his world. "The whale is not the only work of yours that I have seen. I told you I saw two of your paintings at the Royal Academy. One was a lovely seascape—it was called *Ferendisi.*"

"And what was the other?" he asked. "I sent several and haven't heard yet which they mounted."

She opened her mouth to answer, then closed it as the vision of the nude Aphrodite and the nearly nude Adonis flashed in her mind. "I don't recall," she replied haughtily.

"Oh, *that* one!"

Of course he knew exactly which she meant, and the lively light in his eyes told her that he found her primness particularly amusing. And considering the bold way she had spoken earlier in their acquaintance, she couldn't blame him. So Charity found herself laughing with him and describing her aunt's reaction to the Aegean Adonis—though not, it is true, her own. Candor had its limits, even among friends.

He even showed his artist's eagerness for an audience, pressing her for the precise number of viewers who stopped at his paintings, a comparison with the admirers of J.M.W. Turner's works, and a list of the other artists represented. She warmed to the longing in his voice; she knew he was accustomed to spending the exhibition season in London and thought that he must miss the colloquy of his fellow artists. Impulsively she said, "The Academy's exhibition will be open yet for another week. Why don't you go up to town to see for yourself and meet that special client perhaps?"

He paused only a moment to consider this, then shook his head briskly as if banishing regrets. "No, not now. There will be time enough for that in the future, when Anna is settled again. Besides—" he cast her a significant glance, "I've your whale and his Jonah to finish. And the fencing match Saturday, of course."

As they approached Haverne Hall, she considered him covertly from under her lashes. She had promised herself—and Francis—to take a holiday from thinking about the Midsummer fair today. But she couldn't help wondering if Lord Braden was a good enough swordsman to make the St. George audition a true competition. Crispin Hering was, of course, expected to win. But Lord Braden was lean enough for quick motion and all unstudied grace as he strolled beside her in his casual buckskins and soft Indian leather boots. And his hands, of course, were perfect—strong and yet deft. He would be good with a sword. An exciting match for the St. George role, she decided, could not help but increase interest in the Midsummer fair itself. And Lord Braden in motion, she added secretly, could not help but stir excitement among the young ladies in the audience.

"There it is, my studio."

They had come at the Hall from the back, and Charity shaded her eyes to see where he was indicating. "Oh, the old sunroom! We used to have puppet shows there when Kenny's little cousins came to visit. He used to chase us outdoors onto the balcony, and we'd climb down that oak tree to escape him."

The preserving oak still spread its branches over the balcony. She put an affectionate hand on its sturdy trunk. "You see, the rungs are still here. Francis nailed them in, for he feared Ned and I would come to grief climbing down. Even Kenny made use of them when he wanted to sneak out at night."

She gazed nostalgically up at the branches, recalling those childhood adventures, when the almost-grown Kenny was just as boyish as Ned and Francis was left to supply the mature wisdom. "We had such fun."

She glanced guiltily at Lord Braden, wondering if he had had such childhood exploits. From what she knew of his life, she thought it unlikely. But he gave no sign of feeling deprived. Instead, he grinned at her. "It's unfortunate that you are too old and too dignified now to make the ascent."

Charity had never in her life been able to turn down a challenge, even one she knew was unintended. "Too old? You are mistaken, Lord Braden. I climbed a tree only last week to rescue a kitten. It's all a matter of skill—and privacy."

"Privacy?"

"Surely you know the rule—boys up first, girls down first."

Lord Braden considered this somberly, his brows drawn together in a frown. "When I used to climb trees, propriety wasn't really a consideration. But if you insist—"

She had never really supposed he would do it—he was lithe enough, of course, but it was rather at odds with a man's dignity to climb a tree. He didn't even take the easy route, up the rungs, but caught the first branches and swung himself up, something she in her encumbering skirts could never attempt. He was well into the sheltering branches before she remembered his hands, which were necessary not only to finish the whale triptych but also to fence that Saturday. "Be careful of your hands, do! Don't scrape them on the bark—"

His protest floated down from the upper branches. "Really, Miss Calder, I do know how to climb a tree without risking permanent disability."

She strained to look up through the concealing leaves but did not see him again until he dropped onto the balcony and leaned over the wall. He was laughing at her, holding his hand out as if she might jump up and grasp it. "Are you coming? Or have you decided to take the long way through the house?"

Charity sensed the Italian warmth now in his cool voice; the vowels were a bit longer, the consonants gentle. She recalled how tense he had been when they first met—was it less than a fortnight ago? He must have felt so inadequate to the task before him, and he was, like Charity, the sort to hate feeling inadequate. But now he was quick to laugh, quick to tease her about being a coward, showing a playful side she thought he usually kept hidden.

I have been good for him, she realized, warming at the thought. She was used to having a positive effect on people; it was rather her purpose in life. But to make Lord Braden carefree, unreserved—that was especially gladdening.

Now, laughing down at her from above, he looked like one of his own paintings of young gods, slim and golden in the noon sun. He had taken off his cravat and left the lawn shirt open at the neck. Charity's gaze lingered on that tantalizing triangle of chest, with its suggestion of dark curling hair, usually kept concealed. How came this to be tanned as golden as his face? She dropped her eyes, the heat rising in her cheeks as the likely answer came to her. On the Italian coast, she imagined, he dressed even more casually.

It signified adventure, that careless dress, allowing quick escapes and freedom from restraint. She sensed again that foreignness surrounding him like a faint glow, as if the heat of the Italian sun still radiated from his body. She knew he was a gentleman, no rogue at all, but somehow he seemed more hazardous than the proper—or even the improper—English gentlemen she knew.

His recklessness was contagious. She set aside any notions of modesty and decorum and glanced around to make sure the boxwoods encircling the garden concealed her misdemeanor. Then she gathered her skirt in one hand and with the other took hold of the trunk and climbed up the rungs. She lost her sunbonnet before she reached the balcony. But her light sandals didn't slip off, and her feet stayed secure on the thick branch until, taking the hand Lord Braden held out to her, she dropped lightly over the wall.

Once she found her footing on the stone floor, he released her. But that momentary contact was enough. She found that his fingers were callused, rough and smooth at the same time, and left behind a trail of heat on her hand. His merest touch thrills me, she told herself. But along with that illicit thrill came disquiet; she didn't know if she were quite ready to be thrilled, or if, indeed, this was the right sort of man to thrill her, this dark solitary man who was so foreign to her experience. Of course, she reminded herself, I wouldn't want to be so reduced that an ordinary man would thrill me.

"What fun! I hope the doors aren't locked, after all our work!"

But at Lord Braden's touch, the French doors swung open smoothly, and she saw that the old sunroom had undergone a transformation. This studio bristled with evidence of artistic activity, and Charity, usually disoriented by mess, found the chaos oddly appealing. Forgetting for a moment the man who created the place, she squeezed between two easels and made a slow circuit around the sun-filled room, examining each unfamiliar item.

The shelves along one wall, once used for repotting plants, held the artist's supplies: jars of oil paints stuck on sheets of an Italian newspaper, a box of brushes, a clutch of palette knives, a jug of linseed oil with a wide cork stopper. A pitcher and ewer, the water a muddy gray, took up most of the marble surface of a console table. Next to it was a jar of brushes soaking in turpentine. She wrinkled her nose at the sharp smell and went on, stepping carefully to keep from catching a heel in the dropcloths that protected the plank floor.

She stopped at a table strewn with charcoal pencils, their box lying discarded on the floor. She retrieved it and gathered up the pencils, tapping them on the table to even them and then boxing them up. She looked up to Lord Braden's laughing eyes.

"I wondered how long it would take you to begin tidying."

Charity flushed and placed the box of pencils back on the table. "I'm sorry. It's just a habit."

"Don't apologize! It's rather endearing, actually."

Perhaps it was only a half-compliment, but it warmed

Charity. He wasn't a flirtatious man, given to rhapsodies and raptures whenever a lady was in earshot. No, usually he had that slight formality she attributed to his foreign heritage. His relaxed bearing with her was even more of a compliment.

"I do like your studio," she said, clasping her hands firmly behind her back out of temptation's way. "I can see now that underneath the—the disorder, it is really organized in a fashion to suit you. I will wager your last studio was arranged much the same way."

He gazed around him in some surprise, as if he had never really seen this room before. "Yes, actually, I think you are right. I like to keep all my supplies accessible, not away in some cabinet." He crossed to an easel and pulled the cover off, saying over his shoulder, "And I like a southern light. I've already chosen the room I'll use for my studio at Braden, and it is very like this. But then," he added thoughtfully, studying the painting, a barely started still life, "I don't know if Braden Hall is up to this sort of chaos. It's very—precise. A Palladian house, you know. Perfectly symmetric. Geometric order. Manicured and squared lawns."

"You must have a very good steward," Charity commented. "Especially as—" She broke off before she said something impolite about absentee landowners, but Braden looked up from the canvas to laugh.

"Oh, your brother's already taken me to task for that. Says the steward should have robbed me blind, were he not a devout Methodist. But he's done me better than I deserve, I suppose. I should be pleased. But—"

"But?" She wished he wouldn't examine the painting so minutely, that he would move away so she could see it, too.

"But it doesn't look much like a home. Too perfect. Nothing to soften that stark facade."

This, at least, was an art Charity knew something about. "You need a few great flowering trees right in front. Two on one side, perhaps, and one on the other, to break up the uniformity. There is a dome, I imagine?" At his nod, she said wistfully, "I love domes in houses. If only we didn't have a Tudor house—a dome would never fit in a Tudor. Then," she added briskly, returning to his landscaping problem, "a nicely overgrown garden along the drive, tall flowers, lilac bushes."

"Flowers will not be enough to make that museum a home."

"Oh, no. Only living in it will. But once you move in, prop your paintings against the wall, and toss some rugs about, it will no longer be quite so perfect. A house can only be a home when there are people there to muss it a bit."

Finally, with a bit of ceremony, he yanked the cover off a large wide canvas. "This one is closer to completion, but I've been neglecting it of late."

The painting was a seascape, much like the one she had seen in the Royal Academy exhibition, a pretty whitewashed village around a harbor filled with fishing boats. It was a picture full of light and color, and very charming. "Oh, that's lovely. Is that Ferendisi again? You know it very well, don't you?"

"We stayed at a villa there every winter when I was a child. And I still winter there."

Every winter in Italy? No wonder he felt alien here. "Surely you didn't continue after the war started up again."

Lord Braden's expression became abstract, and he gazed at his painting as if someone else had painted it and he were seeing it for the first time. "Actually, we did. We were trapped for two years when I was thirteen; the French had taken Naples."

British subjects in occupied Italy—it must have been terrifying for a sensitive boy. Charity almost reached out to touch him, as if she could soothe away the memory somehow. But she drew back her hand and looked back at the sunny painting. "How did you escape arrest?"

"Oh, Mother's cousin is an archbishop, and so—" that unexpectedly merry grin flashed, and the abstraction was gone—"well-acquainted with lowlife sorts. He got us forged passports and smuggled out letters to my father in Oxford and bank drafts back to us. We weren't in any real danger. In fact, it was rather a lark. Anna got to dance with all the defeated officers who had gone to cover in Lecce, and I spent the time in Florence, studying art. My teacher was in a direct line from one of Leonardo's students." Thoughtfully he added, "The da Vinci connection has added a certain cachet to my reputation as no one else at the Royal Academy school was able to study in Italy during the war."

To Charity, who hadn't even been to France except for one weekend after the war ended, it seemed a most nomadic life. She didn't know whether she envied him or pitied him. "But you must have found it hard to accustom yourself to England on your return."

"Oh, children are adaptable. My mother never learned to feel at home when we came back to England, it's true. Too damp and cold." A wave of his hand included the pretty vista outside—the tender green backdrop of an English spring, the dots of lilac and pink and yellow flowers, the clusters of tan and brown houses, the gentle blue sky. "And all these misty pastels. She used to say the landscape here made her drowsy."

It was odd, she thought, that sometimes Lord Braden spoke of the English as an alien race. With a flash of intuition she wondered if in Italy he spoke of the Italians the same way. But she did not voice this speculation directly. "Unlike those shocking primary colors you have in Italy?"

She knew she had spoken his thoughts when he rewarded her with a quick grin. "Precisely."

The next painting was a closer view of the same harbor, but the entire tone was different. It was at sunset, and the colors were duskier, cooler. Charity reached out to touch the mast of a fishing boat, its sails furled, its deck deserted. The paint was still damp but didn't smudge under her curious touch.

"Such a lonely view, isn't it? Looking back to the harbor

where everyone works. But everyone's gone home for supper and left the boats behind."

Lord Braden didn't like this interpretation, she could tell from his frown. "A painting's a painting. It's not a story."

Well, she saw a story in it, a story about an artist and his necessary isolation from everyday life. "But it captures a moment surely. There's a story in that moment and in why you chose to paint that moment."

"I chose this moment because—because of the composition. The harbor and the beach are the horizontals, and the masts and cliff the verticals. And the light links it all. It doesn't have a story to tell, except about light and shadows and heights and widths."

She had to admit that she didn't have the sort of mind that viewed a scene and saw geometric shapes, and that perhaps the audience saw what the artist never intended. But about the next picture's meaning, there was no doubt:

A ship afire against the black night. The sails were long gone, the masts charred and broken, residual flames fickering along the hull. The smoke was dissipating into shadows in the darkness. It was truly a moment suspended, an interlude between death and burial.

Charity stepped back instinctively, backing up right into Lord Braden. She scarcely noticed his arms going out to hold her up, but she sensed the hard support of his chest against her back and closed her eyes. She dragged in a breath, shut out the vision she had long blocked and, turning her head, opened her eyes.

She could see only the light tan weave of his linen coat, and it was to this she addressed her comment. "Very evocative," she said, in a voice that sounded false even in her own ears. She slipped out of his grasp and, stooping to pick up a balled-up piece of brown paper, added, "That's the one I would choose to send out, were I you. It's almost done, isn't it? Or perhaps the one of the village." Without giving him time to answer, she stuck the paper in her pocket and walked to the door. "We must get back, don't you think? I must stop by the church hall before dinner to see how Crispin's booth-building is doing. Let's take the long way out, shall we?"

And with such light comments she got them out of the door and away from the studio. She knew that he didn't believe her cheerful mien, that he was studying her closely to discern her real feelings. But she wanted only to be away, away from fiery visions and ghastly memories, away from his work and what it revealed.

Chapter Ten

The next morning Tristan added a last dash of white on the smoke, then stepped back to examine the painting of the ship afire. Had he gone too far? If anything, he had erred on the side of subtlety. He had scorned the cheap dramatics of bodies blown through the sky, of limbs floating in pools of blood, of sharks circling. He had seen all that one night from the rail of a ship, after a frigate caught fire and its gunpowder chamber exploded. But this painting was of a later moment, just before the ship sank. There were a few bodies, of course, but they were hardly noticeable, floating darkly against the dark sea, along with the other debris of the explosion.

But perhaps it was more theatrical than he intended or Miss Calder more delicate than he imagined.

No. The Charity Calder he knew would not blanch at a bit of gore. She had only laughed when he described his vision of Jonah's whale, seamen impaled on his teeth. A mere painting wouldn't frighten her. No. This was something else, something personal.

He left the painting to dry there on the easel and, musing, went downstairs to breakfast. He had been making a great point of starting the day with his sister. She was much improved but still likely to lie abed till noon and arise feeling dizzy and useless. So her new maid—the eldest Ferris girl—

had been ordered to roust her out of bed and into clothing by nine.

Tristan had grown used to sullen, silent breakfasts, so Anna's blithe humming this morning made him suspicious. "What plot are you hatching?"

Anna looked up guiltily from her egg cup. "Plot? No plot. I just—I just had a pleasant time yesterday on our excursion. 'Tis true, that folly is a blight on the landscape and entirely out of place."

"That sounds like a quote from Sir Francis Calder."

She shrugged. "Well, he's right. I've given him permission to have it pulled down. I hadn't realized it was in such a state of disrepair." She glanced around her as if the pleasant breakfast room were gray with cobwebs and neglect. "Like everything else around here."

"Oh, it's not so bad now," Tristan said defensively. "All the work and money we've spent have had some effect, certainly."

"But not enough to counteract years of neglect." Her mouth tightened and Tristan knew she was thinking about her husband, who had seen Haverne as a source of income and nothing more. "The tenants' cottages need a great deal of work, and their common land gets flooded too easily. I never noticed such things before. I never knew that the church tower's masonry was in such poor repair—and it's of the Norman era, Sir Francis says, and part of the national heritage. The vicar said it won't take too great a contribution to restore it."

A bit dryly, Tristan said, "You needn't borrow against the harvest for the tower, Anna. That's what the Midsummer fair is to pay for. If that is not enough, we will make up the difference. But the Calders, I think, have it well in hand."

"That's just it, isn't it? The Calders have been carrying their own burden, and Haverne's, too, all this time. It's the earl's duty to maintain the vicarage, but I think Sir Francis must be paying for it."

And probably for the vicar's salary, Tristan noted silently, having seen no outlay for that in the Haverne account books. "And Charity does all the church poor work for this side of the parish and organizes so many of the activities. I know Mrs. Hering helps, too, but some of this should be my responsibility."

"Miss Calder seems to enjoy it, you know. She certainly needs an outlet for all that energy of hers."

Anna nodded slowly. "Yes, you're right, of course. But all her duties have also confined her. You know she cut her season in London short because she was needed here. I wonder if that is why she didn't accept any of the men who offered for her—because she didn't think the village could do without her."

Tristan preferred to think that none of the men that offered for her intrigued her at all, but he agreed that there was something in what Anna said.

"I would not have even known that the church ladies made rag dolls if Charity hadn't told me. I suppose I thought that the church just—just contracted with a dollmaker for a couple of dozen dolls. Do you know," she added thoughtfully, "that poor girls must cuddle sticks bundled up in rags if they haven't any dolls? Charity says that's why so many of them have children at an early age, because they never had a chance to love a little doll."

Tristan laughed, choking on his hot coffee. It sounded like something Charity would say, a little outrageous, a little preposterous, yet somehow insightful. "Well, as many rag dolls as you have made, I predict a population decline in a decade or so. All the girls in the neighborhood will now have their own dolls to cuddle."

"Don't scoff, Tristan. When I think of how many dolls I had—the finest china dolls from Milan—"

"I remember. They filled your room. I wondered how you could sleep with a hundred eyes focused on you."

"And you know, not one of them was special to me. But if a girl hasn't anything else, she cherishes the simplest rag doll. And they are so simple to craft! Still I try to make each one unique in some way, especially the expression. I change the eye color or plait the yarn hair differently, something to give each a bit of individuality. I recalled how annoyed I was at the Gilder ball last year when Emily Mainsell wore the identical dress, and I thought that a little girl would want her doll to be different from her friend's."

This was the longest speech Anna had strung together in quite some time that didn't detail her woes, and Tristan found himself touched by her compassion for the unknown girls. "Superior to her friend's, even. Or so she will believe."

They were doing so well together, better than he might have imagined two weeks ago. They had not been close for a long while, since long before her marriage. Anna was always very much the girl, with no interest in art or horses, the only things he cared about as a boy. But those endless voyages back and forth from Italy must have built up a well of affection which, untapped for years, was available now that they needed it.

And so they could fall right back into that sibling rapport, full of teasing and familiarity, knowing that their relationship had started at birth and would last till death, no matter how they mistreated each other.

He saw the same dynamic between Lawrence and Jeremy when, well-scrubbed and well-mannered, they were brought in by Mrs. Cameron after their own breakfast. Their piping voices as they recited their spelling words were almost identical. Once, when Jeremy hesitated over the consonant cluster in *church*, Lawrence prompted in what he thought was a whisper, "C-H, clunch!"

"C-H. I did real good, Mama."

"Yes, you did, dearest." Anna bent to kiss his dark head and extended her hand to draw Lawrence into the embrace.

"You are the most beautiful mother in the whole world." Lawrence's vow was no doubt sincere but showed he had inherited more than his looks from the silver-tongued Haverne.

Anna rewarded him with kisses and coos, and with a brother's disdain, Tristan wondered if she would ever get over her weakness for flattery.

Lawrence, his duty done, pulled Jeremy away. "Come on, Jerry. Cammie's waiting."

Mrs. Cameron, too dignified to be deferential, announced, "I told the boys I would walk them to the Grange if they spelled all their words for you. We are just on our way out."

"We're going to see Charity!"

Tristan put a protective hand on his coffee cup as Jeremy, unable to contain his glee, gave a few bounces.

Lawrence tugged at Mrs. Cameron's hand, trying to pull her to the door. "Charity said she'd teach us how to do the three-legged race before Saturday so we can try out for the Midsummer games. Her and Ned won it every year for four years!"

"She and Ned. Make your bows, boys." Mrs. Cameron detached her hand from Lawrence's and gave him a subtle shove. Lawrence bobbed a bow, Jeremy followed suit, and they ran off ahead to learn all the tricks from Charity.

Tristan glanced at his sister, wondering if she weren't the least bit jealous to see her sons so enthusiastic about visiting another woman. But Anna, he realized, was content with the boys' performance and kisses and just as glad to cede this particular charge to someone else. At least this affectionate detachment was healthier than their own mother's alternate smothering and neglect. Lawrence and Jeremy would recall their mother as something of a goddess, whose embrace was always scented with perfume and soft with silk. They could worship her, for she'd never spoil her image by sitting down on a dusty floor to tell them a story or get muddy joining in their games.

"Isn't Charity a very good sort of girl?"

He was startled to hear the name that had just appeared in his mind. "So I keep hearing."

"Don't you think she would make a very good wife for you?"

"Subtle, Anna, very subtle. But don't be so obscure. Stop hinting and say what you mean."

"Sarcasm is the lowest form of wit, Tristan. Which means, of course, that it's entirely appropriate for you." Anna preened a bit at getting this insult off, then added severely, "And this is no time for subtlety. Mrs. Hering told me her son was set to ask Charity for her hand any day now."

Tristan used his butter knife to slash a piece of toast into strips. "She won't have him. She's already turned him down."

"Perhaps she values persistence. And if he isn't successful, some other man will be. You're not the only one who recognizes her virtues."

Anna was so positive that he felt a moment's unease. "She does seem to receive offers every week or so. Turns 'em all down though. Oh, I wasn't supposed to tell you that."

"I know all about her offers. Sir Francis told me."

Anna blushed a bit as she spoke of Calder, and Tristan wondered if their conversation had gone beyond conspiracy. Then he dismissed it. She was still in mourning, after all, deeply so. Besides, a good man like Calder would never have a chance with her. He couldn't spin a pretty compliment to save his life, however adept he was at insult. "What makes you think I'd be any more successful than the others?"

Anna dismissed this with a wave of her white hand. "Oh, Tristan, come now. Girls have always thought you handsome. Why, some of my school friends used to talk about stealing kisses from you—and you three years our junior!"

"I wish I'd known that then. They wouldn't have had to steal them."

"And you are an artist. Sir Francis said that's a source of fascination to Charity. And only think how capable she is. Think of how she will enjoy helping you with your work."

Tristan could just imagine Charity ordering his supplies, negotiating with dealers. He'd get the best commissions in the country if Charity made the deals. She would like that, too, he knew, remembering her honest appreciation of his work. "We've known each other scarcely a fortnight."

"Nonsense. Her virtues are immediately apparent. And, dearest, you do need a wife. You live such an aimless life—"

"It's hardly aimless," he said stiffly. "My aim is to paint."

She shook her head, and he knew she was right. That wasn't enough, not for a life. Her voice was gentle but chiding. "You don't even have a posting address much of the year. And you haven't any ties that I know of, except to me, and we neither of us have done well at keeping those tight."

He covered her trembling hand with his own. As difficult as this last fortnight had been and as bitterly as he had resented the responsibility, Tristan knew he owed more to his family than an occasional letter or visit. "Agreed. But that doesn't require a wife."

"Oh, but it does in a way. You've got in the habit of avoiding connections, and a wife like Charity wouldn't let you do that. Oh, I know I'm no one to talk of the benefits of marriage—" She broke off, staring out the window at the newly neat garden. "But you know Charity would be a true helpmeet, and make you a home. You've never had one, so I suppose you think you don't need one. But only think how homey she could make Braden —why, you'd be eager to come back from Italy every year then."

Tristan studied his sister's slender white hand, with its manicured nails and diamond ring. He wondered if siblings ever grew old enough to see each other as adults. He would always see Anna as that delicate, passionate girl who always got her way, even when it was clear she had lost her way. And to Anna, he would always be that restless, obsessive boy who spent too much time alone.

He would have dismissed everything she said, except that he suspected she was right. "This is not, I'll have you know, your idea. I thought of it long ago. And the other day, when I saw my house and couldn't, couldn't think of it as home, I thought of Charity and what she would do with it." Suddenly he said, "It means choosing England, you know."

Anna's brows drew together in a puzzled frown. She had never felt that tug-of-war he knew so well, between the rational pragmatic land of their father and the dangerously passionate land of their mother. But she replied sensibly enough. "Well, Tristan, must there be a choice? You will no doubt spend much of your time in Italy, nonetheless. But you'll know that your home will be safe under Charity's charge. I should think it would make life easier for you."

She withdrew from her pocket a small velvet pouch and, from that, a sapphire ring set with small diamonds. "It's Mother's betrothal ring. Before he died, Father asked me to keep it for you and not to release it until you found a girl of whom he would approve."

"One unlike Mother, you mean."

Anna tried not to smile. But enough years had passed that the utter incompatibility of their parents was more amusing than appalling. She pressed the ring into his hand. "Well, one more like Mother couldn't be found. I do approve, and Father would, too. Charity can't help but make you happy. For she's so happy herself, and she is so generous with her happiness."

He regarded the ring soberly for a moment, waiting for the panic to rise. But he felt peaceful, even hopeful. It was the right time and the right decision, and Charity was without a doubt the right woman.

He closed his fist over the ring and put it away into his coat pocket. He looked up to his sister's dismay. "Anna," he said in exasperation, "I promise you I have no frogs in my pocket or molding peppermints. I'm a grown man. I won't lose the ring."

"Mind you don't pawn it either, as you did your ruby stickpin."

She rose with lofty grace, leaving him to wonder how it was she had learned of every unsavory act he had committed in his youth and why she felt it necessary to remind him of them.

Later, he came into the churchyard from the back, through the little cemetery. There were fresh flowers in front of the Calder family stones, simple blooms, daisies and hedgeroses tied with a long blade of meadow grass. The bouquet was so evocative of Charity, he almost felt her beside him. He picked it up, tugged one errant daisy back into place, and tightened the grass tie.

Then he bent to trace the engraving on one of the smaller stones. Edward Calder, R.N., born 19 June 1798, killed in His Majesty's Service, 12 December 1816, aged 18.

Tristan crossed himself, then dropped the bouquet on the grave and went on to the church hall. Charity was in the habit, he knew, of checking his progress with the whale each evening. He determined to finish the stormy sea this morning and sketch in the fishing boat before the Saturday revelry rehearsal. The sooner he completed the figures in the foreground, the sooner he could demand that she help him finish the background. That would cheer her, if she needed cheering.

Chapter Eleven

By Saturday Lawrence and Jeremy had learned their event so well they undertook with Charlie the job of tutoring the other children in three-legged racing. Charity left them in Francis's charge—he got such enjoyment out of seeing the teams careen into each other—and crossed the green to the tables set up for lemonade and teacakes.

This was only a rehearsal of sorts for the Midsummer fair, but the villagers were enjoying it as if it were the real thing. At least a hundred people were wandering around the sunlit green, enjoying the respite from chores and the casual atmosphere that allowed countess to mingle with cowherd. Not that Anna was precisely mingling. Still in her blacks, Lady Haverne sat like a mourning madonna next to Cammie, watching with only the hint of a smile as the children hobbled along the race course. But she did nod to the occasional well-wisher and even accepted a glass of lemonade from a little boy who had to be retrieved by his jealous mama.

As the sun grew warmer, the villagers gradually discarded their colorful shawls and jackets, their converse, like their clothing, becoming more casual after noon. Pockets jingling with small change, they roamed from table to table and green to churchyard. Near the little lily pond in the center, knots of boys and girls engaged in complicated group flirtations, and over by the statue erected to General Wolfe, the elderly men ogled the ladies and talked about fishing. The children gathered in the center of the green, each group focused on some adult who solemnly demonstrated how to carry an egg on a spoon or hop thirty yards in a burlap sack.

As if to emphasize the link between village and church, Midsummer preparations had spilled across the road to the front lawn of the church. Mrs. Dalton had set a crate under the wall and stood there ordering women to run home and bring back donations to sell at the jumble booth. Charity had already emptied the Grange attics for Mrs. Dalton, but she felt guilty passing by empty-handed and made a mental note to go through the kitchen for more donations.

Mrs. Hering called her over to a table set up to block the way to the privies set in the little hollow beyond the church. Triumphantly she jingled a bowlful of silver and copper coins. "I'm not letting anyone past unless they buy a ticket to the fair!"

Charity praised this ingenious tactic and punctiliously purchased a ticket herself before she went on toward the church.

David Greenaway sat alone, as usual, resting against the church's oldest oak tree. On his knee was a book she knew must be of verse. Charity wondered why he would come to a village activity only to sit by himself and read. She thought it was sad to see him so lonely and started to go over and greet him. But guiltily she stopped halfway and turned back. She had warned him last week that she had made some changes to his Jonah script, and he had only smiled and said he trusted her editorial judgment. But now he would be sure to ask to see it, and she would have to confess just how much revision she had done. Better to wait until the children were better rehearsed so that she could show him how well it had turned out, changes and all.

The vicar was standing on the church steps, gazing out at the party before him. Most people would have seen a harmless village gathering, but from his expression Charity knew Mr. Langworth was on the lookout for pagan activities. It was only a matter of time before he found them, with all these young people gathered together.

Inspired, she said, "Oh, Mr. Langworth, don't you think this might be a good time to hear confessions? Half the parish is here now. Why—why, there is Arnie Potter!" Ruthlessly she grabbed the arm of a lad on his way back from the conveniences. "Arnie, you meant to make your confession, didn't you?"

It was an inspired choice, for fourteen-year-old boys always had something to feel guilty about. Arnie flushed a deep purple and ducked his head, and she wondered what sin he thought she had caught him at. "Yes—yes, miss, I guess I did."

Shoulders slumping, he followed the vicar into the church, and Charity knew a moment's twinge. Well, she told herself, confession is always good for the soul.

She returned to the village green, letting the flirtatious breeze tease the ribbon from her hair and the faint worries from her mind. This Midsummer rehearsal would go perfectly well as long as the vicar remained inside the church (she'd have to find a few of Arnie's more conscience-stricken friends and send them along after him) and sufficient swordsmen signed up for the fencing competition.

One swordsman in particular drew her gaze. Lord Braden was standing on the steps to the church hall, testing his sword against the wall. In his linen shirt and buckskins, he was young and graceful, and she had some poignant sense of what sort of boy this man must have been.

The sight of him, slender and strong like his blade, made her heart race, and it took a great effort of will to turn from him to look for other competitors. There was Crispin, of course, in the midst of a group of girls, showing off his silver sword. And his cousin Jacob Hering, pouring something from a flask into his lemonade.

And her brother Barry next to him—

Barry! What was he doing here? With a quick glance to

make sure their elder brother was occupied, Charity ran lightly across the green. She had only time for a quick nod to Jacob before she grabbed Barry's arm and dragged him out of sight behind the great oak tree.

As soon as they were hidden, Barry squirmed out of her grasp. Sullenly rubbing his arm, he said, "What's so blasted—"

"Barry, what are you doing here? Francis just got a letter from your beadle saying you'd been piking your tutorials, and—"

"I'm here quite legally, I'll have you know."

He drew himself up proudly, and she noticed for the first time that he was a head taller than she. She was still his big sister, however, and knew all too well his stunts. "What lie did you tell this time?"

His grin dashed all his former dignity away. "I said you had the measles and you needed me to come pick up Charlie and take him to stay with Aunt Grace."

"You might have given me a more mature disease, at least." It was a ten-hour drive from Oxford, and she had a fair suspicion what had brought him home. Who, that is. A particular blonde who. "Why are you back again so soon?"

His gaze slid away to focus on the church tower. Even with that holy sight in his view, he was able to lie as boldly to her as to his tutor. "Thought I'd help you earn a bit for the restoration of the tower. You know, try out for St. George. I got my entry fee."

He dragged a coin out of his breeches pocket and held it up as if it alone could make up for all his sins. Charity shook her head, sighing. "You don't think you'll actually win, do you? Just because Molly is set to be the princess? That won't make up for your lack of skill with a sword!"

"You don't know that."

Barry set his chin stubbornly, looking for a moment enough like Ned that she knew there was no use arguing with him. "Well, do try to stay out of harm's way, at least. And that includes out of the way of Francis!"

Barry put on his sweetest smile. "Tell him you sent for me, won't you? To—ummm, help you out with counting the receipts or putting the tables away or something?"

Charity shrugged, refusing to commit but knowing that, as usual, she would probably protect her younger brother. "If you intend for him to believe you, then you must help out in truth. You may take the names of the men who will be taking part in the fencing competition and then arrange pairs for the bouts. No escaping to the Rose and Crown till your own bout is called."

Barry was more agreeable to this than she expected, even pulling a little notebook out of his pocket to use as a scoresheet. "I'm all prepared," he said. "And Charity?"

He pointed to a couple of young men lounging about the distant lemonade stand. "Buzzy and Pookie came back with me. You know, my friends. They'll be staying the night."

Charity groaned, imagining the sort of conversation Buzzy and Pookie would bring to the dinner table. "To help me through my bout with the measles, no doubt. Well, you run home at some point and tell Mrs. Piper to make up a couple rooms for them. But first—" she called out as he started toward his friends, "make up that list of competitors. And if you get hurt playing with a sword, you've only yourself to blame."

Charity went off to check on a few of the less violent events. Francis had brought the three-legged teams to see his favorite event, the boiled-egg spin. He had already set up the long rimmed table for a demonstration match with Malachi Morgan, the defending champion.

Charity was drawn there not so much because her brother was a participant as because Lord Braden was a spectator. He held his sheathed sword negligently in one hand and with the other kept tight hold of Jeremy. Lawrence, clinging to his mother's hand, drew her closer to the table where Francis was explaining the game. Charity smiled, imagining what Anna would think of this scholarly disquisition on the ancient origins of the boiled-egg spin.

Malachi, it was clear, did not regard this as any sort of demonstration. The medal he had won in this event a year earlier dangled from his chest as he divided the stock of eggs into two piles, one for the champion and one for the challenger. His jaw was clenched tightly as he worked, and Charity recalled what the Ferris girls had said about his competitiveness. He had decided not to enter the fencing competition; he probably guessed he would have little chance of winning.

The demonstration had already drawn a crowd due to Francis's skill as a lecturer. Squire Hering was there, laughing at an old joke Francis made about the foolishness of Sussexmen, the usual butt of Kent jokes. Lord Braden must not yet think himself a Susssexman, for all that he owned property there; he was laughing along, too, instead of defending his county.

Charity drew close by his side, almost reaching out to touch him to make her presence known. But she didn't have to after all. He turned, the laughter still warm in his eyes. When he saw her the laughter changed to something else, something that made her catch her breath and wish that they were alone again. Next time, she promised herself, she wouldn't let the past seize her as it had there in his studio. She would think of the future, whatever that might be.

She was tantalizingly aware of him beside her. Her lilac cotton dress, donned for maneuverability rather than fashion, seemed insubstantial suddenly; she could feel through it the warmth of his arm so near her own.

Then Barry appeared at her elbow, full of questions about the relative skills of the fencers. She could only shrug and say what they both knew, that Crispin was the most accomplished fencer in Calder, and barring unforeseen circumstances, would likely win.

She had let her gaze stray again to Lord Braden's expressive face, and when she mentioned Crispin as the odds-on favorite, she noticed how his jaw tightened, quite like Malachi's, as if this inflamed his competitive spirit. "Young Hering is the best of the lot?" His voice was casual, but Charity could see the resolution forming even as he spoke. He meant to beat Crispin.

Barry pulled out his notebook and pencil. "He usually wins this sort of thing. Why? Do you think you can give him a match?"

Lord Braden only shrugged, but Lawrence heard and piped up loyally, "Course we can. My uncle used to teach fencing."

His uncle shook his head, out of negation or modesty Charity hadn't a chance to determine, because Barry had already torn away from their small group. She saw him huddling with his friends Buzzy and Pookie, and she turned with an apologetic smile to Lord Braden. "He's got two friends down—"

"Foul!"

Startled, Charity squeezed through the crowd to the egg-spinning table. The squire, the self-appointed director of the contest, had called a halt to the match. He held one egg up to the light of the sun and peered through it. "I thought so. A foul! Someone has sucked out half the yolk of this egg before boiling. I can see the pinhole!"

As Malachi shrank back, Francis picked up another egg and shook it. "This seems all right." But the third egg and the fourth—so half the eggs assigned to him—all proved to be faulty.

The squire pontificated on this as if he were Galileo and the eggs some new constellation. "The remaining contents have settled in the broader end, thus interfering with the balance and the spin."

Word soon spread that the purity of the turf had been sullied, and Barry and his friends gathered round, waiting for a verdict. Lawrence squirmed from his mother's grasp and grabbed up one of the suspect eggs. He examined it, shook it next to his ear, and proclaimed in a ringing voice, "We've got us a cheater!"

"Hush up," Charlie said from behind him, snatching the egg out of his hand. "You don't know anything about eggs, except they come in a china cup and you break 'em with a silver spoon."

Lawrence took this aspersion to his worldliness with surprising meekness, only turning to stare accusingly at the assumed criminal. A burly young man with a jutting chin, Malachi wasn't about to take this from a child, even a noble one. He protested that just because his mother the innkeeper had prepared the eggs, they should not assume he was the intended beneficiary. "Sir Francis's tenant Mrs. Lambeth supplied the eggs—he could have done the tampering first."

The squire and the Justice of the Peace, who had been called in to adjudicate this little mess, looked up shocked from the heap of eggs sacrificed to the tamper test. "Sir Francis would never cheat," the JP said austerely.

The crowd murmured approval, and Francis flushed. Lord Braden murmured to Barry, "There's a lesson for us all. 'The purest treasure mortal times afford is spotless reputation; that away, men are but gilded loam or painted clay.' "

" 'Mine honor is my life; both grow in one; take honor for me, and my life is done.' *Richard II.*" Barry reddened as he saw Buzzy and Pookie gazing at him in dismay. "I do attend an occasional lecture, you know."

"And he takes lessons with a few actresses in the Shakespearian theatre there in Oxford," Charity remarked. She won a grateful grin from Barry, and Buzzy and Pookie laughed and elbowed each other, muttering, "Shakespeare!"

A decision at the table brought the crowd to silent attention. The JP rose and with a jerk of his finger brought the trembling Malachi to the table. "Mr. Morgan," he said in awful tones, "please take off that medal. I am afraid we must divest you retroactively of your victory last year and award it to the runner-up—Sir Francis Calder."

Too broken to protest, Malachi removed the medal with shaking hands. Charity did not wish to see this humiliation and turned to talk to the countess. But before she could speak, Anna exclaimed, "Oh, what a noble gesture!"

Francis was handing the medal back to his erstwhile opponent. "No, no, Malachi is right. I am sure there were no irregularities in last year's contest, and today there's no reason to suspect one of us over the other." He waved his hand dismissively at the pile of egg shells. "Such anomalies occur in nature. I've no doubt if it had come to a match, Malachi would have beat me hollow again."

"Right," Barry said in a sardonic undertone as Malachi, head bent, pinned his ribbon back on. "Because somehow you ended up with all the anomalies of nature. Francis, you are a sap."

Anna turned on the boy with surprising ferocity. "He is *not* a sap! He realizes how much that silly medal means to the poor man. It's probably the only distinction he's ever had. Why, I think it's quite the kindest act I've ever seen."

Barry had never been dressed down by a beautiful lady before, much less a countess. But he recovered his university man's élan soon enough. He shrugged and observed, "There's that, too," before he gestured peremptorily to his friends and they melted off into the crowd.

Charity's eyes met Lord Braden's and found them laughing. She felt again that tenuous, tantalizing connection between them as if somehow they could communicate without words, with a metaphysical as well as physical language. The thought made her shiver and look away from him, only to collide with Anna's knowing gaze. It was all too public, this connection that should be private. Anna, Francis—the whole village was probably taking note of Charity Calder and the man who made her shiver.

She broke away. "I'm going to announce the fencing competition—that will divert attention from this mess." And then, feeling like the Pied Piper, she led everyone across the green.

A long fencing strip was chalked on the grass at the verge of the green, parallel to the road. A crowd had already gathered, ranging along the strip with drinks and meat pies in hand, calling out to their favorite candidates. Molly Ferris, as befitted St. George's prize princess, posed invitingly at one end of the strip. She perched on the swing hanging from the elm tree, occasionally kicking off so that her russet skirt floated up and revealed her fetching ankles.

By the time Charity arrived, Barry was already organizing the event, gesturing here and there with his unsheathed foil as he called out instructions to the entrants. He passed her a handful of silver, the entry fees collected from the contestants. "I took myself out of the bouts, sis. Didn't think it looked right to be competing when I've made up the pairs. I'll serve as judge if you like."

Charity was too glad that Barry wouldn't be flinging himself in the path of a sword to question his motives. "Perhaps Bookie and Puzzy—I mean, Buzzy and Pookie—can keep track of the scores. And Charlie, you keep the children back, will you?"

Grateful to abandon all those duties, Charity climbed up on the stretch of fencing that served as a hitching post and balanced there, her feet swinging. From this vantage she could see the entire field of combat, and the assembled crowd, too. She kept a wary eye out for the vicar, who might run out of confessions and decide to confront unrepentant sinners directly.

Buzzy and Pookie stood officiously to one side, Buzzy holding the pencil and Pookie the notebook, while Barry called out the first pair, Jacob Hering and Lord Braden. They rolled down their sleeves and pulled on gloves gauntleted to protect their wrists. Then they took up their positions and began the elaborate military salute that opened a bout. Even this harmless display looked somewhat dangerous as the two fencers lunged toward each other and Barry brought his judge's sword clashing against theirs. She knew that they would don masks for the actual bout and that the lethal-looking foils had tiny tips at the end to blunt their points. But the tense stance and intent expressions of Lord Braden and his opponent reminded her that however friendly her St. George competition was to be, it had its roots in martial combat.

Crispin Hering paid no attention as his potential rivals took up their fencing positions and Barry called out, "En garde!" He sauntered up to Charity, sword in hand and a grin on his freckled face. She had been avoiding him all day, ever since Mrs. Williams warned her he was set to renew his suit. She liked Crispin very well; he had been Ned's best friend and was the first boy she ever kissed. But she couldn't imagine marrying him, not a boy she had known all her life, whose ambition was to be a squire just like his father, whose vista extended two miles south to Hythe and six miles east to Folkestone.

Still she let him pull her ribbon loose and tug at one of her curls, just as when they were children together. He stuffed the ribbon in his pocket and regarded her with a laughing challenge.

"Crispin, give it back," she said impatiently, trying to look over his shoulder at the match.

"Come and get it." He stood insolently, blocking her view, his hand stuck in his pocket and the ribbon dangling between his fingers.

"Keep it, if you want it so badly. And do step aside, Cris, I want to see the bout."

"Oho, the lady gives me her favor. So I am to be your knight, am I, my princess?" He leaned closer and pulled an imaginary visor over his eyes. "I'll slay dragons for you, I vow."

"I'm not the princess; Molly Ferris is. You can be her knight if you win." Laughing at his foolishness, she pushed him away. But he lingered beside her, leaning against her knee, trying one-handedly to tie the purple ribbon around his forearm.

Charity was engrossed in the match—Lord Braden had just scored a touché—and when Crispin stuck out his arm across her lap she tied the ribbon automatically in a bow.

Crispin rested familiarly that way, his arm against her legs, his expression reminiscent. "Do you remember when we went dragon-slaying with Ned into the woods at Haverne?" he asked, pulling the strap of her sandal off her heel. "We were shooting arrows into that old treehouse and shouting like wildmen—until we heard Kenny Haverton shouting back. Up there with a chambermaid, he was, and he thought the French had invaded!"

"Hush." Charity pulled her sandal back on, looking quickly over at Anna. But the countess was watching her brother's match intently and couldn't have heard. The always-efficient Francis had procured her a chair from somewhere, and in her black drapery she looked rather like a tragic queen waiting for her knight to die defending her throne.

Charity shoved her own self-appointed knight away. "Now will you sit and watch? Your cousin looks to be getting the worst of it."

Crispin didn't even turn around, remarking with youthful contempt, "I'd back Jake against an *artist* any day."

"Too bad for you and Jake, then, that fencing is an *art*. Because that artist just vanquished your cousin. Five touchés to ones."

"Then it'll be up to me to restore the family honor. And with this—" Crispin held up his arm, the purple ribbon dancing in the breeze, "I'll be sure to take the victory home."

Crispin had never suffered from false modesty, and he did well enough in his preliminary bouts to justify his confidence. But Charity, watching Lord Braden's second match, felt her own competitive instincts thrill. He did not destroy poor Peter Lamb; he merely toyed with him, scoring with an ease that suggested he had ample tricks in reserve. He was all lazy grace, enigmatic behind the mask, able to parry Peter's ungainly thrusting with only a slight rotation of his wrist. Then, suddenly, like a tiger pouncing, he disarmed his opponent, and a murmur rose from the spectators.

Pookie whispered, "I couldn't even see what he did," and Buzzy whistled low and long and grabbed the notebook to record the score.

Not daunted, Crispin strolled up to the mark when the final bout was announced and bowed to the accomplished newcomer. Then he brazenly blew Charity a kiss before he donned his mask.

She felt the heat rise in her cheeks as Lord Braden's glance flicked over her and returned to focus on the ribbon around Crispin's arm. He will think I cheer for his opponent, she thought. But then she saw the set of his jaw as he brought the sword up in salute to the judge and decided not to correct his misapprehension. These last days, he had toyed with her as he toyed with poor Peter Lamb, first reticent, then seductive, then resistant, then all too direct. Let him for once be the one teased with uncertainty.

Besides, it was a novel sensation, to be fought over. Charity could not help but enjoy Polly's envious glances and Molly's petulance as she kicked at the ground under her swing: "But *I'm* the princess!"

Lord Braden pulled down his mask and dropped into a relaxed en-garde position. The first engagement was a quick clash of blades and then a mutual retreat as each assessed the other. Charity also found herself appraising the two men, these men who apparently considered themselves rivals for her affections.

Braden was taller than Crispin but not as broad, and though he hadn't such powerful arms, he was quicker twisting his wrist in a parry and dodging away from an attack. He played a defensive game at first, letting the more aggressive Crispin tire himself out with vicious thrusts and lunges. Grinning, Crispin pushed him back nearly to the end of the strip, clearly expecting a touché by default.

But just before he was forced off the strip, Braden took the offensive. His arm tensed from its relaxed position; he leaned forward, beat aside Crispin's desperate advance, and then, with a swift thrust, came under the arm for a touché. Crispin acknowledged this with a nod, and the bout restarted in the middle of the strip.

This time Lord Braden was the aggressor, tantalizing Crispin into reacting to attacks that never occurred, into parrying thrusts that vanished only to reappear elsewhere. In short order, he scored another two touchés, and Crispin no longer swaggered back to the en-garde position.

In the fourth exchange, Lord Braden slowed the match down. He stood his ground in the center of the field, his blade still except in parry, forcing his opponent into offense. Against this infuriating calm, Crispin's thrusts became more and more desperate, and once he was so off balance following a lunge he went down on one knee. He ended up, after one wild lunge, scoring a touché. Charity could not be certain, but she thought that Lord Braden might have allowed it. His control of the bout was so complete that even his missteps seemed planned.

Lord Braden won the next point with a complex double, feinting a direct hit with the point of his blade and then circling around Crispin's parry before circling back and thrusting the blade home. Charity didn't actually see this—the action was too much a blur for her to distinguish parry from counterparry. But she received low-voiced commentary from the Justice of the Peace, who leaned on the rail next to her. He straightened at this last score, calling out, "Oh, good show!" He added to Charity, "The Italian method, don't you know. Precise point control. You remember that. Pay no attention to where his hand is leading; always watch the point of the blade."

An obedient girl, Charity focused her attention on those

dancing points, and so she was not diverted as everyone else was when Crispin erupted into a snap-lunge, thrusting upward, forcing Braden to retreat. She kept her gaze on the points as the swords clashed, and so she saw the little red tip break from Crispin's blade and fly off into the grass.

The scene crystallized. She could hear the echo of the clash of metal on metal, see the glare of the sun off the blades, but everything was still, expectant, frozen.

She could not move; she could only wait for the engagement to stop, for Barry to call hold, for Crispin to raise his free hand and gesture for a pause. But when animation returned, the attack was continuing, Lord Braden moving back, Crispin pressing his advantage—a greater advantage than he knew. For he could not know, Charity was certain. He was competitive but not dishonorable; he, like the rest of those assembled, had not noticed the loss of the little red tip.

But Lord Braden had. With a sensitivity based on their intense if short acquaintance, Charity translated his momentary stilling, his instinctive retreat, into recognition of his danger. She let go a relieved breath; he would call hold and Crispin would pull up his sharp blade and—

But Braden did not call hold. She could not see his expression under the mask but could imagine it nonetheless: that thoughtful assessing look, then a sudden smile. His stillness only lasted that instant; he deftly turned his wrist and beat aside Crispin's thrust so that the lethal blade slid to the side, barely brushing his arm.

Her unusual passivity ended. Charity jumped off the rail and started toward Barry. She knew where her duty lay; he had to be told about the untipped blade. But something stopped her as soon as she pushed through the crowd to her brother's side. It was reckless, it was irresponsible, it was dangerous—it was thrilling, to watch Lord Braden step forward, his own point dropped, inviting another attack. This was no exhibition, no contest. This was deadly serious and yet the laughter bubbled in Charity's throat. Tristan was courting death with such insouciance. How wild, how romantic, how very *Mediterranean* of him! And somehow she knew it was for her benefit.

Crispin launched another attack, aiming his blade as every swordsmen did for the vulnerable area above the heart. He was fury personified, his free hand clenched in a fist, a cry escaping him as he lunged forward and slashed upward. Tristan stepped back, flashed his blade up in parry, knocked Crispin's to the side, then instantly drew back to thrust forward in riposte.

Crispin's counterparry slid off the handguard, and his unshielded point caught Tristan's right sleeve, slicing cleanly through the linen. It all happened so fast that Barry's startled exclamation was lost in the cheer that rose from the crowd. Tristan deftly, swiftly slipped the point of his blade under the ribbon on his rival's arm. A flick and the ribbon was dangling from the sword; he tossed it up and caught it in his free hand, then, almost as an afterthought, thrust to Crispin's chest for a touché.

Barry brought his own sword slashing down between the combatants. "Hold, I said! Jupiter, Cris, your tip is gone! You could have—"

Crispin yanked off his mask and brought his blade up, staring at the broken point, then at his opponent. Then his gaze shot to Charity, standing beside Barry, still breathless from her knowledge of the danger and her own criminal inaction.

She could hear Barry's remonstrations, Buzzy and Pookie's argument about counting that last touché, the cheers of the crowd, Crispin's harsh breathing, her pulse pounding in her ears. Lord Braden took off his mask; his face was damp with sweat, his breath coming ragged. But he seemed not to notice the tumult around him. He was studying the purple ribbon as if it spelled out some secret only he could read, and he looked up only when Crispin cried out impatiently, "It doesn't matter if the last touché counted! He won! I yield—on all counts."

Crispin let his broken sword fall to the ground. He bowed to the victor, shook his head, and walked off toward the church. Charity saw the brave set of his shoulders and remembered that last year, when she refused his proposal, Crispin had responded with as much confusion as hurt. "But I have never imagined any wife but you," he had said and, "Think how happy Neddy would be, to have his twin and his best friend together always."

Now Crispin had conceded. And the victor was holding the captured token, ignoring the clamoring well-wishers, gently putting aside Princess Molly when she threw herself into his arms. He pulled off his glove and held out his hand to Charity.

It was only then that she noticed the blood that stained the lace of his cuff. Her breath halted, then started up again, easy and slow. She crossed to him, saying calmly, "Molly, give me that towel there. Lord Braden has been cut."

And as she used Crispin's discarded sword to slice a bandage out of the towel and as she concentrated on binding up Lord Braden's slashed arm, she felt his somber gaze on her and told herself, This I know how to do. This at least I can give.

Chapter Twelve

With the highly tuned courtesy essential in a village, the crowd melted away. Barry and Buzzy and Pookie withdrew to a nearby table, still arguing over the scorebook and handing coins back and forth in some obscure banking ritual. Molly Ferris lingered to cast an accusatory look at Charity, but she left, too, when Barry called for her to come share a lemonade with him and Buzzy and Pookie.

So Charity was left alone at the edge of the green, adjusting Tristan's bandage, her gaze focused on the cords the long muscles made in his arm. I should take the entry money to Mrs. Hering, she told herself, feeling the weight of the coins in her pocket against her leg. But she didn't move, except to tie a final knot in the bandage, her fingers brushing against the smooth skin of his wrist.

"Look at me," he commanded, but she only shook her head, staring at the jaunty bow she had tied on his arm. He groaned, then laughed, and with his uninjured arm drew her against him. Against her cheek she felt the rough linen of his shirt, the warmth of his chest, the steady beat of his heart.

"I don't know why your parents named you Charity. You are the least charitable girl I have ever known." His hand tangled in her hair, and she remembered that he still had her ribbon tucked away in his pocket. He whispered, "Will you come with me now, Charity?"

She felt herself on the brink of disaster, and he was urging her over. She wanted to go with him; she wanted to go away from him—she didn't know what she wanted. She felt like Marie Antoinette on the way to the guillotine, except that the executioner was going to ask her if she preferred it quick or slow. This is precisely what you hoped for, she told herself, but she felt an ache in her chest that had more to do with fear than with fulfillment.

It was all too fast, a whirlwind courtship at its whirlingest. For all their crackling conversations, for all their occasional moments of oneness, they had had no courtship. He had never sent her love letters or bunches of flowers; she had never melted into him during an improperly close waltz or felt his kiss even on her hand.

She had no time to prepare for this, to unwrap her heart and examine her feelings one by one. She had never been the sort to make impulsive choices; and yet he expected her to know so soon what was best for her, for him, for them both.

She looked up into his wary dark eyes, saw the shadow of sadness, the glint of laughter, and with the recklessness she had just learned from him, she agreed.

He drew her across the road, down the shady lane toward the bridge that crossed the stream. They were hidden from view here, though she could not forget that the whole village must know where they were and what they were doing.

The overarching oaks muted the noise and the light here—it was rather like a church, she thought. The stream rippled below, gentle now that the flood season was done; she stared down at a leaf floating along in the current. It got caught up in an eddy and swirled helplessly there for a moment before it was released back into the stream.

Lord Braden leaned against the old stone wall and pulled her close to him. Everything paused while he studied her, and feeling challenged somehow, she lifted her chin and stared back. With laughter lighting his eyes then, he lowered his head to kiss her.

This was not her first kiss. Boys had been stealing kisses since she was fifteen, seven of them at last count. That made her, she supposed as she twined her hands behind his neck, somewhat fast. But never had a kiss gone farther than her lips: she might be fast, but she was never loose.

Lord Braden didn't appreciate this fine distinction, and suddenly neither did she. She opened her mouth to his searching and arched closer to his lean body. Her head fell back as he pressed his advantage, kissing the soft skin of her neck and caressing her back with his artistic hands. She was aflame where he touched her, burning where he kissed her, a fire kindling as he held her.

But finally good sense edged back into her consciousness, and reluctantly she complied with a lifetime's strictures. "You must let me go, Lord Braden." She punctuated her less-than-forceful protest with a hand's gentle pressure on his chest, and slowly he loosened his embrace.

"I think it's proper to call me by name when I kiss you, Charity."

She had longed to say his name, had whispered it to herself a thousand times. "Tristan." It was a beautiful and sad name. It will be all right, she thought. This is Tristan holding me.

But then he dropped his hands from her waist, leaving her bereft. "You might also open your eyes and look at me while I propose."

She opened her eyes to meet his, but held her breath, for the first time in her life completely unsure of herself. She felt lost in love, cheated of love, fascinated, frightened. She dropped her gaze to the weedy ground, trying to corral her emotions. But they kept squirming out of her frame.

"You're not attending, Charity."

She looked up, startled, and found that he was no longer smiling. In fact, he looked wary again. "You're not so distracted because you're wording a polite refusal, are you? You should be practiced enough to rattle one off without thought."

She shook her head, more in confusion than in denial. This

was the oddest proposal she had ever received, worse even than Sir Ralph. At least Ralph had gotten around to asking her eventually. But she supposed her own behavior was not beyond reproach, for she was standing there, biting her lips and clenching her fists for all the world as if he were going to cane her instead of offering her his name and his home.

"There's no turning back, is there? Ah, Charity, be charitable with me, won't you? I do want to marry you. Will you be my wife?"

She closed her eyes, waiting for the happiness, the *something* to fill her. Then she opened them again to his intense regard. He looked almost sad as if he were anticipating her refusal.

When she could not speak, he added ruefully, "You know, until this very moment, I did not realize how much I want you to say yes. I need you in my life, I think."

Finally she found her voice. "But you have known me for such a short time."

"I know. But your virtues are so apparent. And I do know my own mind." He smiled, reaching out to stroke her cheek. "I should have waited, I know. But with you receiving offers every week or so, I couldn't be sure you'd still be available." That brief smile never reached his eyes. "Come, girl, put me out of my misery."

She listened again to his words, "I need you in my life," and decided that they were more convincing than she had thought at first, and she looked at his sensitive mouth and remembered his kiss, which had all the passion his declaration had lacked. She touched the bandage on his arm, so neatly binding the wound he had earned for her. He needed her; she thought that might be true.

She had had no practice at accepting, and somehow throwing her arms about him and shouting "Yes!" seemed inappropriate. Very softly, still studying the bandage, she said, "Thank you. I hope I will be a good wife to you."

He was more surprised than gratified, and she glanced up

at him, wondering if he had really imagined that she would refuse. "You will be an excellent wife, I know that." Then he drew her close again and brushed her lips with his.

Charity, she scolded herself, a very handsome man, an artist no less, and one who thrills you to your toes, has just asked you to be his wife. Show a little enthusiasm.

So she stood on her tiptoes and kissed his beautiful brooding mouth, knowing that as long as he held her the doubts would remain in abeyance. Eventually, of course, he released her. Even though they were sheltered from view, there were limits to what a couple could do in broad daylight with a churchyard full of neighbors avidly waiting their return.

"Out of respect for my brother-in-law, not that he deserves any, I suppose we had best wait a few months." His eyes lightened with laughter as he traced her lips with a callused thumb. "You mustn't try so hard to make that impossible for me."

She wasn't sure what he meant but nodded as if she did. Then she, who had never been at a loss for words, didn't know what to say. Fortunately Tristan had left his reserve behind. Triumphantly he pulled something from his pocket.

"I almost forgot your ring. I thought if I weren't enough to sway you, I could always try diamonds. But you are probably too sensible to be swayed by a mere bauble."

The mere bauble was exquisite—a sapphire surrounded by diamonds, quiet and elegant and out of place on her hand. She resolved immediately to let her nails grow longer, even if they interfered with her gardening. Such a ring deserved a better presentation. "It's lovely." She held out her hand to admire it. "I can't wait to show it to Anna."

"Oh, she's seen it any number of times. It was our mother's. In fact, Anna guarded it. She insisted on approving my choice of bride."

"That was kind of her." The ring had been his mother's. That was rather romantic, after all.

"You'd best put it away for the moment. I probably ought

to speak to your brother." He added with a laugh, "You might just slip him the word that I am acceptable, or he could refuse me just out of habit."

Reluctantly Charity pulled the ring off. She tied it up in her handkerchief and tucked it into her puffed sleeve. Checking with her fingers to make sure it was safe, she said, "Oh, I'm certain Francis will take your word for it. It's not as if everyone hasn't guessed what we have been doing out here. If I had refused you, my reputation would be in shreds."

"Neat trick, wasn't it? I wonder no one else thought of it." He pulled her into his arms again, resting his cheek on her hair.

She felt safer like this, more sure. "Kiss me again."

Tristan was taken aback by her bold whisper; she could tell by the stillness of his body against hers. But then he complied, his hand cupping the back of her head, his mouth tender and hard over hers. Her eyes drifted shut and she let the sweet tide of passion carry away her doubts.

There in the filtered afternoon light, sitting on the old stone bridge where three centuries of lovers had kissed, Charity told herself that it would be lovely to have him forever, to kiss him this way, with the warm hush all around and no one left in the world but the two of them. She could live forever in his arms . . .

But then, slowly, reluctantly, his hand slipped down through her hair, and his lips left hers, and she was alone in the whirlpool. The dizziness had to subside before she could open her eyes. He picked up the fist that lay in her lap and brought it to his lips, nibbling a bit on her knuckle until she smiled unwillingly. Then he smiled back—a happy smile, one full of promise and peace.

"Charity." Her name was slurred again in that sweet Italian way, and she shivered. "You mustn't tempt me down such dangerous paths."

"But I want—" She couldn't finish, except to herself. But

I want the danger; I want to tempt you and tempt myself; just for once I want to give into temptation.

He picked up where she had left off. "I want to do this right, you see. I've never done anything the correct way in my life, but this is so important to me I must fall back on the tried and true."

She didn't understand, but he was rubbing her knuckles against his rough cheek, and the sensation was so unexpectedly pleasant that she didn't have the will to ask for elaboration. He dropped a gentle kiss on the knuckle she had scraped assembling a booth, then he rose and pulled her to her feet. "These pagan rituals, even in rehearsals, are stimulating. But I'm sure you've been up since dawn, and we'd best get on with the business so you can get home and rest."

His tone brooked no argument, and Charity meekly took his arm. She decided it was nice to have someone concerned about her health, though she hadn't been ill since she was a child. And if the final kiss at her door was chaste, her dreams that night were not, so she could not explain why she woke the next morning full of dread.

Chapter Thirteen

After church on Sunday, every congratulation added to her confusion. She smiled and showed off her ring and agreed that Lord Braden was the handsomest man in England and she the luckiest woman alive. And she blushed whenever someone added that Braden was the luckiest *man* alive or that the village would be lost without her but she shouldn't pay that any mind. She kept the smile in place when Tristan stood beside her to accept another round of well-wishings and as the two families returned to the Grange for lunch. By then, even her eyes ached with the effort of being cheerful.

Lunch was an informal affair, taken picnic-style out in the courtyard, and quickly broken up. The boys scattered to hunt rocks; the Havertons had been enlisted into Charlie's obsessive quest. Francis took Anna off to see the secret walled garden first cultivated in the sixteenth century. And Charity, left alone on a wooden bench with her betrothed, found her tension only increased.

He, at least, seemed relaxed, stretching his long legs out in front of him and leaning back in his seat. "This is such a comfortable house. A real home, not just a place to live. I know it's your doing, and I know you'll make our home just as warm."

"I'll try," she said, but the words stuck in her throat. She thought of Braden Hall, that perfect Palladian house, and imagined mussing it up a bit, Infusing a little enthusiasm in her voice, she repeated, "I'll try. I—I'm sure it's a beautiful place and only needs a family living there to make it a home."

"A family." He tilted his head to the side as if tasting the word and finding it sweet. "Children. Well, that will mar the perfection a bit. I can't wait to see little muddy footprints tracked into that marble hall. And an old sheepdog asleep across the staircase. That will be the finishing touch for the entry hall."

It was a pleasant thought, their children, a favorite dog, their home. But Charity felt a gnawing of discontent even as she castigated herself for a fool. She just wondered—oh, if that was the limit of his vision of the future, and, if it was, if he knew her very well at all.

Tristan was still looking ahead and west, toward Sussex. "Next time I go to Italy, I shall bring back some flowering trees, as you suggested, to break up the symmetry of that front facade."

This last brought Charity out of her own unproductive thoughts. "Next—next time? Do you plan to go soon?"

He glanced back at her with a reassuring smile. "Oh, not until we're settled in together. The winter, perhaps. That's a good time, for you'll be so busy you won't notice I'm gone." He reached out and took her hand, entwining his fingers with hers. "I used to regret coming back to England because there was so little here for me. Now I can look forward to coming home to you."

Charity slipped her hand from his and folded up each linen napkin into a neat square. She felt his approval warm on her cheek. He sounded so happy, contemplating his future—our future, she reminded herself. And isn't that what I want, to make him happy? Isn't that what I've always wanted, to make people happy? Abruptly she rose and smoothed her skirt. "Let's go make sure the boys aren't getting into mischief. Of course, they are, but it is always instructive to see what sort of trouble they've created."

Never before had Charity had trouble conversing, especially with Tristan, who inspired her with his rare interests and wide experience. But today, when they were newly allied, there was so much she couldn't say, so much that seemed inappropriate to ask her betrothed. She found that every bright comment had to be assembled ahead of time, tested mentally, and only if found safe sent forth.

Tristan suffered from no such awkwardness, talking easily as they walked, holding her hand in his warm grip as if long used to such familiarity. And she relaxed a little when his fingers twined intimately with hers and his smile lightened his dark eyes. Perhaps it would be all right—no, not all right. Perhaps it would be wonderful as she had always hoped.

To distract them both, she told him that the vicar had actually been pleased to hear that Tristan would be St. George. "For some reason he thinks having a peer in the role will make it more English and Christian." When he made a face, she asked, "You aren't thinking of abdicating, are you? That was the whole aim of the contest, you know, to choose a St. George."

"Oh, was that the aim? I thought I was aiming at something else entirely." He took her hand and straightened the diamond-and-sapphire ring that bound them in promise. "But if you want me to play St. George, I suppose I must. I hope the dragon isn't as fierce as your former flame."

"The dragon is made of cloth and plaster of Paris, and Crispin was never my flame," she said, but the slight edge of jealousy in his voice made her smile. She let him keep her hand as they walked between the rows of cabbages in the kitchen garden. "Did you really teach fencing?"

"One of my many attempts to pay for art lessons—fencing teachers, unfortunately, earn less than drawing masters." He gave her a sidelong glance. "I almost regret no longer being poor. You would be the most helpful helpmeet for a starving artist." He gestured round them to the neat rows of plants, the lacy green carrot tops, the purple frills of cabbage. "Look at this garden—I couldn't starve if I wished to."

He must have led such an odd life, not to know that every manor house—every house—had its own kitchen garden. But then, that was why he needed her, to make him the home he never had.

He would never guess, she thought, that she rather envied his impoverished past. Charity had never been less than comfortable in her circumstances, though she had certainly observed and even tried to alleviate poverty around her. But the poverty he survived was of a different order. It was romantic, this talk of starving for art. She wanted to ask more about that past of his, when he was an art student and a fencing teacher, which she imagined as a time of desperation and determination. But probably Tristan never thought of his past as exotic, just as Charity found nothing very interesting about her own life.

"Look." Tristan tugged her over to an old apple tree which drooped over the hedge, the apples still bare green nubs against the darker green leaves. As they approached the tree, Charity heard the plaintive cries of nestlings over the buzz of insects, and then a sharp warning from a bird. But ignoring the mother bird's anger, Tristan pulled her closer.

"See?"

She saw nothing remarkable—a wizened old apple tree, a shaft of sunlight weaving through its branches. But he put his hand in the sunbeam, transfixed. He turned his hand, studying it, against the gray bark of the tree.

Then he dusted off his hands, as if the sunlight were tangible, and returned to her.

How very different they were—she couldn't ever leave the world behind like that, forgetting everything else to pursue one vision. But then, he must see the world just like that—as visions. She thought he hadn't her sense of the world as a unit, every element interdependent on other elements, every part having a purpose in creating the whole. Instead he has, she thought, a narrow focus on life; everything is potentially a subject for painting.

They found the boys by the rocky stream that cut through the lowest meadow at Calder. Lawrence and Jeremy were side by side, sprawled on their stomachs with their hands trailing in the water. Charlie sat a little way back in the long golden grass, cross-legged in front of a pile of pebbles. They were all too preoccupied to notice the adults watching them from the ridge above. It was a pretty scene, the boys so absorbed under the arching blue sky.

"For city boys, Lawrence and Jeremy seem to have taken well to country life. They do delight in catching tadpoles and snatching at minnows." Charity hoped their mother wouldn't make a fuss over muddy nankeens, for as sure as July followed June, those two would be in the water before the day was through.

"Oh, even we denizens of the metropolis can find things of value in the country." He slanted her an amused glance and pulled her down to sit at the brow of the hill. Even from here, they heard the bickering that ever crackled between the Haverton boys. Tristan shook his head. "I wonder that Charlie is able to put up with that constant arguing. I'm tempted to crack their heads together and see if they'll get along better. But he just ignores it."

Charity looked down at Charlie's small figure hunched over his rocks. He picked one up and held it to the sun, then flung it carelessly away. "He's got great powers of concentration." Like you, she added silently. "When he's reading or organizing his rock specimens, he could ignore a French invasion. Besides, his childhood was filled with argument, with all of us about. He seems peaceful now, but when he was a little boy—"

When she faltered, Tristan prompted gently, "He was about Lawrence's age, wasn't he, when the youngest boy died?"

Unobtrusively Charity withdrew her hand from his and

edged a bit away. How had he learned of her brothers' deaths? Not that she had been keeping that a secret. But dwelling on it was useless and sad, so she and her brothers didn't talk about those years, when their family of eight was reduced by half. She supposed someone had mentioned the deaths; perhaps Anna knew the history and had told her brother. "He was a bit older, perhaps. Eight. Joey was closer to Lawrence's age. It was a long time ago."

"Were they like that, always competing, but best friends?"

Charity pulled up wild daisies for a chain, willing her hands not to tremble. "I don't recall. I'm sure they fought. I—" Joey's face, set in pugnacious lines, appeared in her mind, and she said softly, volitionlessly, "I remember whatever wooden soldier Charlie had Joey wanted, so Francis always carved two identical ones. But they would find some minor distinction and both claim the biggest or the brightest." The white petals of the daisy she gripped wavered as if brushed by a breeze. "After Joey died, Charlie threw all the soldiers into the fireplace. So many hours of work for Francis all burned up. I thought he would cry when he saw them in flames."

Finally her words halted, not by her choice, for she had not chosen to speak them, but simply because there were none left. And they were gone now, and she couldn't call them back.

"That must be why Charlie is so quiet now." To her relief, Tristan fell silent, studying the boy below them, little Charlie with his slight shoulders hunched as he examined his specimens. Charity could imagine his intense gaze and looked up to see Tristan's own eyes dark with concentration. "Because he felt responsible. Because he should have protected Joey better."

Charity drew a sharp breath. "Joey—Joey died of influenza. There was nothing Charlie could have done. Nothing anyone could have done. Or I would have—"

She pressed a fist against her mouth, tasting the tanginess

of the daisy stem she still clutched. She was almost grateful to hear him speak again, for his accent's gentle rhythm almost dissolved her harsh words lingering in the air.

"But he wouldn't have known that. He would just know that he should have been a better brother and it wouldn't have happened."

Charity didn't know why Tristan spoke so about a boy he hardly knew. And it angered her, this assumption that somehow he knew Charlie, understood him, when Charity had raised him since he was a babe. She had to freeze the hot words trembling on her lips. They would show only her defensiveness. She knew that however she tried she couldn't break through Charlie's shyness, couldn't teach him to open up to life, to laughter. She loved him anyway, the more so because she feared no one else would. But she couldn't tell Tristan that, couldn't confess her fear that Charlie would always be apart, even in the midst of his family. She only bent her head and focused on her daisy chain, carefully picking off the bruised petals.

But Tristan wouldn't let the subject go. "Would you like him to come live with us?"

With us. It sounded sweet, seductive, strange. "I—I don't know. Francis is his guardian, of course. And he's to go to Eton in the autumn, if he ever learns his Latin."

Tristan looked down at Charlie and shook his head. "I can't imagine him at Eton. It's a hellish place. I only lasted a few months. I was never so happy to set sail for Italy as that year."

Charity stood up, tugging angrily at her skirt. "My other brothers have gone there. It can't be so terrible. Francis learned a great deal, and Barry liked it well enough."

"Francis would doubtlessly learn a great deal on a desert island. And Barry would like any place with a crew team."

Tristan rose also and held out his hand. But she pretended not to see it. It wasn't polite, but then neither was his comment, which intimated that he knew better than she or Francis what Charlie needed. With an effort she concealed her feelings. "Well, you might get your wish. The vicar tells me Charlie is hopeless at Latin. And he shan't be allowed in if his Latin is poor."

"Smart lad."

That flashing grin was so attractive she almost gave in and forgave his effrontery. Then she heard a splash and looked down to see Lawrence standing in the stream, pulling a laughing Jeremy down with him. "I know they'd end up wet! There's something about water that magnetically attracts boys."

As if to prove her right, Charlie jumped up with a whoop and joined the younger boys. Charity's volatile emotions had to be pushed aside while she and Tristan ran down to make sure that Jeremy didn't get the worst of the ensuing water fight. It was a half-hour before they all started home, the adults now as wet as the boys.

Back at the Grange, Charity kicked off her ruined slippers, tied her wet hair back with a string, and glanced over at Tristan. He had carried the exhausted Jeremy most of the way home and now stood in his muddy boots holding the boy as Anna fussed about calling for towels and hot water. Jeremy rested his dark head on his uncle's shoulder, his eyes closing despite his valiant vows to stay awake.

Charity felt a rush of tenderness that frightened her. The rueful smile, the streak of mud on his straight jaw, the cling of his damp shirt to his muscular arm, the kiss he dropped on Jeremy's forehead before handing him over to Cammie—it was all so sweet and so compelling and so very dangerous.

Chapter Fourteen

Rehearsing the children's play was painstaking work, especially in that restless hour after their release from the schoolhouse. Few of Charity's twelve actors could read well enough to use a script, so she patiently read each line and pointed to the appropriate child to repeat it. Fortunately once she had reworked Mr. Greenaway's play, none of the children had to say much. She had excised most of the soliloquys and long descriptive passages, relying on action rather than narration to advance the plot.

Children really were much better at moving than speaking, she decided, sitting back on her heels on the oak floor of the church hall. Lawrence and Jeremy were sitting in the front of Mr. Padden's old rowboat, straining away at imaginary oars, bellowing as if they were truly pursued by a leviathan. Behind them were two girls, gesticulating wildly and shouting. Jack Moresby, who played Jonah, thrashed convincingly on the floor, pretending that the whale had caught him in its teeth.

"Curtain!" she called out, and though there was no curtain to drop, the children took this as permission to become themselves again. Jack jumped up and announced that he was hungry, and Jeremy whined about his unquenchable thirst. Lawrence dropped his imaginary oar and turned around to yank on Mary Moresby's beribboned ringlet—he really was very much like his father, worse luck. Mary kicked him in the shin, and only Charity's intervention prevented a rift in her theater group's solidarity.

When they had collected all their belongings and gotten into a ragged line, she announced, "Tomorrow we will learn Act II, and by the week's end we will be able to perform it altogether."

Jeremy waved his hand for her attention, then pointed to the three canvases that, still covered, took up most of the stage. "But Charity, when do we get to see my uncle's whale?"

"When we've made it through the entire play without making a single mistake, then I will unveil the masterpiece. It isn't complete yet, anyway. I think he means to put the hand of God in there to chastise the whale for chewing on Jonah."

Too late she saw that the artist himself had come into the church hall. The sun was filling the door behind him, outlining his slim form; an artist to the last, he had waited until the fullest light was gone to seek her out this afternoon. She wasn't sure if she were piqued or relieved by this. Both, she guessed; all her feelings were so ambivalent, seeing Tristan only made her wonder if she had lost all sense of herself since his proposal.

She busied herself ushering the children out the door. Jeremy tugged on Tristan's sleeve as he passed. "I know you'll paint God's hand just right."

Teasingly Tristan asked, once the door had closed behind his nephews, "The hand of God, is it?" He kissed her cheek once, quickly, a fiancé's casual caress, then her mouth not so quickly, then, with a sigh, released her. "This triptych of yours is getting more populated every day."

Two days of betrothal had taught her to long for his kisses but to fear them, too. There was the simple but profound physical pleasure to be enjoyed, the sweet thrill that rippled from his mouth to her heart and even elsewhere. There was a deeper desire, to know more of him, to let her hands wander from their safe harbor on his arms to unexplored territory, to let his kiss roam further, too. And there was the pride of knowing that he wanted that, too, that when he held her he loved it, that when he let her go he regretted it, that he anticipated a day when he could hold her always.

But his kisses also awakened a strange dread in her heart. He wanted her, wanted to marry her, and she must want that, too. Yet she knew what marriage meant; it meant giving herself to him. And she wasn't at all certain which self he meant her to give.

She recalled his comment finally. "Michelangelo painted God on the Sistine ceiling, didn't he? And it would be a great lesson for the children even if it's not quite true to the Biblical text."

"All these references to Michelangelo are gratifying, Charity, but rather misplaced. I don't aspire so high. Did you know," he added, uncovering the whale's swinging tail, "that God on the Sistine ceiling is modeled on Leonardo da Vinci?"

Charity took a guilty pleasure in this revelation. She loved artistic gossip. "It sounds blasphemous."

"Not to artists. We think it quite apt. On whose hand should I model God's?"

"Donatello." She decided to ignore the blasphemy involved in modeling God's hand on any sculptor's, no matter how great.

"Unfortunately I haven't any memory of Donatello's hand. Perhaps I shall just use da Vinci's. That one I can call to mind, for I had to copy that panel of the ceiling when I was a student."

She sat down on the edge of the stage and arranged the pages of the revised script in order, hoping he would pick up his brush. But he only frowned at the blank corner of the canvas where she supposed the hand of God was meant to go.

"You don't need a model, then? You can paint it from memory?"

"Yes, and lucky you are that I can. Otherwise the Midsummer play would have to wait for me to sail to Rome with my easel and come back with a reproduction of Michelangelo's work. Not to mention," he tugged off the cover on the adjacent panel, revealing a quite fiercesome whale with a gaping, sharp-toothed mouth, "that I would have to catch a whale and tie it up in the harbor."

"But isn't that the way most artists paint? From life?"

He shrugged, using his index finger to trace the outline of a hand on the empty corner of the first panel. "Some do. They drag their easel down to the seacoast to do a seascape, and they set their fruit up on a table to do a still life." He frowned at his invisible outline and redid the thumb. "They might finish the painting later, but the fundaments—" He paused to reconsider the unfamiliar and possibly un-English word. "The important parts are composed on the scene. But I don't do that. I think I must have a good visual memory. Or a good imagination. For I don't think," he added, glancing back with a grin, "that I have ever seen a whale."

The subject reminded her how different this man was from anyone else she had ever known. The mental process he spoke of was as foreign to her as his dark Italian eyes. "Do you really just paint the scenes you've remembered or created in your mind?"

"I suppose that is what I do." He gazed at the panel as if he saw something other than a half-completed painting. "Is it so strange? If I know something well enough, I just look at the canvas and see it there, and paint what I see. I might alter it, of course."

"But the critics say your paintings are realistic."

"Wait till they see our whale friend. And besides, my paintings merely appear realistic. If all I do is copy, if I add nothing of my own, then it doesn't matter who painted it, does it? A real artist can't stop with the truth. He must transform it to make it art, rather than just—a picture."

Chin on fist, Charity considered this. She valued truth as a rule, but she was more likely than most to—oh, not to transform it but to manage it. Her negotiations with the vicar over Midsummer had contained quite a bit of *managed* truth, she recalled. She had never before thought of that as an art. "I do think art must require more than that. Mr. Greenaway certainly transformed the whale story, but I don't know if that made it art. Anymore than my changes to his story have achieved art."

"As fond as I've gotten of Jonah's whale, Charity, you must admit it is not the most promising material with which to start."

She was still intrigued but troubled by this artistic dismissal of the reality of reality. "But surely with portraits you must stay very close to reality. The subject will want to recognize himself."

Laughing, Tristan pulled the cover back over the canvas. "You'd be surprised. When the painter comes too close to reality, the subject always claims it is not a good likeness at all. That is why I've never painted portraits. I would likely expose their secret vices, and they would be outraged and refuse to pay my fee."

He jumped lightly off the stage and held out his hand to her.

"But aren't you going to work?"

He shook his head. "I've been working all day. Now I want to have some tea and talk about our future."

Our future. Those words he liked so well were fraught with tension, with promise, and yet he seemed not to notice. "But—but the future includes the Midsummer fair, you know. And that backdrop must be done very soon."

Impatiently he pulled her to the edge of the stage. So positioned, she could do nothing but step off into his arms. He let her slide down against his body and then gently set her on her feet. "It will be done soon, as long as you don't add in new features. Do you know how long it took Michelangelo to paint his picture of God?"

The contact with his hard lean form reassured her, and she even managed to answer practically, *"You* have only to paint the hand."

By the time they reached the Calder drawing room, she had pledged not to promise the children any additions to the great triptych, and her hand rested comfortably in his. But even as she teased him with her desire for an octopus hanging from the whale's tail, she realized she was putting on an act of sort. She was *managing* herself, creating from herself a more appropriate picture of the happily betrothed young lady.

And the worst of it was, she wanted more than anything to confess it to Tristan, to tell him how strange she felt in this new role, how inutterably *stupid* she was not to be happy in truth as well as in pose, and how she wished he would hold her and kiss away the doubts.

But what a greedy, grasping girl she would seem if she gave voice to such complaints! And yet, perhaps she was a greedy, grasping girl after all. All her life she had always wanted more—more praise, more gratitude, more acclaim, more love. All her good works couldn't conceal that selfish child in her who demanded what she couldn't get. And it was greedy to look across at a man who cared for her, who wanted her for his wife, and say, "I want more."

She poured him a cup of tea with a hand held rigid. As he took it with that sweet smile of thanks, she contemplated pouring out her absurd woe. But what would she say? That she longed for something more from him? Some great epic romance? Some gamble on passion?

But she couldn't gamble at all, couldn't risk the words she had framed in her mind. She imagined him drawing back, his dark eyes remote again, his response careful and appalled. That greedy Charity wasn't what he wanted, of course; he had proposed to another Charity entirely, a generous girl of good cheer, who wanted nothing more than to give him a home. Nothing more.

So she said nothing at all, except for assenting murmurs as

he talked about that home, about the conservatory he intended to make into a studio, about the ruined square yard of stone wall Francis insisted was Roman and made Tristan promise not to replace.

"The village is just right for you to do your good works. Still we won't be so far that you can't keep up your activities here."

She couldn't help herself. "Just what I long for. His and hers villages to maintain." She dropped her gaze at his sharp look, and when he asked what she meant, she shook her head. "Nothing."

He frowned but apparently decided not to pursue the subject. "We'd best forego a wedding trip for the time being, by the way. I don't want to leave Anna alone just yet."

Charity's voice was as blithe as her thoughts were bitter. "But what about this winter when you leave for Italy?"

"She won't be alone then. She'll have you. And you'll have more outlet for that energy of yours—" He pulled her hand away from her needlework. "I don't think I've ever seen you with idle hands. What are you working on there? Part of your trousseau?"

"We Kentish girls finish our trousseaus by our fifteenth birthdays." Charity gently detached her hand from his to hold up her handiwork, a large white tube patched together from old shirts and pillowslips. "No, this is going to be the body of your dragon. It will be filled with paper, you see, and the neck will be of plaster of Paris, so you can easily slice it through with your sword."

From her pile of rags she pulled out another shirt to add to the tail. Yanking off the strip of lace down the front, she rolled it up and put it away in her sewing box. She held the shirt up to display the frayed elbows and torn sleeves and the stain on the back. "Charlie's rock-hunting shirt. Do you know, ten years ago it was Ned's best shirt. He wore it only to church. And then he outgrew it, and Barry inherited it. He sneaked out of Matins one morning to go fishing, and it was never the same again."

She tore the sleeves off and began to stitch the rest to the dragon, remembering all the times she had darned this particular shirt. "Charlie hasn't anyone to hand it down to anymore."

She looked up to his sympathetic gaze and, flushing, looked back down at her work. How self-pitying she must appear, almost in tears over an old shirt! Something about Tristan made her weak, that was all; was it that she was not nearly as strong as he imagined?

Suddenly she asked, "If you were to paint my portrait—not from life, but from—from your mind, what would you paint?"

He was startled. "I told you, I don't do portraits."

She didn't know why, but she persisted. "If you did, what would my portrait show?"

He shook his head, then humored her. "Your portrait would show—oh, all your virtues, I suppose."

"But what would the scene be?"

He shrugged, still obviously puzzled by her insistence. "Well, I don't like posed portraits, with the subject gazing out. I think I'd have you engaged in some task—gardening, perhaps."

"You haven't ever seen me gardening."

"I told you." He was still polite, but his voice was edged with impatience. "I have a good imagination."

Not so good, if he only imagined her doing what she did every day of her life, weeding and pruning and clearing. "Why gardening?"

"Charity, gardening would be a—metaphor, do you see, for your virtues. Thrift and good sense, hard work and sunniness."

"Describe the picture."

He shook his head again, annoyed but unwilling to say so.

"Describe. Well, I would paint you in that garden west of the house, the one with the sunflowers—"

He closed his eyes, and she saw his brow furrow as he concentrated, assembling in his mind the picture he would paint on canvas, were he the sort to paint his beloved. Then he opened his eyes and gazed at her, eyes narrowed. "I can't really picture you now. The garden, yes. But not you in it."

It seemed to trouble him as much as it troubled her, and instinctively she sought to soothe, to explain, to promise better later. "We could walk out there again, and then perhaps it will be clearer—I will be clearer."

But she felt the chill well up inside her. This mythical portrait that he would never paint had already accomplished one purpose: she knew what she had suspected all along. He didn't know her, not as she really was. And he couldn't even imagine her.

She knotted her thread and broke it, then hid her fists in the sleeves of the shirt. She had decided, she realized, sometime during his flattering catalogue of her virtues.

"There will be time for that when we are married." He reached across to touch her cheek. His caress still thrilled her, more now, when it was so agonizingly clear she would know it no longer.

Hidden in the shirt, her hands began to shake, and she gripped the dangling sleeves to still the tremors. She couldn't bear it. She jerked away from his hand as if his touch burned her.

"No. I can't marry you after all."

As if she had broken loose, she felt free, disengaged from whatever followed. It was a liberating feeling, to be outside of this experience, but odd, too. She had become alien to herself.

Her hands had stopped trembling, so she started ripping the seam from the arms of the shirt. She spoke her thoughts into the utter silence. "That didn't hurt nearly as much as I thought it would! I think that must mean it is the right thing to do, don't you?"

Very evenly, Tristan said, "I'm afraid I didn't quite get your meaning there. Perhaps you could repeat it. One of your few faults is a tendency to speak too quickly."

Carefully, as if she were addressing a foreigner, Charity said, "I don't think I would make a good wife for you after all."

"Are you trying to tell me you wish to call off our wedding?"

"Not our wedding, for we've not even set the date, so how can we call it off? No, only our betrothal. I've forgotten how one conducts such matters—well, I daresay I haven't forgotten, as I've never broken off a betrothal before. But I have an etiquette book in the library, and I'm sure that will tell which of us should send the notice into the *Gazette*. The fair thing, it would seem, would be for me to do so, if you have already sent in the betrothal announcement."

"Why?"

She started to reply, but he stopped her with an abrupt gesture. "No, don't tell me why you should send in the notice. I don't give a tinker's damn about that. Why do you want to call off our marriage?"

She dropped her eyes to her needlework to escape the force of his black scowl. "Because it's clear I will not suit you."

"Don't give me that etiquette prattle." He rose and came to stand towering over her. "It's not clear at all that we should not suit. All along I've said what an excellent wife you will make."

His very height was a threat, and she didn't like being threatened. She found anger easier than regret, and besides, she hated that term. "An excellent wife. Well, I don't think I would make you an excellent wife. And you think so only because you don't know me."

"I know you perfectly well."

"No. Or you wouldn't think I would make you an excellent wife. I won't, because I'm not the person you think I am."

It made perfect sense to Charity, even as it broke her heart to say it, but Tristan didn't understand. He moved back a step to a less intimidating stance and shook his head. "Come, Charity, you are having a joke with me. Or bridal nerves, or some such. You can't confess you have some secret vice, for I know you haven't."

"It's not a vice. It's only—oh, just accept this, Tristan. I won't make a very good wife for you, and you won't be happy."

Some of the tension left his face as his hands, which had been clenched, opened in a resigned gesture. "I'll take the chance. In fifty years, if I am not happy, I will admit you were right."

Charity wasn't in the habit of acting impulsively, without thinking through the actions and goals and consequences. She was at a loss, unsure herself why she had to do this. She only knew she didn't want him to stand there looking hopeful and defiant and a little hurt. She couldn't look at his face and gazed instead at his hands, open in welcome, in supplication. That was no better. She stared down at her needlework.

"I am sorry. I know it isn't fair, but I couldn't abide it any longer. I've made an absolute mash of this. I just can't be what you want me to be or only what you want me to be. I thought perhaps I could, I hoped I could. I realized just now that if I couldn't keep it up for a week, I would spend my life struggling to hide."

"To hide what? You aren't making any sense!"

She pulled the seam ripper all the way around the arm and let the sleeve fall to her lap before she could gather the words to answer. "Oh, that, for example. That I'm inconsistent. That I don't make sense. That I'm not sensible, at least not without trying very hard."

He closed his eyes as if to block out a vision he didn't

want to remember. "I think you are just anxious about the marriage. All brides are, or so I hear."

"I am not just anxious. I am trying to tell you that—that you don't want to marry me."

He opened his eyes then and regarded her narrowly until she dropped her gaze back to her needle. "What do you want?"

It was a new question, one she never expected to have to answer. Her words came slowly. "I want—" How selfish he must think her, assembling a shopping list of desires and whining when it wasn't filled. "Oh, I just want more, you see. And you don't. I mean, you don't want a wife who wants more. What an awful life that would be. But—but we could remain friends. Then I wouldn't want any more."

This last thought cheered her. They needn't after all lose that connection they shared. "I do make an excellent friend, I think, and without trying very hard at all."

Tristan put his hand on the back of a chair as if to give himself some support. "I don't understand you."

"I know. That is what I have been trying to tell you."

His supporting hand curled into a fist on the upholstery. "I knew you would say that. I knew it. And if I tell you that I don't worry about all your worries, that I will marry you nonetheless, you will tell me that if I understood you I would feel differently."

She didn't answer, for that was indeed what she would have said.

"That I am lucky to be allowed my escape. That someday—soon, if I've any claim on sense—I shall thank you for this."

"You will," she agreed, though the bleakness of his expression gave her pause. Gratefully she recalled the etiquette of the situation. She laid her needlework on the end table and pulled off the sapphire ring. With a gentle finger, she traced the golden circle, then held it out to him.

He looked at the token and finally took it. "You are determined to do this, then? And you won't tell me why?"

"I have told you why." Guilt made her impatient; she wanted only to have this encounter done. She should never have accepted him in the first place—he deserved better than this—but she saw no other remedy than to unmake the mistake quickly.

He jammed the ring into his pocket and strode to the door. "You are right then, I don't know you. For I would never have imagined that you, with your sweet face and manner, could be so heartless!"

The door closed, and after a moment, she rubbed the tears off with the back of her hand and rose. She still had to explain this to Francis, and he was even less likely than Tristan to understand why she couldn't marry.

Just then the drawing-room door crashed open and she found herself trapped in the burning gaze of her erstwhile fiancé. "What you are complaining about then," he said, as if their conversation had never ended, "is that you think I will not love you."

Charity took a prudent step back until she felt her chair against the back of her legs. Then she sat on the edge of her seat, poised to run. "I wouldn't say I was complaining precisely."

"Implying then. When you said you wanted more, that is what you meant."

Charity clasped her hands in her lap and stared down at them, evaluating his inquiry. Love. Such a small word, to fill such a large gap in her. "I suppose that is part of it."

"Well, then. That's fine. I have no doubt I will love you."

Charity's breath caught in her throat. "Oh, how sweet of you to say so!"

His expression was still taut, but he brought the ring out of his pocket with a flourish. "Then put this on and we'll set a wedding date. An immediate one."

Charity pushed back in her chair till her back touched the

upholstery. She looked regretfully at the ring but made no attempt to take it. "But that doesn't change my mind."

Tristan pressed the fist with the ring against his forehead. "What do you want from me, you heartless vixen?"

"Now there's no call for that, you know." Knowing she had behaved unconscionably added an edge to her voice. "You have called me heartless twice now. And I'm not that at all."

Tristan was bitter, despairing. "Then what does that heart of yours want? I told you I would love you. What more do you want?"

"Something more. I don't know." So she would not have to look at him, she studied the misty June day outside the window. "Love at first sight, perhaps."

"That might be hard to arrange," he answered acidly, "as we've met any number of times already. Why isn't the other good enough as it's all we can have now?"

Charity shrugged helplessly. "It should be enough. For anyone else it would be enough. But you see, don't you now, that is why we would not suit. I am not very like you imagined, am I? Being loved—merely loved—isn't new for me. People usually do come to love me, you must have noticed. I don't mean to boast," she added hastily. "Because it isn't anything to boast of. I work hard at it, and usually I succeed. But just once, I'd like not to have to work at it—I mean, if I am just going to be the same after this, then I may as well stay with what I have. At least I will not be disappointed. Oh, I'm not explaining this well at all. Couldn't you just perhaps consider me a bit tetched and have it done?"

"No. I can't. You've taken this too far to drop it without explanation." Tristan's eyes were hard and glittering now with his anger. Anger was better, she dimly recalled telling herself recently; perhaps he had discovered that, too. "You need only have told me that you didn't want to marry me— God! only two days ago—and it would have been put to rest.

But you told me you would be my wife and let me think you meant it."

"I did mean it, or I wanted to mean it—Oh, Tristan, I can't explain. But please let it go. If you think you need a wife, you can find another easily enough. There are dozens of girls who would do you well right here on the Kent coast. Good sensible girls, who can make you a home and be happy doing it. You'll find a replacement to suit your purposes if you would only look a bit farther afield."

This bit of advice did not assuage him. Savagely he jammed the betrothal ring back into his pocket. "And will you so easily find a replacement for me? Or will that prove impossible? I'm only the latest of a series, I recall. I expect none of the rest suited either. They didn't understand you, is that it? I should write them and tell them they are lucky in that, for in my experience, you hardly improve on more intimate acquaintance!"

Although that was exactly Charity's point, hearing him rephrase it so brutally brought her to her feet in affront. "Thank you, Lord Braden, for making this so easy for me. For I know I shall never regret turning away a man who is so quick to insult a woman just because she has declined the honor of being his wife!"

From the shamed, stubborn set of his face, it was clear he knew he had gone too far. But with the air of a man who would as soon hang for a sheep as for a lamb, he said just before he slammed the door, "And I will never regret being refused by a girl who, all evidence to the contrary, believes she is too good for mortal man!"

Chapter Fifteen

Tristan was beyond shock. Instinctively he turned his horse south down the winding road out of the village. He hardly noticed the tall pastoral hedgerows and rolling fields until they suddenly ended at the brow of a rocky cliff. Below was the solitary beauty of a sandy beach. He dismounted to stand at the edge, waiting for the salt breeze to clear the dizziness from his mind. But when the vertigo remained, he guided Giotti to the steep path leading down to the beach. The chestnut, who had carried him uncomplainingly across the Italian Alps, dug in his hooves and refused to follow.

No one cares what I want, Tristan thought with a self-pity he recognized as particularly childish. He yanked at the reins, and with a whinny of protest, Giotti picked his way down the cliff.

In recompense Tristan took Giotti on a gallop along the beach. But the ferocity of the ride only enflamed his raging thoughts.

"I want . . . love at first sight," she had sighed, exactly like the silly dream-spinning girl he knew her not to be. Silly, fickle, vain, emotional, inconstant: exactly the sort of woman he wanted to avoid. Love at first sight—

The horse's hooves kicked up sand and saltwater, the mist stinging Tristan's eyes. He didn't want to think of having to announce this fiasco to his sister, to his nephews, to the world at large. He had always cherished his privacy, almost resenting his new fame, glad to inherit the title so he could sign his paintings in that impersonal fashion. Even writing the announcement of his engagement and sending it to the *Gazette* was difficult; retracting it—God, one day after he'd posted it—would be humiliating.

He found himself thinking in Italian as he always did when he was angry—another legacy of his histrionic mother. In his mind he heard his thoughts run like the long heart-rending lamentation of a Venetian gondolier deprived of a fare. He cut the flow off. Reining in his horse, he forced himself to continue in precise, clipped English, so much more conducive to rational thought.

Barely winded by his hard ride, Giotti dropped his head to graze on the sea oats that edged the beach. Tristan walked away, the hard-packed sand crunching under his boots. At the remains of an old pier, he sat down on a battered pylon and contemplated the great gray Channel, dreaming of escape. In a month or so he could be in Italy again, away from these incomprehensible English, away from the cold gray northern seas, away from the odd silvery light that filtered through the mist, away from Charity and the hurt she had dealt him.

He scooped up a handful of pebbles, automatically checking them for fossil material to interest Charlie. But they were just pebbles after all, and he tossed them one by one into the water and watched them disappear under the surf.

What had she said, this other Charity, the one he didn't know? Oh, yes, exactly that. "But you don't know me." What dark secret was she hinting at? Some ruinous love affair?

No. Her kisses, though sweet, were not those of an experienced woman. And besides, if that were her secret, she would be sensible enough to confess that, and he hoped he would be sensible enough to accept it without condemning her.

She had no secret vice, he'd make book on it. She'd lived all her life in a village where everyone knew her. This suffocating intimacy didn't allow for secret vices or secret virtues either. Tristan, the perpetual outsider, been there less than a month and already knew where smuggled brandy was sold, where cockfights were staged, and which Ferris girl liked interludes in the hayloft.

He had learned this last not from a personal experience, being too occupied with the Calder girl to do more than take appreciative notice of the nubile Ferris girls. No, his informant had been the wily Crispin Hering, hoping, no doubt, to scotch Tristan's chances with Charity. For a dark moment Tristan considered how much better off he would be had he gone along with that scheme and been discovered by Charity in flagrante delicto with the blonde maid. He would still be missing one betrothed, but at least he would have had a bit of fun—and a reason anyone could understand.

Instead, he was left unfulfilled and uncomprehending. You don't know me, she had said sadly. And if you did, you wouldn't want to marry me. It was incomprehensible. Of course he wanted to marry her. She was exactly the wife he'd never thought to dream of but had recognized right off as right for him. An excellent wife—how she had flinched when he said those words, as if he had insulted her.

Could that be it, that after all she had decided that she couldn't be an excellent wife to him? Did she think his standards were too high, too inflexible? But she did it all already, making a home, nurturing a family. He wouldn't expect much more than that—oh, of course, wives had a duty that maidens didn't. But from the cling of her embrace, he couldn't imagine Charity balking at fulfilling that, or even considering lovemaking a duty. His pulse quickened just remembering her passionate response to his kiss, her bold demand: "Kiss me again." It couldn't be that which frightened her, surely.

He had promised to love her, and she wasn't much impressed. Everyone loved her, she said. From another woman, that might sound vain; in this paradoxical Charity, it sounded poignant. Sad.

She hadn't, of course, reciprocated his promise. For a moment Tristan gave into the most anguishing possibility of all—that she didn't think she could love him. And if that were so, of course they were better off apart, for he was old-fashioned enough to believe that lasting love was necessary for a happy marriage.

Almost reluctantly, he rejected that. If she didn't care for him, he would have to let her go. But she must care for him, or nothing in the world made sense. He recalled their conversations, sparkling with spoken and unspoken contact, with an intimacy they hadn't had to earn. And he remembered those few kisses, shimmering with passion's promise—no, they had shared too much. Their caring wasn't entire yet, for they'd only known each other these few weeks. But surely she, too, had felt them on the brink of something new and profound. But that must be less—or more?—than she wanted.

Love at first sight. That was what Kenny had professed for Anna, what Tristan's parents had used as an excuse for their impossible marriage. Charity couldn't want that ephemeral and absurd emotion, not the Charity he knew. Not when he offered her something lasting and complete instead. But therein lay the conundrum—if she did prefer the other, then she really wasn't the woman he thought he knew, the only woman he had ever thought might share his life.

"You don't know me . . ." How sadly she had said that. The anger seeped out of him like the sand through his fingers. He had wanted to believe that she would come to him complete, without any edges to cut up the peace she brought him. He had needed to see her as fitting the world in a way he had never fit, one with nature and her fellows, belonging. He wanted only to add her to his life to absorb that completeness, that serenity.

But he had never really wondered what she needed. And if he had, he would have supposed—oh, that she needed nothing, really. She was complete already. She needed a husband of some kind, of course; girls were supposed to marry. But otherwise, she was so cheerful. Not always, of course. She still grieved for those lost boys. But she had never asked for his sympathy, never asked for anything, except that once, when she asked him to kiss her again.

But then she wouldn't ask, would she? He hadn't known her long, but he knew that much. She offered help; she didn't ask for it. She might eventually get what she wanted, but not by requesting it.

Perhaps that was all. She wanted more than he offered—more than nothing. And she didn't want to have to ask for it.

And she had concluded that he was not likely to give it to her.

It was a brutal realization. He had fallen short somehow, without even noticing. He had disappointed her. And she thought it best to cut her losses and cut him out of her life.

He might have known it had all been too easy. He hadn't even had to court her in the usual manner, with flowers and love letters and tiny tokens of esteem. He had asked so much of Charity and hadn't considered what she might want out of courtship and marriage. If he had to do it all over again—

Tristan let another handful of sand sift out of his cupped hand. Would he do it all over again? Knowing now that she wasn't likely to be a source of stability and calm in his life, that she might bring her own complications to complicate his life? Knowing how right he was to be wary of connection and how deeply this connection had already wounded him? Did he still want her as his wife?

The wave of longing that swept over him was answer enough. All he knew about her, and all he didn't know, made her essential to his life. Oh, yes, if he had the chance, he would do it all over again, but only better: treat her more worshipfully, perhaps, recite her poetry, bring her flowers.

He remembered Kenny playing Romeo to Anna's Juliet, and ruefully shook his head. It just wasn't him. And Charity wouldn't accept it anyway. He imagined the ironic glint in her eyes if he suddenly started playing the adoring swain. She would tell him it was too little, too late. He'd had his chance and mucked it up and didn't deserve another.

He wasn't used to speaking his feelings; he was a painter, not a poet. He had thought she would read his heart as she read his mind. But perhaps she didn't know him well either, or she would never have suggested that he could find a replacement for her. The thought would be laughable if it weren't so painful, that any other woman would quicken his senses and fill his heart as she already did.

But perhaps he'd given her no reason to believe that his regard was deep and true. It had all happened too quickly for him to understand himself. Now, when it would do him no good, he could admit that he wanted her, needed her, cherished her—loved her, although he had never framed that thought until he knew he'd lost her. His feelings had been different from what he thought love would be—they had been peaceful, not tormenting. Well, now he felt tormented enough to be convinced this was indeed love.

But he couldn't tell her that. She wouldn't believe him. She wouldn't want to believe him. She had already made her decision and wouldn't go back on it just because he started declaiming poetry. If she, too, was hurt by this, she wouldn't gamble on him again.

He really should just leave it all behind, go back to Italy, lose himself in his work. Staying here would be to risk rejection again, to renew the pain every time he saw her, to torment himself with regret.

But to leave would be to give her up, and that he could not imagine doing.

Despair made him restless; he rose and walked along the edge of the surf. Ironically, its comforting rhythm reminded him of Charity, of her wisdom, of her strength. He imagined confiding his folly with that other Charity, asking her counsel. He could almost hear her consoling voice, inventing excuses he hadn't thought to offer, analyzing his mistakes ...

She would tell him that his first mistake was to assume that he knew her, when he knew only what he wanted to know. His second was to rush his fences, forcing an ultimatum before he had a chance to realize his first mistake. His third was to imagine that his needs were paramount—Now, he could almost hear her chiding, does that sound loverlike?

She would tell him to do what he had never thought to do—to consider whether this proposed marriage would benefit her life nearly as much as him. Could she ever have wanted to marry him?

He stopped to watch the waves smooth away the footprints he had left in the sand. He had never been particularly vain, even about his art, so he dismissed his looks as irrelevant. As an artist, he knew how easy it was to create an Aphrodite or an Adonis either with paint or with cosmetics. But not an evocative expression, an intriguing face, an infectious smile: those lingered in the imagination but were almost impossible to recreate. Charity—now she had that sort of beauty. Her features weren't at all symmetrical; those dimples unbalanced everything, making her smile a little crooked. But so radiant . . .

He wrenched his thoughts away from his own feelings and back to hers. But he sensed Charity felt the same way, that true beauty shone from within. At least she liked his hands; often he'd caught her gazing approvingly at them, paint stains and all.

In fact, the paint stains were what attracted her. She admired his art, admired him for being artistic. Such conversations they had about art. He wasn't used to talking about his work; even his exchanges with other artists were mostly technical, not substantive. But Charity genuinely enjoyed discussing his paintings, his education—he closed his eyes, thinking how self-absorbed he must have been. Did they never discuss her work, her education?

Then he imagined what his friend Charity might say to that: she didn't want to talk about her own life. She found yours exotic, enticing, art and Italy and adventure. Think of the guidebook she annotated, for a place she had never been. No one else she knows lived such a life. She was fascinated by you.

Cheered, he retraced his steps to the old pier. Fascinated—she often asked him about Italy, her close questions betraying her hunger for description beyond what guidebooks reported. That was good; he knew Italy far better than he knew England. He had been a tour guide himself one destitute summer after the war, leading a group of aging British tourists through Tuscany. Charity would love that story, and he resolved to tell her if he got the opportunity.

And he would make sure he got that opportunity. Briskly he dusted the sand off his breeches, whistling for Giotti. As he led the chestnut back up the cliff, he reminded himself of her passionate response to his embraces, her intense interest in his work, the laughter they had shared, the exchanges of ironic looks, the sparkling conversations. Sometimes the involuntary intimacy had even frightened her, he thought, recalling how she had withdrawn when he had spoken of little Joey. He had been too intuitive that afternoon, sensing her feelings of having failed the child. She couldn't let him near enough to comfort her.

Without vanity, he concluded that, blind as he had been, no other man could see her as well as he could. And no other man would as well appreciate her—the known and unknown Charity.

Halfway back to Haverne, he had determined his course: a courtship with all the proper elements, only surreptitious. He would win her back without her ever realizing she was still in the game. She wouldn't resist his renewed pursuit because she would never recognize it as such.

Chapter Sixteen

For the first time in her life, Charity felt the chill of public disapproval. Those same people who didn't cock an eyebrow when she gave away scandalous Gothic novels to encourage literacy, who contributed uncomplainingly to her fund for parish bastards, who understood when she turned away the proposal of the finest men in the area, shook their heads over this latest event.

Mrs. Hering, Mrs. Dalton, and Mrs. Williams, as representatives of the older and wiser members of the parish, arrived at the Grange ten minutes after the news of the broken engagement got out. Ostensibly they were there for a Midsummer committee meeting, but no matter how often Charity asked for reports of rag dolls and jumble booths or destiny cakes, the ladies could only talk of her folly.

They accepted tea and cream biscuits but not Charity's decision. "I was not surprised when you refused my boys," Mrs. Hering conceded. "They are boys, and you grew up with them, and Crispin especially must seem almost a brother to you. But Lord Braden—why, what objection could you have to him? So handsome, so talented, with that lovely estate only a few miles away!"

Charity didn't know how to defend herself, except to say once again that she had realized they would not suit. Mrs. Hering set down her teacup with a decisive rattle. "Nonsense.

You'd suit well enough eventually. You grow to suit, don't you see? You can't expect perfection straight off, especially in a man!"

"Especially in a man!" Mrs. Williams echoed, and Mrs. Dalton nodded sagely in agreement.

"Men never do get perfect, no matter how we nag! So don't go expecting it, or you'll only be disappointed."

Charity was hard-pressed to hold her temper in check, but she managed to get a consensus on the banquet menu before the ladies left, trailing advice behind them.

"It's none of their business, after all," she told Cammie, who had come by to support her during the onslaught.

"Of course it is." Cammie peered calmly out the window at the puddled courtyard, finally empty of visitors. "The Grange is the center of the village, and the Calder family is central to its welfare. So your welfare, my dear, is central to every villager."

"I can make my own decisions, and they are likely to be sensible ones, even if—"

"Even if not a single soul understands why." Cammie turned away from the dreary vista and regarded Charity soberly. "Explain to me why this is so sensible."

Charity poured herself another cup of tea, but no compelling answer appeared in the meantime. "It is sensible, it is. Tristan's a good man, but he doesn't really know me. And I don't know him."

"A long engagement would have solved that. In fact, a short engagement and a long marriage would have been an even better solution."

Abandoning her fresh cup, Charity rose from her defensive position behind the serving tray. In a napkin, she gathered up the biscuits to deliver to the children at the play rehearsal later. "No. I knew right away I'd made a mistake. I didn't feel properly."

"What do you mean, properly?"

Charity tied the ends of the napkin into a square knot before she replied. "I was unsettled. I didn't want to see him or be with him. And that doesn't augur well for a life with him, does it?"

"You'd be surprised." Cammie didn't explain this cryptic comment, adding gently, "You have the right to be happy, you know."

"I am happy. Oh, not right at the moment, but I would be if everyone would just leave me be. I wasn't happy, not at all, when we were—" The word stuck in her throat but she forced it out. "Betrothed. Oh, no, is that the vicar?" She squeezed past Cammie to peek out from behind the curtains. Head down, Mr. Langworth was picking his way among the puddles in the lane. In his black caped greatcoat, the vicar looked rather ominous. "Oh, I can't talk to him as well. He'll just shake his head and say that all this Midsummer foolishness has overset me. I'm going to the church hall to build a few more booths."

"Take your umbrella!" Cammie called as Charity escaped through the drawing-room door. "And wear your pattens. It's dreadfully muddy out there."

Charity did not need this estimable advice, only replacing her slippers with a pair of walking boots before entering the misty afternoon. The rain had stopped finally. A few shafts of sun poked bravely through the clouds as she wriggled through a space in the high hedges, yanking the basket of biscuits and peppermints after her. Then she was in the meadow, free from any chance encounter with concerned neighbors, free from disapproval and interference.

The run across the long grass overheated her, and she knelt to splash her fevered cheeks in the deep pool formed where beavers dammed up the spring. This was the best fishing hole at Calder, rocky and cool, shaded by willows and wych elm. Drinking in the clean wet scent, she recalled other damp afternoons spent here with her brothers, fishing or just listening to the deep throb of the bullfrog and the trickling of water through the dam. She could almost hear Ned's bouncy step behind her—

It wasn't Ned at all, but Crispin Hering. A fishing rod balanced on his shoulder, he walked into the grove, whistling softly. He stopped when he saw Charity. Then, insolently, he took up whistling again, settling himself not far away and pulling a live worm from his shirt pocket. His tune trailed off finally. "'Hullo."

"Hullo."

"I've decided to marry someone else." Contemplatively Crispin watched the worm wriggle at the end of his hook, then glanced back at Charity. "I haven't decided whom yet, but someone else. So you'd best not count on me to make you another offer."

"I hadn't the least intention of counting on you." Charity's tone was lofty, but she bent her head so her hair fell forward to hide her face. She was ridiculously hurt; she had never meant to marry Crispin, but she had also never meant to earn his scorn.

"Don't you want to know why?"

It was apparent that he had a set-down speech planned, so she didn't give him the satisfaction of an answer. He didn't need one. Casually dropping his line into the water, he jiggled it a few times before he said. "Because we have enough stupidity in the family with my brothers. And you, my girl, are stupid. Stupid, stupid, stupid." He jerked his fishing rod with each repetition until Charity wanted to seize it out of his hands and break it in two.

"I am not stupid."

"Of course you are. Here you are, almost of age, still in your brother's house, still taking care of others' children. Oh, I know why you wouldn't take one of us. Dickon is hopeless, and Davey's younger 'n you, and I—well, I'd've done you well enough, but I—"

He broke off, swallowed hard, and went on, "Oh, I know you look at me and think of Ned, and I reckon you shouldn't think of sad times, or your brother either, when you look at your husband. I understand that. But none of that signifies with Braden. He ain't the man I would've chosen for you—well, I'm the man I would've chosen for you—but he'll do. He's artistic, and you like that, and he'd talk to you of all those bluestocking subjects you enjoy, and he doesn't seem likely to beat you. He'd probably even be good to you. Hell, I did my best. Told him all about Polly Ferris's predilection for haystack romance. I even told her he was hers for the asking—"

Charity actually thought Crispin's machinations sweet, if ineffective. At least she hoped they had been ineffective.

"Didn't even notice her, 's far as I can tell. Only had eyes for you and all that tripe. And you know, Charity, I've always meant to marry you, at least until today, and I still had at least one eye for the likes of Polly. Of course," he added with an illustrative wink, "I would've closed it, had we married."

Charity's heart ached full in her chest, and she couldn't say why. Every word Crispin said, about himself, about Tristan, hurt her.

"Anyway, I wouldn't have let him win at fencing if I didn't think he'd treat you well."

This at least had the effect of diverting her. "You didn't really let him win."

Crispin pulled in his line and flicked the worm to restore it to life, then cast again. "I might have, if he hadn't beat me first. I'd decided, see, that if I couldn't have you, I'd rather lose you to some foreigner than to one of my cousins. Then I could tell myself it was just because I couldn't teach you Italian or take you off to my Italian villa or paint your portrait." He regarded her with honest puzzlement. "But he can. So why aren't you wedding him?"

Charity looked at the familiar face of her oldest friend, at his candid blue eyes, the unruly fair hair, the obstinate chin—such a dear face, so English and true—and then she closed her eyes. In the darkness she saw another face, one more exotic, more dangerous, with watchful dark eyes and a tender mouth. "Because—oh, Cris, you have given far more thought to what sort of husband he'd make me than he ever did. All he considered was what sort of wife I'd make."

"That's the problem?"

She opened her eyes to meet his astonished gaze. "Well, it seems to argue a lack of care for my feelings."

Crispin just shook her head. "What an idiot you are. I don't suppose any man thinks of that much, for we expect the lady we've chosen to martyr ourselves for will tell us what sort of husband she wants. And newly sheared sheep that we are, we'll comply with her every wish. For a sennight or so, at least." The tug on his line seemed to inspire him, for he tugged back and said brightly, "Maybe it's not too late to get him back. I'll drop a word in his ear if you like, though it didn't help Polly any."

"Don't you dare!" The prospect left Charity gasping like the fish Crispin had just expertly reeled in. "I've made my decision, and I shan't change it."

"Oh, no, you'd never change your mind, would you? At least not for some stupid reason like the one you just gave me."

With great dignity Charity got to her feet. Brushing the clinging moss off her skirt, she said coolly, "I thank you for your sage commentary, Mr. Hering. Though I have never asked for your advice, I know I shall always be privileged to receive it."

"You could do worse."

With this cryptic comment, Crispin applied himself impaling another worm.

She spent an hour alone in the church hall, pounding nail after helpless nail, building a booth that would probably stand up to explosion and hurricane, so well-nailed was it. Her ears were ringing and her palm stinging by the time the children came in, stomping their muddy feet on the clean floor.

She blessed the self-centeredness of children. Even Lawrence and Jeremy said nothing about her short-lived betrothal. They were too busy begging for real oars and boasting that their play would be the greatest event at the greatest Midsummer ever.

The rehearsal went quickly, and with a bit of time before the children were due home, she set them to making paper boats to carry candles on the village pond Midsummer Eve. She went from one child to another, kneeling down on the floor beside them and guiding their little hands. "Put them in the basket here when you are done, and I will tell you what else will occur at Midsummer."

They were young enough to love hearing the schedule again and again. So she started counting off events on her fingers. On Friday evening next, the children's games would be held, and prizes awarded to the first five finishers (the first eight if more than five finished) in each event. Then in the evening the great Beltane fire would be set on the green and the participants would hold hands and circle the blaze. "Then we all chant—"

Before Charity could finish, the children seated on the floor before her burst into unison: "Green is gold, fire is wet, fortune's told, dragon's met."

"And then we float the candles!" Lawrence cried out. "Wet fire! To tell our fortunes!"

Charity looked around to make sure the vicar wasn't about to overhear. "Yes, yes. These boats and their candles is one way we tell our future." Despite Mr. Langworth's objections, she hadn't been able to strip Midsummer of all its fortune-telling traditions. Almost every ritual, it seemed, had some prediction attached. She had culled a few of the less appealing ones from the agenda: no one really liked eating the locust seedpods they called St. John's Bread, and the local tradition that said the number of seeds predicted how many children each woman would have and how many her husband would sire, had led to some marital disagreements in earlier years. She had also persuaded Margo Ashton to forego the colorful turban and tent and instead merely interpret everyone's fortunes with the candle boats and the destiny cakes her husband the baker provided.

"And then the banquet happens. Between each course we will sing songs or perform tricks. And after that—"

"St. George!" Jeremy cried out. "My uncle!"

"Yes, Jeremy, your uncle will play St. George." Charity felt a sting somewhere near her heart, recalling the day—only last Saturday!—when Jeremy's uncle had won that role. Sternly she reminded herself that she would have to bring the costumes out of the choir loft and let them air out and remember to give scripts to Squire Hering, who was to play the king, and Molly Ferris, the princess. And Tristan, of course, would need a script, though St. George, a man of action, not conversation, had only a few lines. "And after that will be your play, and I don't need to tell you how much we're all looking forward to that."

"And then what?" Mary asked, getting up to dump a skirtful of boats into the basket.

"Well, after that, I imagine you'll all be going to bed!"

The chorus of protests that greeted this made her chuckle. Her laugh sounded rusty, as if she hadn't practiced it for weeks. "Well, if you aren't going to bed, what will you do?"

"Dance! With the grownups around the fire!"

"And stay up till midnight!"

She took advantage of this discussion to dismiss them, knowing that in their excitement they would run all the way home and hardly get wet at all, no matter how hard the rain was falling.

Lawrence and Jeremy, however, halted at the door. "Uncle Tristan!" Jeremy cried, and Charity's heart took an unaccustomed jerk. "Have you come to walk us home?"

"In a moment or so." He stood in the open doorway, blocking the meager light, shaking mistdrops from his bare dark head. Producing a handful of coins from his pocket, he said, "You run down to the bakery and get some cakes. But stay there to eat them, won't you? Otherwise they will get all soggy in the rain."

It was all done so adroitly that Charity hadn't time to escape. She bent to pick up the paper boats left on the floor, hoping her consternation didn't show in her face. After she dropped the boats into the wicker basket, she looked up to see that he had not moved from the entryway as if he was unsure of his welcome.

But then he smiled and came forward, and she straightened her shoulders. They neither of them needed to be embarrassed just because they had been betrothed and weren't any longer.

She hoped her pose of ease was as creditable as Tristan's. As was his wont, he was dressed casually, hatless, with a jacket but no waistcoat, his cravat knotted in that careless way that was all the more artistic for being entirely artless. She focused her attention on the shoulder of his gray jacket. But at his first words she glanced up, startled.

"I must apologize again. I fear I must have said something unforgivable yesterday, though I recall it not at all."

Without thinking, Charity replied, "You said—"

Tristan's face suddenly lightened with laughter. "Oh, Lord, don't repeat it. I have been taking comfort in my poor memory! But I do apologize for whatever it was. I hadn't any right even to argue with you, much less to insult you. It's entirely within your rights to decide you don't want to marry me. In fact," he added with a winning smile, "I thank you, as you said I would. I'm glad you realized this before we made any lifelong vows."

He was merely acknowledging what she knew to be true, that he was better off without a wife who wasn't right for him. Somehow that gave her little comfort. He had recovered quickly from his disappointment, considering how furious he had been only a day ago. "You are being very good about this."

He shrugged. "I haven't any choice, have I? I'd like to maintain friendly relations with you, so I can't sulk. We were friendly, weren't we, before I so precipitously demanded more?"

"I—I thought so."

"And you said you wanted to remain friends."

Charity recalled saying something of the sort to ease her way out of their betrothal, not that it had given him any immediate comfort. She often remained friends with former beaus; Terence Wetherby had been her favorite escort in London, and Crispin would always have her affection. But Tristan was different because they had been betrothed for those two days, because they had both imagined being so much more than friends. But she couldn't look in his hopeful, wary eyes and tell him she really thought it best that they never saw each other again. This sort of confusion, a distant voice reminded, is just what got you engaged in the first place.

But his voice, so warm now, so encouraging, drowned out the warning. "I shouldn't like awkwardness between us to cause discord. Anna and my nephews have grown attached to the Calder clan. I think Charlie is a good example to the boys, for he controls his temper so well, and they both of them need to learn that."

Charity shifted the basket to the other arm and rearranged the paper boats so they wouldn't crush each other. "Charlie does very well with the boys. He has come out of his shell a bit. I suppose it's because they look up to him as older and wiser. He is so used to being dismissed as just a child. But I think the boys will not regard our relations at all."

"But Anna will feel awkward, I know, if she thinks you and I are at odds." He added coaxingly, "Oh, you needn't worry that I will bother you again with unwelcome proposals.

I'm not like that poor sap Hering. I can take no for an answer."

He smiled and raised his hands as if in surrender, and Charity felt the sadness again full in her heart. It was the mention of Crispin that did it, she thought. She said brightly, "Oh, Crispin's decided I'm too fickle for his tastes. He would not save me from drowning now, I think."

"He seems to have taken this rather worse than I," Tristan said with a laugh. "Then I can take his place as former flame, can't I?"

She had no choice but to nod, and, as if this were an invitation, he crossed to the stage where she had set the basket. But he didn't come near her, only vaulting lightly up on the stage and walking to his triptych. "Come see what I did this morning. I was in an utter fury of activity. Don't know why."

She was curious enough to ignore the irony of his voice. She came up beside him as he pulled the cover off the middle panel, the one with the whale's great grinning mouth. What was new was the two little men impaled on the teeth. "Tristan—oh, Lord, I can't think what the vicar's going to say."

"He will say that the artist should make a full confession and repent. Come, now, *cara,* you did say the children liked a bit of gore in their Bible stories. And look at the expressions. Worthy of Hieronymous Bosch, I'd say, if I weren't so modest."

Bending closer, she could see the terror on the tiny faces. One looked exactly like Charlie when he had to visit the dentist. She had to laugh, but that wasn't enough to distract her attention from his casual endearment. *Cara.* It only meant that he meant them to be friends. He couldn't be so casual were his heart in shreds.

How easily, after all, he had moved back to friendship. Perhaps they never should have imagined that they could share anything more.

His mind must have been running in the same direction because he asked, with a quick glance at her, "Did your brothers take it any better than young Hering?"

"Oh, Charlie was worried only that he would not be able to exploit your nephews' labor any longer—he has recruited them to dig in the chalk formations for fossil materials. Francis only said that he knew all along it was too good to last. He hasn't said a word about it since."

Tristan shook his head with wonder. "He really is a much better brother than you deserve."

Her laughter was still rusty, but she found it oddly relaxing to be with Tristan. She always had to work so hard to be admirable, to be exemplary, and if she fell short, she knew how many people she would disappoint. But Tristan couldn't possibly become any more disappointed in her. "I know. I've never seen such restraint. He must be biting his tongue off. But he figures the rest of the populace will pick up his slack, and they have."

He regarded her sympathetically. "Has it been very bad?"

She gazed again at the fierce whale and his piteous victims, fighting off a wave of self-pity. "Cammie said the people in the village have—oh, a proprietary interest in me. That means, I guess, that they own me. It's all I deserve. I've been telling them how to live their lives since I was in pinafores, and they must be glad of the chance to turn the tables."

"You tell them—" His voice was suddenly low and fierce, and she was startled. He should be her most vociferous accuser; he shouldn't be feeling defensive for her. "That you know what is best for you. That you can make your own decisions."

Partly to ease the tension, partly to cover her own confusion, she laughed lightly. "Oh, I have been too arrogant, I think, and I deserve a comeuppance."

He dropped the subject without inquiring how his jilting could be considered her comeuppance. He was trying so hard not to accuse her or blame her; she saw the effort in the tense set of his jaw. But he resumed his friendly tone as he covered the panel back up. "Well, we must demonstrate to all that we neither of us nurse hurt feelings. If we go back to our earlier relationship as if it had never been disturbed, then they will have nothing to talk about."

Charity was more versed in the ways of villagers and knew that a resumption of their friendship would cause even more talk. But his expression was so hopeful, his manner so open, that she could only agree. She worried that he, too, had been exposed to intrusive comments and friendly advice these last two days. He must have hated it all.

Impulsively she invited him back home for tea. But he only smiled and shook his head. "No, I must take my nephews home, then go back to work. I hope I haven't painted myself out for the day because I'm tired of staring at that ship painting, and I mean to finish those last touches this afternoon." He said ruefully as he opened the door for her, "Extremes of emotion are not conducive to the artistic temperament, at least not my artistic temperament. That is another reason I am endeavoring to take a rational view of all this. I feel more creative already."

She lingered there, her hand near his on the old door. No wonder he desired a peaceful home, if his artistic temperament was such a sensitive instrument, ready to flee at the least disturbance. Used to soldiering on no matter what, Charity found this attitude alien and fascinating. "It must be very trying to have such a delicate creative process so easily overset. Surely many artists do their most impressive work under stress. Think of Michelangelo, who turned his anger at the Pope into those great frescoes. Don't you wish that you could harness emotional energy like that, instead of wasting it?"

His dark eyes glinted in amusement at her sensible observation. "You are right, of course! And surely it's all that separates me from Michelangelo, isn't it? But alas, I seem only able to waste my emotional energy in brooding and kicking walls and beating my nephews. Not very hard," he added at her startled look. "Had I no nephews, however, to waste my emotions on, perhaps I, too, would be painting the Sistine Chapel."

It seemed from his bantering tone as if he had exhausted all his anger at her. She hoped he had, especially if it affected his work. But it was lowering to know that a day was all it took to restore his equilibrium. "You are teasing me."

"Never!"

"Well, even if you are not Michelangelo, I would not like to be an impediment to your art."

"No need to worry." With a light imperative hand on her back, he urged her out the door into the misty afternoon. "I've a commitment to meet, after all, for the Midsummer painting. And so do you." At her startled glance, he added, "Don't you recall? You were going to paint the background. That middle panel is done, except for your work. Tomorrow, after you rehearse the children, I'll bring the paints you need and get you started."

"But—but—" That promise she made a fortnight ago, a lifetime ago, came back to haunt her. She had so many other things to do in the week before the fair; she couldn't take this on, too. Still, she had promised, and she had never yet gone back on a promise—or at least a promise she could keep.

Ignoring her hesitation, Tristan called to his nephews, who had been jumping with both feet into every puddle this side of the bakery. Then he whistled, and his grazing horse came trotting over from the green, tame as a dog. Swinging lithely into the saddle, he said, "I shall see you tomorrow, then."

Charity murmured something affirmative as he cantered off, promising his running nephews that he would let them win the race home. But she wondered if she could really bear to meet him to work on the painting, that constant reminder of who he was and what had passed between them. She would have to, she decided. She owed that much to the children, who were working so hard on their Midsummer play. And she owed that much to Tristan, who was being so forgiving about the wrong she had done him.

Chapter Seventeen

On Saturday the children made it almost all the way through the play without stumbling. Charity was giving them the promised glimpse of the whale triptych when the black-caped schoolmaster emerged from behind the crates in the alcove and clambered up on the stage. She took one look at the fury in his face and said, "Go on home now, children. I'll show you more tomorrow after church—if you promise not to tell any grownups!"

The children filed out solemnly, much as if they were still in Mr. Greenaway's school, several casting looks back at their angry teacher. Charity pulled the cover straight over the painted panel and turned to face him. She had been dreading the moment he learned of all she had done with his play. Better they have it out now than in front of the entire parish on Midsummer Eve.

He didn't give her a chance to greet him or to divert him. His hands balled up into fists, he advanced on her, stopping short only a few feet away. "What have you done with my play?"

She almost shot back that she had improved it, for she didn't like feeling crowded by any man. But it would do no good to anger him further. In a reasonable tone, she answered, "You told me to revise it to fit the occasion. Therefore I simplified the language so that the children could speak the lines. It was also rather long, almost three-quarters of an hour, so I cut some of the soliloquies."

"Some! You cut them all! I couldn't believe what I heard those stupid children recite—so simple, so short. My soliloquies were gone, gone! Every last line—all my lovely poetry!" His fists opened; he turned his hands over and gazed at his palms as if somewhere in them were the lost lines.

"But at the outset, you knew this was to be performed by children. You did give me carte blanche to make what changes I deemed necessary. And I kept the structure of the story exactly the same, only I combined some of the arguments Jonah has with the sailors—"

"The most polished part of all! If only you knew how I labored over that portion, you would not be so blithe!"

Charity thought that since he had written the whole play in less than a week, she had probably labored over it more than he had. She, at least, had given some consideration to performers and audience. But one glance at his tightly clenched face told her that Mr. Greenaway was not in the mood for home truths. "I've still got the original script. You must think of this as the children's version, and the original as the adult version. Think of the possibilities!"

"Possibilities! I wrote this to be performed so that I could hear my words spoken. And what did I hear? Distortion. Reduction. Corruption!"

Fury thickened his voice and tensed his shoulders, and she knew a moment's anxiety. She had seen such anger in men's eyes before, though never directed at her, and she knew it could presage violence. Unobtrusively she moved back toward the edge of the stage, closer to the open window so that, if need be, her screams could be heard.

Such precaution was probably needless. This was David Greenaway, the ineffectual schoolmaster, whom she had pitied but never feared. He was so very angry, however, and some vestige of guilt made her feel all the more vulnerable. Soothingly she said, "Well, you needn't worry, I—"

"No, don't! Don't you try that! Don't you try to—to *manage* me!" He took a step forward, clenching his fists in front of him. "You do that with everyone. Everything. You always think you know what is best for everyone. For the village, for my school—distributing those Gothic novels at the commencement ceremonies last year! Gothics! For my play! For my play!"

Something in her responded to his anguish. She reached out to him in conciliation, in apology. But he flung her hand aside. "No! I won't have you talk me out of this. I want my name off that—that travesty! I shan't be associated with it!"

"Mr. Greenaway, let's be reasonable. If you don't want to be known as the playwright, I can't insist. But—"

"And I shan't let you use my title either!"

"Jonah and the Whale?" At this, Charity's sense of the absurd got the better of her. "Well, it's hardly your title, is it? I think the Scriptures had it first."

"Don't you laugh at me! Don't you—"

As he raised his hand, she stepped back, forgetting how close she was to the edge. She felt the floor vanish under her back foot, then in that moment of blind panic heard her name and running steps.

She found herself caught up in Tristan's arms, firm and secure. "Thank you," she whispered, then, in a stronger voice, added, "I'm fine. You may put me down."

He did but kept his arm around her shoulders while she found her footing. The residue of terror seeped away as he held her. She took a deep breath and nodded to him, and then drew back closer as Mr. Greenaway dropped off the stage next to them.

She couldn't believe it, but he was still angry, and didn't moderate his tone even in the presence of another man. "You deserved that, after what you did to my work. You deserve worse. And you'll get it."

He started to shove past her, but Tristan shot out a hand to block him. "Don't threaten the lady, you cur. And don't ever, ever think of touching her again."

Greenaway was too angry to mind the warning and yanked himself away, in the process brushing Charity with his arm.

With lightning swiftness, Tristan grabbed him by the lapel of his scholar's cape and hauled him up. "You haven't learned your lesson, have you, schoolmaster?"

The uppercut connected smartly with Mr. Greenaway's jaw, jerking his head back and clattering his teeth together. Charity resisted the urge to cheer, especially when he picked himself off the floor and stumbled out, whispering, "You'll regret this, Charity Calder."

As the door slammed behind him, Charity tried to rearrange her face in sterner lines. "I suppose you think that was the appropriate response to this situation."

Rubbing his knuckles, Tristan grinned down at her, his dark eyes alight with triumph. "It must be, or it wouldn't have felt so good. It's all he deserves, threatening a woman. Don't worry, I won't let him near you again."

Shaking her head, she took his fist and turned it over to gently stroke one red knuckle. When the red faded to pink and finally disappeared, she dropped his hand with an exasperated laugh. "Paint! I though you might have broken your hand and ruined your career."

"A paltry sort you must think me, to break a hand on a jaw like that."

"Where did you learn to box?"

"I told you Eton was a hellish place. The Etonians took exception to my accent, you see." As he said that, she heard a slight deepening of that elusive accent. "That's all I learned in three months there—to fight." He smiled at her disbelief. "Stood me in good stead in all those fights on the docks in Naples."

As if this were an everyday encounter, he retrieved the leather bag he had dropped and began drawing out his brushes. He was so very nonchalant, fluffing the bristles up as he approached his painting, reaching out to grab up the palette he had left on the table. But he seemed brighter somehow, at least in Charity's vision. Perhaps it was only the afternoon light streaming in through the windows or the reflected glow from his eyes. But there he was, gleaming, burnished by triumph.

"Thank you," she said finally. "He—he frightened me."

"You didn't show it. Help me, *mia,* if you are feeling up to it. You've got a good start on the background, but there's so very much more to do. Why ever did I propose a triptych?"

He was so casual she almost missed that sweet Italian endearment, but then she realized he was trying to comfort her without alarming her. He would know that work soothed her best. She took up the blue-daubed brush he prepared for her and came to stand next to him at the painting. And after a few moments her hand stopped shaking and she was able to paint the sky instead of just making streaks on the canvas.

Only then did he move farther away to fill in the fingers of God. And only then did he mention the confrontation with Greenaway. "I take it he objected to your direction of his play."

"Yes. But you were there, weren't you, when he first gave it to me? You recall I told him that I would have to make it fit the children better."

"You did say that. And he agreed." He reached out his brush and dabbed a bit of pink on her nose, and as she laughed and tried to rub it off with a rag, he added, "Don't let him worry you. You did the best you could with it. He is typical of his sort—he thinks whatever he produces must needs be art."

She tucked the rag away into her pocket, still troubled. "But he is right, you know. I do always think I know best. I do—manage things. I always have. No one's ever minded before, or at least no one has ever said so."

He stopped painting and gazed at her, then slipped an arm around her waist so that his palette was dangerously close to her muslin'd hip and his mouth was dangerously close to her ear. His tender words stirred her hair. "Charity, *cara,* you are what you are. And I for one wouldn't have you one whit less than that."

She felt his lips brush her temple and unthinking lifted her face to meet his kiss. But before their mouths met, he pulled away, laughing. "Oh, I forgot I haven't the right to do that anymore. Amazing how quickly I became accustomed to it."

As if nothing had happened, he went back to his painting. When she only stood there, her anguish knotted in her throat, he glanced over at her as if nothing had happened. "Charity, we've six days till Midsummer Eve. And I'm sure you have many other tasks to finish before then. The play, for example." And then, as she slowly began to paint again, he went on, "Jeremy has learned the whole thing, you know, not just his own bellows. He recited all three acts for his mother and me yesterday, with Lawrence supplying the whale noises. I think it is much better than anything written by that—*oca pocco cotto.*"

It sounded like an insult, and Miss Falesham had taught her none of those in Italian class. Charity found herself smiling. "What does that mean?"

"Undercooked goose. You see how much Italians love food—insults and compliments both take the form of food."

By the time she had filled in the background behind the whale, he had taught her how to call someone a stupid beef, a sweet biscuit, a nagging tripe, and a limp fish, along with the associated hand gestures. By the time Tristan pronounced her accent perfect and her gesticulation worthy of a Neapolitan longshoreman, she had nearly forgotten the ugly incident that preceded his lesson.

As the afternoon went on, they fell silent and applied themselves to their work. Painting was a lulling activity, drawing Charity into a world of color and light and almost no sound. Once Tristan spoke absently to her in Italian, and she smiled and decided not to embarrass him by asking for a translation. It must be the Italian part of him that paints, she thought, for he had never before confused his languages. She stepped back, looking critically at her daubings next to the precise lines and curves of his work. Perhaps when she knew more Italian herself, she would make a better show as a painter—and understand Tristan better.

Chapter Eighteen

Tristan was doing his best to persuade Charity that she had a future in painting theatrical backdrops when they were interrupted. He wasn't ungrateful to see his nephew shuffle in, dragging a picnic basket behind him. It meant he would have another hour in Charity's company, even if he must needs share her with Lawrence, too.

The boy planted himself before the stage, arms crossed over his chest. "Cammie made me bring you tea."

Charity looked startled, as if she had never meant to be occupied in the church hall through teatime. "Well, that was kind of her! And of you, too, Lawrence."

But Lawrence wasn't to be cozened out of his sullens. His benevolence, it turned out, was really a punishment for having refused to do his lessons that morning. "Jeremy got to go rock-hunting with Charlie, and I had to bring you tea! It's not fair!"

He howled that eternal lament once more for good measure. Tristan groaned while Charity wrinkled her nose and resorted to bribery. She sat down on the edge of the stage and began unloading the basket. "Come it beside me and have a crumpet. See, I'll spread some apricot preserves on it."

Even the famous apricot preserves didn't divert Lawrence from his grievance. Through a mouthful of crumpet, he reiterated, "It's not fair. He always gets his way because he's younger and everyone likes him best."

"Everyone likes him better," Charity corrected, exactly as Mrs. Cameron would. "With only the two of you, there can be no best."

It was a measure of her distraction, Tristan thought, that she did not anticipate how Lawrence might misinterpret her grammar lesson. "So you like him best, too, don't you?"

"Be quiet, Lawrence," his uncle said unsympathetically. "And close your mouth when you chew."

Lawrence subsided into mutterings, slumping down next to Charity on the stage. The adults resumed their conversation, Charity noting a paint spot on Tristan's hand that didn't match any part of their project. "What are you painting now? I mean, of your own work."

With curious Charity, secrecy was the best policy—if fascination was the aim. "Oh, it's a study of brown."

"Of brown? Brown what?"

"The color brown. Or rather the colors. Fascinating, the brown spectrum is. I'm starting around gold and ending at sable."

Her confusion was pretty enough to sketch—wrinkled forehead, chewed lip. "But what are you painting? What is the subject?"

He shrugged and quoted yet another master, this one a radical who contended the human face was merely an arrangement of circles and half-circles. "Oh, subject doesn't matter. Only composition and chromatics count."

Bored with this artistic discussion, Lawrence begged another crumpet. As Charity leaned over to get it, something gold slipped from the demure neckline of her blue cambric gown. "What's that?" Lawrence demanded, half-rising from his perch. "Around your neck. The necklace."

Charity's cheeks pinkened as she replaced the gold circle under her bodice. "Just my locket. Now shall I spread preserves or—"

Secrecy was a lure to little boys, also, and little earls especially hated being kept in the dark. "Let me see it!"

Tristan sensed one of Lawrence's patented temper fits coming on and rose, speaking sharply to head it off. "No. Now sit down, boy, and behave yourself."

The tone that always subdued Jeremy only fired his elder brother. He lowered his brow and snaked out his hand and grabbed at the gold chain, his fingers leaving smudges on Charity's pale gold skin. Instinctively she pulled back from the attack, and Lawrence, triumphant, ashamed, jumped off the stage and dashed away, holding up the broken chain.

"Where's the locket?" Charity whispered, pressing a hand searchingly against her heart. But the locket had not fallen safely into her gown.

"Get back here, Lawrence." Roughly Tristan grabbed his nephew's arm and took possession of the chain. Then he forced Lawrence to his knees on the floor under a half-built booth. "Find it. It must have dropped here somewhere."

Charity was pale and trembling as she started to join the boy's search. But Tristan took her arm and eased her back into her seat. "It just fell under that booth. He'll find it—" he raised his voice— "if he knows what's good for him."

He had seen the intrepid Charity shaken already once today, but he had learned how to comfort her—quietly, unobstrusively, without drawing attention to her vulnerability. He sat beside her and held her hand as she watched Lawrence's search.

When Lawrence emerged from under the booth, her shoulders drooped in a release of tension. Head bowed, the boy trudged back to them. "Here it is. I'm sorry, Charity. I didn't mean to break it."

She took the little gold locket from him and held it clasped in her fist for a moment. Then, slowly, she opened her hand. "It's just the miniatures of my brothers." She took her other hand back from Tristan and faltered with the latch. "Come here, Lawrence."

The boy sidled close to her arm. "See? That's Ned. He was my twin. And there's Joey. He was our youngest. That's all, Lawrence. Nothing exciting after all."

Lawrence stood gazing at the little pictures—two boys, both dark like Charity, one very young and one nearly a man. "Do you mean they're dead? But that boy—he's my age!"

"Yes, but he wasn't sturdy like you, and the influenza took him. He died late one night—it was a long time ago." She closed the locket with a decisive snap. "Why don't you run and tell Cammie you accomplished your mission? Perhaps she will let you chase after Charlie after all."

As Lawrence made his escape, Tristan rose and began to clear away his supplies. He couldn't stay next to her without wanting to hold her and let her cry on his shoulder. But he knew better than to let his tenderness overwhelm them both; she needed understanding as much as sympathy, someone to listen to her for a change.

The locket rested in her lap as she fussed with the broken link, taking it off the chain then slipping it back in and trying to squeeze it shut. When she finally spoke, her voice came muffled as she bent over the necklace. "Poor Lawrence. He doesn't mean to be so difficult. He just hates to be denied. Neddy was just the same. He could never abide the word *no*. I learned that soon enough—whatever he was told not to do, he had to do."

She dropped the chain next to the locket and raised her hands to her hair, pulling it back and plaiting it with quick jerky motions. She still didn't look at Tristan, only gazing at the stack of booths near the window. "It's just that word *no*. You should use some roundaboutation instead. I could always work Ned around without saying it if I had time. Papa never liked to tell him no either. But when he wanted to leave school and join the Navy, Papa kept saying no. The war was over, but he just couldn't let him go. He loved him best, you see, and we'd just lost Joey. I think I might have talked Papa round—what else would Ned have done with his life, if not joined the military?"

She picked up the chain again, threaded it through the locket, and held the broken ends together in her fist. Finally she stuffed it in her pocket. "But Ned couldn't wait. He ran off and volunteered on the first ship he saw in Portsmouth Harbor, an old ugly corvette bound for Riga. It just blew up one night—old gunpowder, they said. He hadn't told me what he was planning. It was the only secret he ever kept from me. If only I'd known, I would have stopped him." She finally looked at him then, not in accusation, but he could see the anguish in her eyes. "I never let myself imagine what it must have been like for him that night. But your painting—it was like that, wasn't it? Terrifying, with no escape. Burning or drowning."

There was no use apologizing, but he knew nothing else to say. "I'm sorry you saw it."

"No, no. It's not your fault. It must be a great painting if it felt so true. But that's the danger, isn't it?" She felt in her pocket for the little gold circle, opened it up, and studied her brothers' faces. "I keep trying to forget that. If it's true, if it's real, it will hurt sometime, no matter how much I try to make it right."

Knowing it was inadequate, he offered the obvious. "But if you can't make it right, it doesn't mean you've failed. You don't have to take all the world's burdens on your shoulders."

"Oh, I know." She glanced at him now, her smile a little crooked. "I know that the world would go on turning without my help. I'm not essential at all—oh, don't pay me any mind. I'm just a bit blue-deviled because I saw the date today and realized that Ned's birthday is Saturday. He'd be coming of age."

Tristan envisioned the date carved on the headstone in the churchyard: June 19—Saturday. "But you are twins. It's your birthday, too."

She looked startled as if this had never occurred to her.

"Well, yes, I suppose so. But we don't celebrate it anymore. I visit the graves, but that is all."

He found it so intensely sad he could hardly keep from gathering her close and vowing to banish all sorrow from her life. But of course, she would recognize the emptiness of that. Sorrow was inevitable in life. She just hoped for a little happiness, too, and that she wouldn't have to make it all herself.

So he only jumped off the stage and held out his hand to help her down. "Now that the hand of God is done, I feel inspired to another divine work. I think I will try to use the last bit of sun on that brown study of mine."

She gave him a sidelong glance as they left the church hall. "You work too much, you know."

"Finally! Finally I understand what is meant by that old English aphorism, the pot calling the kettle black."

This made her laugh, and he felt cheered. Perhaps he made her happy after all. At least he could divert her on those few occasions when she let herself feel sad.

She didn't let go of his hand as she usually did, as she was supposed to do, but held it shyly until they entered the public road. "Tristan, will you do me a favor?"

"Anything," he swore. "Within reasonable limits, that is."

The ironical glint was back in her dark eyes. "This is reasonable, I think. Would you teach me a bit of Italian? I mean, more than just insults."

This he hadn't expected. "I suppose I could. I don't usually speak it in England."

"Not even with Anna?"

"No. I doubt she's fluent any longer. But I imagine I could. Why?"

She took a deep breath as if ready to confess to a crime. "I learned it at school but haven't had much call to keep up with it. Oh, I've read Dante's *Inferno*, but I don't imagine Italian is still spoken that way."

"I don't imagine it ever was, even in Dante's time." Just

before they reached the gates of Calder Grange, he said, "I should have known you would ask me that."

That annoyed her as he figured it would. She regarded him through her dark lashes, suspicion all over her face. "I am glad you find me so predictable."

"Oh, predictable you are not. Once I might have called you inconsistent—in fact, I think I did."

She didn't look away, but color crept up her cheeks at this reference to the unmaking of their betrothal.

"But now I see that you are consistent. Not, oh, symmetrical, mind you." He held the gate open for her, musing, "Only, well, designed with a logic I haven't come across before but is nonetheless logical. I cannot predict a thing about you, but when some facet of you is revealed I think, yes, that makes some unlikely sort of sense. Some harmony that echoes the harmony of the universe."

She liked that better as he hoped she would. She would not give over to flattery; she used that so much herself she could sense Spanish coin from far away. But objective appraisal—she liked that. She wasn't used to having anyone study her so closely or analyze her so well. But then she hadn't known an artist before. Lucky for him, observation was his stock-in-trade.

To keep his compliment unmawkish, he added, "And so I realize that a thrifty girl like you would *naturally* prefer to get her Italian lessons for free."

Her pleased look vanished and she put on a vexatious face. But he saw the laughter in her eyes and knew he was making progress. She took more pleasure in his company than she ever had before. Now he just had to convince her how significant that was.

Just as Tristan was turning back toward Haverne, Charlie Calder caught up with him to thank him for a fossil he had sent over with Jeremy. "The ammonite is a fine specimen of an extinct species. I can see just how closely it resembles the modern pearly nautilus, *Nautilus pompilius*, that is."

"I thought you were a dead loss at Latin."

Charlie ducked his head. "I can't abide Virgil, but the genus and species of mollusks are simple. Could—could I ask you a bit of advice?"

The boy looked so brave and abashed Tristan could hardly say no, though he would have liked to refer the boy to the much wiser Sir Francis for counsel. Apparently this way the sort of question one didn't ask an elder brother, however wise.

"You went to Eton, didn't you?"

Having expected some excruciating question about the physical changes of pubescent boys, Tristan had no appropriate answer prepared. Finally he came up with one. "Yes. For a few months. After that I was privately tutored."

"How did you manage that?"

"I don't recall, actually." At Charlie's disappointment, he tried harder. "We usually spent the winter in Italy, so that first autumn I just left. I think that was the year the French took Naples, so we couldn't escape Italy for a couple years."

"That's no good then."

Charlie's disappointment was a bit of a sting. Charity at least had found the story fascinating, how they hid their British passports under the floorboards and spoke only Italian, even to each other, so that he hardly remembered his English when they got out.

But Charlie's intent came clearer when he said with a crooked grin, "It's not as if I can contrive a war just to keep from Eton. Why didn't you go back when you got home?"

"Oh, my father paid no mind that I never went back to school. He hadn't much respect for the Eton education as so many of his students had come from there."

"When you say you were privately tutored, what do you mean?"

"I studied with an art master in Florence, and then in London. I was supposed to have a tutor in Latin and the rest of the academic subjects, but I can't remember having one after my mother died. Father kept me sharp in mathematics, but I still can't conjugate a Latin verb."

Charlie's eager nod worried Tristan, so he added, "It would not be an ideal sort of schooling for most. I wanted to be an artist and cared for naught else. Most boys aren't so focused in their studies."

"Most boys don't study at all." Charlie kicked scornfully at the graveled drive. "Especially not at Eton. They only cane the younger boys and make them cry. I know. Barry's told me. I wouldn't fit in because I want to learn."

Tristan could only agree, though he suspected Charity would not be pleased. "It's a sad case when you have to avoid school to learn. But you can't just end your schooling at the age of twelve."

"I want schooling. I just don't want school." Charlie chewed thoughtfully on his lip, then nodded. Some decision had been reached; Tristan only hoped he would not be blamed for it.

"Charlie, wait." Tristan glanced back toward the Grange; Charity had already vanished inside. "Before you go off to meet your future, I've a favor to ask you. How effective are you at diversionary tactics?"

Charlie considered this question with gratifying seriousness. "I always talk my brothers out of thrashing me. I expect I'm effective at diversion."

"Good, I have an assignment for you then. Only it's your sister, not your brother, you must divert. On Saturday next, after Midsummer."

Back at Haverne, Tristan walked silent as a cat past the schoolroom, but it was to no avail. The sharp-eared boys had heard him coming up the stairs and were waiting for him at the door to his studio.

Lawrence hung back, looking chastened, but his brother cried, "Uncle Tris! Can I have a peppermint?"

Tristan had taken a trick from Charity's arsenal and kept peppermints handy, finding them to be an effective means of closing the boys' mouths when necessary. Jeremy was young enough and fetching enough to get away rifling his uncle's pockets, but Lawrence knew better than to test his credit.

"Give one to your brother," Tristan reminded Jeremy, who had found his prize. "What would you say, boys, to an excursion to Dover Monday? I've got to make a stop at the shipping office, but there will be time to visit the market. You can each have a half-crown to spend."

Dover, full of soldiers and sailors and Frenchies and seagulls, was one of the most exciting places in the world as far as the boys were concerned. Jeremy started listing all the places he wanted to visit and items he meant to buy, but Lawrence only frowned and unwrapped his peppermint. Finally he said, "I could take Charity's chain to the jewelers to get it fixed. Will that take more than a half-crown?"

Tristan answered gently, "I don't think so. That's a good idea, Lawrence. If you take it Monday, you'll get it fixed before Saturday. And Saturday will be the right day to give it to her."

"No, Friday." Jeremy's mouth came muffled around his candy. "Friday's Midsummer Eve and the fair."

"Exactly. She'll be too busy Friday to be bothered. Saturday, all her work will be done, and she'll be free again. Now if you leave me to paint and are very good for Mrs. Cameron, we'll take my phaeton to Dover instead of a carriage."

"I get to sit next to you!" Jeremy cried. "I said it first!"

Lawrence was inclined to argue the point, but he did so reasonably enough, without striking any blows or calling names worse than "sticky-face Jerry." Jeremy responded with equal civility, citing precedence and authority for his case like the nattiest London barrister.

What good boys they have turned out to be, Tristan mused.

Once he had thought them both merely loud, dirty creatures, the only distinctions between them that the bigger one was louder and the little one dirtier. Now they were individuals to him—well, they were still loud, and as for dirty, he supposed he should make them wash off all the peppermint residue before they left. But under the lint-stuck sugary glaze, each had his own face. Lawrence's was pugnacious, his nature shown in the conflict between golden hair and brown eyes; Jeremy's was elfin, his dark gaze darting quickly, curiously around him.

Before the boys lost their tempers or got disgustingly sticky, Tristan picked them up one at a time and faced them toward the backstairs, then unlocked his door. Back in his studio, he prepared to work, changing into his painting clothes, mixing his oils, assembling his palette, clearing his mind.

He lit a lamp, for the studio was darker than he liked. With the approach of summer had come the clouds this land was known for. No rain, but fog in the morning, haze in the afternoon, mist at night, fading down to meet the gray sea: this was the England he remembered, the one that created Constable and Turner with their vaporous backgrounds and ambiguous edges. He had always thought his art required more light than this, so he had done most of his painting in sunny Italy. England was for conducting business.

But perhaps he was more adaptable than he realized. Here he was in England, on an overcast day, and ready to paint. He was even experimenting with painting at night and finding it feasible. The radiance cast by his vision—and by two dozen candles and five lamps carefully arranged—could more than make up for the lack of sun. The trick, he supposed, was choosing an English subject.

Preparations completed in just the precise order, he carried the lamp past several unfinished canvases with scarcely a twinge of conscience. He set the lamp on the shelf, tilted the shade to reduce the glare, and yanked the green baize cover off his new project. It was the study in brown—a dull color, some might say, hardly worthy of the fabled Hale palette. But it required an eye like his to discern the splendor in that prosaic hue. Brown—oh, it had its own prism, from the near-black clod of rich Kent soil through the robustness of burnished parquet to the pale gold of sunlit skin.

"Mixing the colors is all," his ancient Florentine master used to tell him. "Look at Michelangelo—now he was an alchemist of color." (Gioberti had been old enough to recall when Michelangelo's paintings glowed, before the soot of the ages had dulled and sophisticated his colors.) But Tristan knew that distinguishing the chromatics was just as essential, and he could close his eyes and see all the shadings and distinctions and contrasts that made up the brown spectrum in his memory.

It was not prosaic at all, this color brown, for it started with gold, the gold of the sun-blessed cheek of a girl whose bonnet never stayed on her tumbled dark curls.

Chapter Nineteen

All Charity needed at the end of a long, trying day was the sight of her brother sprawled at her desk in the parlor, eating nuts while marking on her best notepaper. "Barry, for goodness' sake, what are you doing here again?"

Barry glanced up guiltily and hid his scrawlings under a book. "Had to bring Charlie back from London," he said with a grin. "You'll be glad to hear you're over the measles. Hey, what's this about you giving Tristan back his ring?"

She had forgotten that, when Barry left Sunday, it was with the anticipation of a new brother-in-law. What a long week it had been. "We decided we wouldn't suit."

"Stupid. Wouldn't suit. Well, I'd say you'd suit to an inch." She opened her mouth to tell him to stubble it, but he had already veered away to another subject. "Charlie's just telling me about the Midsummer Games. Doesn't know much. Can't even tell me who's in the children's events."

Now that he was pointed out, Charity realized her quietest brother was curled up in the hooded chair, cradling a large crystal in his arms. "I told you," he said wearily. "Charity made me sign up for the obstacle race. That whole pack from over Elham way is in it, too. Mary Moseby's supposed to be in the eight-and-under girls' egg toss, with the other girls eight and under!"

"Big help you are. I just want to know who's the best in

each event. Willie Morris and Perry Laidlaw—is that a good wheelbarrow team? I mean, I want to cheer for the winners, not the losers."

"Very sporting, Barry," Charlie said acidly. "Well, I can't help you much. It's not as if these people are my *friends.*"

No, Charity thought sadly, not your friends. Just children you have known all your life.

"What about the three-legged race?"

Charlie perked up at this. "Well, actually, I think Lawrence and Jeremy have a chance at that. I've been teaching them how to walk together, and they don't fall down more than once each race. And Jerry's pretty good at the six-and-under sack race, I'd say."

Charity smiled at him, relieved that he'd had to adopt the younger boys this way. They fought over his company, and that had to be balm to his fragile spirit. She regarded even Barry more benevolently now. "Cook's son is in the sprint. You might think to cheer for him."

"Is he good?"

"Well, he's been dodging her wooden spoon for ten years now," Charlie said with a laugh. The Calder cook was known for rapping any hand, even Sir Francis's, that edged toward her cooking. "I imagine he's the quickest boy in Kent by now."

"Good!" Barry said, pulling out his sheet and scrawling something.

He wrote so quickly that Charity could tell he wasn't making notes on Classical Rhetoric or Euclidean Geometry. She shook her head. "Barry, if you come home next week for the fair, when are you going to have time to study for exams?"

"Study?" Barry looked up with brow furrowed, as if this was a foreign word. "Oh, don't worry. I'm a Calder, remember? I always have it under control."

She suppressed a sigh. Some how that wasn't much of a consolation. "What is Francis going to say when he sees you?"

"Already saw me. Didn't say anything. Oh, he said, 'You home already? Tell your sister I've gone to Haverne to check on the livestock. I'll probably stay to sup there.' " Barry brightened, pleased with himself. "What do you know! I remembered to give you the message! Sure was distracted, our Francis. Seemed to think it was my Summer Hols already."

"And you did nothing to correct his mistake?" Charity asked.

Barry jumped up, stuffing his notes in his pocket. "My mother didn't raise any idiots. 'Cept you, of course." He dodged away, though she only flung a scowl in his direction. "I shan't be home to supper either. Meeting Jacob at the Rose and Crown—and I'm late!"

"Barry!" She shook her head, wondering if he would ever be mature enough to be released into the general population. "You can't go wearing your traveling clothes. Do change first."

"Right, right. Don't wait up. I'll be late!"

"And loud," Charlie murmured. He flashed an oddly adult smile at his sister, then, holding his crystal securely, he loped out of the parlor.

After dinner, when the light was fading from the sky, Charity put the finishing touches on St. George's dragon. It still needed to be painted red and stuffed with paper, but as it lay limply across her lap, she could imagine how fierce it would look in the Midsummer parade. She wondered if her actors had been studying their scripts. The squire had been playing his part for years and could probably recite it in his sleep, and Molly had sworn to have hers memorized before the final and only rehearsal on Thursday. But Tristan—

As she took tiny stitches to make wrinkles in the snout, she remembered that she had been sewing the tail when she broke off her engagement. In such prosaic details was her short engagement told. They had become engaged during a rehearsal and unengaged over a cloth dragon. And, perhaps, they became friends again next to a painted whale.

"Miss Calder?"

Bess, the upstairs maid, was at the parlor door, holding up a crumpled sheet of paper. "I just went into straighten up Master Barry's room, and in the pocket of his breeches I found this paper. I thought it might be important, and as I was going home, I thought I'd leave it with you. He'll likely be searching high and low for it."

Bidding her an absent goodbye, Charity studied the page Barry had left behind. Here was the list of events of the Midsummer games, the names of participants, and after them a series of numbers: 2-3, 5-2, 3-1. She'd seen enough Racing Forms in her time to recognize this pattern and what it meant.

The Rose and Crown's dark taproom on a Saturday night wasn't really a place for ladies. The air was thick with cigar smoke, the tables were cluttered with tankards of ale, and the men at the bar turned and stared when she walked in. But Charity had crossed that threshold more than once in her youth to collect her father when he forgot to come home.

She located Barry at the table her father used to haunt. His chair was tipped back against the wide leaded window, but clattered down when she sat next to him. He and Jacob Hering were already a bit disguised, but blinked owlishly at her.

"Charity, this ain't really the place for you. Let me get you a drink." Barry raised his hand to call for another tankard of ale, and Jacob pushed his glass over to her, in case she'd like to share.

"No, thank you," she murmured, glancing around her. Only when the waiter came and left did she drag the paper out of her pocket and slam it down in front of her brother. In a low, angry whisper, she asked, "What's this, Barry? A racing form on the Midsummer games?"

Barry snatched it up with a guilty gasp. "Where—where did you find this?"

"In your breeches. Or rather Bess found it."

When Barry only shrugged, she gave way to exasperation, kicking him under the table. At least she thought she was kicking Barry; Jacob jerked back, aggrieved. "Ow, Charity, leave me be, will you?"

"Tell me, Barry, or—or I'll tell Francis, and he'll cut off your allowance quicker than you can wink."

"Aw, Sis, don't be such a prude. So we're getting together a little flutter on Midsummer. I made six pounds off Tristan's fencing last week just from keeping my ear to the ground and hearing he used to teach it."

"He *taught* fencing?" Jacob's face took on the same sulky look he wore after Charity turned down his half-hearted proposal. "You might have told me before he cut me to shreds in front of Molly."

"You might have told *me* that you were going to cut me out with Molly soon as my back was turned," Barry retorted, then glanced quickly at his sister.

But she cared naught about his adolescent passion for the future star of Drury Lane. "You can't seriously expect to make book on the girls' egg carry and the six-and-under sack race!"

"Just a bit of sport—something new—the girls run truer to form than most of the nags at Newcastle." Barry smoothed the wrinkles from his form, sullen again. "I can't quit on it, Charity; I'm keeping the book. I've already taken bets and gotten seven of the lads to toddle down from Oxford next weekend."

"Seven?" Charity's heart sank. All planning to stay at Calder Grange, no doubt. But that was the least of her worries. "You've already started taking bets?"

"Yes. And you know what that means."

She rubbed at the headache on either side of her forehead. If Barry reneged on the bets now, he would be violating one of those strange rules that made up a gentleman's code of honor. Besides, if she knew her brother, he'd probably already spent some of the money.

Barry exchanged his sullen look for one more calculated to

wring pity from his sister's heart. "You can't tell Francis. You know if he knew he'd expect me to do the honorable thing."

"I know he'd expect you not to get in such a coil in the first place. I suppose you're part of this, Jake?"

Jacob nodded. Crispin, too, then. And half of Trinity College, Oxford, no doubt. A dark suspicion stabbed her. "You weren't planning any—any interference with the results, were you?"

Both boys drew up scandalized at this as if it were inconceivable that someone who could bet on children's races might tamper with them, too. But neither of them was faking outrage, and a bit of dread seeped out of Charity.

Barry must have sensed he was in the homestretch because he leaned forward and said coaxingly, "Think of it, Charity. Seven down from Oxford, all plump in the pocket. I'll see that they each buy something from the jumble booth and put money in the poor box, too."

"And they're sure to buy lots of ale," Jacob put in helpfully.

Charity was thinking feverishly, trying to come up with a solution to the coil her brother had handed her. He didn't even seem to understand how deep he had dug himself, making book on the Midsummer games. She couldn't call a halt to it; she knew Barry and knew he would somehow see the only honorable route as continuing his scheme surreptitiously. All she could do was try to contain it.

"All right, Barry, you listen to me. I won't tell Francis, and I won't tell the vicar. But don't bring anyone else into this—this syndicate of yours. Half your proceeds go to the Tower Restoration Fund. And after the fair is over, I want you back in Oxford studying hard until the term is over. Is that understood?"

Barry's sigh was heavy and heartfelt. "Half my proceeds? Damn, Charity, you're brutal." One look at her face, however, and he conceded. "Oh, if I must. I should by rights get a portion of everything my friends spend, but I will forgo that if I must."

"You must."

As she left, she caught sight of David Greenaway in the nearest corner, slumped down over his tankard. The lamp on the table illuminated his face and the dark bruise over his jaw. Charity refused to feel guilty about that bruise; he deserved it, just as Tristan said, for thinking he could threaten her right there in the hall of the church that her family had supported for centuries.

He was glaring at her. She put up her chin and stared him down. Only when he finally looked away did she leave the taproom, hoping she would have nothing more to do with him.

When she met Francis in the lane leading to the Grange, Charity was glad the darkness hid her face. Francis had always been good at ferreting out guilty secrets. But he didn't even comment on the scent of ale and cigar smoke that clung to her. He agreed with her nervous observation about the coolness of the night and gave absent replies about the state of the Haverne livestock and the conversation at the Haverne dining table.

"Oh, yes, Anna—she asked if she could come along with you on your parish work Tuesday."

Charity stopped halfway up the front steps. "Whatever for?"

Francis gave her a shove to get her going again. "She says she wants to be more involved in the parish benevolence. You have an objection to that?"

She was taken aback at his sharp tone but wasn't about to annoy him by taking issue with it. "No, not at all. It's just—well, she's never taken an interest before. And she is still in mourning."

"How long does that last anyway, mourning?"

Charity was weary and wanted only to go to bed, so she pushed open the front door as she replied, "For pity's sake,

Francis, we were in mourning for years and years. Surely you noticed how long it lasted."

Stiffly he said, "I don't know that it's the same, mourning brothers or a parent, and mourning a husband."

"A year in blacks. But I suppose etiquette wouldn't preclude her joining the Midsummer committee and making poor visits. I'm going to put tickets to the Midsummer fair into the poor baskets, remember, so I'll expect a couple pounds' contribution from you to make up for it."

"Whatever you say. By the bye, Braden said you've been helping him paint that backdrop for the children's play."

She stopped with her hand on the bannister. "So?"

Francis put out the lamps, except for one to help Barry negotiate the stairs when he found his way home. "So you seem to see more of him unengaged than you did when you were engaged. You have the oddest way of breaking off with a man, little sister."

Chapter Twenty

"I did warn you that some of the cottages are quite decrepit." Charity held out a restorative cup of tea to Anna. Even here in the pleasant Calder drawing room, Anna looked shaken by their visits to Haverne tenants.

"I shouldn't have been so very surprised," Anna said faintly, sipping gratefully at her tea. "Truly, I am glad you took me on your rounds. I didn't know that Haverne's people could be living in such dreadful—"

As the countess's words trailed off, Charity cursed her own ill-considered agreement to take Anna on the Tuesday afternoon sick visits. As soon as she saw that Anna had dressed in the finest muslin as if for a social call, Charity should have realized that city-bred Anna was only being polite in asking to go along. Now her lace fichu was wilted and spotted with soot, and her eyes had that haunted look Charity remembered from weeks ago.

Sympathy made Charity solicitous, and she reached across the tea table to touch Anna's lovely white hand. "Will you stay for a true tea? The Midsummer committee will be meeting here to make sure all is on schedule for Friday evening."

"Oh, yes. I told Tristan to come by for me at four. He's in Dover now consulting with a banker and will be able to tell me how much money is available for refurbishing the cottages."

Charity was taken aback. She realized that Anna meant to make her home here now, but this was homebuilding with a vengeance. "It will cost a fortune. Some of the cottages haven't been redone since Kenny's grandfather's day. When they can, Francis and the squire send their hands to do some structural work, but that's only just kept them standing."

"It has been good of you and your brother to take up the duties that we Havernes have neglected. But they are our duties, and we should be performing them." Anna lifted her chin, very much the grand lady again. "Lawrence must learn to be a better earl than his father or grandfather because, God willing, he will be earl longer. So I must set a good example. I will take over the visitations for our people."

This declaration, composed as it was of haughtiness and gratitude, silenced Charity. The good Lord knew Charity had often complained, if only to herself, about being overworked. But paradoxically, Anna's returning strength made Charity feel uncertain.

She stared blindly at her needle flying through her darning. If Anna could take over half the sick visits, just like that, then someone else could come and take the other half—the woman Francis eventually took to wife, for example. And then where would she be, if Lady Haverne and a new Lady Calder continued poaching her duties?

Free. She would be free to do as she wanted to do, without worrying about the Christmas carol service and the leaky school roof. She could start a new life without regret for the old.

She had only a moment to wonder what sort of new life she could want without any purpose to it when Anna cleared her throat delicately. "Now, dear Charity, I must thank you again. Oh, for so much, but for one thing in particular. I was thinking of Kenny this morning—praying for his soul, actually." The blush only enhanced the purity of her ivory skin.

"I went to the church and lit a candle—I know what you're thinking!"

Charity smoothed away the irony that had wrinkled her nose. "I was thinking how strong you are; you said his name and didn't cry."

"Liar. You were thinking that Kenny needs it, and a dozen other candles, too."

This was close enough that Charity wondered if she had lost her ability to hide her thoughts. "I never thought him bad. Only a little wild. But surely that was what made him so—so Kenny."

"Yes! You told me that first day that no one blamed me for loving him. Now I realize why that helped me so. I had been thinking what a fool I'd been. And I was a fool—oh, not to love him, but to let the love blind me. I was afraid if I let myself know him truly, I would stop loving him. We married so quickly, you know, in such a heat, just as my parents did. And when my parents got to know each other, they found they didn't suit each other at all. So I preferred to love blindly." She was pensive for a moment, touching one manicured nail to her teeth then jerking it away. "Now I see that I could have helped him more. His parents had indulged him so, and his friends, and no one had ever made him live up to a higher standard. I should have made it clear what I expected from a husband."

Charity was used to taking responsibility for the world, but she was surprised to recognize this in another. "It wasn't your fault, surely. Kenny should have known that a good husband—" She bit down on "respects his marriage vows" and swallowed hard.

"Oh, but I might have helped him grow up, if I'd told him what I expected of him. He must have thought that I didn't care enough to fight for my rights to him."

As Anna's voice faded, Charity heard an echo of her own persistent remorse. "Oh, Anna, please don't be thinking you could have prevented his death. It's such a relentless thought, and you'll never be rid of it, so just don't start. We all have regrets, and life just goes on."

Anna nodded thoughtfully, then fixed Charity with a significant gaze. "Yes, it's true. We all make mistakes."

"Not Francis." She didn't know why she said that, only that she wanted to divert Anna from discussing mistakes like betrothals and broken betrothals. It seemed to work, for Anna had tilted her head inquiringly.

"My twin Neddy and I used to say that," Charity explained hastily, for her assertion sounded bombastic. "You know, Francis is always so good. He's a good farmer and a good student, and, you wouldn't credit it, but a good dancer. Why, he taught me to waltz. And what's best is that he doesn't really know. There's not an ounce of conceit in him. You can understand why Ned and I always wanted to poison him."

Anna laughed dutifully, but Charity could see she didn't really understand at all, possessing as she did only a younger brother whom she probably never desired to poison.

"Sir Francis is indeed a modest man, considering his many fine qualities." The countess wound the cord of her reticule around her finger, and Charity realized they'd backed away from those tense subjects of Anna's husband and brother. Francis would doubtlessly be surprised to know he was at the center of two ladies' conversation.

"I'm surprised, in fact," Anna went on, "that some girl hasn't snapped him up long since."

As she couldn't ring for a real tea until the other ladies arrived, Charity had to damper her hunger with a few nibbles of a cream biscuit. She had somehow forgotten to eat lunch. "Oh, we've been in mourning forever. And I don't think he believes he will attract much interest should he step into the marriage mart. He thinks he's nothing special, only a country baronet without any great fortune or looks."

"His looks are very creditable," Anna said in a tone of great objectivity, her fingers still winding and unwinding the reticule cord. "He is always so impeccable. Hardly a rustic."

Charity shrugged, for Francis's looks seemed no more inspiring than her own. "You are kind to say so. He will probably turn his mind to acquiring a bride after harvest, now that we are out of mourning." She frowned, imagining a new Lady Calder here in the house, and hardly noticed Anna's returning gloom.

Then the knocker sounded and the rest of the Midsummer committee arrived for tea. The other ladies greeted Anna warmly but with the respectful reserve due to the highest ranking noblewoman. Anna accepted it all graciously, even suggesting that they share luncheon with her on the morrow.

Charity recalled that she had planned three major summer projects upon her return from London: overseeing the Midsummer fair, preparing Charlie for Eton, and coaxing Anna out of her self-imposed isolation. It looked as if, in another week, only Charlie would remain undone, and the summer had not yet officially begun.

At least she had a few minor Midsummer disasters to cope with over tea. Some children had gotten into Mrs. Dalton's crates of jumble booth donations—Charity gazed innocently into her cup, knowing her acting troupe was probably at fault—but she promised to have everything sorted again by Wednesday.

Her bosom heaving with outrage, Mrs. Williams reported on mercantile perfidy. Mr. Ashton, the baker, had abruptly raised the price on his destiny cakes, knowing that it was too late for the committee to order them elsewhere. So much for Christian benevolence, Charity thought, and decided this required an Old-Testament sort of punishment. "Mrs. Hering, you are so good at this. Could you just somehow let Margo know that we won't be requiring her fortune-telling services if her husband doesn't return to the agreed price?"

Mrs. Hering, eyes gleaming, agreed to attack the baker at his most vulnerable point. "Margo does love to play off her airs, pretending she's got second sight. And Ashton's a fool for that woman. He'll do anything for her."

In a murmur of agreement, the meeting broke up. The ladies were lingering at the door, exchanging last-minute plans, when the vicar came walking up the drive. "Oh, Lord, we're in for it now," Mrs. Hering said irreverently. "He's got his Jehovah face on."

Indeed, the vicar was looking wrathful, and Charity knew a moment's unease. Had he heard about—when she thought of how many things he might have heard about and disapproved of, she felt a chill. I can manage it, whatever it is, she told herself, and greeted him with a cheerful smile.

But Mr. Langworth permitted himself only a nod and refused to come past the foyer. "I'm glad you are all here, ladies. I come only to say I've called a meeting of the parishioners tonight after evensong. I think this Midsummer nonsense has gone too far, much too far. And I think you will agree with me when you hear the most disturbing report I have just heard."

He fixed Charity with an angry, sorrowful look, and she felt faint. This was not the vicar's ordinary anti-pagan rant. He was deeply angry and deeply troubled.

She closed the door behind them all and leaned weakly against it. It could only be Barry's gambling syndicate. Nothing else she had done would cause the vicar to call a special meeting.

She felt the vibrations of the knocker against her cheek and dispiritedly opened the door. Tristan came in, taking her hand and raising it to his lips.

"Anna said that something is wrong."

He has forgotten he's to speak Italian to me, Charity thought irrelevantly. She made an attempt to pull herself together. "No, no, nothing important. The vicar is upset again about the fair." She glanced around, realizing that they were standing in the foyer. "Do come in. Would you like some tea?"

"Charity, tell me what has happened." He still had her hand and gripped it imperatively. "Tell me."

She gazed down at their joined hands, feeling some comfort flow from him to her. She wasn't used to confiding in another, especially about her own troubles and mistakes. But this was Tristan. He had already forgiven her much more than this.

Still the words caught in her throat and emerged so softly he had to bend his head to hers to hear her. "Oh, it's rather a muddle. I think I might have pushed Mr. Langworth too far this time . . ."

He pulled her down to sit on the window seat next to the door and slowly, with much coaxing, got the whole story from her. He wasn't shocked, which was comforting, but he understood that some members of the church might feel differently. "I think we had better find your elder brother and tell him before he hears from someone else. This is his concern, too, you know. And you'll need his support at that meeting tonight."

If Charity had any doubts that she would have her brother's support, Francis made short work of them. Beyond calling her a dolt, he made no more criticism of her actions. He rose from his chair in the drawing room and paced along the periphery of the room. "You should have told me. But of course, you probably thought it would be of no use. I've hardly noticed you or the boys this last few weeks. I've been so damned distracted by my own affairs."

Charity was startled to hear such a *mea culpa*. She had never really know that her brother had any affairs that didn't have to do with the Grange or the village or the historical research he was doing on Kent in Saxon times. But of course he must have a bit of his own life, and he had a right to it, too. "No, Francis, I didn't tell you—oh, because I knew you'd be angry at Barry and probably make him do something he didn't want to do."

"I might have, at that. Or I might not, I don't know." Francis paced off another couple lengths of the room. "I would probably have let him go ahead and meet the bets he'd already made because he was in so deep anyway. But I wouldn't have allowed him to take any more bets or to bring his friends to see the events. And I never in a thousand years would have thought of making him donate some of his winnings to the Tower Fund."

"Only Charity would think of that," Tristan agreed, as if her ingenuity pleased him. That almost made her smile—he always appreciated her view of things. He sat down on the arm of her couch, a warm comforting presence at her side, speaking gently as if he had forgotten that they were not alone in the room. "And poetic justice it would have been, *cara*. Unfortunately, that makes it seem as if you condoned what Barry did."

"I guess I did condone it." She wanted to feel angry, to blame someone, but she had instead a deep sense of dread, of inevitability. "How do you think the vicar found out?"

Francis shook his head disgustedly. "Oh, Barry probably had a dozen of his local friends enlisted, and one of them must have split on him. He never has had a lick of sense. It's Neddy all over again, isn't it? But I'd never thought you'd consider me like Father, that you couldn't come to me. Though as worthless as I've been lately, I can hardly blame you."

Charity let go of Tristan's hand and reached up to intercept her brother in his pacing. She tugged on his arm, pulling him down to sit on the couch next to her, wanting to erase the remorse on his face. "No, no, Francis, it's my fault. I should have told you, but I thought I could handle it myself without any help."

They were both chagrined to hear Tristan laughing. Francis drew up straight and inquired exactly what was so amusing in all this.

"You're just such a pair. Neither of you is at fault here, for pity's sake. Barry is to blame, and he's safe off in Oxford and leaving you to handle the muddle he has made!"

Francis said, "Well, that's as may be. But it is our doing if he's so irresponsible. We had the rearing of him."

"And you're both of you only a few years his senior. You expect too much of yourselves, and so does everyone else. I think no one, including the vicar, has any right to complain if you fall short." Tristan rose and pulled Charity to her feet. "You go rest for a bit. I'll see if the vicar can be persuaded to call off this absurd meeting. This isn't the Inquisition, after all."

But a little while later Francis knocked on her bedroom door and told her that the vicar was insisting that he inform his parishioners of this new development. "Don't worry, Charity." Francis leaned wearily against her doorframe. "Everyone in the village loves you, you know that. They might chide you, but that will be all."

If that was all, Charity thought as she entered the church that evening, it would be more than enough. Only about fifty or so of the parishioners were assembled, but among them were the most prominent. Charity sat in the pew where her family had sat for generations, with Francis next to her, and Charlie, who had insisted on coming, beyond him. Just behind her were Tristan and Anna, making their allegiance clear even before any accusations were announced. Tristan kept his hand on the back of her pew, so that she had only to lean back to feel his gentle surreptitious caress on her neck. It was very wicked, but sustaining, too, especially when the vicar began to speak.

Mr. Langworth was no longer the old prophet thundering doom. No, his halting speech was all the more painful to Charity, because she knew he was deeply distressed. He said that he had received a report, from an impeccable source, of gambling on the children's games at the Midsummer fair, and that more troubling yet was the news that a member of the organizing committee had condoned it.

Charity was expecting this, as she was expecting the parishioners to crane their necks trying to see which of the four women on the committee looked most guilty. But she wasn't expecting the vicar to pause and call Mr. Greenaway forward.

The schoolmaster strode to the pulpit and, with more confidence than he had ever before shown, described Barry's scheme and Charity's participation. Charity recalled now that he had been in the taproom when she had accosted her brother. Mr. Greenaway must have been straining his ears to the bursting point, for she had made certain to keep her voice low. She wondered what he would say if she rose and pointed a finger at him and accused him of the sin of eavesdropping. But that was probably not really a sin, however perfidious it was. And Mr. Greenaway was scrupulous to confine himself to the truth, without exaggeration or embellishment. Only his self-satisfied expression indicated that he was more than just an objective witness.

Still his reedy voice echoed in the ancient sanctuary, and each accusation echoed in her heart. She had been baptized in this church, buried her loved ones here; she had hoped one day to be married here—this should indeed be her sanctuary, and it had become instead an inquisition.

When he finished his statement, Mr. Greenaway shot a triumphant glance at her and returned to his seat. He had gotten his revenge after all.

The vicar did not add to the accusation and did not call for any particular action. He did not even demand the cancelling of the Midsummer fair, though he permitted himself a few comments on the corrupting influence of pagan traditions. He reminded them of God's mercy, of Charity's long service to the village, of her family's difficulties these last years. Certainly Charity was not wont to behave as impulsively and erratically as she had these last weeks, he said. Perhaps so many sorrows had overset her judgment, and thus their judgment should not be harsh.

The heat rose in Charity's face. The veiled reference to her short-lived betrothal could not be mistaken, and even Tristan's quick grip on her shoulder did not mitigate her shame. To have that raked up again and used as evidence of her instability—this was worse than anger, this pity. If she had done wrong, she would accept her punishment. Just let it be quick, without these endless earnest preliminaries.

But the parish needed it, if she didn't, needed to justify whatever it planned to do. The Justice of the Peace spoke first. He was her mother's cousin and had dandled Charity on his knee. But he shook his head and said that she had erred in keeping this scheme to herself and even more in seeking to have the church profit from it. Mrs. Williams rose, too, not to denounce Charity, of course, but to suggest again that she had used poor judgment. Charity knew that Mrs. Williams had resented having a younger woman chairing the Midsummer committee, but still the criticism stung, all the more perhaps because it was true. At least Mrs. Williams did not suggest herself as a successor. Mrs. Hering was her candidate to direct what remained of the Midsummer preparations.

Tristan's hand slid to Charity's arm, gripping and releasing as if through his touch he could pass on a little of his strength. She wondered if he understood all this village justice. The worst punishment might be disapproval, but she dreaded that. He was not really one of them, she thought, and he would not dread disapproval. But she leaned back against the firm clasp of his hand, knowing that if nothing else he understood how hard this was for a girl who had known no other home.

Then his hand slipped away from her as he rose. She realized that he had appointed himself her defender, and she blinked back the tears that stung at her eyes. She couldn't listen to his defense, knowing that everyone would be remembering that once, not very long ago, they had been betrothed.

She didn't want to break down in front of all of them. Quietly she slipped out of the pew and out through the side door into the churchyard.

Chapter Twenty-one

It was one of the longest days of the year, so the sun was just setting when the meeting broke up. On instinct, Tristan followed the path through the gravestones in search of Charity. She was sitting half in darkness, hands clasped in her lap, on the bridge overlooking the stream where he had made that first unromantic proposal.

He wasn't used to seeing her so still, and it stopped him for a moment. She was always so busy, so cheerful, a small efficient bundle of energy. But now she was just sitting there, still and alone, her back to him and the church. He felt the ache rise in his throat, and he wanted to demand that she give him all that pain she was holding in that straight little body and strong little spirit.

But he knew something now of her pride and her sense of herself. He took a seat beside her, close enough to touch her but not touching. Her face was pale, but the ironic glint was back in her eyes as she turned to greet him. "You are very brave, to associate with the heretic."

"Idiot." To his mind, his response was insufficiently sympathetic, but it made her smile. He touched that curved lower lip with his thumb, wanting to kiss her, but thinking she would cry if he did. "You are officially forgiven. Back in charge."

She was startled and not as pleased as he had hoped. In

fact, she pulled away from his hand and turned away, hunching her shoulders as if to ward him off. He felt stupidly wounded, as if she had returned a gift he had given her.

At least her voice was determinedly light, though she kept her back to him. "You must have been very eloquent."

"Devil a bit. I'm never eloquent in English. Not in Italian either, for that matter." He couldn't help but brush aside the feathery tendrils of hair, to trace the vulnerable curve of her neck, to say with his caress what he couldn't say aloud: that her hurt was his hurt, that she should let him take it from her. She shivered under his fingertips; he drew his hand across the nape of her neck under the ear to the stubborn line of her jaw. Just for a moment, she bent her head and let her cheek rest on his hand.

Very gently, he added, "I merely suggested that you had never once thought of your own interest in this matter, or in any other matter either. And that Mr. Greenaway had his own reasons for bringing this accusation."

"He said nothing that wasn't true."

"Neither did I. And the truth is that he is rancid with jealousy because you can teach his pupils and he can't and because you can write a play and he can't. Say the word," he added, lowering his voice to a melodramatic whisper, though he meant it entirely, "and I will break his neck."

"It would serve you square if I did say the word and you had to go off and find him." Charity was feeling better, he could tell from the ironic tone that lightened her voice.

"He might be hard to find after all. I caught him as he was slinking off and suggested that if he valued his life he might find another set of pupils to bore stiff."

This news cheered her. "He will be leaving then? Oh, that means then that we—" she broke off, then started up again, "that *they* will have to employ another schoolmaster for the fall term." She was still studying her clasped hands, but she didn't avert her face from him now, and he could see the uncertainty, the anger, the guilt she felt. "Tell me who else spoke."

"Francis, of course, took the blame as Barry's guardian. I think he must be auditioning for Early Christian Martyr."

That surprised a chuckle out of her, quickly suppressed. "He's a very good brother."

"Very good indeed. And Mrs. Hering said that she knew you'd done it to protect Barry and her boys, too, and that you'd been doing it all your life and no one should expect that you'd stop now. She expressed the intention of going home and boxing a few ears, and no intention at all of serving on any committee that didn't have you at its head. And Mrs. Dalton concurred."

"Mrs. Williams?"

"Mrs. Williams recanted her position and decided to support you. Probably she did not relish heading up a committee without any members at all and the fair four days away." He knew he sounded as cynical as he felt, but whatever the outcome, he had found this public forum as unfair as a public hanging. And it exacted the harshest penalty from Charity. She had, he was sure, never been found lacking before as she had worked her life to live up to everyone's expectations.

However straight she kept her little shoulders, he knew this incident had shaken the foundations of Charity's world.

So though he wanted to tell her to just brush it off, as he would brush off a bad review, he knew that this mattered too much to her. "They felt guilty right off. I think no one meant to go through with this. And they were relieved to vote to have you back, even the vicar."

"They think no one else can do the work."

Her hard tone was new; so was the sigh that stirred against his hand. He had never seen her like this, so subdued, so sad. He stroked her cheek, wishing he could still see her face. But the gathering duck concealed her from him. "Charity, it was near unanimous. It is an endorsement of you."

"How kind."

She didn't sound grateful. But then she leaned back against him as if keeping her back straight and her chin up these last hours had wearied her beyond discretion. He knew better than to take advantage of this; he let his hand drop to her shoulder in a casual caress but made no move to embrace her. "What do you mean to do?"

"I mean to—I don't mean to return to the position of organizer." She shook her head at his automatic protest. "Tristan, they were right, you know. I shouldn't have allowed Barry to make book. It was a corruption of the whole idea of the fair."

This time he couldn't help himself. With an arm around her waist, he pulled her against him, resting his cheek on her hair. "You only did what you thought right."

"I know. That's exactly the point, Tristan. It never occurred to me to ask anyone else, not even Francis. Not even you. Certainly not the vicar. I thought I could balance it all, that the extra money would make up for what Barry is planning and that no one would be the wiser. Poor Barry." Her voice came muffled against his arm. "I expect his syndicate will be defunct now."

"Serves him right."

"So all my machinations have come to naught. My crime is exposed. The Tower Fund gets no great gambling revenue. Barry will have to do what he thinks is dishonorable—"

"He'll just have to give back the money he collected," Tristan pointed out. "And if he's spent it already, Francis will ante up. I hope he extracts a pound of flesh when he does it. What a nodcock Barry is. Are you sure he is your brother?"

"I should think there would be no doubt. I've spent the last three weeks acting like a nodcock myself. Oh, Tristan." Her back pressed against him as she sighed. "I think I have lost my way. I have always, always known my place, and now I don't know where I am."

"Here with me."

It was all the declaration he could let himself make. He didn't want to take advantage of her vulnerability now, still less to add to her confusion. But it was enough for the moment. She nestled closer and said with a wavering chuckle, "Yes, I am here with you. You have turned out to be an *excellent* friend after all."

"And without even trying." They were on dangerous ground here, reminding each other of that one explosive confrontation, and he thought it best to change the subject. "What will you do then, about the fair? I hope you don't mean to stop painting with me, when we are so close to finishing."

"I expect I can't stop that now or quit rehearsing the children either. But I will let Mrs. Hering tell me what else she means for me to do. Or Mrs. Williams, if Mrs. Hering won't serve. I will certainly no longer be in charge."

"There is no need to punish yourself."

"It's not punishment, exactly."

"Then no need to punish *them*, either, by withdrawing."

She laughed again, more truly this time. "I don't mean to do that either. I will do what I'm told to do, all that must be done. But I have been fighting this Midsummer battle, and all these other battles, for so long. I am weary of it suddenly. It has all taken up so much of my mind, I've hardly room for my own thoughts and notions." She sat up suddenly, pulling away from him and gazing around in the twilight as if this scene was too familiar and yet newly strange. "I think I must leave this place. Or I shall end up leaving myself."

It was what he wanted to hear. Still he worried that she was reacting to a long and frightening day. "Why must you leave?"

"It is—" Her voice wavered again, then she began again. "It is just like remaining in my parents' home. Only they are gone, and it is Francis's home, and I am welcome always, and even necessary at times. But it is not mine, no matter how I try to make it so. I think I must make my own place. But first I must find it."

He might have offered to take her there, but he had learned

subtlety lately. Instead he bent to pick up the handful of flowers he had dropped earlier. "Look what I have."

The rising moon cast quite a ghostly light on his now-bedraggled briar roses. He almost laughed at her frown—it was such a Charity sort of frown, showing bemusement and far less sadness than before. "Those are from the altar, aren't they? I put them there myself."

"And I stole them myself. Turn your head away, *carissima*."

Startled but acquiescent, she looked down at the moon-dappled stream. He tangled his hand in her hair, pulling it loose from its pins, threading the blossoms into her curls. This was more improper than anything he had ever done, for when he had kissed her they were betrothed and now they were merely friends, however excellent. But she didn't protest. She only shivered as his fingers slipped down her neck, still twined in the thick silk of her hair.

She let go the breath she had been holding and turned to face him. He tilted her chin up with one finger and, in the most objective voice he could manage, observed, "How pretty you are. The moonlight is so pale on the roses, and the night so dark on your hair." He traced a path from her ear to her lips with a callused thumb, watching her eyes all the time, seeing them widen and then half-close. A sensualist, he thought, and traced the gentle bow of her mouth.

"You look quite Dionysian, with those flowers in your hair. That the flowers come from the altar makes it all the more provocative."

Her eyes flew open. "Tristan! You are so—so wicked." She reached up to touch one of the roses but didn't remove it. "To make me a pagan with altar flowers is almost sacrilegious."

"But you're forgetting it's Midsummer. And Midsummer is pagan, however you tried to convince the vicar otherwise. Did you know, those pagans used to cover altars with flowers, armfuls of flowers. And do you know what they used to do on those altars?"

"What?" In her eyes was a mix of wariness and eagerness. "Licentious things."

Even in the moonlight he could see the color that crept up her cheeks. But the look she gave him was pure Charity—pragmatic and ironic. "Well, if those flowers were mostly roses, I think your pagans must have had a rather prickly time of it."

After only a moment she joined in his laughter. But too soon her laughter faded and she stood up, shaking her head so the flowers fell out of her hair. He caught one and held it out to her. With a blush she took it and hid it away in her pocket. "I'd best stop at the vicar's to tell him what I've decided. And Mrs. Hering, too. I hope they can manage to keep from brangling for the rest of the week, for I am determined to stay quite in the background."

"This I shall have to see," he murmured, picking up another of the fallen roses and pocketing it. "Charity in the background."

She stopped halfway across the bridge and looked back. "What do you mean?"

"I mean, *mia cara,* that, like the moon tonight, you shine too bright to be anywhere but in the center of life."

And with that, he let her go, following at a discreet distance just in case David Greenaway had plans for more revenge.

Chapter Twenty-two

The dragon was a great success, at least with Lawrence and Jeremy. They came over to knock on it and test its weight by tugging on the pole. Charity explained that Jacob had volunteered to haul it around during that evening's parade and the play. "You must remind your uncle to be very careful to behead the dragon and not Jacob!"

Now seasoned performers, Lawrence and Jeremy had accompanied their uncle to the village green to sustain him during his single rehearsal as St. George. Charity was glad to see the boys had made Tristan learn his seven lines and could prompt him when he hesitated.

Tristan refused, however, to don St. George's chainmail vest and helmet with visor. "I'll wear it this evening if you insist. But I'm not going to wear armor at high noon in June!"

No gentle reminders that St. George would not be so craven had the least effect, especially when the squire added his objections to a dress rehearsal. Even Molly, who was to play the king's daughter, said her gauzy costume might be damaged or dirtied if she put it on early. So Charity gave up the idea of a true dress rehearsal. One size of armor probably fit all, and if it didn't, Tristan had only himself to blame.

He did well enough, after all, without the chainmail, though in his buckskins and loose shirt he looked more a corsair than a knight. Though he recited his promise to save Princess Molly in an inappropriately ironical tone, Tristan took a good swath with his saber when he pretended to cut off the dragon's head. His nephews cheered, the squire-king applauded, and Princess Molly swooned.

"Very nice," Charity called out. "Now pretend to pick the head up on your sword and walk toward the bonfire. Everyone will follow you in a parade. Be sure and shake the head about as you go, for I've stuffed peppermints in there for the children to grab."

"You mean I'm going to have little wretches like these—" Tristan indicated his excited nephews, "digging around at my feet? You won't mind, I hope, if I leave off my best boots."

"When do I throw my arms around my rescuer?"

Molly threw a coquettish glance at Tristan, who accepted it with a smile and an outstretched hand.

"Not now!" Charity caught Molly's arm as she rushed past. "The king must give his final speech and then the dragon must dance around headless, and then perhaps—but no need to bother in rehearsal."

Charity turned to meet Tristan's amused glance and suppressed an answering smile. He was teasing her with his ironic loverlike speech to Molly. He was sending her a message, and if she couldn't yet translate it accurately, she thought it held good tidings. It certainly wreaked havoc on her heartbeat.

His easy manner was a contrast to that of the squire and even Molly, who treated her with the exaggerated civility one offers a recovering invalid. Three days after that meeting in the church, Charity felt like an alien in her own village. The ordinary pleasantries seemed forced, and she felt people were going out of their way not to ask her for help. Even Jacob and Crispin, who had been her friends all their lives, acted awkwardly around her, as if they thought she might blame them.

But Tristan was Tristan, her friend despite it all. He had

never really been part of this village or part of her past, and so he didn't see her as—as a fallen angel, or whatever in was her neighbors saw when they looked at this new Charity. Every day, just when she had run through the few tasks left to her now that Mrs. Williams led the committee, he bore her off to show her some improvement he had made in the whale painting or asked her to take him to the prettiest spots in the countryside. He was starting, he said with grin, a series of English paintings and thought a landscape might be in order.

Each time he asked for her opinion on a possible landscape vista or made her laugh at some scandalous gossip about her favorite artists, she felt less like the parish pariah and more like herself again. She thought she might never regain that sense of utter belonging, but she no longer felt so disoriented at its loss.

Even now, when he professed that he had to finish a painting before the festivities began, he lingered beside her. Sheathing his wicked saber, he reminded her to practice her Italian.

"But Tristan, do I truly need to learn how to abuse coachmen and haggle with vendors before I learn more of the grammar?"

His smile flashed and that slight accent deepened, as it always did when he told her about Italy. "Before you learn aught else."

He couldn't kiss her here on the village green, but he bent toward her as if he would like to, and she waited breathless for him to say something significant. But he only tickled her under the chin and said, "When you are in Naples and Rome, you will understand why I started your lessons at that point."

When he said that, she could almost imagine it, a future away from this village, a future that involved travel and adventure and arguments with Italian hackney drivers. Miss Falesham, her old schoolmistress, had written recently, indicating her desire to sell her school and retire to a nomadic life. And, oh—oh, there were other possibilities. She wondered what Tristan would say next winter if she arrived unannounced at his villa in Ferendisi. . . . But this was no time to consider such a future.

Not that she was consumed with details. Her Midsummer duties had been reduced to making sure the St. George play and the children's performances would not shame the parish. Out of some mingling of pride and penitence, she had not interfered in anything Mrs. Williams had decided in these last few days. Mrs. Hering, out of solidarity or perhaps only spite, was being just as reserved, and poor Mrs. Dalton and Mrs. Williams were near frantic.

Fortunately, she thought as Tristen and his gamboling nephews departed, her extensive early preparations had left little for the others to do on this last morning beyond booth set-up and personnel assembly. Already the men of the parish had laid the kindling for the cooking fires that would flame across the vicarage lane and set up the spits to roast the suckling pigs. The Hering boys had assembled a makeshift stage at the edge of the green for the plays, leaving plenty of room for the audience to sprawl on the grass. Charity had decorated the platform with laurel boughs and other greenery, so that all was in readiness for the evening performance.

Unfortunately Charity's own idleness meant she had all too much time to contemplate the sharp turn her life had recently taken and to worry if she was headed the right way—and if Tristan lay in that direction.

Since that very moment when she so firmly set him free, she had known only ambivalence. Her emotions darted more erratically than the fairies; she could hardly trap them long enough to identify them. Remorse, yes, for causing pain when she should soothe it. Desire, yes, to have him in some elemental way, joyously, without all the hesitation and regrets. Fear, yes, always that, fear not that he didn't know her, but that he knew her too well. And hope? Yes, that too had escaped from her Pandora's box. But she wasn't ready yet to discover exactly what it was she was hoping for.

Idle hands, she told herself, are the devil's workshop, So she surveyed the green to find a task that needed doing. Ah, there was one. The flower beds at each corner should be weeded before half the county saw the village in disarray.

She knelt down and attacked the weeds as if they were her own unruly thoughts. Just yank them out and toss them on a pile, she told herself. But while her hands obeyed, her mind didn't. It kept dwelling on her last encounters with Tristan, on her impulsive revelations, on his quiet sympathy, on the trust and ease she felt in his presence—and the danger.

He had become, in fact, the sort of friend she had always tried to be herself. But he was also fast making himself indispensable, and that was not a very friendly thing to do. In fact, if he kept this up, he could very well break her heart.

That heart leapt when she heard a phaeton drawing up in the adjacent road. But the footsteps that came up behind her then were not quick and light like Tristan's. Only Francis walked across a green as if he were pacing off the length of a barley field.

"I'm going to Dover this morning. I'll stop off at the jeweler's and get your chain fixed if you like."

Charity sat back on her heels and considered her brother. He was buttoning his plain dark coat over an unprecedentedly fashionable cravat. She thought of teasing him but resisted. He looked too tense to take it in the proper spirit.

"Tristan promised to make Lawrence take care of the repair. So that's one less stop for you to make."

"I was planning on stopping there anyway." He paused, waiting for some response from her. But she was too preoccupied to decipher his message. Eventually he added, "Braden's a bit weary of Lawrence's antics, I expect."

Charity picked up her pile of weeds and shook it, dislodging the topsoil from the roots. Then she brushed the dirt back into the plot. "Lawrence's antics would weary a saint. Tristan does his best, but he's had no experience at this. He alternates between sternness and sympathy. Lawrence needs consistency, I think."

"Lawrence needs a father," Francis said abruptly. "And Jeremy, too. They've never had one to speak of. Braden does his best, but he's only an uncle, and he'll be leaving eventually. They need someone who will stay. And so does she."

Charity stripped off her gloves and rubbed at her eyes. Surely they were filled with sawdust to have been blind to this. "That's why you're visiting the jeweler's. Francis, I never dreamed—"

He jutted out his chin, but his words were more defensive than defiant. "You are thinking that I am aiming rather high."

"I am thinking no such thing. Why, Anna would be lucky to have a man like you, so good and true and intelligent."

Francis was too sensible for false modesty, so he discarded it. "Well, I thought so, too. If I didn't, I would never dare to approach her." Francis paced off a few more rows of barley with renewed purpose. "She'll realize that this is for the best. Lawrence will be able to grow up on his own land, or next to it, anyway, and I can manage it for him until he's of age. I can manage her affairs, too—from what Tristan has said, they're in a sad state. And I've experience enough rearing boys to handle hers."

His case sounded completely persuasive. Anna would see that Francis would make the perfect husband, efficient, cheerful, faithful. The perfect husband . . .

Something Tristan had said echoed in her mind. "Francis, are you auditioning for the role of Early Christian Martyr?"

He turned stiff and forbidding as he always did when his pride was stung. "I don't see the need for levity."

"I only mean that it seems you are sacrificing yourself, taking on a mismanaged estate, rearing two neglected boys, rescuing Anna from her own folly."

Francis nodded. "Yes. And, as you say, if she is sensible, she will agree that her best course is to marry me."

Charity sat back on the walk and drew her knees up under

her gown Indian style. The she regarded her dear, deliberate brother, restlessly prowling the path. They were so much alike and so quick to make the same mistakes. "But, Francis—"

"But Francis what?" Not one to waste a moment, Francis checked his purse to make sure he had enough for a suitable betrothal ring.

He was too confident: Anna must admit she had no rational choice but to marry him. Charity foresaw a temptation to fate. "But Francis, what do you want?"

Annoyed, he stuffed the purse back in his pocket. "What do you mean?"

"What are you going to get out of this marriage? Besides the rewards of a job well done. Why do you want to marry Anna?"

Francis flushed and looked away. "I don't know what difference that makes."

"Have you ever proposed marriage before?"

Sulkily Francis dropped onto a stone bench and crossed his arms over his chest. "No."

"Really?" Charity made a disappointed face. "When you were first at university, Mama worried that you would offer marriage to that acrobatic performer you met at Astley's Circus. She said acrobats know how to ensnare a man—" With their legs, in fact, her mother had said.

"I wasn't so foolish even when I first went up to Eton! I didn't need to offer marriage, for one thing, and for another—well, I just couldn't imagine introducing her to my mother and my sister."

"I would have thought you very dashing indeed," Charity said.

"Mother would not have agreed. But I needn't point out that even she would find nothing ineligible about Lady Haverne."

She let this pass. "No proposals made. And how many have I received?"

"A couple dozen or thereabouts. I've lost track. So?"

"You must agree then I have a deal more experience in this proposal business than you have."

More than most men, Francis could acknowledge superior wisdom in a woman, even his sister. But this he couldn't concede. "I can't imagine you know better than I what a proposal should sound like, since you've never heard one that pleased you."

Charity pulled her gloves back on and returned to her weeds. "That's so. All I heard from my prospective husbands was how helpful I would be." She yanked viciously only to realize she had denuded the lavender patch. "And apparently all you mean Anna to hear is how helpless she will be."

Francis rose to pace again. "You know that's not what I mean."

"I do know." She replaced the abused plant and tamped the dirt down around it. "I know that you have your own selfish reasons for wanting Anna. But she has never seen you fight for the last raspberry tart, so she will consider you a martyr rather than a man."

He gave this the consideration it deserved and finally allowed, "Well, I don't want her to think that. I do have my own reasons—"

"What? Oh, I know she is beautiful and all that. But she always has been, and you've never paid her the least attention."

"I would never pay attention to another man's wife," Francis said, head held high, "not that sort of attention, anyway."

"Francis, will you cut line? There's more involved than the absence of Kenny. Anna is no mind reader. You must tell her why you want her." Even as she spoke, she knew she had been as guilty as he, assuming that a lover should not have to explain such things.

Preoccupied with his own situation, Francis did not join in her moment of revelation. "She is beautiful, and naturally I admire that. But she was one of those frivolous London ladies who never give a thought to anything but their furs and fashions. I couldn't admire that." His words came carefully weighed; he was unused to speaking so judgmentally. "That was Haverne's influence. He wanted her to be a child, to keep him company. Since he's gone, she's had to grow. And she has, remarkably. Don't you think?"

Charity nodded, but her brother was looking out west toward Anna's home and didn't see. "I couldn't care for a woman who had no consideration for her own people. Those of us who are fortunate enough to be guardians of this land—" He broke off the sermon. "She's trying so hard to take responsibility now. She insists on deeding a hectare of prime land for the tenants' vegetable garden. That took foresight. She's learned that rough as it is, this life is truer than she's used to. and she's coming to value that."

It was all very moving. "But Francis, what is it about her that dazzles you? That makes your heart thrill?"

He flushed a fiery red. "I'd hardly tell that to my sister!"

Charity gave an exasperated sigh. "Just tell it to Anna, will you? Believe me, she will not be scandalized."

From his shrug, she knew she had persuaded him, though he would never admit it. "Am I too precipitate? It hasn't been half a year since Haverne's death."

With the acuity of one miraculously restored to sight, Charity perceived that Anna was already expiring with impatience. "Surely you can come to some understanding now. You know how high your credit is, Francis; no one will ever question the propriety of anything you do."

Francis reached down to ruffle her hair in an awkward expression of gratitude. "You don't think that you and Braden— he's still hanging about, I can't help but notice. Our children could be, what do they call it, double cousins."

The leap of hope was too dangerous to allow. "Oh, I don't see any profit in regret."

Fortunately their youngest brother thundered into view before Francis could take issue with this or suggest an alternative.

"I thought you two would be here!" Charlie planted himself between them, obstinacy set in his mouth and chin. "I'm glad I found you both together. Now listen." From his breeches pocket he took out a much-folded page and opened it. In a authoritative voice, he read, "I am not going to Eton. Instead, I will study privately with Mr. Champfeur, the retired schoolmaster in Deal." He added in an normal tone, "You remember him, Charity. He came last year to see my agate collection and told you then that he tutors scientifically minded boys. He's a very accomplished geologist."

"I remember," Charity said faintly.

Charlie returned to his script. "Mr. Langworth's sister lives in Deal and keeps house for boys who go to the choristers' school there. He thinks I can have a place with her. I shall visit home every Sunday so you can be sure I am well."

Francis was taken aback by the stand of his most passive sibling. "But Charlie—Calders always go to Eton and then to Oxford."

Handsomely Charlie allowed, "I shall consider Oxford. Cambridge is better known for its science masters, however."

In his unostentatious way, Francis was just as school-proud as his brother Barry. "I shan't hear of Cambridge, Charlie."

"But Mr. Champfeur? You will agree to that?"

Francis and Charity exchanged glances and then identical helpless shrugs. "Have we any choice?" she asked. "You've made a hash of your Eton prospects. Deliberately, I've no doubt. Well, Francis, if you're agreeable, I'll ask Mr. Champfeur over for tea and pursue this. He did seem a worthy man."

Charlie wasn't one to leap about with glee, but he nodded graciously. "Thank you, I assure you it will be for the best." With dignity, he turned on his heel and marched back to the Grange.

"He certainly laid down the law to us," Francis observed

once he was out of earshot. "But how will he bear up? He's so shy."

Charity imagined him in a Deal boarding house, thirty miles from his protective siblings. Of course, Eton was even farther away and likely a harsher environment than Mr. Champfeur would provide.

Francis had the same thought. "He knows himself best, I suppose." He gazed at the straight back of his little brother. "If he maintains that attitude, I don't think anyone will trouble him."

Charity waited until he had left for his errand before she rose, spilling flowers from her lap. Francis, Anna, even Charlie: they had all decided to start new lives. She wondered if she had the courage to follow their example.

Chapter Twenty-three

One of the tasks Mrs. Williams assigned to Charity was selling admission tickets. So it was that she greeted her brother Barry when he arrived from Oxford just as the games started at five. He paid for his ticket with exaggerated care, counting out the pennies and laying them in her hand, and then giving her a quick, shamed grin. This was, she thought, his way of apology.

"Where are your seven friends?"

"Didn't come. I didn't want any more trouble, you know. Hey, is that Lawrence and Jeremy in the three-legged race? I've got to see this!" And he loped off, leaving Charity to wonder how he had managed to deal with his friends, whether he had quietly agreed to carry out the bets anyway. Then she decided she'd rather not know.

Charity had only to look over the village green and the church lawn to know that everyone in the parish, and many from other parishes, had turned out for the fair, all wearing the green sprig that signified Midsummer. It was a success, despite the change in leadership.

The light breeze tugged the silver ribbon holding back her curls. Distractedly she pulled it out and, combing her fingers through her hair, retied it at the nape of her neck. A good crowd, rising laughter, a cloudless sky of that particular Kent blue—if the ale held out all evening, and the candles and the destiny cakes foretold good news, they might just avoid disaster.

Certainly there were shillings aplenty being spent at the booths that lined either side of the green. Mrs. Dalton's jumble booth was popular, and there was a long line of girls at the ring-toss booth that offered rag dolls as prizes. Charity waited to make sure that each girl who played the game walked off cuddling a doll. Today was not the day for scrupulous honesty in prize-awarding. They had a supply large enough, she was sure, for every poor girl in the county.

She waved to Mrs. Hering standing militantly at the ale booth and blessed the woman for rationing the precious liquor to a tankard per person per hour. No one would get foxed on that meager amount, and their supply would last all night.

She saw Tristan and Anna over by the race track and, smiling to herself, wandered over to join them. She wondered if Francis would take Anna aside this evening and make his proposal or wait for a less public occasion. She sobered, recalling the last public occasion that they had all gathered on this village green and the proposal that had taken place then. It seemed so long ago, and she hardly remembered the girl who had received that proposal with more trepidation than triumph. That girl had been so frightened of the future, or reaching for a dream and finding it hollow, of changing her life and finding it unchanged—or too changed. She had been so certain of her place, and so uncertain, in the end, of herself.

Now she saw Tristan sweeping his nephews, still tied at the ankle, into a victory hug. Here among the fair broadfaced sons of Kent, he stood out as exotic, though he wore the same country casual dress. He would never really fit in, she realized, no matter how many ties he established here. But that was what she had always admired about him, after all, his otherness. Through him, through his art, she had gained entrance to another world.

What she would do in that other world, whether he would

share that with her, was not something she could determine now. Finish the old business first, she told herself.

When he saw her, Tristen flashed her a grin and held out his hand. But Lawrence and Jeremy reached her first, hopping across the divide to collapse clinging to her legs. Laughing, she peeled them loose and knelt to untie them. "I am so proud of you both! First place in your first Midsummer event!" She couldn't forgo a bit of a moral lesson along with her congratualations. "And it's all because you two worked together as brothers, as a team."

Cammie, who had been sitting under the shade tree, came up to add her own commentary. "Yes, boys, Charity is right. Perhaps you can apply the same camaraderie to your spelling lessons."

The boys looked dubious, but the effect of the victory hung on. Still in accord, they seized Cammie and Charity and pulled them over to the obstacle course, proclaiming that Charlie was in the finals.

As they waited for the contestants to line up, Charity outlined for Cammie the future Charlie had planned for himself. She forced down the lump in her throat and spoke as gently as possible. It meant a new future for Cammie, too, once Charlie left home, especially if Charity followed his example.

But Cammie, watching the last of her Calder charges tug up his drooping stockings and take his mark, did not lament. "Good for him. I must say, I worried I would have another year of trying to force him to study his Latin if Eton wouldn't have him. I daresay this Mr. Champfleur can find some way to connect the classics to geology and have better success." With a firm hand on Lawrence's shoulder, she pulled him out of face of another boy who dared to root for someone other than Charlie. "Lawrence, all this shouting will distract Charlie from the race. Now muzzle it and just watch."

Immediately Lawrence hissed to Jeremy to quiet his cheers, and the two squatted down together beside the track in rapt silence. Cammie waited until the opening gun sounded and the older boys bounded past. "Lady Haverne has been kind enough to ask me to remain to teach her sons until they are ready to go off to school. So I will be remaining at Haverne—for a short time at least."

Charity saw the gleam in her old governess's eyes and knew that Cammie had long since guessed Sir Francis's intentions. She would be back at Calder soon enough if Anna accepted his suit, for Francis would never have his wife and her sons living away from him—and he would never leave Calder, even for a larger estate a half-mile away. And soon enough there would be little Calders for Cammie to teach. The cycle of life would go on, even without Charity to turn it.

Charlie was the first contestant to re-enter the green, bounding over the hay bales and under the hitching post. With typical painstaking, he ran around rather than over the water trap, avoiding the disqualification for wetness. Then, disheveled and perspiring, he crossed the finish line and, like a seasoned victor, accepted the congratulations of the Haverton boys. He glanced wryly at his sister. "Everyone else stopped for lemonade at Mrs. Wiggins's house. They'll be coming along soon."

So it was that when the vicar, with a grudging smile, handed out medals at the ceremony following the games, Charity's protégés collected their share. Lawrence and Jeremy swaggered like conquerors with their medals on their little chests, and even Charlie condescended to show it to his sister when she asked. Barry clapped him on the back, saying jovially, "Knew you could do it, Charlie. I was betting on you." He shot a glance at his sister. "So to speak."

Lawrence and Jeremy claimed her before she could respond to this. "They're lighting the bonfire! Hurry, or we'll miss it!"

Charity kept tight hold of Jeremy's hand, a little guilty to use him so. But her ruse worked. When they gathered with the other young people around the bonfire for the First Rogation, Jeremy had planted himself and Charity right next to his uncle. And when everyone joined hands, hers was clasped in Tristan's firm grip.

The circle moved slowly clockwise around the bonfire as the fragrant logs burst into flame. The chant she had taught the children rose, though she only whispered it, and Tristan only listened. It was a riddle, listing Midsummer paradoxes that reflected her own tangled emotions:

> Green is Gold.
> Fire is Wet.
> Fortune's Told.
> Dragon's Met.

And as the flames danced before them, and the sunset blazed beyond, she struggled with her own riddles. How could the familiar seem so alien now? And why was Tristan, the man she turned away, still here, still so kind, even more intriguing than before?

As soon as the circle broke up, Lawrence begged, "Ask us what that means, Uncle Tris."

"What does that mean?" Tristan kept Charity's hand for a moment but turned to his nephew with every evidence of attention.

"Green is gold, you see, because this is Kent and we farm, and so the green fields are precious to us."

"Like gold," Jeremy interposed. "Ask us how fire can be wet."

"How can fire be wet?" Tristan smiled over their heads at Charity.

"We'll show you." They each grabbed one adult and dragged them toward the little lily pond in the center of the green. "We folded those boats, us and Charity," Jeremy explained. "Let's light them."

Tristan gravely helped him to hold the candle against the fortune-teller's taper, then Jeremy set it in a boat and gave it a shove. Lawrence helped by wriggling his fingers in the water to start up a tidal wave, and the little boat set sail for the opposite shore. Tristan, Lawrence, and finally Charity launched their own boats, and Jeremy said, "Now we must each make a wish. If the boats make it to the other side, we get our wishes."

Margo broke in sternly, "Not this year. This year I'm to read the candlewax to determine the future. No wishes allowed."

Jeremy looked so downcast that Lawrence whispered fiercely, "You can still wish, Jerry. Just don't tell *her.*"

Out of fellow feeling for Jeremy, or so Charity told herself, she closed her eyes and sent up a wish as mingled as her emotions. Let me find a new way, and let him forgive me.

She opened her eyes slowly, sensing from the warmth on her face that Tristan was watching her. All through this Midsummer ordeal, she had felt his quiet, supporting strength. Would he leave now that it was over?

It wasn't dark enough yet to appreciate the full effect of the candles in their little boats on the water. But the flickers of flame and their reflections seemed to set the pond on fire. The little boats bobbed gaily on the waves Lawrence and Jeremy made with their hands, and soon enough the four little boats made it unscathed to the other shore, where Margo had taken up her position. She picked up Lawrence's candle and peered at the trickles of wax along the sides. "Riches and good harvests," she said, and for Jeremy, "A pony and plenty of hay."

"Let's trade, Jerry," Lawrence said immediately, but Margo had blown out their candles and picked up Tristan's.

"Fame and fortune will be yours."

Tristan accepted this with a thoughtful nod, and Margo studied Charity's candle with religious intensity. "I see—I see an adventure. Answers."

Charity couldn't help a certain disappointment. She had rather hoped that Margo would continue in her conventional vein and predict a future with a tall, dark, and handsome man. But adventure—well, that was a start.

"So you see, Uncle Tris," Lawrence said in the lecturing voice he had borrowed from Francis, "The fire's wet and the fortune's told. All that's left is the dragon's met—and you do that."

"I?" Tristan assumed an expression of innocence. "I don't want to meet a dragon. I don't like dragons. They're too hot."

Jeremy, earnest as always, pulled at his arm in distress. "But you are to be St. George! Don't you remember? We taught you your lines." He regarded his uncle anxiously, his lower lip caught between his teeth. "Perhaps we should go over your part again."

Charity had to laugh at the horror on Tristan's face. She intervened before Lawrence could join in. "No, boys, remember what I told you about overrehearsing? And if he doesn't remember his lines, you can always prompt him. Now look, the banquet is starting. Run on over to the children's table or you won't get a seat."

The boys' small bodies disappeared into the crowd, reappearing a few moments later at the children's table, set safely away from the tempting bonfire. Jeremy waited for his brother to choose a seat, then sat down next to him, among boys wearing caps of green leaves and girls clutching the rag dolls the countess had made for them. The countess's sons were greeted with friendly disdain, for they were among the youngest there. Charity smiled, seeing how meekly Lawrence took this treatment from the sons and daughters of his own tenants. And Tristan, following her gaze, spoke her thoughts aloud. "There will be time enough for him to learn to be toplofty. First he should learn how to make and keep friends."

Tristan took her arm and steered her through knots of girls who stopped talking when she was near, toward a table where Charlie sat all alone, still wearing his medal, waiting for the banquet to begin. He was spreading his rocks out around the vase of flowers that served as a centerpiece, oblivious to the tumult around him. No, Charlie would not sit at the children's table; he had not considered himself a child for years.

Charity smiled at Mr. Perry, the fiddling mason, who was strolling about playing the traditional St. John's fanfare. He gave her a strained smile. With the candor Tristan always engendered in her, she said quietly, "The village is disappointed in me."

Impatience flickered over his face. "Ignore them. You weren't put on this earth to make them happy."

"I rather thought I was." Suddenly she smiled. "*They* certainly thought I was."

He touched her hand under the table. "Well, you make me happy." After a brief pause, just long enough to send a thrill through her heart, he added, "Sitting with me and trying to divert my thoughts from my great performance, I mean."

Before she had a chance to ask what else made him happy, Polly intervened, setting the great bowl of cuckoo's foot ale in front of them. She made a great show of bending down, so all those who had assembled at the table could see how her pale green dress displayed her bosom, lit white and gold by the flaming torches. The serving girls, as usual, had lowered the necklines of their costumes and put flowers instead of just leaves in their hair. Well, Midsummer was a festival of fertility, and Polly was definitely the picture of that. If she weren't careful, one of the local lads would take her up on it.

The squire rose, holding up his cup of ale up for the traditional Midsummer toast, and Mr. Perry cut some sharp notes on his fiddle, imitating the sound of the cuckoo. All the children chimed in, raucously calling, "Coo-coo, coo-coo."

Charlie, noting Tristan's puzzlement, whispered, "Dip your cup in the bowl. Don't worry, it's only spiced ale." He must have felt his sister's admonishing gaze, for he added, "I only sip it myself."

The squire waited until everyone was holding up a cup. Or almost everyone. Charity saw that the vicar, sitting at a nearby table, kept his hands ostentatiously clasped and his cup empty. "I toast to the cuckoo and the rebirth of summer."

Mr. Perry, standing in the middle of the circle of tables, struck up the traditional cuckoo song. The song swelled up, led by a few members of the church choir, and Charity softly sang the old words as she had sung them almost every Midsummer of her life:

> Summer is a-coming in.
> Loudly sing, cuckoo!
> The seed grows,
> The meadow blows,
> And the woods spring anew.
> Sing, cuckoo!

Her throat closed up after the first verse, and she couldn't sing anymore. Her father had always joked that Midsummer was a fertile time for Calders, as his twins had been born early the morning after a particularly enjoyable fair. It was the cuckoo's foot ale that brought on the birth, her mother had claimed—and the dancing around the bonfire, of course.

To the accompaniment of other old rounds, the girls of the parish served the other courses of the banquet. There was the sweet omelette made with almonds and honey, and the heavy brown bread topped with great dollops of butter, and a suckling pig for each table—a wealth of country produce, donated by the local farmers and prepared by their wives.

Last year Charity never had a chance to eat, so busy was she directing the serving of the banquet. But tonight Charity was idle enough that she could see how the gruesome sight of the suckling pigs, their mouths stuffed with apples, impressed the children and how the constantly replenished bowls of ale impressed their fathers.

It was quite a feast, and when it was done, Margo and her husband the baker brought out the destiny cakes on great platters covered with cloths. At each table, the diners reached under the cloth and grabbed a cake sight unseen. This was yet another Midsummer fortune-telling technique that the vicar disdained, waving his hand dismissively as the platter was held out to him.

Charlie got a hat and gravely said it meant he would soon be a scholar. Tristan got a key and speculated hopefully that he would be elected to the Royal Academy, the key to artistic fame.

Charity, however, got a square. Everyone at the table offered a different interpretation of this prosaic shape. One man—a stranger from the next village west—said it looked like a coffin to him, but the others shouted him down. A treasure chest, a house, a trunk. "No," Charity said finally. "It's just a box. Pandora's box. And all that's left is hope."

"I still think it's a trunk." Tristan took it from her and held it up to the torchlight. "I'm an artist. I live out of a trunk. I can tell one when I see it. This means you are going to take a trip." Then he took a bite out of it and handed it back to her, no longer quite square.

She could only laugh at his effrontery, but the familiarity his gesture implied brought hot color to her face. He didn't give her time to protest, rising from the table to say, "I suppose I must get into that armor. I don't suppose you'd like to help?"

Charity blushed even more hotly as her tablemates laughed and offered their opinions on this proposition. Fortunately Charlie was back to studying his rocks in the dim light and didn't hear. It was only a bit of Midsummer raillery, after all, she told herself. She would hear much worse as the night darkened and the ale diminished.

So she only reached over and shook her brother's shoulder. "Charlie, go and help Lord Braden with his costume. No, don't worry, no one will take your rocks." Her assurance didn't assure Charlie; he regarded his tablemates suspiciously as he handed her his prizes. Then he followed Tristan across to the church hall.

She swept up the crumbs of the destiny cake and carried the dishes to the huge vat of water near the cooking fires. Mrs. Williams was sweaty and harassed, gesturing to the serving girls and calling to the men carrying heavy trays of dirty dishes. Charity dutifully offered to help, but Mrs. Williams only shook her head.

It was time to set up for the St. George play anyway, Charity told herself, leaving the banquet behind, beckoning to Jacob at his cousin's table. Without too much stumbling he made his way out of the banqueting area and down toward the stage. Fortunately he had no lines, only the job of carrying the dragon about the stage, and he was sturdy enough to do that even when his mind was muddled.

Charity gathered up a couple of youths to help her light the torches and set up a few chairs for the elderly around the stage. In the gathering darkness, the ring of torches cast an eerie glow on the scene. The vicar would not like that, she thought. It looked like a habitat of Dionysius, with the lush greenery and the flickering flames and the deep darkness beyond.

Nonetheless the vicar was in the audience when the squire and Molly made their entrance onto the stage. Charity stood on the side with Jacob Hering and Tristan, willing the rowdy youths to quiet their catcalling. The squire, full of authority of kingly purple robes and an evening's worth of ale, waved his arm. "Silence, you knaves, or I'll feed you to the dragon!"

This was the perfect introduction for Jacob, and when Charity poked him he propped the dragon's pole on the crook of his elbow, as if he meant to joust, and swaggered onto the stage. At the sight of the towering dragon, red and furious, the rowdy youths hushed and children drew closer to their fathers. The squire, his broad grizzled face triumphant, his crown atilt, turned to Princess Molly. "Woe is me, my daughter, that I must live to see your slaughter."

That was Tristan's cue. As Molly simpered and looked woefully brave, he vaulted on to the stage, sword drawn, and stepped between her and the dragon. Molly clapped her hands to her bosom, in the process pulling her bodice down another inch. "Good youth, good sir, spur on your horse and fly to take another course. The dragon, foul and fierce and sly, will grind his jaws to make me die." Jacob, holding the dragon out before him, bobbed his knees to make the fierce monster dance, and Molly drew back in a pretty display of anguish. "I beg of you, be off in haste!"

Tristan flourished his sword and bared his teeth, and Charity breathed a tiny sigh of relief. She had worried all along that Tristan wouldn't enjoy his participation in her play, that he would associate it with their short betrothal and the trouble it had caused. But he was overacting quite as much as Molly, with the sweeping gestures and fierce expressions that a provincial audience loved. He looked very much the knight errant with the red-crossed coat of mail shining like his silver sword. At the last minute, he had left off the helmet he had never stopped complaining about, so his dark hair gleamed in the torchlight. And though his tone was still ironic, he spoke his lines without a stumble, and he glared at the dragon as he proclaimed, "My horse, my cross, my sword, and I will bring this monster forth to die."

But Jacob just stood there, beaming foolishly, his dragon drooping from the end of the pole. Charity groaned softly. She had to wake him up. In her pocket she found a rock, and with the aim of a cricket bowler, she flung it, glistening in the torchlight. It struck Jacob on the back, startling him into action. Charity heard "That's my pyrite!" but the protest was lost in the children's gasp as the dragon reared toward Tristan. Tristan made a great show of swordplay, feinting to the left and to the right before aiming carefully and slicing across the dragon's neck.

Jacob let out an audible sigh of relief as the dragon's head tumbled off, leaving him unscathed. Molly and the king embraced—the squire enjoying it most—then she threw her arms around Tristan. He bore it stoically, or so Charity thought, until a quick trill from Mr. Perry's fiddle signaled the start of the parade.

Tristen poked his sword through the dragon's mouth and held the head aloft. "All come to celebrate the extinction of hell's fires!"

It was a rousing line and got everyone up and following Tristan when he leaped off the stage and strode across the green. Charity remained behind, watching as he faithfully shook the head to release the peppermints for the children who scrambled along in his wake. He looked, Charity thought, every inch the hero, and he even gave the appearance of enjoying the role.

By the time the torchlit parade snaked around back to the stage, she had already begun preparations for the second play. Barry, Jacob, and Crispin cursed as they hauled the heavy canvas backdrops across the green, stumbling into each other in the dark. When Tristan saw them manhandling his paintings onto the stage, he sheathed his sword, yanked the chainmail vest over his head, and joined them. "Put the middle one there, Barry. Yes, there, in the middle. No, that's upside down. By God, if you put your foot through the whale I'll kill you."

Glad of his authoritative presence, Charity left the set design to Tristan and gathered her performer around her beside the stage. She wet her finger and brushed a shard of peppermint off the face of her star, Jack Moresby, and helped the Haverton boys change into the striped jerseys that proclaimed them sailors. Mary Moresby, another seaman, objected at the last minute to having her ringlets stuffed under a cap. "Fine," Charity said coolly. "We have plenty of seamen. You may go sit with your mama and watch."

The threat worked; Mary pulled on her cap and assumed a piratical expression, which Lawrence and Jeremy tried to imitate. The other seamen lined up in the order they would be sitting in the boat and promised not to fight until after the play was done. When they were all standing at attention, chins down on chest, shoulders braced, she said, "Don't move. I'll be just a moment."

Jacob and Barry were wrestling the rowboat in front of the backdrop, with Tristan directing its exact placement. As Charity walked through the audience, she heard the gasps that greeted the unveiling of the whale triptych. Well, she thought with mordant humor, at least no one will ever forget *this* Midsummer. They will forever recall it as the one with the man-eating whale.

When she saw the vicar sitting with Mrs. Dalton, Charity felt in her pocket for the script she already knew by heart and brushed aside Charlie's bits of pyrite and mica. She took a deep, steadying breath. This was a gesture of reconciliation, but it could be so easily interpreted as something else. And the vicar's expression when she approached him was not conciliatory—guarded, rather, as if he no longer knew how to deal with her. It didn't matter; she held out the script to him.

"Mr. Langworth, I need your help."

He didn't say that she should have asked for that long since on many matters of more import, but his nod was a little curt.

In for a penny, in for a pound, she told herself. "I meant for the squire to read the words of God in the play, but then I realized that might be somewhat—blasphemous." Oh, no, she thought, seeing Mrs. Dalton's startled face, now they'll think I'm criticizing the squire. "For an ordinary man, even one as good as Mr. Hering, to take on the role of God. But for a vicar it would be no different, would it, than reading the words of God during the sermon?"

The vicar opened his mouth to protest, but Charity didn't let him. "If we don't have God's words, then this will be just another, umm, sensational play about a man swallowed by a fish. It will have no moral import. But if God is in it, then, then—" she added bravely, "it will be godly. Do say you will read the words." She forced the script into his hand. "Do you see, I've underscored your lines—I mean, God's word—in red. You have such a powerful voice; I think you can sit here under the torch and merely speak them."

The vicar was noncommittal, only scanning the lines as she used her last desperate weapon. "Indeed, I think that it might be all the more effective, to have God's word ring out from the middle of the audience, as a reminder that He is with us always."

Mr. Langworth glanced up at this, and a curious light shone in his eyes. "So I am to perform. In the role of God."

My word, Charity thought, he is as starstruck as Molly. Fearful of hexing this piece of good fortune, she bade him a quick thanks and sped back to the less divine performers.

Charlie was waiting for her. He had crawled about the stage in search of his rock and trusted her no more with the rest of his treasures. She handed them over, but reminded him he had promised to supply the storm noises for the play. She showed him the bucket of large stones, which he examined with professional interest. "Charlie, please. You just shake the bucket when it's supposed to be thundering. I'll take care of the surf noise."

At her signal, the squire, still in his royal purple robes, introduced St. Catherine's own rendition of that great Biblical tale, "Jonah and the Whale." Some notion of fairness had made her insist that he identify the author as David Greenaway and herself as merely the adaptor and director. Tristan, standing next to her, gave her arm a squeeze as the squire intoned that the backdrop was painted by Lord Braden. "And Charity Calder," Tristan whispered in her ear. "We should give credit where credit is due."

His breath against her cheek, his generous words, made her color up. She wished that this could be over so that they could have some easeful time alone, without the specters of Midsummer or David Greenaway or Jonah's whale looming over them. Then she could thank him properly for his kindness, and—and ask him for more. She would visit him, she vowed to herself, when she traveled to Italy, no matter how improper that was. And there, in the heat of the Italian sun, they would start again, away from this village that claimed her and restrained her and kept her from herself.

As the squire bowed and left the stage, Charity wrenched her mind back to work. She signaled to Jack Moresby to lie down on the stage as if asleep. The vicar, a born actor, took this as his cue, and intoned, "Arise, Jonah, go to Ninevah, and cry against it."

Jack rose and stretched and looked befuddled, then when the vicar repeated the line, he put on a terrified expression and dashed downstage. Charity gave Jeremy, the first sailor, a little shove, and the ship's crew clambered on stage and into their boat. Jack approached, glancing all about him as she had taught him, and in a carrying whisper asked Lawrence, "Can you take me to Tarshish?"

The play went well. The children remembered most of their lines, no one fell out of the boat, and the vicar made an impressive voice of God. Charity let go of some of the tension that had gripped her all day. Soon Midsummer would be done and without disaster—without transformation, too, it was true. But the fair would soon be over, and she would be free.

Tristan was still standing behind her, watching over her shoulder as his nephews rowed furiously. He laughed, and the flickering light outlined the dramatic planes of his face and the curve of his smile. Did he want another chance, too? As Francis said, he was still here. It was enough to give her hope.

There was a burst of applause, and with the aplomb of seasoned stars, the children joined hands at the edge of the stage and bowed. Charity clapped until her hands hurt, then kissed each child coming off the stage. "You did wonderfully well," she said before she dismissed them to their families. "The best Midsummer play ever."

Before he took his nephews home, Tristan bent to whisper

in Charity's ear, "The triptych is yours, *cara*. I can't imagine where you'll place it, but I never want you to forget this Midsummer."

Pausing for a moment beside her, Francis was quick to congratulate her, or so he said; his real role turned out to be spoilsport. "I've told Barry to see you home when you're done here."

It was no use, but she tried anyway. "But, Francis, what about the dancing?"

Francis shook his head. He was distracted, looking past her to the crowd at the bonfire. "You know that's not for girls like you. The activities get heated there by the fire, and I've more important things to do than to try to peel some foxed farmhand off you."

Charity retorted that she was quite able to deal with farmhands herself. But then she saw his fists clenching and unclenching, and recalled that a proposal was the most important thing he must be planning to do. No need to add to his anxiety with resistance.

Still, her sense of anticlimax grew as everyone removed to go dancing and she was left to pick up the discarded costumes. Even Cinderella danced till midnight. She stomped around the stage, feeling childishly resentful. She had expected more of this night than a square destiny cake and kisses from children.

But as she pulled the covers down over the great triptych, recalling the hours they spent painting, she had to smile. This was hers now; Tristan had given them to her. And she supposed that was better than a glass slipper and a pumpkin coach.

Any slight hope that she might still be able to get a dance or two with Tristan if he returned was dashed when Barry vaulted onto the stage with Jacob and Crispin to tow. They helped her douse the torches but wouldn't hear of lingering. "No, no, don't worry," Barry said. "We'll just come back after we take you home, sis!"

So she trailed along home like a good girl, cursing the social system that let her younger brother drink and carouse and denied her even a single dance in the Midsummer firelight.

Just as the lane up to the Grange crossed the stream, Crispin leaned toward her, his eyes clearly bloodshot even in the dim light. "Just tell me where that Greenaway fellow is, and I'll search him down and rip 'im up a bit for you. Just tell me."

He stumbled on a speck of dust in the lane and fell onto her. With a muttered curse she shoved him away. "I don't need you to fight my battles, Crispin Hering. Especially—" she added, as he stumbled backward, flailing as if she were the whale and had swamped him with her mighty tail, "since you can scarcely stand up."

Crispin balanced for a long moment on the edge of the road, then with an "uh-oh" he tumbled into the stream. "Some protectors you are." She shook her head and, leaving Crispin to be rescued by his friends, went on home alone.

Chapter Twenty-four

In that tantalizing moment before full sleep descended, she almost ignored the tap at her window. But curiosity proved stronger than drowsiness, and she shook herself awake. In the darkness the window was a gloss of moonlight; the casement was open just a crack. "Come out, Charity."

At once wide awake, she ran to the window and threw it open, almost knocking Tristan from his perch on a ladder. "What on earth are you doing here?"

Hands gripping the window sill, he gazed up at her innocently. In the moonlight his dark eyes danced with laughter. "Midsummer's not over yet, *cara*. I wanted to invite you to my picnic."

"Tristan, we can't have a picnic. It must be near two o'clock!"

His face fell. "Then what am I to do with the champagne? And the strawberries?" In a sudden, decisive motion he grasped her wrist. "No, I can't let them go to waste. You must come along."

He was ruthless, Charity realized with a thrill. "I'll climb down myself," she promised, afraid he might try to sweep her over the window sill. She waited until he had descended. "Move back," she whispered into the cool air.

"Charity, I have to hold the ladder for you. I'll look the other way, I promise."

She was too disoriented by the whole experience to question any part of it. So, glad of her tree-climbing skills, she stuck one foot out the window and found the ladder rung. Then, all too aware of her billowing cotton nightgown, she made a quick descent into his arms. She couldn't deny the tremble of her body but sought instead to disguise it. As he set her down on her bare feet, she said, "Oh, it's so chilly! And the grass is wet!"

Immediately he pulled off his gray riding coat and draped it over her shoulders. She pulled it close around her, savoring the warmth of him in the linen. "Will you give me your boots also?"

His brows drew together, but a smile quirked the corner of his mouth. "A heroine should not make such complaints when she's being abducted. Your concern should be for your virtue, not your feet."

Even in dazzlement, Charity retained her pragmatism. "Well, young Lochinvar, unless you want my brother also concerned for my virtue, you'd better move this abduction farther from the house."

He tugged her through the shrubbery edging the side drive and down the service lane. Outlined against the darker sky was the patient Giotti, laden with saddlebags but still somehow dignified. As his master approached trailing a young hostage, he dropped his head as if disavowing any acquaintance.

Drawing deep breaths, Charity leaned against Tristan's arm as he adjusted the saddle. She was too athletic to attribute her breathlessness to anything but excitement. And it was exciting, to be stealing away while the rest of the sensible populace slept off a Midsummer Eve, to be out in the misty air in her nightgown, to feel the hard warmth of a man against her, though she could barely make out his features in the darkness. "Where is my horse?"

In answer, Tristan put his hands on her waist and hoisted her into the saddle. Before she could protest, he sprang up behind her, reaching around her for the reins, leaving one arm snug about her waist. He nudged the horse into a trot and they left the safe confines of Calder behind them. "I don't provide mounts for my captives. Only champagne."

It was all too outrageous to protest and too magical to resist. So she leaned back against him, savoring the hard support of his chest and the security of his arm around her. Above, a half-moon silvered the clouds and cast pale light over the hills. The air was scented with wildflowers, the night alive with the songs of crickets and the rhythmic beat of hooves. She was drowning in sensual delight, and with a longing sigh realized there was more to come.

More to come: the glow of the great Midsummer bonfire off in the dark south sky, the little grove of silver birches arching toward the brook, the soft cotton blanket he spread there, the strawberries bursting sweet in her mouth, the champagne drunk from the bottle for lack of glasses. And Tristan, his eyes alight, stretched out beside her, his callused hand caressing her bare arm. He spoke Italian slowly and sensuously so that she was able to understand nearly every word. It was so much like a fantasy that she knew she would never believe it in the morning. So she simply savored it, lived it, knowing that soon she could do no more than yearn for the vanished dream.

"Why are you doing this?" she whispered, and the moment broke into shards like a mirror.

"Midsummer madness." Her distrust, her disillusion couldn't dismay him. He uncurled her fist with gentle fingers. "You want me to do it. And I want to do it. Must there be some other reason?"

But she knew better; she knew him better. He once spoke of friendship, but friendship was never so dangerous. This was temptation. And this was deliberate. This must be his revenge, to make her regret her refusal for the rest of her life.

As soon as she formed the thought, she dismissed it. Tristan wasn't cruel; he wouldn't hurt her so deliberately. Perhaps he meant this as a lesson, a lesson she had to learn: that desire felt like fear; that love frightened as well as fascinated her.

Her feelings for him were so paradoxical she could only express them in a clumsy riddle. If he could solve it, then he could know her. "Abduction—it's not an act of friendship. More of passion."

She was disappointed and relieved when he rose and moved to lean against the curving trunk of a birch. But at least he recognized this as a riddle. He tilted his head inquiringly to the side.

"Passion. You keep using that word. You implied last week that I didn't feel sufficient passion for you. I wondered then what you meant." When she remained silent, he added, "I expect you meant did I want to take you to bed."

She was glad of the dark that hid her fierce blush. That wasn't the solution to her riddle, not really, only a little piece of it.

In the same impersonal tone, he continued, "Passion. Well, if that is what you wanted all this time, we might have avoided all this grief. Of course I wanted to bed you. I spent the requisite amount of time admiring how small and yet how strong you are, and wondering if you'd be as good at that sport as you are at, say, climbing trees. I imagined what it would be like to kiss that lovely mouth and feel your lithe little body open to me. I still imagine that, as a matter of fact. There, does that make you happy?"

She felt his anger blazing across the darkness and didn't understand it. Blindly she shook her head, her loosened hair spilling to her shoulders. "It's just—that is what has been missing. You have been so good, so kind to me. But no passion."

His breath came out in a harsh laugh. "If you knew how difficult it's been for me—Come here, Charity."

Warily she regarded him, a dark form against the pale tree. He had not come to help her up or hold out his hand to her;

he only waited. Slowly she stood, slowly she crossed the separation. Only when she stood beside him did he reach out to her and draw her in.

The wind shifted, and the strains of an ancient melody came on the breeze. They must still be dancing at the bonfire, she thought. Tristan was still against her for a moment, listening to the ghostly music, then he eased her into a slow, sensuous dance in the meadow.

We have never danced before, Charity thought, and yet they moved together as if they had long been intimates. This was a dance like none she'd ever known, with the breeze teasing her nightgown and his hands teasing her bare arms, and the moon casting its faint radiance on them. Still moving to the music, Tristan bent his head to kiss her, lingering tenderly at her mouth and drawing her even closer.

After that first kiss, Charity leaned weakly back against the support of his arms and lifted her head, wordlessly seeking more. But his eyes burned so hot she couldn't see him, and she closed her eyes as he bent closer and trailed kisses across her cheek to her mouth. With the sweet pressure of his kiss, of his body against hers, her resistance slipped away. She knew the swell of his desire, her own pulsing response—

And then he let her go and stepped back, breathing hard. "I don't know what that's meant to prove," he said before she could protest. "That I, like any red-blooded man, am aroused by a nubile girl in my arms? That you are also aroused? Is that some sort of epiphany for you? Charity, men and women are meant to feel this way. It's how the race survives. The physical connection—oh, it's the easiest connection of all, and the least important."

She tried to step back from that harsh assessment, but the birch tree was behind her. She let it hold her straight-backed, and read in his somber eyes that he couldn't mean what he said. "It's so trivial to you?" she whispered.

His dark eyes softened, and he drew her back into his arms. He didn't try to kiss her, only to hold her, his cheek against her hair. "Oh, it's important. But because it's you I'm holding. Otherwise it would only be a moment."

"I knew . . ." She couldn't complete the sentence, even in her own mind, because once she said them the words couldn't be taken back. And she had already caused so much pain by making irrevocable actions based on fleeting, if fierce, emotions.

But Tristan wouldn't let her rest in this half-understood haze of contentment. "Ah, Charity, it's such a lovely night, and you are so beautiful. Tell me what you want. Let me give you what you want."

His husky voice thrilled her as much as the caress of his callused hands on her bare arms. "I want—" She closed her eyes tight, letting the darkness conceal her wantonness. "I want you tonight. To kiss me and to hold me and to—"

She couldn't finish, but she didn't need to, for he was already obeying, drawing her down onto the soft blanket, sliding one hand along the sensitive nape of her neck, the other along her side to the curve of her hip. She tasted his lips for a long minute, then he withdrew to kiss her neck, the hollow of her throat. "Let me," she whispered softly as he started to unbutton her nightgown.

But he pushed her ineffectual hand away. "No, *cara*, you have no work to do here. I will take care of it all. You just rest—"

And she did, letting the sensations wash over her, surrendering to his seduction. It was new to her, this surrender, but she knew, as she knew nothing else, that Tristan would not hurt her.

"Mia cara, mi' amore, tell me what you want. Tell me."

She heard her soft voice saying words she had never imagined saying, that she wanted to touch his bare skin, that she wanted them to be naked to the night air. And whatever she asked, he gave her, gently and lovingly gratifying every wish. This is what I meant, she thought gratefully, this is passion.

And it was only the night breeze across her fevered body

that recalled her. The cool brush across the heat he left reminded her of who she was, and who he was, and why they could not go on. For an agonized moment she was caught between desire and decision, and then, inadequately, she touched the back of his dark head, the crisp curl of his hair, and whispered, "No more."

He rested his burning cheek for a moment between her breasts, then sat up and pulled his shirt on. She sat hugging herself, her face flaming. "Are you angry?"

She heard rather than saw the smile quirking his mouth. "No."

He felt around the ground and produced her nightgown, pulled it over her head, stole a kiss as her mouth emerged, and eased her arms into the sleeves, sliding it down past her hips. His hands were efficient where they had once been evocative, and she felt the loss as well as the comfort. He tugged the gown straight around her legs, pausing to tickle her bare feet. "I want only what you wanted."

"Only?" she echoed plaintively.

"Perhaps just a little more." She heard the Italian lilt again and knew he was smiling.

That decision had taken all her strength, and when he drew her to her feet, she swayed against him. He guided her to his horse and helped her into the saddle, then returned to their bower to gather up the blanket and picnic basket. He was the practical one now, tidying up after their incomplete passion.

As they rode back to her home, she rested her head against his chest, hearing his heartbeat's reassuring rhythm, his soothing murmur. But she also heard the echo of his demand in the cool night. *Tell me what you want.* "Tristan—" She took a deep breath and tried again. "Tristan, I know now that I was wrong. I shouldn't have done what I did. Not tonight, I don't mean that. When I told you that you couldn't give me what I needed. When I told you I wanted more."

"Hush, sweeting." His arm tightened around her waist as he forestalled her confession. "This isn't the time for that.

And you don't have to justify anything. We did nothing shameful."

"I know!" she cried, looking up at him to prove her lack of shame. "I don't feel that. I feel—I feel regret, that I hurt you before, that I didn't explain how frightened I was, that I didn't let you have time to discover that yourself. I want to—"

"Not yet. Sweetheart, don't say it yet."

The ragged edge of his plea silenced her. He didn't want to hear whatever avowal she was about to make. Sulkily she said, "You don't know how hard it is for me to ask."

"Don't I? I do. I know you always anticipate what others want and never think to ask for yourself. I know. But not tonight, Charity, Not tonight."

And with that, and a gentle good-night kiss at her window, she had to be content. She nestled into her lonely bed, watching the breeze stir the drapes where he had been, waiting for the despair to take her. But she waited in vain. She had asked and been refused, and her heart hadn't broken. She didn't even want to cry. He didn't mean to hurt her, she knew that now, and his denial wasn't meant to make her despair. Tomorrow, she thought as she fell asleep, tomorrow I will ask him properly. On bended knee.

Chapter Twenty-five

Charity awakened with a warm sense of well-being, and after a moment's concentration remembered why. Tristan had swept her away last night for a midsummer rendezvous. It was decidedly improper and deliciously wicked. And she knew what she always hoped: that he could take her to other worlds just by taking her in his arms.

Her maid entered with chocolate and a handful of wildflowers with a note tied to it. "His Lordship—the handsome one—brought it over this morning," Jenny said, plumping pillows while trying to read over her mistress's shoulder.

Charity smiled and held the note up. "Go ahead and read it."

"That's not fair. It's not in English!" Jenny gave the pillow a disappointed smack and drifted out the door.

But Charity had the benefit of Miss Falesham's instructions and Tristan's recent tutelage. " 'I cannot sleep a minute this night. My mind and heart are filled with the memory of your lovely golden'—*còrpo, còrpo*—" She had to resort to the Italian lexicon on her night table to translate. "Body, oh, my word, I'm glad Jenny isn't Italian. 'Your lovely golden body and your delicious mouth.' I should burn this, Tristan Hale." But she couldn't, for the closing read, " 'Forever your worshipful captive, T.' "

She rose with renewed purpose. She had made a mistake,

and it was her responsibility to correct it. But the timing wasn't yet auspicious, not so early in the morning. If he truly hadn't slept all night, Tristan would need to rest to be in a receptive mood. So, humming the closing aria from *Così fan tutte* with its chorus "happy forever after," she descended to the sunny breakfast room.

She was glad to see Francis in the same mood as he sat buttering his toast and whistling. "I gather you got the answer you desired," she remarked as she took her seat.

"It was as you foretold: my noble sentiments got me nowhere, but once I explained my baser motives, she fell into my arms."

"No caveats at all?"

"She did worry that she is older than I, but I assured her that I am much more mature, so we will achieve a balance."

"Oh, Francis," Charity sighed. "You are incurably honest. It's fortunate that you don't intend a career as a rake."

He offered her a slab of sirloin, but when she declined, he speared it himself. "I wanted you to be the first to know, but I had to content myself with Barry as a confidant. You must have been dead asleep. I banged on your door but you never answered."

She lifted her teacup to her lips to hide her guilty blush. "Barry was sober enough to listen?"

"He nodded at the appropriate moments. Up early this morning, even, unlike you. Did he tell you he plans a walking tour of Wales when his examinations are done?"

Charity decided not to worry what mischief Barry would get up to with all of Wales at his disposal. "A wanderer, he is. Just like his elder sister! I hope to be off soon too—but not to Wales. Italy. Much more adventurous."

Francis's mouth tightened, but he didn't bother to repeat his edict that traveling to Italy, even with Miss Falesham, wasn't a proper adventure for a young lady. "You know you have a home here, no matter that I marry. Anna already loves you as a sister and—"

"Well, of course this will always be home," she said gaily. "But now I can leave it—and you—in loving hands. I can go away in good conscience."

"I haven't much to say about it after today, I suppose," he said gruffly. He reached under his chair and brought up a package wrapped in striped paper. "Here. If you're to be a wanderer, you might as well learn from the best."

She took the gift but only stared at it.

"Come, girl, have you forgotten it's your birthday? You are one-and-twenty, and my guardianship is done. Not that you've ever needed any guarding. But I will be glad to be liberated from all those unfortunate devils and their eternal applications for your hand. Well, open it."

"Francis—" Her mind filled with memories of other birthdays, when Ned would wake her at dawn proclaiming, "We're a year older!"

Sensing tears, her brother took the package and ripped the paper off. "I know you say you don't want to celebrate it. But some birthday you'll get over this and want to be cosseted and gifted. And you'd likely never mention your change of heart, so we shall injure you unwittingly. Accept it, Charity, and have done."

It was time to move out of Francis's house, she thought resentfully as she took the red leather-bound book; he had learned to read her too well. *Journals,* the gilt letters on the cover said. But the frontispiece was more enlightening. "To Miss Charity Calder, on the occasion of her coming of age. May your journey through life be a meandering one. Lady Hester Stanhope."

"Francis, where did you get this? It's her travel journals! Privately printed! Endorsed to me!"

Without a thought to good manners, she opened the book there at the table, reading of the famed explorer's journey through the Middle East. She hardly heard her brother's offhanded admission. "Oh, we correspond, you know. She was kind enough to read and comment on that monograph I wrote on Pitt the Elder's feud with Robert Walpole. She was Pitt the Younger's niece, you'll recall."

But Charity was already deep into an account of how the Druse tribe of Lebanon adopted Lady Hester and made her their prophetess. She was surely the only former debutante, Charity decided, to have become a religious icon.

"Some parts are rather raw, but now that you are a mature adult, I expect you will pass them right up as tedious. Page eighty-four," he added as Charity began flipping through the book.

Page eighty-four contained nothing raw at all, except a description of the camel meat Lady Hester once encountered at dinner. Charity went back to page three and paid no more attention to her brother's teasing.

Her other brothers catapulted in, Charlie carrying a specimen box, Barry fresh and fragrant from a dawn fishing trip. He sent the footman Phipps off with his string of trout and turned to his sister.

"What a great Midsummer Eve! Never got to bed because I heard those fish a-calling. You been making more trouble, Sis?" Barry asked this quite as innocently as if he had not been at the center of it. "Crispin told me to tell you he won't be marrying you no matter what. Said that dunking in the brook was the last straw."

"I've told him that for years," she said crossly. "Barry, do wash your hands. You've got bits of worm up to your wrists."

Barry looked with surprise at his hands and took himself off toward the kitchen. "Well, Cris said he wouldn't have you if you begged him on bended knee," he called back through the swinging door. "But then he said you might as well give it a try."

Charlie cleared his throat for attention, then he shoved the specimen box across the table. "Felicitations, Sister."

Touched, Charity opened the lid and took out a magnificent quartz, broken in half to show the hexagonal crystals flashing red and blue. "Oh, Charlie, this is your prize! I can't deprive your collection of this!"

"I knew you'd say that." He took back the box, shook out a little square of cardboard, and handed it to her.

She read aloud, "On permanent loan to the Calder Collection from Miss Charity Calder." Her voice trembled a bit, but her countenance remained admirably straight. "Do you mean my name will appear in your collection? Why, we could call this the 'Charity crystal'!"

Her brother drew back a bit, "The 'Calder quartz' will do. We don't want to confuse the viewers. It will be the centerpiece of the collection, on black velvet with the card underneath. I intend to convert one of the plowsheds into my museum."

Francis was explaining why this was unfeasible when Barry returned and realized the import of the gifts at his sister's place. "Dash it, Charity, why didn't you write to remind me? I would have brought you something, a Trinity scarf perhaps."

"It's enough that you're sharing the day with me."

"You're right, that's plenty enough. Pass me the marmalade, won't you? My birthday is next month, which gives you ample time to plan. I'll be back from my walking tour of Wales—"

"Your walking tour of Welsh pubs," Charlie muttered, holding out his hand. "You'd best give me the Calder quartz back, Charity. You wouldn't want to drop it."

"Certainly not when it's put me on the brink of geological fame." She gently transferred the crystal back to its donor and rose. There were a wealth of chores to attend to before she gathered her courage and offered Tristan her heart. After lunch, she decided; that would give him time to rest up and her time to steel her nerve.

"Well, the laundry has no regard for my new consequence. We're washing all the sheer drapes today."

Charlie and Francis exchanged alarmed looks, and Charity

exclaimed, "I promise I won't ask any of you to take them down. Phipps will help us without a single complaint."

"That is what servants are for." Barry nodded his thanks to the footman and began sawing the head off his steaming trout. "To do the tasks we can't abide. Where's the cat?"

"Don't toss it on the carpet, for goodness' sake." Charity grabbed a plate from the sideboard and interposed it under Barry's offering.

"Trinity College never countenanced such barbaric manners in my day," Francis muttered. "You'd think he'd spent the last term in an alehouse." With a significant look at the laughing Charlie, he added, "You may help the maids boil as many sheers as you like, Charity, but be properly dressed for tea at two. You must divert Mrs. Hering when I go to purchase that pasture from the squire."

"Francis, really, I have better things to do." But he was already out the door. So much for my birthday, she thought as she followed him out. But Mrs. Hering was indeed a far tougher negotiator than the squire, who would, out of her presence, likely trade the pasture for a good hunter. And they could have a good coze, discussing all the events of the fair—well, not *all* of them. Just the ones before midnight.

And if she waited until four, she wouldn't disturb Tristan's painting time, she told herself, secretly relieved to have the moment of truth postponed.

At two she stood waiting in the entry hall, arrayed in a gown of shadow-striped silver muslin sure to distract the fashion-conscious Mrs. Hering. Instead of Francis, however, the opening door revealed a groom with a note. The tea was off, the squire having been called away, and Charity was free to boil her sheers.

I'll just surprise Tristan in his studio, she decided, and put on her bonnet. Perhaps that won't put him in a loving mood, she thought, and took her bonnet off. Her dilemma was resolved when Charlie burst in, disheveled and breathless from his long run.

"Charity, come quickly! Haverne—it's all ahoo—the countess is crying—I told Jem, he's bringing the gig. Hurry!"

As Charity expected, agitated noises greeted her as she approached the Haverne drawing room. But as she sailed across the threshold, ready to reorder the chaos, she stopped short. There was a party in progress, spilling out onto the terrace, complete with pink and white bunting and crystal punch bowl, no doubt the most unusual assembly Haverne had ever hosted.

Charlie, laughing when he had previously been anxious, tugged her into the crowd toward the people who had come to help her celebrate her day. Uncomprehending, she held out her hand to the squire and Mr. Langworth, offered her cheek to Mrs. Hering and Cammie and Anna, bent to hug the Haverton boys, shook her head at her secretive brothers. So many friends were there: a few tenants in their Sunday best, Mr. Perry playing sentimental ballads on his fiddle, all three Ferris girls in their crisp maid uniforms, Crispin chatting up the always amenable Polly—what would his parents think if Crispin took *her* as a substitute for Charity?

Aunt Grace bustled up with her fragrant cushioned embrace and her horrified whisper, "Is it true? You aren't marrying that lord?"

"I think so, Aunt," she said absently, her gaze drawn mesmerically to Tristan standing on the edge of the party, laughter lighting his eyes.

"You think you aren't, or you think you are? Really, Charity, now that you are of age, you must learn to be more precise—and less precipitate."

Borne away by the Haverton boys, Charity could not respond to this. Lawrence sat her down in a chair by the window, and, clambering up on the sill behind her, he put his hands around her neck. She flinched then felt the cool of metal against her throat and heard the snap of a clasp. "I got your necklace fixed. I paid for it myself. You didn't lose the locket, did you?" he said, climbing down.

"No, dearest, it's in my jewel box."

"This is for the jewel box, too." Jeremy elbowed his brother out of the way and handed her a little red clay heart. "It's a pin. I made it. It says 'Love' on the back. L-O-V-E."

"It's lovely, Jeremy, thank you." She pinned it to her bodice and turned to accept felicitations and a heavy volume from Cammie.

"It's a guidebook to the Vatican, with engravings of the Sistine Chapel. Very improving. I wish I might see it. Perhaps when Charlie builds a stone bridge to the Continent."

Always she was aware of Tristan, of the warmth of his gaze, the tension of his slim form. Polly blocked her view, however, twirling a gaily printed sunshade. "I hear the Mediterranean sun is bright," she said significantly, closing the parasol and handing it over.

Charity thanked her, musing that if the entire county thinks I'm going to Italy, it must be true. She raised her gaze to meet Tristan's, just as Lawrence announced, "My uncle has a present, too. I'll show it to you."

"No, I'll show it to her myself." Tristan crossed to take her hand and pull her to her feet. To Lawrence, he said, "You'd best apply yourself to cozening your future steppapa. He's not so indulgent as I."

"But he has guns. He's going to teach me how to shoot."

"Not till I'm a league away, I hope. Come, Charity, let me show you your gift."

Even away from the curious crowd, Charity could not bring herself to speak her heart. Just as well; Tristan apparently had other plans for her. He pulled her into his studio, and she looked about, enjoying the careful chaos. She didn't even feel the need to tidy up. Still—"Tristan, should you leave your brushes to dry on that dusty shelf?"

He grabbed the dustrag from her hand before she could apply it. "My brushes will be fine. Now come here and see. I didn't have time to frame it; in fact, it isn't even dry. I was up till dawn finishing it. But that was all right," he assured her with a grin. "I couldn't sleep anyway."

Her color rising, she approached the easel he indicated. The canvas, about two by three feet, was covered with a baize cloth, and with a flourish he pulled it off.

She felt his arm tense under her hand and reassured him. "A painting is the best gift you could give me." It was that study in brown, she realized, almost disappointed. The canvas glowed with that most prosaic color. And perhaps the subject was unimportant, as Tristan said, but this was very odd. Two girls kissing?

"It's me," she whispered ungrammatically. "I don't remember—"

"Don't you?" Tristan's voice was urgent, his hand stealing around her waist. "How could you forget? I couldn't. See the dirt the boys tracked in? And the broken vase? And you were wearing a brown riding habit."

"But the mirror?" Memory glimmered. So much had changed since then: Haverne Hall had been in mourning, the entrance hall shabby, the boys so wild, Anna sunk in melancholy. But she'd just come from London where everyone had liked her so well, and she'd been so pleased with herself she gave into a silly impulse and kissed her image in the smudged mirror. "You were watching, you—you voyeur!"

"Artists are all voyeurs. We're given lessons in lurking and creeping about unnoticed—do you remember now?"

"You must have thought me very vain."

"Well," he confessed with a laugh, "I thought you very odd. But charming. In a vain way."

She did look charming, that doubled girl in the painting, her dark eyes alight with laughter, her pretty mouth curved in a kiss. Gamine, engaging—and very vain.

His left hand stole around her waist and clasped the other, pulling her close against him. She turned in his arms to look at him. "You aren't going to call it *A Study in Brown*, are you?"

"I expect you like *The Kiss* better."

He brushed her mouth with his own, and she drew away, breathless, to admit, "I do like kisses better than studies."

"You might take up studying kisses." And he kissed her again, lingering this time to give her lips a thorough study. But then he raised his head. "I—I forgot. I must explain the painting. You are distracting me from my script."

"Your script?"

"You are not the only playwright here, my darling. None of this romance comes naturally to me. So I wrote out my script last night. I had a most productive night, though frustrating."

"You truly wrote a script?"

"One for your brothers, too. The painting ... the painting ..." He turned her to face the canvas. "Ah, yes. When I first caught sight of you, you were bestowing a kiss on that charming girl in the mirror. I was captivated but confused. Such a very unusual thing to do in someone else's home. But—no, don't explain, for I think I know better than you why you did it."

He took a deep breath and exhaled it slowly, so she could feel the rise and fall of his hard chest. "It was because you loved yourself. No, it's not conceit. It only makes sense, after all. You are lovable. But not for the reasons you think—not because you are so kind and sweet and helpful and clever. It's because you love life so well, so you must love yourself, because there is so much life in you. And you teach us all to love life, too."

Her heart was so full it came up to her throat, and she could speak only in a whisper. "But why did you paint this?"

"I tried to paint other things. I tried to finish my other paintings and couldn't. So I thought I'd paint you. I tried to paint you nude, as Athena, but I would have had to rely on imagination—this was before last night—next time I will paint you blushing, for you do it so well, Charity. Where was I? Oh, the kiss. Well, finally I gave into the vision. I knew it would be considered mawkish by the critics, even if I did call it a study in brown and even if the double image is so precise—next to impossible to achieve, I assure you. The composition is fascinating, don't you think? But the subject—pure sentimentality. Old Crome could have painted it."

"No, he couldn't."

"No, he couldn't. Because it was my vision. Charity, don't you see, it was the first glimpse I ever had of you, and I couldn't escape it. It was so evocative of all I admire of you."

"I understand now." He had memorized her.

"No, you don't. You can't. I haven't gotten to the part of the script where you understand. Then you throw your arms about me, you see. Not yet!" He held her off with a firm hand. "You told me once that you wanted me to fall in love with you at first sight."

"And you told me it was impossible."

"It wasn't impossible after all. That's why I couldn't paint anything else, because that is the vision I fell in love with weeks ago. I just didn't recognize it, never having fallen in love at first sight before."

The admission she had awaited all her life was as fulfilling as she had hoped. She slid her hands up his sinewy arms toward his shoulders. "Is it time yet?"

He caught her hands in his but he didn't push her way. "Only another minute. I have to tell you why I was wrong and why you were wrong—that's the best part." He paused to find his place in his mental script. "At first, I just knew I had to make you my wife. I'd never really had a home, you see. I don't just mean a house, but a place of peace. A place in someone's heart. I thought you might have room in that generous heart for me. But it was only when you denied me that place—how cruel you were! but how right—did I realize that if I wanted love from you, I must love you back. And not just as others love you, for your good sense and good deeds. They love you for what you do—all your angel-of-mercy acts. I learned I had to love you for what you are. And you are no angel. I knew that as soon as I kissed you. You are a woman of passion and mystery—you are, Charity, you mystified me well enough. I had to investigate you and contemplate you, but now I know you well enough to love you truly. Even if you did treat me brutally."

"I was afraid," she murmured.

"Afraid?" He brought her hand up to touch his heart. "You didn't want me to understand you. No one ever has, not really; they only see what you let them see."

"I was wrong to pretend that you were the one at fault."

"But it was the best thing for us both. What were we thinking, to get betrothed after a fortnight's acquaintance? We must have been mad. You were right to call a halt to it, though at the time I didn't think so. I needed to consider whether I could make room in my heart for you—the real Charity, and find a way to take my place in your heart. Now it's been nearly a month since we met, and we are so much wiser now."

"How am I wiser?"

"Ah, because you have learned patience. And you've learned to ask. From the first you wanted a miracle from me; you wanted me to read your mind and know what you wanted in a husband, and you wanted me to be it straightaway. You thought husbands came as a package, created all complete. Men might be that way, but not husbands." He turned her to look out the window at the hills rolling gentle under a blue sky. "It's the difference between that, a work of nature—" Then he turned her, unresisting, toward his painting of Ferendisi—"and this, a work of art. Art must be crafted, shaped by the human touch. You thought that it is magic, that I wave my paintbrush and a picture appears. But it's much more work: I must make measurements and calculate proportions and mix paints and make compromises, for while my vision may be limitless my ability certainly isn't. And sometimes I make mistakes and have to scrape them off or paint them over. But you know that now since you helped me to paint Jonah." His kiss just brushed the nape of her neck, and she shivered.

"It takes the same sort of effort to make a husband. And sometimes it's the work of a lifetime."

She twisted in his arms to study his intense dark eyes, his tender mouth, this solitary man who couldn't be alone any longer. "I'm lucky, aren't I, to find a man who needed only a month's worth of shaping."

"Oh, I expect I'll need a few corrections throughout the years. Wait, I'm almost there. I hope you're impressed. Romeo proposed in half this time: I counted the lines. That reminds me, it's time to go out onto the balcony."

"Oh, no," she cried, holding his arms. "Let's stay here. I think your studio is the most romantic place in the world."

He glanced around at the disarray of unfinished work and untidy supplies and shrugged. "You have but to ask, my love. I will kneel, however, whatever you say."

And he did go down on one knee, just as she had planned to do herself, except that he looked so much better, so slim, so graceful, his burning eyes lifted to her. "I knew from the start, my treasure, that you would make me happy. Now I think—I know—that I will make you happy, too, if you will only let me. So, Charity, I shan't ask again if you will do me the honor of being my wife. Now I ask you if I may have the honor of being your husband."

Finally she heard her cue and answered it. She threw her arms about his neck, and he fell back on the floor under her kisses. They lay tumbled there amidst the scattered charcoal pencils, her hands clasped behind his neck, her legs entwined intimately with his.

When they paused for breath, he managed to say, "I'm glad I wasn't hanging off the balcony after all. I take it that's an affirmative answer."

"Yes," she murmured in his ear. "Oh, Tristan, I do love you, I've waited to say that for so long—" She sat up and tucked her feet under her skirt, recalling last night's resolution. "Oh, I meant to propose to you! Last night, but you wouldn't let me!"

He lay there, his curls black against the paint-stained oak flooring, and reached up to stroke her cheek. "I wanted to let you. I wanted you to ask me for what you wanted. But I had everything planned: the party, the painting, the proposal. I couldn't let you spoil it! Now, now, you may ask for anything you want, for my script ended with the kiss. And the happily ever after, of course."

Charity squirmed down beside him and rested her cheek against his chest. His arms tightened around her, and she felt the accelerating pulse of his heart. "Anything I want. Oh, what could I want? I'm perfectly happy as I am."

"There must be something you want."

"A short engagement."

"Just my thought. Fortunately it's Saturday. Well, it's not fortunate at all; I planned for your birthday to fall on Saturday this year."

"Absurd creature," she said lovingly. "But you are right. The banns can be posted for tomorrow's service, and for two Sundays after that. No, Tristan, I shan't be married by special license, no matter how romantic that sounds. The vicar would never forgive me for setting a bad example again."

"As you wish, my love."

"But I don't want to wait until the mourning for your brother-in-law is over."

"Why should we when my sister isn't?" Tristan said. "They'll probably run off to Gretna, so abandoned to common decency they are."

The thought of Francis eloping made her chuckle, and she felt him shake with answering laughter. "How utterly perfect we are together."

"No other demands? I mean, requests? Not one?"

He was so watchful again, his arms tense about her, that she applied her mind to finding something, anything, that could possibly make her happier. Her gaze fell on the painting of Ferendisi. "Oh, Tristan, I know you wanted to move to Braden right away. But I have always, always, wanted to see Italy. Do you think we could?"

He sat up, pushing her away, but only to feel around in his coat pocket and pull out a leather packet tied with black string. "Another birthday present."

She fumbled with the tie and extracted a whole sheaf of papers. On the top was a pair of tickets on a ship from Southhampton to Naples, leaving the Monday evening after the third Sunday banns could be posted. She regarded him suspiciously. "You were very sure of yourself, weren't you? You have been—*managing* me all along!"

He shrugged modestly. "I mean to apply myself to anticipating your every desire. I anticipate that you want to kiss me again, for example."

She complied, dropping an absent kiss on his lips, then returned to examining the travel papers. "Oh, it will be such fun, taking our wedding trip in Italy! You must show me all the places you love and everywhere you've ever painted, especially the romantic places."

He drew her back in his arms, brushing her temple with a kiss. "I promise I will take you to every romantic spot in Italy."

"What luck you know Italy so well. I mean to write a guidebook." She turned her head to kiss his hard, tender mouth. "For brides," she murmured. She felt his mouth under hers curve in a smile and pulled away to see it.

"Oh, better and better. Then you'll have a purpose for the trip. And you must have a purpose, Charity Calder. Otherwise you will no doubt feel bored and useless."

She loved his teasing: this lightheartedness was something she had given him. So she only nestled into his arms, her head against his chest so she could hear the rapid beat of his heart. "Tristan, do you truly mean to paint me in the nude?"

He considered this, brushing her hair back from her face

with a gentle hand. "I think I will have to. If you don't mind. Think of what fun the sittings will be."

"Imagine what Aunt Grace will say when she sees me in all my glory on the walls of the Royal Academy."

He straightened at this suggestion. "I was planning a private exhibition. Very private." After further consideration, he decided, "No nude painting. I couldn't do the subject justice. Once in awhile, nature doesn't need any embellishment from the artist. Only enjoyment. And I intend to have plenty of that."

And in his burning eyes, Charity saw visions of passion, romance, delights untold, and knew that they had a lifetime to make them real.

SUSPENSE IS A HEARTBEAT AWAY—
Curl up with these Gothic gems.

THE PRECIOUS PEARLS OF CABOT HALL (3754, $3.99/$4.99)
by Peggy Darty

Recently orphaned Kathleen O'Malley is overjoyed to discover her long-lost relatives. Uncertain of their reception, she poses as a writer's assistant and returns to her ancestral home. Her harmless masquerade hurls Kathleen into a web of danger and intrigue. Something sinister is invading Cabot Hall, and even her handsome cousin Luke can't protect her from its deadly pull. Kathleen must discover its source, even if it means losing her love . . . and her life.

BLACKMADDIE (3805, $3.99/$4.99)
by Jean Innes

Summoned to Scotland by her ailing grandfather, Charlotte Brodie is surprised to find a family filled with resentment and spite. Dismissing her drugged drink and shredded dresses as petty pranks, she soon discovers that these malicious acts are just the first links in a chain of evil. Midnight chanting echoes through the halls of her family estate, and a curse cast centuries ago threatens to rob Charlotte of her sanity and her birth right.

DARK CRIES OF GRAY OAKS (3759, $3.99/$4.99)
by Lee Karr

Brianna Anderson was grateful for her position as companion to Cassie Danzel, a mentally ill seventeen year old. Cassie seemed to be the model patient: quiet, passive, obedient. But Dr. Gavin Rodene knew that Cassie's tormented mind held a shocking secret—one that her family would silence at any cost. As Brianna tries to unlock the terrors that have gripped Cassie's soul, will she fall victim to its spell?

THE HAUNTED HEIRESS OF WYNDCLIFFE MANOR (3911, $3.99/$4.99)
by Beverly C. Warren

Orphaned in a train wreck, "Jane" is raised by a family of poor coal miners. She is haunted, however, by fleeting memories and shadowy images. After escaping the mines and traveling across England with a band of gypsies, she meets the man who reveals her true identity. She is Jennifer Hardwicke, heiress of Wyndcliffe Manor, but danger and doom await before she can reclaim her inheritance.

WHITE ROSES OF BRAMBLEDENE (3700, $3.99/$4.99)
by Joyce C. Ware

Delicate Violet Grayson is hesitant about the weekend house party. Two years earlier, her dearest friend mysteriously died during a similar gathering. Despite the high spirits of old companions and the flattering attention of charismatic Rafael Taliaferro, her apprehension grows. Tension throbs in the air, and the housekeeper's whispered warnings fuel Violet's mounting terror. Violet is not imagining things . . . she is in deadly peril.

Available wherever paperbacks are sold, or order direct from the Publisher. Send cover price plus 50¢ per copy for mailing and handling to Zebra Books, Dept. 4230, 475 Park Avenue South, New York, N.Y. 10016. Residents of New York and Tennessee must include sales tax. DO NOT SEND CASH. For a free Zebra/Pinnacle catalog please write to the above address.

WAITING FOR A WONDERFUL ROMANCE?
READ ZEBRA'S

WANDA OWEN!

DECEPTIVE DESIRES (2887, $4.50/$5.50)
Exquisite Tiffany Renaud loved her life as the only daughter of a wealthy Parisian industrialist. The last thing she wanted was to cross the ocean on a cramped and stuffy ship just to visit the uncivilized wilds of America. Then she shared a kiss with shipping magnate Chad Morrow that made the sails billow and the deck spin...

KISS OF FIRE (3091, $4.50/$5.50)
Born and raised in backwoods Virginia, Tawny Blair knew that her dream of being swept off her feet by a handsome nobleman would never come true. But when she met Lord Bart, Tawny saw at once that reality could far surpass her fantasies. And when he took her in his strong arms, she thrilled to the desire in his searing caresses...

SAVAGE FURY (2676, $3.95/$4.95)
Lovely Gillian Browne was secure in her quiet world on a remote ranch in Arizona, yet she longed for romance and excitement. Her girlish fantasies did not prepare her for the strange new feelings that assaulted her when dashing Irish sea captain Steve Lafferty entered her life...

TEMPTING TEXAS TREASURE (3312, $4.50/$5.50)
Mexican beauty Karita Montera aroused a fever of desire in every redblooded man in the wild Texas Blacklands. But the sensuous señorita had eyes only for Vincent Navarro, the wealthy cattle rancher she'd adored since childhood—and her family's sworn enemy! His first searing caress ignited her white-hot need and soon Karita burned to surrender to her own wanton passion...

Available wherever paperbacks are sold, or order direct from the Publisher. Send cover price plus 50¢ per copy for mailing and handling to Zebra Books, Dept. 4230, 475 Park Avenue South, New York, N.Y. 10016. Residents of New York and Tennessee must include sales tax. DO NOT SEND CASH. For a free Zebra/Pinnacle catalog please write to the above address.

THE ROMANCES OF LORDS AND LADIES
IN JANIS LADEN'S REGENCIES

BEWITCHING MINX (2532, $3.95)
From her first encounter with the Marquis of Penderleigh when he had mistaken her for a common trollop, Penelope had been incensed with the darkly handsome lord. Miss Penelope Larchmont was undoubtedly the most outspoken young lady Penderleigh had ever known, and the most tempting.

A NOBLE MISTRESS (2169, $3.95)
Moriah Landon had always been a singularly practical young lady. So when her father lost the family estate over a game of picquet, she paid the winner, the notorious Viscount Roane, a visit. And when he suggested the means of payment—that she become Roane's mistress—she agreed without a blink of her eyes.

SAPPHIRE TEMPTATION (3054, $3.95)
Lady Serena was commonly held to be an unusual young girl—outspoken when she should have been reticent, lively when she should have been demure. But there was one tradition she had not been allowed to break: a Wexley must marry a Gower. Richard Gower intended to teach his wife her duties—in every way.

SCOTTISH ROSE (2750, $3.95)
The Duke of Milburne returned to Milburne Hall trusting that the new governess, Miss Rose Beacham, had instilled the fear of God into his harum-scarum brood of siblings. But she romped with the children, refused to be cowed by his stern admonitions, and was so pretty that he had the devil of a time keeping his hands off her.

Available wherever paperbacks are sold, or order direct from the Publisher. Send cover price plus 50¢ per copy for mailing and handling to Zebra Books, Dept. 4230, 475 Park Avenue South, New York, N.Y. 10016. Residents of New York and Tennessee must include sales tax. DO NOT SEND CASH. For a free Zebra/Pinnacle catalog please write to the above address.

A Memorable Collection of Regency Romances

BY ANTHEA MALCOLM AND VALERIE KING

THE COUNTERFEIT HEART (3425, $3.95/$4.95)
by Anthea Malcolm
Nicola Crawford was hardly surprised when her cousin's betrothed disappeared on some mysterious quest. Anyone engaged to such an unromantic, but handsome man was bound to run off sooner or later. Nicola could never entrust her heart to such a conventional, but so deucedly handsome man. . . .

THE COURTING OF PHILIPPA (2714, $3.95/$4.95)
by Anthea Malcolm
Miss Philippa was a very successful author of romantic novels. Thus she was chagrined to be snubbed by the handsome writer Henry Ashton whose own books she admired. And when she learned he considered love stories completely beneath his notice, she vowed to teach him a thing or two about the subject of love. . . .

THE WIDOW'S GAMBIT (2357, $3.50/$4.50)
by Anthea Malcolm
The eldest of the orphaned Neville sisters needed a chaperone for a London season. So the ever-resourceful Livia added several years to her age, invented a deceased husband, and became the respectable Widow Royce. She was certain she'd never regret abandoning her girlhood until she met dashing Nicholas Warwick. . . .

A DARING WAGER (2558, $3.95/$4.95)
by Valerie King
Ellie Dearborne's penchant for gaming had finally led her to ruin. It seemed like such a lark, wagering her devious cousin George that she would obtain the snuffboxes of three of society's most dashing peers in one month's time. She could easily succeed, too, were it not for that exasperating Lord Ravenworth. . . .

THE WILLFUL WIDOW (3323, $3.95/$4.95)
by Valerie King
The lovely young widow, Mrs. Henrietta Harte, was not all inclined to pursue the sort of romantic folly the persistent King Brandish had in mind. She had to concentrate on marrying off her penniless sisters and managing her spendthrift mama. Surely Mr. Brandish could fit in with her plans somehow . . .

Available wherever paperbacks are sold, or order direct from the Publisher. Send cover price plus 50¢ per copy for mailing and handling to Zebra Books, Dept. 4230, 475 Park Avenue South, New York, N.Y. 10016. Residents of New York and Tennessee must include sales tax. DO NOT SEND CASH. For a free Zebra/Pinnacle catalog please write to the above address.